**VAMPIRE GOD**

**REBEL ANGELS BOOK FIVE**

**In the realm of the gods, the final game for the Crown has begun.**

Violet is running out of time. In a court of godly Seraphim, the only way to survive the trickery and secrets of The Burning Temple is to seduce the despotic Emperor's sultry shifter son. Yet is he as much a prisoner as her in his Gilded Cage?

Violet must undertake the Test by Monster to become a bodyguard to the Emperor: a Fae Knight of the Seraphim. If she fails, her vampire and angel lovers will be tossed into the Abyss. At last, Violet meets her creator, and the dangerous truth is revealed...

When the Emperor threatens to wipe out every world and start a new Eden, time is up. In the final battle, Violet could lose everything.

# FANTASY REBEL

FANTASY REBEL

VAMPIRE GOD: REBEL ANGELS BOOK
FIVE@copyright2019RosemaryAJohns

The moral right of the author has been asserted.

ISBN-13: 978-0995557987


Book Cover Designer: Rebecca Frank
Fantasy Rebel Limited

rosemaryajohns.com

# 1

Vampires? Angels?

I'd become their huntress, princess, mage, and at last I'd discovered that I was their god.

In the deadly Realm of the Seraphim with the ancient and cruel angel gods, who played with life and death like a game, I could either fight or die their slave.

And that made the gods bastards, after all.

In the beginning, I'd believed myself human. The gamer and developer, lost in make-believe. Half vampire, half angel, I'd still lived out a human geek life, until my powers arose phoenix-like on my twenty-first birthday.

I'd sacrificed my mum and dad, as well as my Crown in the Angel and Under World. I'd swept away the Legion of the Phoenix to free the brainwashed lost boys.

Yet now I was the one caught in The Burning Temple by a despotic Emperor: a pet monster, in a realm of gods and monsters.

*Hiss.*

A blazing arc of fire cut across Court One in the Seraphim's Burning Temple. I howled, yanked backwards by the snaking leg shackles, which bound me to Mischief.

I stumbled, squelching across the floor, which rippled as if it was alive; Mischief's wings flared in alarm: violet ghosts in the gloom. When Mischief caught me, I clutched onto his silver tunic. He swung us away from the fire, whilst we tangled in the clanking shackles and tumbled onto our arses.

I flailed, and my palm was sucked into the insides of the latest room in the Pleasure Pavilion.

*Nope, not thinking of being swallowed by a python.*

I wrenched out my hand with a shudder, wiping the stickiness down my black leather trousers.

If it was a bastard *Pleasure* Pavilion, where were the chocolate unicorns, live gaming tournaments, and my blokes in a blissed pile of feathers, fur, and kisses...?

My stomach rumbled: in my current starved state, I'd lick and suck the chocolate unicorns, until nothing would be left of them but their horns.

Instead of those *pleasures*, Mischief and I had been trapped together in a screwed-up show for the angel Seraphim, who believed themselves gods: The Angel Games.

For the last three rooms, Mischief and I had battled Seraphim, booby traps, and our worst nightmares come to life. We'd been separated from the rest of my family, as soon as we'd been dragged inside the Seraphim's domain.

I couldn't even sense my bonded and Marked Irish angel, Rebel, or my vampire, Ash, who was so close to bonded that my blood called to his.

Since I'd learnt that the sassy voice in my head — J — who'd raised me better than anyone in Jerusalem Children's Home, was truly the seed of Jahael, Emperor of the Seraphim...making the Emperor my creator...I also hadn't heard a word from J.

*His silence shanked me.*

The magic, which wound coldly inside me caressed by shadows, reached out to stroke Mischief's.

Mischief startled, before he smiled. He curled around me, as I brushed his long silver hair off his forehead. He was trembling, although he fought to hide it.

In the Angel Games, you either worked together...or lost.

Mischief and I had lost against the last Seraphim who we'd battled because in a routine, which would've made most clowns stomp their giant feet with jealousy, we'd each pulled in different directions against the shackles: both trying to lead.

Mischief had led the rebellion in the Underworld, just as for centuries he'd helped his people, although always from the shadows. Now that Mischief had revealed his true place — not as a lowly Undeserving, but rather as the bastard son of the Emperor of the gods — did he surge with the same power that had blasted through me ever since we'd entered the temple? The need to prove himself worthy at last?

*How dangerous was he?*

Mischief was an Archduke. He'd brought us to this realm to save our lives, but now that we were trapped here, did Mischief hunger to finally rule?

It sucked if he did because so far Mischief hadn't been raised up as an heir, he'd been mocked as the entertainment.

Mischief shuddered, pressing closer to me.

This Serpent Chamber was our punishment for failure because Mischief had been trained to be terrified of snakes.

Yet Jahael was Mischief's dad. So, for Emperor, read *prick*.

Was Jahael watching us — his creation and his long-lost son — suffering for him in his Angel Games?

Mischief gasped, as the Pavilion rolled us against the scaly walls. I caught Mischief's lower lip between mine, biting hard enough to explode his popcorn crackling blood shuddering through me, just like his tremors: his desire chased away the fear. When his hands clasped mine, he was

3

lost in me; the feel of being snake-swallowed forgotten.

*Take that Your Imperial Worship Me Because I'm a Narcissistic Unstable Dictatorness.*

Mischief was mine, yet he alone had never kneeled for me. I didn't need his worship, only his love.

*Hell, I loved him.*

Yet the Seraphim were too powerful for me to keep him safe.

Could I keep any of my family safe in this realm? Could even *I* survive?

The son of a god and a vampire god had become no more than a sideshow.

*And wasn't that a bitch.*

Giant metallic glowing eyes swirled, Cheshire Cat style, out of the dark above our heads.

Mischief stiffened, whilst I swallowed with difficulty against my parched throat. Nothing as ordinary as food or drink — or sunlight for Mischief because that's what angels fed on — had been left in the Pavilion as rewards. Maybe no one in the Angel Games lived long enough to need them.

I'd put in my order for a Meat Feast pizza and tequila as soon as the tall glass gates at the end of the Pavilion melted open.

"Trust me, Holy Competitors, whilst you wallow in your fruitless rutting, you risk burning as the Damned, rather than the Divine." The smooth, aristocratic voice boomed from bowed pink lips, which floated below the silver eyes. I smirked at the Overseer of the Angel Games, whose magic tingled across my own. He'd been the only haughty constant of the games...nothing but eyes and lips...watching and guiding. *But why was he throwing a brat tantrum?* "You're approaching the centre of Court One and The Abyss. Will two of royal blood die as whores?"

*Abyss* wasn't sounding like Lollypop Land for Fairies. And dying wasn't on my to-do list.

"Sorry, bro, but I don't take orders from freaky

4

disembodied body parts. Plus, *wallowing in fruitless rutting...*?" I caressed Mischief's sensitive wings, until he arched against me. "If you weren't just the voyeur but had the balls to be part of this feathery ride, you'd know that it's worth living for, even bringing my fam back to life."

The Overseer's eyes narrowed. A blast of cool mint, sweet with honey, blew Mischief and me back.

*Crack* — my head slammed against the wall.

I groaned.

"Oh, here's an idea, beastly deity," Mischief cradled his nose, which had smacked into the scaled wall next to me, "how about *not* taunting the powerful Overseer, whilst we're trapped in the angelic *Hunger Games*?"

I shrugged. "We're already caught in your nightmare. What's the worst that Twinkle Eyes can do?"

Mischief sighed. "And you consider it's *I* who needs a gag?"

The Overseer's lush lips chuckled. "We have only been playing, brothers and sisters. What else does one do with toys?"

When boa constrictors slithered out of the floor, Mischief scrabbled backwards, and I yelped, hauled after him by the shackles. This was just like the snake attack at the witches' house, as if the Overseer had reached into Mischief's mind and plucked out a horror to punish us both.

*Yeah, Mischief might've had a point on the Overseer baiting.*

Mischief whimpered, scrabbling at his own chest, whilst the snakes coiled up his trousers. I growled, unsheathing Star, my dagger. Then I took a breath, before I plunged it through the squeezing coils.

The snake exploded in a spray of glitter.

*Cheers and polite clapping.*

Wearily, I looked up to see our Seraphim audience

5

shimmering in and out above our heads.

Invisible, the Seraphim only made their presence known at victories or failures: which had this been?

Each angel god had six silvery violet wings, which fluttered more like arms. Red-dyed feathers had been woven into their silver hair, which matched the crimson satins that flowed off them, as if they were flaming matches. I quailed before the rolling waves of buzzing *power*, which called to my own.

Ever since I'd entered The Burning Temple of the Seraphim, there'd been a static thrumming beneath my skin. As soon as I'd battled in the Angel Games, it'd blazed through both angelic and vampiric sides of my nature. It'd sung to me of something deeper inside: a craving to meet my creator.

*To take Jahael's power.*

My breath hitched, and I shivered.

Why the hell was I coming over all *Game of Thrones*? Perhaps that's why Jahael had refused Mischief and me an audience, and perhaps it's why I was so desperate for one.

The Seraphim faded back to invisibility, even if I could still feel the bastards *watching*. The burning power dwindled too, until I reined in the autocrat and remembered Mischief's personal fear had just come to life.

I ran my hands down Mischief's tremoring arms, stilling his hands, which had gouged scarlet furrows down his pale chest. His eyes were glazed, and I knew that he was lost in the Lower Vault of Castle Drake with the snakes... I'd rescued him then too. Except, he hadn't believed that it'd been out of love.

*Did he believe it now?*

At last, Mischief's gaze focused on me. "Why would you save me, when I brought you here?" I hated the insecurity in his eyes. "I should be no more than your prisoner or hostage after I—"

"Trapped us in this freakshow of a realm?"

Mischief gave a short nod. "How can you trust a sly traitor?"

My gaze hardened. "Who said anything about *trust*?"

Mischief flinched. "We need to survive together. Then we'll rescue *our* fam because you can pretend that you don't care but you have *their* back, as much as you have mine. You know what though? I'll kick your arse if you go searching for Jahael as a Sith mentor for your dark side."

Mischief bristled. "How precisely do you know that he wouldn't be a Jedi?"

"Pleasure Pavilion with torture rooms Yoda scream it doesn't."

Mischief's lips quirked into a grin, which he couldn't hide fast enough. He pouted. "Childish." Then he curled his hand into mine. "Do you imagine that this is the greeting I hoped for from my father? Hated by my mother and scorned by the other mages for my *feminine* magic, simply because Jahael enjoyed walking amongst other worlds and creating bastards...like me."

I licked my dry lips. "Being shackled to me and thrown into death games isn't your deepest desire? Why not? I'm legendary."

I tangled Mischief's legs with mine, tumbling him over in a flash of leather. He laughed, rubbing his hands down the tight trousers, which I'd been dressed in, before I'd been shoved into the Games. Then he traced along my top that glistened with purple diamonds in the outline of six Seraphim wings, which pulsed when danger was near.

"I shan't call you *beast* anymore," Mischief mused. "Or my Sailor Moon. How about—"

"Your god?"

Mischief hissed. "Tempting, although blasphemous, but no... You will be my *sultan's jewel*."

I snorted. "Your daddy's the sultan."

"Who's seeded inside *you* as well... Wait, are your diamonds pulsing or are you just pleased to see me?"

I peeked down at the angel wings that were threaded onto my top.

*Hell...*

"Don't let us interrupt your scintillating drama," the Overseer drawled. His eyes widened into spinning vortexes. *Why did his sarcasm remind me of Mischief's?* "You're worshipping the *Fire God*, may his will always stand, through your battles in the Games, although one would've thought it was through your—"

"Sassy charm? Epic violet boots? *Love?*"

"It'll be the boots," Mischief muttered. "Knee-high leather... We've all got a thing about your boots. Although, maybe *he* should be worshipping *your* boots...?"

"I thought we weren't taunting all powerful pink lips?"

Mischief shrugged. "That was before the snake trick. Now I fully intend to make it out of Court One and to hurt him with more than words."

"Holy Competitors, I merely fulfil my duty, as must you." *Was that concern in the Overseer's voice?* I grinned. "And if you love, then *burn* with it."

Light flared through the room.

Blinded, I raised my arm over my eyes. My top flashed a warning.

*Screech.*

I rolled Mischief to the side, as a flaming crimson creature with a horn on its head swooped past him.

I paled, whilst my pulse thundered. "Either I've been sucking on the crazy juice, or that's a—"

"Dragon," Mischief snapped.

"I was going with *My Little Unicorn's on Fire*."

Mischief arched his brow. "We may wish to work on the survival part of our plan now."

*Screech, screech, screech.*

Three more dragons, like they'd been set alight and were pissed about it, plunged out of the gloom.

Mischief threw me to the side this time. He howled, as he was caught between the dragons' burning shanks. I slapped at Mischief's singed feathers, putting out the embers, whilst he hissed.

*Screech, screech, screech.*

Mischief and I stared at each other. *Three more dragons?* What was this: *Snow White and the Seven Freaky-horned Dragons?*

I gripped Mischief's hand. "Bastard run..."

Mischief and I stumbled through the undulating room, the leg shackles clanking and tugging painfully, towards the glass gate at the end and the only exit into the inner room of the Pavilion.

*Please, let it open...*

A dragon swooped overhead; its sharp claws scratched along my scalp in fiery brands. I tripped, but Mischief caught my elbow pulling me on towards the gate.

*Clang, clang, clang.*

"Open sesame!" I pounded on the glass. It'd never worked before, but sometimes even a god was desperate enough to reach for the classics. "Divine knocking on heaven's door, bitches."

*And sometimes, less of the classics.*

Mischief twisted me to face the Serpent's Chamber again. "I always imagined that I'd make a noble St George." He cast me a sidelong glance. "Until you came along and slew the dragons for me."

"Looks like you'll get your chance." I tightened my hold on Mischief's hand. "Unless we're now playing the role of damsel sacrifice, and I swore that I'd never be the damsel."

The dragon brothers snorted, as they turned as one: they had no problem working together, but then how long had they been trapped down here? Unless, they were only illusions, as the snakes had been.

The dragons felt real enough, however, as they soared towards Mischief and me. When the dragons' mouths opened, shooting out flames towards us, we recoiled — trapped against the gate — and I howled against the heat of the towering inferno.

# 2

When Rebel had trained me as a huntress, he'd taught me that killing should only be to save others, or else you'd become a monster too. During an apocalypse, Mischief had fought to stop me transforming into Lucifer's beast who was infected with a spark that enthralled men to sacrifice their lives. Here in the Pleasure Pavilion, however, the Seraphim killed for sport.

*And Mischief and I were their playthings.*

The heat of the dragons' breath scorched my skin and singed my hair in a stinking rush. I screwed shut my eyes against the brutal blaze.

*Couldn't breathe, couldn't breathe, couldn't...*

Mischief's fingers slipped from mine in the dark.

My heartbeat — *thud, thud, thudded* — in my ears, drowning out the rumble of the flames. I scrabbled, clawing along the glass of the gate to reach Mischief again. If this was my time to go out in a blaze of glory, then I wanted...*needed*...to know that he stood at my side.

Still, this was the last room before the centre of the Pleasure Pavilion and the final battle to win the Angel

Games; it'd be an epic fail to be killed, when the end level boss was just through these gates.

I clasped Mischief's wrist, edging his stiff fingers between mine.

*"Trust me,"* the Overseer's supercilious voice whispered like winding silk into my mind.

I jolted, as the gate melted. Then I was tumbling through, away from the seven dragon brothers and the Serpent Chamber and into the final room of the Pleasure Pavilion.

*Oomph* — I landed hard on the ruby floor.

For long moments, I lay gasping and choking.

Lips caressed against mine, sucking away the burns, blisters, and pain...healing me.

I struggled to open my eyes, whilst Mischief vibrated with the dual agony of his own roasting and mine as well: his Angelic Power took my pain. His skin was waxy pale with the effort. I stroked his hair, which was damp with sweat, behind his ear. At last, he broke away with a shudder, before resting his head on my chest.

"The Overseer did promise that we would *burn*." Mischief tilted his head. "But then, I imagine that he must have to compensate for something, since the insufferable bully lacks anything but eyes and a mouth."

I shifted to my knees, remembering the Overseer's secret whisper.

Why had the Overseer saved Mischief and me? We should be dragon fodder, but the Overseer had allowed us through into the final room, even if he'd used my own demands for *trust* to skewer me.

*Had the mysterious bastard been helping us all along?*

I glanced around and then whimpered.

I shoved myself back against the sparkling wall, which rose above my head so high that I couldn't even see where it ended. When seven blazing dragon statues burst from the walls, I clutched Mischief's tunic, yanking him closer. The vast chamber stunk of sulphur; the smoke from the statues

12

stung my eyes. The Pavilion was spherical, and in its centre was the deep Abyss. I shivered at the blackness.

*Was it as deep as it was high?*

When I'd lived amongst the humans, I'd designed a computer game, *Angels vs Vampires*, where vampires had crawled deformed out of a pit to be battled by the golden perfection of angels. I'd since learnt that there was no such thing as perfection, and that in the epic war between angels and vampires *I* was the Protector for *both* sides.

*Yet here was the pit.*

Delicate fingers caught my jaw, turning my chin away from the gaping Abyss.

Mischief studied me, before kissing me tenderly, just once, behind the ear. "My, have I lost all my charms, that our impending death at the hands of whatever hideous creature slithers out of the depths takes up *all* of your attention, jewel?"

I spluttered with laugher. "Not in the land of belly dancing centaurs." I rubbed my thumb over his wingtip, and he leant into me with a sharp intake of breath.

"Exhibitionist," he sniffed.

"Prude."

"The Abyss, unless your *impending death* has less value to you than the hardness in your trousers, brother, is where the Fallen are damned." The Overseer's eyes shone out of the blackness below us.

I jerked: how had I known that, when I'd designed my computer game? Humans called Fallen angels *vampires*. Had J, who'd been seeded in me by Jahael since birth, also brought memories of the Seraphim?

I choked on the clouds of smoke, which drifted from the dragon statues, then licked across my dry lips.

How long had it been since I'd had anything to drink?

"You thirst, sister?" The Overseer's voice softened.

Had he caught my thought? *Was the bastard reading my mind?*

13

*Fluffy puppies snuggling out of the pit, all my fam safe, and...*

The Overseer chuckled. "By His wing, I am no jinn. I assure you, I have no reason to compensate for anything...so, I can be merciful. Drink."

The ruby floor dipped to create a pool of crimson water.

I shook but I forced myself not to dive on the water. "Not on your freaky eyes, bro. If witches have taught me one lesson, it's don't take drinks from your captors. Poison me once, yeah?" Mischief's hand hovered over the pool, and I swiped it away. "Seriously? I had to watch your crazy arse drinking at the Head Coven and not even know..." I couldn't help the way that my voice wavered. Suddenly, my neck was warm with the awareness of the Seraphim shimmering in and out and feasting on my distress. *Was Jahael watching?* "You could've died and..."

"You almost sound sincere in your concern." I startled at Mischief's hesitant tone, as he scrutinized me. With a lifetime of mistreatment by Glories — female angels — did he still not understand that I'd meant my love? Could *he* ever truly love a Glory? "Drinking was less painful than the alternative, as it will be now. Or is this a case of: you can lead a beast to water, but you can't make it drink?"

Stung, I reached for the water.

"Without using your hands," the Overseer commanded, smugly.

I flushed: what was this, *Domination 101*?

Mischief rolled his eyes. "Allow me to be your Official Taster."

His cheeks blushed, as his pink tongue lapped at the pool.

*Titters.*

Mischief's shoulders hunched, whilst the Seraphim crowded closer.

14

I got Mischief's humiliation because I was a queen, but he was an Archduke, and these were *his* people. Returning the long-lost bastard, he hadn't expected that they'd throw a parade, but being shamed and tortured had to be a boot to the balls.

Note to self: no more pissing contests with the Overseer. He didn't need a prick to be one.

Mischief curled his wings around himself as if in comfort against the *catcalls*.

Screw Mischief being my taster. If he could become the Seraphim's dog for me, then I could for him: we'd be their bitches together.

I bowed my head over the pool; the water smelt sickly sweet of roses. Before I could take a long lick, however, soft feathers tickled my nose.

Mischief's wing hovered beneath my face like a feathered bowl with water pooled in its softness.

I shot Mischief a glance.

Mischief shrugged. "Hands free..." I grinned as I lapped at the rosewater, taking care to suck at each feather because a bitch has to be grateful to her squire. I fluttered my eyelashes at Mischief, who groaned at the sensation, struggling not to spill the water. "Insufferable minx..." Suddenly, Mischief slumped, wrapping his wings around me. "I m-may have made a t-tiny miscalculation..."

"What the hell...?" I shook him.

Mischief's eyes were glazed, as he wheezed. The six purple seraphim wings on my top pulsed. "Now you tell me, bitches?" I pinched one of the diamonds, and it *squeaked* indignantly. "How about an early warning system next time?"

My gaze became blurry too; a numbing sensation crept through my body from the pins and needles in my toes to the tips of my fingers.

*Nope, not getting good tinglies from being right about the bastard water.*

15

Violet and black spiralled inside me in righteous fury at the Overseer; it buzzed beneath my skin. The Overseer asked for *trust*, but in The Burning Temple, there was nothing but deception.

"Only cowards poison." I shot an arc of violet flames towards the traitorous eyes.

The eyes blinked out, before appearing in blazing fury above our heads, whilst the giant lips hissed, "In the name of the Most Worshipped Love, the Emperor, I merely anointed you, fit to meet the Damned." The lips quirked. "Surely anything worth winning is hard? Or would you like me to make it easy for you, insignificant ones?"

"Let me think about that... *Of course, I wish you to make it easy*," Mischief panted. "I've always been insignificant: please, go ahead and try to shame me into the hero's way. You have no idea what I've sacrificed or the true battles that I've fought, none of which have been upon stages for applause. So, *easy* it is."

I didn't expect the Overseer's huff of laughter. "So be it. Easy for you, hard for your...owner."

"Wait," Mischief's eyes widened, "I didn't mean—"

"Too late." When Mischief straightened, no longer affected by the drugged water, he shot me an apologetic glance. "The Abyss is opening: here captured Fallen are punished or discover redemption." *I tensed: was Ash in the black freeze?* I couldn't bear the thought of him alone down there. "One final fight for the Emperor's glory. Then the winners will be free, and the losers become their spoils."

"How about a dramatic rock-paper-scissors tournament instead?" I forced myself onto my feet next to Mischief, even though I swayed. "Twister? *Risk*, but I'm holding Australia, bitches."

"A power mad empire builder...what a shock," Mischief murmured, before holding up a finger. "However, I would slay all with my rock-paper-scissors moves: it's all down to patterns and psychology." His grin was sly. "I excel at

16

reading both."

"Silence!" The Overseer boomed. "You speak in cursed riddles. There's no game but battle in the Fire God's Glory."

*That didn't sound like bastard <u>Risk</u>...*

When the Overseer's lips faded, an explosion of smoke burst from the Abyss. I clutched the wall, peering through the haze.

Two Fallen soared from the gloom, christened in ash and majesty, rather than crawling from the pit, as I'd always imagined. Here was judgement and death, shackled at the ankle like Mischief and me. The battle that Jahael had seeded in my mind all my life: angels vs vampires.

Yet it was a battle that I no longer believed in. Hell, I *loved* a vampire. I loved...

*Ash...my* vampire was free from the Abyss — *safe*.

Black surged through me, howling to touch him, kiss him, *taste* him, until I knew that he was mine again. I was heady with the need for connection, after being blocked from my family in the Pleasure Pavilion. I bit my tongue, sucking on my own tangy copper, whilst struggling to calm my vampiric nature.

I gasped, as Ash landed; his olive skin and sable tumble of hair was daubed with soot, like his black shirt and trousers, which hung in tatters. He still had his shooter strapped around his waist, at least. He quirked an eyebrow at me, with a twitch of his crotch. "I've missed you too, Violet, but my eyes are up here."

I laughed, as I circled my arms around his neck, laying my head against his shoulder; the steady beat of his heart soothed the storming black inside. His citrus and clove fragranced wings cocooned me: just for a moment, I was *home*. "All the better for checking out my biteable arse?"

"You know it, babe."

I pinched the soft skin at the base of his wings, and he yelped. "Already you want to remind me of the butter knife deaths still owing? We're already in the *Running Man*..."

He kissed the top of my head. "Then I may as well go out swinging, my precious Monkey Muffins, Pikachu, Wookie—"

I growled, and Ash dodged backwards, but not before I heard it: the *giggle* from behind Ash.

Ash stilled, wetting his lips. "About that..." He jangled the shackle on his leg, dragging out a smaller vampire's foot from where a vampire was hiding behind Ash. "I discovered family down there. They've been forcing us to fight together."

*Family?*

My pulse pounded; my hands tremored.

Had they pulled Harahel out of the Under World or Anarchy from the Pure...?

Sighing, Ash turned, gripping the other vampire by the shoulders and hauling him in front of me.

My breath hitched, as I flushed both hot and cold.

Lucifer — my dad, who'd ruled as the tyrannical king of the Under World, until I'd betrayed him to the Matriarch, my mum — fidgeted, rubbing his foot backwards and forwards across the floor. His spiky ash blond hair was grimy, and he only wore a tiny pair of black leather shorts, rather than his terrifying flaming armour or horns. He looked even younger than me now: diminished. He rocked onto his heels, finally raising his gaze. "Honey, I'm home."

*Slap* — I slapped him across his cheek.

All this time, I'd been devastated to imagine how the Matriarch was breaking Lucifer, even though he'd taken everything from Ash: even his little sisters.

I hated Lucifer, and yet...I loved him too.

And I hated him for that.

*Why did he have to love me?*

Lucifer's eyes gleamed, but the tears didn't fall. "Huh, we'll agree that daddy deserved that." He dug his fingers over the handprint, as if to bruise the pain deeper. "Didn't I always promise that you'd be glorious? Look at you, my monstrous daughter, the golden girl of even the Seraphim. I wish..." He hesitated, glancing down. It was so unlike

18

Lucifer's towering power in the Under World that I shook: *had* the Matriarch broken him? His voice was soft and fragile, "...The Glories hurt and trap us. Everything's pain. On my fangs, I only wanted to save the Wings and Fallen."

"Are we all done with the war crimes tribunal?" Mischief lips were tight, although he stroked the back of his hand down Lucifer's crimson cheek.

When Mischief twisted Lucifer's head to the side, Lucifer stiffened but allowed it: **ML** was tattooed in angel blood at the base of his neck.

*Hell, no...*

My eyes widened. Lucifer had been Marked again, just as I'd Marked Rebel against his will, and Drake had been Marked as the Matriarch's ever since he was young: *a bed slave*. This was why Lucifer had rebelled in the first place and Angel World had been divided into civil war.

I noticed then the purpling around Lucifer's eyes, and the way that the word **FIRE**, which had been branded across his chest between his pink nipples, looked livid and wrong, as if it'd been branded across a second time, then daubed with a paste that stopped it from healing.

Lucifer's Fire: The Matriarch had stolen it...*was still stealing it...* That was why Lucifer seemed so small: no fire lights or turning other angels to ash.

*He was powerless.*

Then why wasn't I doing the happy dance? *Why wasn't Ash?* Lucifer controlled — tamed — at last?

Lucifer arched into Mischief's hand like he hadn't been touched gently in a long time. "I should be spanking cross with you, and we both know that's our scene, for fighting for me and not running like I ordered when the others betrayed me." My cheeks flushed: Lucifer didn't know that Mischief, the angel he'd desired to bond with, had in fact been the spy who'd planned the entire rebellion against him. "Now look at all the trouble you're in, my darling pet."

Mischief drew back; his gaze became hard. "I'm not your

19

pet. I never was and..."

"Not until the Sheriff of Nottingham takes on Robin Hood at a charity dance off will he *ever* be," I smirked.

Lucifer backed against Ash as if for reassurance. "There's sassy and then there's just plain rude."

Suddenly, my head became even woozier; I whined.

Mischief gripped my elbow, holding me upright. "How many brownie points did I lose for leading you to drink poison?"

"You *drank*?" Ash arched an unimpressed eyebrow.

"You dare drug my daughter?" Lucifer howled up into the dark.

I startled. Despite the loss of his powers, Lucifer still had the goosebump effect when he freaked out.

The Overseer's eyes blazed out of the black. "You should know about drugging, whore of the Matriarch," the Overseer sneered, cold and cruel in a way that he'd never been when he'd spoken to me. "Your Marked Glory kept you in such a delirium, how long was it before you even noticed that you'd been snatched as our Emperor's plaything, *Star*?" Lucifer winced at the *Star*, which the Matriarch had called him as well. *No way would I ever call him that.* "Now fight because every word that falls from your damned lips inspires me with the desire to skip to your punishment after you lose."

Hell, my dad might've been a psycho who deserved every punishment...but fam was fam, and no matter how much I wanted to kill the kernel of love for him, I couldn't. I'd thought that I'd never see him again, and now that he was here, I couldn't fight or hurt him when he was defenceless.

I met Ash's gaze, and he nodded.

Before I could tell the Overseer just how deep into the Abyss he could shove his command, Lucifer pouted. "Oh goodie, both a fight and a punishment...? *Hmmm*, I think I'll pass. Hurt me if that's what gets your rocks off, but the only thing I have left is my daughter. And she hates me." I flinched. "I'd topple worlds just for her to allow me to battle

20

by her side."

Why were my eyes burning, and my throat tight?

Ash grinned, lounging against the wall next to Lucifer as he examined his nails. "When's room service? I'm starving."

Mischief snorted. "You missed Happy Hour."

*What had I promised myself about taunting the Overseer...?*

"If you do not complete the Angel Games," the Overseer's voice was dangerously low, "you'll be immolated: offered up to the one who loves us all."

The ground began to shake, just as the diamonds on my top throbbed and *squawked* out a warning.

I slapped my top into silence. "I asked for *early* warning, bitches."

*A rumbling roar.*

The Overseer's lips grew wider and wider, threatening to swallow us whole, as lava spewed from the ruby encrusted walls.

Ash hollered, swiping at his singed wings. I fell onto my arse, whilst the world shook hellfire. Lucifer dived over me, covering my body with his wings: I stilled at the familiar scent and warmth of his feathers.

Then the world burst to flames.

21

# 3

When the seven dragon brothers burst from the Serpent Chamber into the centre of Court One — the glass gates melted into a pool by their flames — at the very moment that the Abyss choked smoke and the walls bled lava, I had two choices: kill the predators or tame them.

The silver magics, which squirmed inside me and nipped at the same time as they caressed, murmured that I *could* tame them. The shadows fluttered inside, excited at the thought, whilst I shifted disquieted by it.

*Should such power be leashed?*

I'd been forced into a collar before and yanked around on a chain.

It sucked.

*So, why did I now crave to be the one holding the leash?*

*Clink* — Ash hauled Lucifer away from me by his ankle.

Lucifer yelped, stumbling to Ash's side. Instantly, I missed the security of his wings, which had sheltered me.

Ash pulled out a tiny fork from his jean's pocket: Devil's Trident. With a flick of his wrist, the fork twisted outwards until he was almost as tall as Ash; the weapon forged from living bone with three prongs, and a sharpened bottom, glistened with energy...and death.

*I bastard hungered for him.*

I licked my lips, edging closer on my knees. I could taste the trident's charcoal-like musk and feel the ghost-like memory of his shaft in my hand, whilst he'd squirmed with bloodthirsty delight at my own dad's attempted murder.

Even if it had been to stop an apocalypse.

"It's fight or die time." Ash gripped Devil so tightly that his knuckles became white. "Like fight or shag, just not as fun."

"*Yours, take me, win,*" Devil whispered, insidious in my mind.

*Even our weapons couldn't be trusted.*

I met Ash's steady gaze: he knew Devil was attempting to worm his way back to me. Devil fed off desires and darkness, twisting them. I was enough of a monster already without the trident playing the One Ring temptation card. Yet when Ash had stood next to Lucifer as his Brigadier, Devil had been Ash's weapon.

Ash was a true soldier: he could control the darkness.

Ash swung the trident away from me, shaking him for good measure, whilst he whined. "Sorry," *Ash didn't look sorry,* "dragons, lava, quake: surviving first, *your weapon is bigger than my weapon* showdown second.*"

I nodded. The poisoned rosewater cramped my stomach, blurring the world like I was underwater.

But then, I'd already fought a battle under the ocean in Castle Drake. The Seraphim wanted to make this hard for me...? They had no idea what I'd already battled against.

*Screw them.*

When the dragons soared overhead in a flaming formation, Mischief grasped my hand, dragging me backwards, just as I surged forwards. We fell in a *clanking* tangle, hollering in unison at the jolt to our ankles.

Nope, not missing the irony, when we couldn't manage

anything else in melodic harmony.

"*Together*, you witless beast." Mischief smacked his hand against the floor, then winced. "Or have you forgotten the purpose of this game?"

I raised an eyebrow. "I thought I was your jewel?"

"We shall all be nothing but ash if we don't battle as one."

The dragons wheeled around, before tossing their heads; flares shot from their horns like rays from the sun. They snorted, soaring directly towards me.

I froze, whilst Mischief's wings wrapped around me, as if they could be any protection against the blazing nightmares.

How much of this was Mischief desperate to show off his skills, just in case his dad was watching?

**The Fae Angel has a point, Violet-sweets.**

*J...? Where the hell have you been...?*

**You missed my fabulous self?**

My hands curled into fists to control my shaking. J had been in my head, even before I could understand words: a soothing presence, who'd explained the world to me when no one else had. Without J, I'd have been lost, abandoned amongst the humans, who I'd never understood: the freak.

Yet I'd discovered since coming to this realm of the gods that J had never truly been mine. He was the seed of Jahael, making me the Emperor's creation: a half angel, half vampire god. Jahael had seen everything that'd happened to me and had never stepped up to save me.

Like the Seraphim at the games, he'd only *watched* my suffering.

Was J anything more than a spy?

*I hate you, J...for not telling me who you are. You get that, yeah?*

*Silence.*

Even with the heat of the dragons and Mischief's trembling wings around me, I felt the silence more intensely

24

than the world around me falling apart.

**Hate me but listen to me. I'm the only one who knows the truth of this realm and I'll always love you.**

*Then why the disappearing act?*

**That asshole Emperor listens and watches through me. If I hide behind the walls that you built in your mind, then you're safe.**

*But he's you—*

**Let me read you some godly realness: I'm his seed, but I've grown alongside you. I'm no one but my glittery parade of hotness self.**

**Did you expect that I'd be anything but a rebel now?**

I couldn't help the smile.

*Then help me.*

**In this Arabian dream, your perky ass will only survive by remembering your bonds: The Silver Angel became yours when you saved his magic from the spell casters.**

*Mischief thinks that we're bonded...?*

**That's because you are, Violet-oblivious.**

**Act the divine: seize the power and don't trust anyone. Plus, you're welcome: no more drug trip for you.**

I blinked, and the Pleasure Pavilion drew back into focus, as the pins and needles faded: J had drained the poison from me.

*The Bitch of Utopia was back.*

Magic itched beneath my fingertips. I glanced at Mischief, before touching our palms together. He jumped, as my silver called to his. I stepped backwards, weaving the gossamer strands of our magic and uniting it between us.

I laughed, soaring on the thrill, as shivers cascaded through me at the sensation of our sparking magic joining; it quested, stroking down my wings. I spun the strands into

25

spinning discs.

Mischief grinned. "I've always wanted to take a dragon for a walk."

*Screech.*

The dragons swooped towards us like scorching death, but Mischief and I stepped forward, shoulder to shoulder, arcing the discs out into seven sparkling leashes. I could sense each of Mischief's movements before he made them: the throbbing of his blood and the thrumming of his magic.

J had been right: we *were* bonded.

Exhilarated with the rush of Mischief's magic, I hurled the leashes at the dragon brothers, even as the heat of their flames seared my cheeks.

I screamed as I was yanked off my feet in the wake of the dragons, dragged behind the leashes. Mischief held tight around my waist, however, flapping his wings and steering the dragons around.

Hell, Mischief *was* taking them for a walk.

I'd tamed the dragons, just like I'd known that I could. I hadn't killed for the sport of the invisible Seraphim.

*That's how we take them down, Hackney style.*

Mischief landed the dragons behind Ash and Lucifer, who turned with widened eyes, as the dragons huffed one final defiant breath, before crouching down on their front legs.

*They were bastard kneeling...*

I vibrated, burning with a god-like power. Was this why Seraphim played these games to experience such thrills?

Mischief pressed the leashes into my hand, before kissing my knuckles. He sparked with dark splendour. "You may be rash, thoughtless, and domineering..."

"You're now into negative brownie points..."

"But you're also a miracle." He scrutinized me in wonder at our new intimacy, whilst our silver tingled across each other for a final time, before mine *snapped* away from his and back inside.

I was cold at the loss: I needed Mischief closer again. "Miracles are a con."

"But you, Dragon God, are not."

I jolted. *Dragon God*? The ancient powers inside me stirred, warming at the name.

Ash pointed Devil at the kneeling dragons. "You win: your weapon is definitely bigger than mine."

Devil whined.

"Yay for you: you're quite the little dragon whisperer. What other talents are you hiding, missy?" Lucifer pouted. *How painful was it to see my strength, after his own had been taken from him?* "There still needs to be winners and losers, or you won't escape here. So, control those creatures and burn me already."

"What in Crazy Cat City, bro?" I stared at Lucifer, suddenly numb.

"The deal," Ash hissed. "You swore to me..."

Lucifer stepped in front of Ash, as if protecting him, even though he looked tiny in nothing but his shorts and without a single weapon in his upturned hands. "*Burn me*," he howled.

Lucifer's desperation and self-hatred shanked me.

Yet I understood it.

I met his gaze, as tears trembled on his eyelashes. Then I threw down the leashes. *Why had I ever wanted such power?* "Not if the world toppled."

Lucifer screamed, launching himself on me in a whirl of feathers. Ash tumbled after him, dragged in his wake.

"Fight me," Lucifer whispered, clinging onto me more in an embrace than an attack. "Burn me."

Ash and Mischief grabbed my dad's wings to pull him off me, but he wrapped himself limpet like and whimpering around my shoulders.

The only way to end the battle in this searing hot Abyss

27

was for one side to lose. Lucifer was offering himself up as a sacrifice, just as he'd once used his own spark to force the Fallen to offer themselves and their loved ones up to him and his light.

*Was this atonement?*

But why did *I* have to be the one to deliver it?

I swallowed; the back of my throat ached. My fingers trembled, as righteous violet fire sizzled along my arms, bursting across my palms.

*Crack* — I backhanded Lucifer.

The blow blistered his cheek, yet he sighed like I'd kissed him. I struck him again, splitting his lip.

"Burn, burn, burn..." he muttered like a benediction.

I hit him once more, swelling his eye and knowing that he was giving this to me — victory and freedom from the Games — through the price of his flesh.

Lucifer whined, before biting his swollen lip to hide the pain, even as his eyes half-closed.

The rubies flared, before the lava cooled to rock, and the ground stilled.

Lucifer had won, by losing for me. I refused to let my own tears fall. The Seraphim had witnessed enough of my pain.

Then Ash was dragging Lucifer away from me, shaking him back to befuddled consciousness. "You promised," Ash snarled. "You owe it to every single Fallen that you killed." Lucifer flinched. *"You don't choose to die."*

How many times had Lucifer been reckless with his life, hoping for death?

This time, I couldn't stop the tears. Let the bastards have their screwed-up fun.

*Once I was free, I'd take this realm apart.*

Lucifer fell to his knees, bowing his head. "Remind me."

Mischief gasped. Lucifer had never knelt: he'd been King of the Under World. Ash had knelt to him. *What the hell had changed?*

28

I scowled. "Not to sound greedy on the whole kneeling thing, but that's usually *my* deal, Mr TridentPants."

Ash ignored me, stroking over Lucifer's hair. Then he wrenched back Lucifer's head. "We had a deal. You're a tyrannical Big Bad but you never break bargains."

"I thought we were clear on not making deals with the devil?"

Lucifer shifted, struggling to stay still with the same energy as a toddler in timeout. "Yikes, you're so strict. What's with the Dom voice? I didn't save my daughter from the Legion of the Phoenix, and this was my chance to save her. You can ease up on the hair pulling; it's not one of my kinks."

Ash only pulled more firmly; Lucifer *yipped*. "Don't ever pretend to be the hero."

"How could I...after I broke my perfect dark Brigadier?"

"I. Am. Not. Broken,' Ash gritted out, shooting white beams of electric light from Devil into Lucifer on each word.

Shocked, I watched as Lucifer arched in agony, juddering on his knees.

Devil screeched in delight. "*Pain, pain, pain.*"

"You're only half way through your sentence: you won't die before that." Ash's voice was hard and flat.

Mischief marched towards Ash with the same determination as me; his jaw was clenched with rage.

Yet Ash had stopped his assault, and now ran the tips of his fingers down Lucifer's bruised cheek with surprising tenderness. "Is this enough for now? Are you sorry?"

Lucifer's eyes were bright with tears, as he shuddered. "I wish that I could lie..."

Ash's eyes became flinty, as he stepped back. White hissed along the trident again.

Devil wriggled, eager to feast on Lucifer's agony. "*Make him sorry...*"

I banged away the trident, hissing as it seared across my hand. "Not a chance. Slow down the torture train because

I'm blasting the bitch off the rails."

Ash sighed, shrinking the Devil's Trident, despite his wail of protest, and slipping him back into his pocket. "Your dad asked for this, Violet. It's what he needs."

Black blasted tsunami through me, tingling my gums. "My bitch of a mum twisted him to *think* that it's what he needs." I surprised myself at how tightly I clutched Lucifer as I fell to the floor next to him. He flushed, before melting into the hold. But maybe it was the way that Mischief mirrored me, like we were still connected, wrapping his wings around Lucifer on the other side, which made Lucifer start to *purr*.

Lucifer needed love, as much as pain: cycles of revenge and reward and punishment had kindled the civil war between the vampires and angels for centuries. If I was going to stop it, I had to try something new.

"Wow, I have to say, I never thought that I'd hold you again, pet..." Lucifer nuzzled closer to Mischief.

Mischief raised an imperious eyebrow. "Not your pet." Then he added more gently, with a teasing smile, "After all, I *am* royalty."

Lucifer spluttered, before gaping at Mischief. "Now I know that you didn't go bonding some *other* king..." His hands tightened around Mischief's wings.

Mischief's grin tipped over the line into Smugsville: but then, he had waited his entire life for this. "Why would I want to do that? I'm already an *Archduke*."

Lucifer paled. "You're the Emperor's son...?"

"You always were quick." Mischief tapped Lucifer on the nose. "How interesting that I now outrank you, *pet*."

Lucifer shuddered, but didn't draw back. Instead, he burrowed closer into Mischief's wing. "You always were a sassy brat."

*Boos and hisses.*

I started, staring up at the Seraphim hordes, who'd

materialised in fluttering fury. They glared down at us, jeering taunts.

Love clearly wasn't as popular as suffering in the Angel Games.

"Let's crack on with the show, bitches," I snarled. "You want blood? Come and have a go if you think you're hard enough." I bounced to my feet, dragging Mischief with me, as I swiped shadows in a phoenix spray at our disappointed audience.

They howled, covering their faces, as the shadows stuck to their cheeks, or crawled down their flowing satins, until the Seraphim knocked into each other, desperately trying to shake them off their private parts.

Lucifer giggled, until a single Seraphim soared out of the Abyss, landing in front of us. Then Lucifer blanched, recoiling.

"I believe myself *hard* enough." That cultured, arrogant voice...whilst the Seraphim raised his eyebrow over eyes that blazed silver and pursed his pink lips, and I knew that *he was the Overseer*.

I took a step backwards. My shadows faded, just as the Seraphim melted back to invisibility.

So, the Overseer did have a body — and a prick — after all.

The Overseer slunk towards us in richly embroidered indigo satin trousers and tunic; his eyes sparked against his dusky skin and lustrous hair, which glistened with woven sapphires. A large sapphire pendant hung around his neck like a collar.

If I'd had a lamp to rub, he'd have been the perfect jinn.

*With all his trickery, why should I trust him that he wasn't?*

Yet I hated the way that my pulse quickened, my palms sweated, and a blush crept up my neck. When the Overseer's gaze met mine with a tentativeness that I hadn't expected, and he smiled with such radiance that I couldn't help my own lips curling into a smile in return, I almost forgot the nightmare that he'd put me through in the Angel Games.

Almost.

*Slow clapping.*

The Overseer slouched against the wall, scrutinising us. "Do you know why your audience calls for your blood?"

"They're not nice?"

The curl of the Overseer's lips betrayed the smile that he was fighting to hide. "By His wing, you worship the Emperor through your battle, but the Games must always end on high drama. The Matriarch's whore was snatched to ensure a stunning climax. I'd imagined that the bastard or the Fallen whore would've killed the father."

I stiffened. The Seraphim had planned this final showdown...? Lucifer hadn't been playing the martyr because he'd had the smarts to know the score: he'd been the sacrifice.

*They'd always meant for him to die.*

"Sorry...yeah, actually *not sorry* to disappoint."

The Overseer fidgeted with the pendant around his neck. "It is the classic ending." There was something rehearsed about his words.

*Was his trying to tell me a secret?*

The Seraphim had come for a blood sacrifice, but I'd given them a snuggling. Did they think that they could control the Queen of Chaos...?

*Lame.*

I was my dad's daughter, after all.

I shrugged. "What can I say, bro? I prefer a happy ending."

The Overseer cocked his head; the jewels in his hair jingled. I quivered with the desire to run my fingers across them. *Why the hell was I so drawn to the bastard?*

"How unexpected: you mean that." The Overseer tapped

32

his fingers thoughtfully on his pendant. "Since there are now three whores…"

When all of my blokes hissed in outrage, I bristled. "What is it with your *whore* obsession? Are you a eunuch or can't you get a girl because normally you're nothing but swirly eyes?"

The Overseer straightened. Silver crackled across all six of his wings, dancing in electric waves.

*Dialling down the Overseer-taunting…*

"*Owie*, that prickles." Lucifer rubbed at his arms. "You know, champ, poking the Overseer never ends in anything but spankings."

The Overseer smirked. "You can still burn through *love*. Perhaps another type of happy ending…?"

*He didn't bastard mean…?*

"Not happening." Ash hauled Lucifer up, pushing him protectively behind him; *I didn't miss that.*

"Seconded," Mischief said, coldly.

I raised my hand. "And this bitch is passing the motion of *hell no*."

Flames shot from the Overseer, dancing across my skin. My knees buckled, as I howled.

"Desist," Mischief commanded. "I hoped to find my family here but all I've discovered is petty tormentors."

The flames faltered.

"You've no idea what lives in the whispers and shadows of this realm, brother, and the torment is far from petty," the Overseer's voice was soft, before it hardened again. "If you do not perform, then you shall all become *my* spoils."

My flames faded.

The freaky Overseer *had* tormented us throughout the Angel Games: if my family didn't obey, then we'd become his slaves. There'd been something about the way that he'd said *spoils*, however, as his gaze had flickered to mine, which hadn't fitted with his cruelty.

*Who was he?*

33

*"The Seraphim are watching,"* the Overseer's voice coiled through my mind again. *"Play along."*

But I was done playing. I wouldn't sacrifice my family to save myself or humiliate them on the word of a stranger.

"One," I held up my middle finger at the invisible Seraphim — Rebel would've been proud of me for the rude finger work, "no kinky strip shows are happening for your angelic pervs." I waved at the invisible Seraphim. "Two..." I raised a second finger, and Lucifer sniggered. "We won, so get us out of here already."

The Overseer prowled closer. "One..." The Overseer matched my rude finger work with an insouciant indifference, "...without the strip show you're my spoils. And two..." He held up his second finger. "...If you won, then the Fallen lost, which means punishment: I shall wrap them in the dark and keep them as ornaments in my Gilded Cage."

Black oozed from the Abyss in a burning slick, which stuck to Ash and Lucifer's feet, slipping up their legs and cocooning them.

Ash had been blinded by the witches at the Head Coven. How could I let him be trapped again in the dark?

Mischief and I moved at the same time, stalking to the Overseer and slamming him — *crack* — against the wall.

The Overseer's gaze slid across Mischief and then to me. "Foolish brother and sister..." He murmured.

The Overseer's wings hissed, before flares jumped into the base of my neck. His magic didn't soothe mine, silky soft, like Mischief's did. Instead, it shocked and jolted, until I screamed into an agony of silver.

# 4

The desolate land of feathers and bones, which had haunted my nightmares and waking visions, baked beneath the fireball sky. My clammy fingers tightened around the opal windowsill, as I leant further out of the Gilded Cage's window. When a cool breeze whispered across my skin, I shivered, despite the heat.

How could we escape, when the world outside was deadlier than even the Seraphim?

I shuddered at the remembered sensation of ticklish feathers and the *crack* of wing bones snapping underneath my feet.

If this was the real realm of bones and feathers, did that mean that I'd embrace the darkness...? Betray my fam? Trigger an apocalypse?

Was I death, the End, destroyer? Or could I choose to be birth, the Beginning, saviour?

What if I was always meant to be *both*?

I'd awoken fuzzyheaded that morning from the buzz of silver, which the Overseer had sparked into my brain with his magic whammy, in the indigo sheets of a chamber in the Gilded Cage. I'd stared around at the cool white lines and silver arches of Court Two: one step closer to the heart of the Temple.

*And Jahael: my creator.*

Except, had Lucifer and Ash been mummified in shadows and hung from the Overseer's ceiling? I'd shaken my shackle free ankle, missing the familiar weight, *clink*, and connection to Mischief.

*I bastard wanted Mischief back.*

My skin tingled between my shoulder blades at a sudden movement in the bone valley below. Shadows stalked just out of sight beneath the too bright sun.

*Monsters*, the Overseer had said.

The Seraphim needed to watch their punk arses because they'd allowed a monster inside now too.

I peeked at the sumptuous bowl, which perched next to me on the windowsill; it was filled with chilli tortilla chips, peeled grapes like eyeballs, and rich dark chocolate slices in an unholy mix.

When my stomach growled, I groaned.

Hell, the Overseer wouldn't even need to tell me *no hands*: I was going into this deliciousness headfirst...or I would be, if not for the two words that'd been traced in sugar next to the bowl: **TRUST ME.**

And I thought that *I* was a demanding bitch.

**If the Silver Sultan wanted to hurt you, girl, he wouldn't have freed your hoochie mama ass from the Angel Games.**

*Claimed as spoils, J, not freed.*

**Who's truly free?**

**Everything in the Temple of the Divine is politics, and everyone knows politics is all slutty lies.**

*Even gods play that game? Ambitious bastards.*

**They have nothing but time to play. The problem with the glorious assholes is that some of them ride it hard enough to break its dick.**

**You have to choose who you can trust to bring the happy instead.**

*Trust? The Overseer has already poisoned me. I'm not in the mood for an Alice in freaking Godland tasting session as well.*

**Eat, or don't. But without Arabian Nights hooked on your spark, you won't get an audience with the Emperor.**

**Play the pretty boy and play the politics.**

**What's one more Wing kneeling at your feet?**

Uncomfortable, I tugged my hand through my ash blonde hair, which had been streaked with violet by the Seraphim.

Could I play the Overseer — use my Angelic Powers to make him love me or at least loyally sacrifice for me — so that he'd submit?

*Should I...?*

I hated the thought that any of my fam had followed me anything but willingly; yet they were now trapped in The Burning Temple, and the only way that I could protect them was to gain a position in the hierarchy.

The Overseer offered that. He'd spoken secretly to me...*unless, he was already playing me...?*

I took a deep breath, before I snatched up the bowl, stuffing a handful of tortilla chips into my mouth — *crunch, crunch, crunch* — and sighing on the taste explosion.

*Screw it, even if it was poisoned, it was worth it.*

I hesitated, before spinning around with narrowed eyes at the sound of quiet footsteps outside the archway.

The grille whispered open.

Two blurs of olive leather, silky red hair, and fox tails bundled me backwards onto the bed.

*Oomph* — I grunted, winded, although I clung onto my bowl of treats.

*A bitch has her priorities.*

The two vampire fox Halflings slunk up my body. The brothers — Blaze and Spark — had untamed waves of red hair down to their waists, pointed ears and tails that stroked me through their slashed trousers.

Spark licked along my neck, before feathering kitten kisses along my jaw. "Missed you, missed you, missed you..."

I relinquished my hold on the bowl, placing it onto the floor, whilst plopping a grape into Spark's soft mouth. "Even peeled for you, bro."

Spark purred, licking at my chilli dust fingers and sucking, until I shivered. I moved my fingers in and out, until he released the last one with a *pop*.

I flushed, quivering with elation that my fam was with me — *safe*. Except, had they been, here with the Overseer? I remembered the Overseer's coldness towards the vampires in the Angel Games: the cruelty of his punishments.

*Had I failed the Halflings already?*

I ran my hands over Spark, who leant into the touch with a sigh, and then Blaze, who squirmed, whilst checking for flinches that they couldn't hide: signs that the Overseer had harmed them.

Finally, Blaze batted me away with a hiss. "Will you leave off fussing. The worst Gabriel's done is snuggle us at night, the big Jessie."

I stiffened. "You're on first name terms with your captor now?"

The ancient powers spat and sparked that *my* Halflings had been...*what*...?

*Snuggling* with the enemy?

"Don't be daft," Blaze snorted. "He—"

"Nay, she's not daft." Spark blinked up at me through his thick lashes. "Our Keeper's protecting us because she..." He caught himself, before rubbing his ears under my chin.

"...Likes our foxie hides in one piece."

*Loves...?*

I'd heard it, even though Spark had been quick to hide his painful yearning.

Hell, all I knew was that joy spiralled at the feel of Spark nestled in my arms. It wasn't the same as the love, which blazed through me for Rebel, Ash, Mischief, and Drake... It was softer, just like Spark.

But it burnt as brightly.

Blaze snatched Spark by the scruff of his neck, rolling him onto his stomach. Then he sank his teeth into his brother's arse.

Spark yelped, scrabbling onto my shoulders, like I had a magic teeth extraction spell.

Of course, he was right: it was called Bitch Voice.

"Teeth out of arse, or my hand will be connecting with *your* arse," I snarled.

Reluctantly, Blaze drew back. Was he pouting? That was a cute look with his fox ears...and high up on my List of Things Never to Tell a Halfling.

I pulled Spark into my arms. He whimpered, at the same time as casting an indignant glance over his shoulder at his brother. "Stop with the Thor and Loki impression. Why the sudden need to cannibalise your bro?"

"I've warned him enough that my fangs would be taking a trip to his backside," Blaze muttered, like a chastened school...fox, except that his tail still bristled with anger. "That numptie's been weeping and wailing after you, ever since Gabriel took us in, risking his own godly neck. Yet even now he has to pretend. Will you not see that Gabriel's as much a prisoner here, as we are?"

The Overseer — Gabriel — was as trapped as us? Had Gabriel truly been working to free us from the Angel Games? For the sake of Blaze and Spark?

"But the bastard's in *charge* of the Games..." I spluttered.

"Aye," Blaze leant over me, drawing his hand gently

39

down the back of my arm, even as he rubbed his nose in near apology through the feathers of Spark's wing, "didn't he pass on our messages?"

"*Trust me*," Spark murmured, his gaze hopeful. "It's what *you'd* say. So, then you'd know that it was one of us. *Trust...*"

I was going to hurl.

*Why hadn't I recognised my own words shanking me in the back?*

"I'm sorry," I whispered. "That was genius-1000, but I was riding the deity dragon, and the rush addled my brains. I might've made a teensy-weensy mistake with Gabriel."

Blaze growled. That was both intimidating and hot. "How teensy-weensy?"

"I screwed-up your escape plan: I didn't — *exactly* — win the games. I might've rebelled, instead. And that epic fail makes me Gabriel's spoils." Blaze bared his teeth; no way were they going near *my* arse. "Maybe he's been babysitting the vampire Halflings, but he's also been lynching full-grown vampires: the bastard has been hurting my dad...and Ash."

Blaze instantly stilled: I hadn't forgotten that Blaze was Ash's fanboy. He clenched his fists, bowing his head.

Spark threw himself off me, sore arse forgotten, as he wrapped his wings around his brother. "Ash will be safe, safe, safe..."

Blaze nodded. "I'll make sure of it." Then he knocked his brother sprawling to the floor with a *yelp* and marched to the archway. "Get your numptie self in here, Gabriel."

I jumped up, reaching for Flight. My sword hummed in my hands, heating and wriggling as she readied for battle.

Maybe I shouldn't have stirred the Ash Pot: Blaze had a bastard death wish.

When the grille slid open, Gabriel sloped through with his hands clasped behind his back. He didn't meet my gaze. Instead, he cast a furtive glance at Blaze.

What the hell had happened to the Seraphim of the Angel Games, who'd unleashed judgment on me?

Apparently, he was busy scuffing his bare feet against the legs of a satin armchair, which sprawled next to the bed.

He glanced up only to wave a hand at the opal blinds, which *clacked* down like a glimmering waterfall: the sun gave vampires a bastard of a migraine.

*Did Gabriel truly care?*

"Where's Ash and the other lads?" Blaze shoved Gabriel into the armchair, straddling him and nipping at his neck.

*What. The. Hell?*

Gabriel in his Overseer Mode would've blasted Blaze with fire, rained down lava-wrath, or at least not wriggled with blushing shame.

With the power that he had, Gabriel was *allowing* himself to be dominated by a vampire, Halfing or not. What use could that be to his *politics*?

"On my wing, it's the least punishment that I could conceive. Besides, it means that they're free of the Abyss. Do I not at least rate gratitude for the risk?" Gabriel ran his hands up Blaze's thighs, tangling his fingers through Blaze's tail.

"Snuggling rights denied, bastard." I sheathed Flight, although I circled closer. A warm, earthy scent of amber prickled the back of my nose. It wasn't harsh, like I'd expected. Instead, its velvety richness relaxed my shoulders, until I almost sank down to bury my head in Gabriel's broad wings. *Why did I ache to protect him, as much as I feared him?* "What punishment? Where's...?"

"The true *bastard*?" I startled at Gabriel's blistering return to Overseer fury, as he swept Blaze into a bridal carry with four of his wings. Blaze snarled but couldn't break free, as Gabriel stormed to a second window, whose blind snapped up: it looked out over a tiny courtyard. Blaze whined at the sudden light. Gabriel was as mercurial and volatile as the volcano that he controlled; any submission that he granted Blaze was no more than play. "He's taking a child's punishment. But then, perhaps you believe him

41

weaker than me? My half-brothers and I are punished with the dark and have been since we were born." He couldn't mask his shudder, even though his gaze was hard. "Tell me, have you spoiled your *family* so with the light, that they'll break at its absence?"

Gabriel waved casually across the courtyard at a row of low windowless cells behind steel doors.

Kids were locked in there as punishment? *Gabriel* still was? And right now, my family was trapped in the dark, even Ash. I'd tried to save him from the nightmare that had broken him under the witches, only to ensure this torment.

At last, Blaze managed to wrestle free, glaring out at the cells.

*Crack* — I slammed Gabriel across the windowsill, clutching him around the neck.

His throat bobbed under my hand, as he swallowed.

"Let them out now," I demanded.

"If you had only followed my direction, sister," Gabriel rasped, "I'd have no need for this petty show of vengeance. But everything is appearance or did your time in the human realm quite melt whatever brains the Fire God granted you?"

I shook, struggling to resist the waves of amber, which ached through every feather that Gabriel was to be *cherished*.

Yet where the hell had that come from because I wasn't the type of bitch to do the whole romance package, even if the way Gabriel's ebony eyelashes curved onto his cheek made me want to kiss him, until he looked up at me: *wanted me too*.

Was that his Angelic Power: to make others think he was weaker than he was? *Mischief had pulled the same trick*.

"You're not my brother." I let go of Gabriel's throat. Anael — my true half-brother, who I'd discovered in Mage Drake's castle — was somewhere alone in this labyrinth of temple courts. He'd never even been allowed out of the castle before: *how would he be able to survive?* "I already have a

42

brother."

Gabriel's gaze softened. "You're a Child of the Seraphim, who my father seeded. It's not a full sister, but I rather think I have some claim."

I stumbled backwards.

*How could you tell me to trust the sexy sultan, J? He's—*

**Archduke Gabriel, son of the Emperor. *My* fabulous son...and Mischief's half-brother.**

*If he's Mischief's brother, why did he humiliate Mischief? And don't give me the politics line because I know personal when it's hurting my bloke.*

**You should know the rivalry between siblings, Feathery-treasure. Plus, only one son can be seen to have the strength.**

**As I still have all Jahael's memories, however, I'll hold my hands up: I'm not playing Switzerland in this war.**

*Have you ever been?*

Gabriel massaged his throat, tapping at the sapphire choker, whilst studiously ignoring Blaze's death stare. "I'm the Firstborn," he explained, although the mirth didn't reach his eyes. "Lucky me."

Suddenly, the gate at the back of the chamber burst open, and a kid Wing with flowing onyx hair tumbling across his face soared into the Gilded Cage. He circled above my head on tiny violet wings, giggling. He was dressed in an identical indigo satin outfit to Gabriel, except for his choker. "Foxies!" He chorused, diving gleefully on Blaze and Spark.

"Archduke!" Blaze and Spark singsonged back like this was a practised routine as familiar as family.

*Maybe it was.*

Why did my chest ache that I'd missed out on their new connection with Gabriel and his brother?

*Hell, these were Mischief's brothers too.*

I couldn't help the grin, as the newest Little Brother Archduke (and how many sons and daughters did Jahael

43

have?), landed in Spark's arms, petting his ears and squirming, until Spark crouched down onto all fours. Little Brother Archduke squealed with delight, as he jumped onto Spark's back and rode him, holding onto his tail, as if it was a rudder of a ship.

I masked my laughter as a cough: marking that as Official Blackmail Material.

Then I glanced at Gabriel warily. Would he turn on the Big Brother stern-face at the interruption? *Tame* his little brother, as he had Mischief?

Instead, Gabriel sauntered to the armchair, stretching out in it with an indulgent smile. I shivered at the glimpse of the bloke behind the illusions, tricks, and deceptions: to something honest and real.

*To his love.*

He'd just shown his belly: the soft place to shank him. *Was I the only one who'd know to use that against him?*

The Little Brother Archduke, whose long hair had been caught back on one side with a pearl clip, tumbled off Spark and swooped towards me, clasping me around the waist.

I froze.

Blaze snorted. "The rascal's a hugger, not an assassin."

I relaxed, smoothing my hand across the boy's wings, as he purred and nestled closer. Why were my eyes prickling with tears, simply from his small arms around my waist and the memory of the Broken kids that I'd saved? When I ran my hand along his back, however, he flinched.

Just like I'd feared Spark and Blaze would, if they'd been injured.

*Who was hurting the Emperor's son?*

Silver stormed, violent with shadows; I steadied my breathing to force it to calm again. I cupped the back of Little Brother Archduke's head, pressing a kiss to the warm crown.

Then he pulled back from me, slipping his hand into the pocket of my jeans like he was the Artful Dodger. Except, he'd left something behind, rather than stealing it.

I inched my fingers into my pocket, feeling the edges of a feather. At the touch, Rebel's bond slammed through me: love with such force that I had to fight to stop my knees buckling.

What magic was in this feather... *Rebel's feather?*

*How did the royal kid know Rebel?*

Little Brother Archduke kept his gaze down as he ambled to Gabriel, perching on his lap. Gabriel enclosed him in all six of his wings, rocking him backwards and forwards. Gabriel's face was lit with a radiant smile like the sun, and I was desperate for him to turn such warmth on me as well.

It was so different to his usual derisive defence of sarcasm.

*Nope, no doubting that this was Mischief Mark Two.*

Although, maybe with a more psychotic flavour... Unlike Mischief, however, his older brother was full Seraphim, rather than only half, and had been brought up in this freaky temple by Jahael, and I'd stake my perky arse on the Emperor not being Mr Unconditional Love.

Yet despite that, Gabriel had risked his position as Firstborn to save Blaze and Spark and then to help me in the Angel Games, even if I hadn't understood the message.

And still didn't *trust* him.

I shuffled my feet, pulling my fingers away from the Rebel bonded feather with difficulty and rubbing my palms down the front of my trousers instead. "Cheers..." I muttered.

"Holy, holy, holy day: *thanks* from the creator's favourite new toy." I winced at the sharpness of Gabriel's tone, yet his radiant smile was turned on me now, and I swallowed at the strength of the tingles surging through me: the hunger to show him how *precious* he was.

I shook my head in confusion.

Wait, stop the besotted bus: when had I ever thought of anyone as *precious*?

I sniffed at the soft amber scent suspiciously. Yet I still

45

wished that I could bottle his smile and wear it around my neck in the pouch, along with my sister Jade's angel necklace.

I shrugged.

"Would it be thanks for freeing you from the Angel Games, saving your family, or having the Guardian travel through Gateways in search of..." Gabriel wrinkled his nose. "Tortilla chips."

I grinned. "All of the above."

"Why, the feathers and bones shall turn to milk and honey." I rolled my eyes at his theatrics. "Maybe you are the Queen that Spark wept for nightly."

"*God*, bro, I've been upgraded."

Gabriel sighed, before grasping his Little Brother Archduke by the chin and tilting his head. "Diniel, as much as you delight us with your presence, do you have permission to visit me?" The Archduke — Diniel — screwed up his nose, as if in deep thought, whilst he bit his lip: *no way did he have permission.* "Because I know Istafil, our Beloved Imperial Favourite," and I'd never heard anyone manage to make a name sound more like a curse, "banned you as punishment, or did your magic advance to memory alteration, and she's conveniently forgotten quite how much she detests us?"

"Well, I hate her too!" Diniel pulled away from Gabriel. He was shaking; his small fists were clenched, even though tears pooled in the corners of his eyes. Gabriel startled, as if horrified that his teasing had led to his brother's outburst. "The Mongrel Witch doesn't scare me."

"She shall, if she ever catches you calling her that," Gabriel hissed.

I glanced between them.

Witches *did* scare me because I knew the terrible things that they could do...that they *loved* to do.

"What's the deal with this bitch?" I asked.

Gabriel's mouth tightened. "I hope that you never need
46

to know the answer to your question. She rules over the Beloveds in the Forbidden Court — my father's toys — just as she has dominion over his children."

"Toys?" I glanced at Diniel, whilst I struggled not to growl. "You're not talking about his collection of Star Wars Lego and remote-controlled dinosaurs here...? You mean a bastard harem."

Gabriel wouldn't meet my eye. "It's tradition."

"So's eating Brussel sprouts at Christmas; it doesn't make it right."

Spark padded closer, running his hand over Diniel's wing. "Let's get you back to the Forbidden Court."

Diniel shifted off Gabriel's knee with a sniffle, before sadly clutching Spark's hand.

"Wait..." Gabriel surged up, swinging his brother around and holding him fiercely to his chest, before dropping him down again. "I'll take him back. We'll brave the Mongrel Witch together." Diniel gasped, scandalized, before sniggering.

Unexpectedly, the wings on my top pulsed; the diamonds *squealed*.

*Danger*.

I drew Star, my dagger, whirling around, whilst I waited for the enemy to attack.

"Don't worry, my lambs," the sultry but spiteful voice sprang from the shadows, which slowly rose into the burning shadow of a woman. Diniel whimpered, clinging more tightly onto Gabriel's hand. "I'm already here."

*Istafil had been spying on us*.

My top vibrated even faster against my skin in warning.

*How long had she been listening?* Did she know that Gabriel had helped us?

Spark and Blaze circled closer, protectively.

The fire shadow sashayed towards Diniel and Gabriel with a swing of her hips. A fragrant Damask rose scent snaked round me; I choked. "Two bad little sons, their pets,

47

and a naughty daughter, who need to be reminded of love's burn. After all, I am the *Mongrel Witch*, isn't that your name for me, my Flames...?"

"Bastard, no..." My eyes widened.

I hurled myself in front of Diniel, just as Istafil blasted towards Diniel's chest winding ribbons of fire.

# 5

Growing up in Jerusalem Children's Home, I'd weave stories about the mum and dad who'd abandoned me at birth. Fantastical and thrilling, the more I told them, the less I had to believe the nagging reality that no one wanted to adopt the freaky-eyed orphan.

Yet there was another type of kid in the home: the ones who had parents, but who'd spent their lives making up stories in which they'd been born orphans.

Because it's family who can hurt us the most.

I cringed, closing my eyes and expecting Istafil's flame ribbons, which had shot across the Gilded Cage, to burn me.

When instead, nothing seared me, and even the diamonds on my top had stopped vibrating at the danger, I cracked open my eyes.

*Why had the bitch held back on the barbecuing?*

Gabriel shuddered next to me, sweat beading on his forehead. He still clutched Diniel to his chest, but silver burst from the vortexes of his eyes, which swirled as they

49

had in the Angel Games, shielding us in a protective bubble that reminded me of the golden one that *I'd* generated to protect Drake and the angel kids in battle against Lucifer.

*Had that been a Seraphim skill?*

The gleam of the bubble cast the cool white and blue of the arched room in a fairy moonlight, just as it held back Istafil's flickering ribbons.

The fire shadow's flames snapped back in irritation. "You know better than to interfere with a chastisement, lamb." Istafil's voice had hardened; I shivered. The bitch was taking the wicked step-mother role a little too far. "Your tricks are for Court One alone. Now drop the shield and return your brattish brother to my care."

I snorted. "Not happening, Cruella."

"Please, Violet..." I swung around to stare at Gabriel. I didn't know if it was the *please* or the *Violet*. But I knew then that Istafil had a higher status in Court Two than Gabriel, and that his reaction to save me and his brother had been pure instinct. "Put away your dagger."

I glanced down at my hand and my white knuckles around Star's hilt. Shakily, I forced myself to sheath Star, which was bastard hard when there was a fire shadow in the room.

Isafil's shadow slowly took form: A Seraphim with flaming wings and ruby ribbons, which wound around her body; her floor-length hair was the same ruby as the ribbons, whose long lengths weaved like cobras about to strike with shining jewels for eyes. Sickeningly fragranced wafts of rose clouded the Gilded Cage like an invasion.

At last, Gabriel ran his hand — just once — over his brother's shaking shoulder, then he blinked. His eyes settled, as the bubble faded.

Istafil darted forward, wrenching Diniel away from Gabriel.

*And Gabriel let her.*

Diniel wailed, as Istafil twisted his sensitive wing tip,

forcing him onto his knees. "*Foxies...*"

Spark leapt forward, but Blaze caught him around the waist, pinning his hands. Spark snarled and thrashed.

"I'm sorry, lad," Blaze nipped at his neck.

"So, this Mongrel Witch thing..." I didn't miss Istafil's cringe. "Is that because you're a bitch *and* buttugly?"

Istafil almost raised her hand to check that her Miss Slutty Arabian Princess face hadn't erupted into boils: *vain*.

"Such language." Istafil's false outrage couldn't hide the undercurrent of malicious spite, as she scowled at Gabriel. "It makes me wonder what naughty little birdie first taught the Archduke here such an insulting name for me..." Gabriel paled. Istafil rapped her nails, as if in thought, on Diniel's still twisted wingtip. I shuddered in sympathy. "I dedicate so much time and effort to your training and yet all I see are two disobedient, defiant, and disrespectful sons. Our loving Emperor will be most displeased."

Gabriel hurriedly dropped to his knees.

Why did it make my guts roil at how wrong it was to see Gabriel kneeling before Istafil, whilst she stared down at him with an infuriating little smirk?

It was as wrong as it would be to see Mischief kneel. Especially when Gabriel was kneeling out of fear for his brother.

Istafil had discovered Gabriel's belly and she was shanking him in in his softest part.

"My apologies, Favoured One. We deliver ourselves to your chastisement. Please punish us as you see fit. Thank you for taking the time to train us to be good sons for the Emperor."

Istafil's ribbons writhed more wildly in excitement. She gave a satisfied smile.

*Time to wipe that off her face...*

"So, you're looking for a new nickname? How about Medusa? Because you've got that whole snake vibe thing going on. Or Baby Doll because if you're the despot's chief toy, you're more or less a blow up—"

"I'm the Favoured Beloved!" Istafil snarled, hurling Diniel to the floor and booting his wings out flat — *punishment position.*

My breath caught. When Gabriel slid onto his front as well, stretching out his wings next to Diniel, his velvety amber scent shuddered through me calling *protect, protect, protect,* until my silver screamed.

I clenched my fists to stop myself drawing my shank again and diving on Istafil to defend both Archdukes.

When I glanced at Blaze and Spark, I could see that they were struggling just the same: they clung to each other, hiding their faces in each other's necks.

Whatever begged me to *cherish* Gabriel, despite knowing his power, wasn't about him being the godly son of an Emperor, although it was about *love.*

All I knew was that he was mine, and he was about to be hurt. And he wouldn't even allow me to stop it.

"Curiosity costs. If you wish to know why I'm called *Mongrel,* then you pay." Istfil's ribbons whipped out.

*Swish — crack.*

Gabriel jolted. Blood peeked through his feathers, where the rubies on the end of the ribbons had bitten in, like belt buckles.

My pulse thundered, as I remembered the *swish — thud* of Rebel's flogging in the Bailey by the cat o-nine tails, which had clawed scarlet down his back.

"I'm a hybrid: both witch and god. Surely you didn't believe yourself our Emperor's first creation, dear heart?" Istafil simpered. Why the hell did that sting, as if I wanted to be special to my...creator? Like she'd caught my thought, Istafil laughed. "They all so prettily line up to be the Emperor's toys in the end."

52

*Swish — crack.*

When the ribbon whips hit Gabriel's other wing, he bit his lip to hold back the gasp. Angel wings were as sensitive as a vampire's claws or a bloke's prick. *It had to be bastard agony.* So, why was he frightened to make a sound? Then I saw the tears in his eyes, and that was worse because he must've learnt that he wasn't allowed to yell out, or even to cry, during his *chastisements*.

How many times had Istafil done this to Gabriel and his brother?

*Why did Gabriel allow her to?*

Istafil's look was suddenly sharp, as her gaze narrowed on me, assessing. "I'm the Fire God's favourite toy, even if he never asked permission to play. And as soon as I have a son..."

*Swish — crack.*

Gabriel convulsed under the strength of the blow, curling away with a whimper.

"Poor little lamb prefers that I take this to the Emperor after all?" Istafil crouched over Gabriel, stroking the tears from his cheeks with mock tenderness.

*Could I at least burn her hands...?*

"Sorry, Favoured One," Gabriel gasped, forcing himself back onto his front.

She straightened. "When I have my *own* son, the Fire God's promised that I shall be his Empress."

"Oh well," I gritted out, "if he's *promised*..."

Istafil's vicious self-satisfaction dropped as she gaped at me. Then every single one of her whip ribbons raised in fury, before she twisted them, bringing them down towards Diniel.

"Hold the hell up..." I hollered.

To my surprise, the ribbons hovered just above Diniel's

53

quivering wing.

Istafil sighed. "Do you think I have nothing to do apart from deal with childishness today? Dear heart, a party in your and your bastard brother's honour is arranged for tonight — let's call it, an introduction into Court Two — and I do so very much more than look breathtakingly beautiful."

"So, get polishing the party hats." I *shooed* her with my hands towards the gate.

"You are a strange creature." She tossed her hair behind her shoulder. "Much like the Irish angel whore: our newest Beloved. So sweet tasting and yet he actually believed that he could fight my touch..."

Violet burst through me: it scented the air, pounded in my veins, and it was all that I could see.

Istafil had Rebel in her harem and had been *touching*...

I roared, launching myself at Istafil, who stumbled backwards, only to find my hands catch on nothing, as Gabriel netted me in silver.

"Guilt by association." Gabriel gingerly forced himself back onto his knees with a grimace. "If you spill a drop of the Imperial Favourite's blood, you will be punished, and if she chooses, your whole family will be punished alongside you."

As the violet faded, although not the ache in my chest at the thought of Rebel trapped in the Forbidden Court — a toy — with Istafil, I got why Gabriel didn't fight back.

By trying to protect his brother, his brother would suffer far worse. It was screwed-up and better than any leash.

Tentatively, I felt through the bond to Rebel.

*Shame, despair, humiliation...*

Shocked, I gasped. Then glared at Istafil, craving to take out every ounce of pain that I'd experienced through the bond on her.

I might not be able to take her blood, but there were other ways to make someone hurt, and I was the Queen of Hurt. Plus, risky escape attempts, and I would save Rebel from the Forbidden Court. His love ached through me from the feather in my pocket: I missed him, as badly as I missed the wings that Mage Drake had stolen from me.

I inched my fingers into my pocket to stroke over the feather, then jolted at Rebel's message, which murmured through my mind like a love poem at the touch: *Feathers, sweet Jesus, I hope you can hear this. I'm trapped in the Forbidden Court with a young fellah, Sablo, who's no older than Haman...he can magic these recordings, and I'd rip out every feather if it meant that you knew you weren't abandoned. I'll find my way to you. But, until then, this is my Reasons Why I Should be Off Your List of Asses to Kick. Number One: I love you and...wait, the Mongrel Witch is coming back...*

Tears pricked my eyes, and my pulse quickened, as the recording cut off.

What had Istafil done to Rebel? Had she discovered Rebel's trick? And I hadn't missed Rebel's anguish about a kid the same age as his brother being held as a *Beloved* in the harem.

Rebel had taken the risk to smuggle out the message to me, however, because he loved me enough to ensure I knew that I wasn't abandoned.

*So, I'd take the risk to set him free.*

Except, Istafil must've been doing her witch mind reader thing or else she knew enough about manipulation to know my next move because she *tutted*. "Only Beloveds and bodyguards are allowed within the Forbidden Court. If anyone else touches a Beloved without permission, their hand is struck off. Maybe Fallen hybrids aren't bright enough to know the meaning of long words like *Forbidden*?"

"I'm the Dragon Queen," I forced myself to reply calmly, "I know the meaning of regime change."

Istafil stared at me. Then she spun to Gabriel who was watching me with an inscrutable expression. "Now, what do you say?"

"Thank you for shining your beauty and kindness on us
55

and correcting our faults," Gabriel intoned.

"Seriously," I rolled my eyes, "you make them recite that? Here's another long word I know: egomaniac."

Istafil's hair burst into flame: *bastard anger issues*. "You must present this creature...your sister, as well as her bastard brother...at the party tonight." She ran the back of her hand down Gabriel's arm. "Let's have some fun, sweet lamb. Unwind and relax. You're so tense."

"No," Gabriel whispered, "they're not ready."

Istafil's claw-like nails bit into Gabriel's welted wings, as she held him close, and at last he wailed.

I jumped forward, before stopping myself, as the ancient powers inside me howled to sweep Gabriel away from her cruel parody of an embrace.

Finally, Istafil let up, patting Gabriel's head. "There, there, lamb. You'll bring them to the party, and it shall be songs and dancing and... If your new brother is not tame yet, then I'll simply tame him myself. In fact, I relish the chance to train such a pretty one." I swallowed bile, as Istafil twisted around to Diniel, dragging him to his feet. "Brat, if you don't wish to spend your time in the Forbidden Court with me, you may spend it in the dark."

"*No...*" Diniel wailed, as Istafil swept through the archway towards the cells.

Gabriel painfully pushed himself up. He looked...*guilty*. And I got that because he hadn't saved his little brother from the dark.

I truly understood now how much of a prisoner he was.

"I..." Gabriel stopped, fidgeting with the hem of his top. "I apologise for my cowardice and—"

"Enough of that." Blaze caught Gabriel before his knees could buckle, supporting him to the bed. He wrapped his arms around his waist, licking up his neck. "She uses you against each other. It'll damage your position in court if you can't control—"

"Mischief," Spark whimpered.

"I am aware." Gabriel ducked his head. "As soon as I'm able, I shall allow your family free of the cells. I should never have put them in there and for that, you have my apologies. One thing I never want is to take after Istafil."

"So, what now?" I dropped next to Gabriel, stroking a sapphire behind his ear, which glistened in his hair. "Because a bitch like that shouldn't be controlling the board."

"She'll use you both to weaken me and gain strength for her own position with the Emperor, until she can bear him a child. She doesn't believe that you and I will be able to tame Mischief or can become the new power: we must show her that she's wrong."

I nodded because my mouth was too dry to form words.

Tonight, I'd go to the Step-Mum from Hell's party, impress the Seraphim, and tame Mischief. I'd break my promise to never force someone to submit against their will. And I'd do it because the gods, Istafil, and for all I knew *Jahael himself* was watching for Gabriel and me to slip up.

Plus, if I didn't, Mischief would be broken under Istafil's training. *Yet how much harder would it be to break him myself?*

Did Jahael know the dangers in his courts? The truth of the Angel Games and the cruelty of his Imperial Favourite? Or was the party tonight my first chance to meet him and discover whether out of all the gods, the Emperor was the deadliest?

# 6

The bone-white moon beamed from the ruby-tinged dark of the night sky; spectre fingers crept across the silver arches of the Gilded Cage. The opals embedded in the roof glowed and hummed lullaby-soft.

I shivered in the cool that at tonight's party I'd be honoured, and Mischief would be humbled.

*And I'd be the bitch who'd put him in his place.*

Mischief pressed another amethyst bead onto my midriff, stoking the skin with his elegant finger first.

When I'd been left alone in the Gilded Cage with Mischief, I'd discovered the outfit, which Gabriel had laid out for my introduction to Court Two: a purple fringed belt and bra that *jingled* every time I moved, a flowing chiffon skirt and ballet shoes.

If Gabriel expected a belly dance, then he'd get the Seven Kicked Asses, rather than the Seven Veils.

On the bed, there'd also been an ornate box of beads. Mischief had stuck the amethyst beads to my skin, until I'd become a gem encrusted doll: another one of Jahael's playthings...or Istafil's.

Mischief glanced up at me through his hair, before bending over my hands and fixing the final two gems onto my palms. Then he kissed each tenderly.

My breath caught.

"My jewel." Mischief cradled my hands to his cheek; his gaze sought mine. "I belong to you in all ways that could conceivably matter, as you belong to me. My father — how he is seeded inside you, as well as whatever we need to do to survive and protect our family — *nothing* changes that."

*Did he know?*

Had Mischief worked out that *his* was the sacrifice that I needed in order to move closer to Jahael?

Why did I always need to hurt someone to save my people? Was that what it meant to be a leader? People as pawns? But wasn't that an abuse of power: *the exact thing that I'd fought against?*

Yet Mischief could never be a pawn because he was as much a leader as me. And he'd granted me permission to hurt him.

My eyes burned with tears, as I pulled Mischief closer. The kiss was petal soft, infused with Mischief's love and understanding. Our magic twined in gossamer curls, crackling like popcorn. I nibbled on his lip, but he pulled back.

"Just don't take pleasure from your actions, since I know that you'll be tempted." I froze: unable to swallow, or even deny. His smile was crooked. "You know quite well how you've thrilled in power before: it's an aphrodisiac to any Glory, and I can't suffer at one's hand, if I know they rejoice in it."

Mischief had been abused by his bitch of a Glory mother. The Legion of the Phoenix had been a psycho cult but it'd also been a refuge, which had saved Mischief from Glories: like me. Every moment that he placed himself or his love in my hands was a gift.

"Never, bro."

Mischief's nod offered more trust than every time he'd fought at my back. "I may be the bastard Archduke but my Firstborn brother appears to have inherited the same traits as me." Mischief's gaze darkened. "He's traitorous, scheming—"

"Snarky?"

Mischief sniggered. "Oh, the padawan has much to learn about the power of the sarcastic putdown." Then he grabbed me by the waist, dragging me closer. "He's *dangerous*—

"By His wing, I consider myself safe as...well, there *is* nothing safe in this realm. Except perhaps you, *brother*." At Gabriel's mocking voice from the archway, Mischief and I startled apart with a *jingle*.

I stared at Gabriel, as he swaggered towards us in midnight-blue robes, which swept the floor. The robes were threaded with the same sapphires that shone in his hair, and his wings glinted like they'd been oiled. The warm aroma of amber made me gasp for breath: I stepped towards him, magnetized.

Gabriel had pulled off one hell of a powerplay.

Where was the Seraphim who'd knelt in punishment position before Istafil or submitted before Blaze? How many roles was Gabriel forced to play to survive?

*How many would I be?*

Mischief pulled a face as he hunched his shoulders like an unimpressed teenager on his brother's prom night. "Go ahead and believe me *safe*. After all, leopard seals look cute, but they'll hunt humans."

Gabriel scrutinized his brother, before sniffing. Then he pulled out of the pocket of his robe a tiny sapphire jewelled thong.

I didn't even want to think how those gems would feel on a bloke's private parts.

I grimaced. "What kinky panties you like to wear in private, Gabriel, is none of our business..."

Gabriel almost smiled, before his blank expression

slammed down again. "May His glory protect me; the Firstborn would not wear such a shameful thing. It's for the bastard Archduke, of course." Mischief hissed, backing away. "It's fitting for your status as my spoils, *brother*."

I winced. I had risked my life and family in Castle Drake to save my own half-brother, Anael. I knew how fiercely Mischief had fought to help his brothers, despite the hardships of the Legion. Now he had new half-brothers, and I hated the flash of pain in Mischief's eyes, which he instantly buried, at the rejection.

*Because I knew what it felt like to be rejected by a sibling.*

Yet was Gabriel treating Mischief like this because of Istafil, his own political machinations, or because he truly despised him for being a *bastard*?

Mischief's voice was low and vibrated with fury, "It's interesting how much you loath me, *brother*, when you know so little about me. In fact, when you've cared to discover nothing about who I am. It's almost as if you loath *yourself*."

Gabriel marched across the chamber towards Mischief, who simply tilted his chin higher in defiance.

*Crack* — Gabriel slapped Mischief, splitting his lip.

"Hold your tongue, bastard." Gabriel's breathing was ragged. His earlier softness had vanished to be replaced by a violent volatility: his eyes were dilated, as if he was drunk or drugged.

Mischief was right: Gabriel was *dangerous*. Could I trust him to hold to our plan and not to take it too far?

I caught Mischief's gaze and willed him to keep silent for once.

*But on that day unicorns would rap "Stairway to Heaven".*

Mischief licked lazily at the beaded blood. "Fiery, aren't you, brat?"

And that was how to explode a god.

Gabriel's six wings spread like an outraged swan's,

61

sizzling with energy that prickled my face and frizzed my hair. "You wish to challenge me, brother?" His voice was suspiciously calm. "Kill me, perhaps?"

*Jingle* — I leapt between them with a frantic wave of my hands.

"Time out, or you'll both be put on the naughty step."

Two near identical eyebrows raised at me.

"We'll settle it by Shifter Duel." Gabriel tossed the thong onto the bed.

Mischief shrugged. "What's that? Transformations at dawn?"

Gabriel snorted. "Has your education been so deficient that you don't even know such a simple rite?" Mischief flushed. "Oh yes, I'd forgotten that you're nothing but a bastard raised amongst the Non-Divine. *My advantage*."

Instantly, Gabriel shifted into a giant white lion, whose head almost touched the opal lights on the roof. He shook his ivory mane, crouching on muscular haunches, as he glowered at us with bright blue eyes.

*Hell...*

I swallowed, jingling my way backwards into Mischief, who caught me, resting his head on my shoulder.

*Roar.*

The lion's warm breath blasted against my cheeks, smothering me in a rich, earthy scent that clawed me down from the panic because this was Gabriel rocking the Aslan look: his go-to shifter form. And now that I'd calmed enough to study his majesty and beauty...*he was legendary*.

Until I remembered that Mischief was meant to be battling him.

When I twisted around to Mischief, however, he only shrugged.

"This was meant to convince me that you're less of an alpha poseur *how* precisely...?" Mischief sighed. Gabriel

62

shook his mane like Mischief was an irritating fly. "Or are you attempting to prove that there can be only one leader in your pride...? Don't fret, I've no intention of stealing your place or your crown."

In a spray of silver sparkles Mischief transformed into a toy-sized fluffy unicorn.

*The wallad was going to get his stuffing ripped out.*

I groaned, but Mischief strutted with all the swag of a warhorse towards Gabriel. Then he looked up at the confused predator above him with his huge eyes. "How about we rebel, and the unicorn lies down with the lion, brother?"

With a *growl*, Gabriel swiped his paw towards Mischief; his claws would tear Mischief apart...

I dived forward, snatching Mischief by his miniature twisted horn (ignoring his *squeak* of protest), and hauling him to safety. "Game over, Mr Plushy-100. It's time to put away the toys."

Mischief sneered at me, although on his unicorn face even that didn't come off as more than endearing, before changing back to his angelic self, sprawled across my lap. He couldn't meet my gaze.

With one final shake of his mane, Gabriel shrank down into his Seraphim form. He pinned his brother with a piercing stare. "It appears that you are indeed *insignificant*."

When Mischief recoiled like the words had been a whip lash, I stroked down his wing.

"Mischief's my fam," I said, "whether you choose to claim him as yours or not."

Gabriel gave a tight nod. "Then you need to tame him. The Burning Temple is one of whispers and secrets. If you're ever granted audience with my father, then know that he's guarded by the Knights of the Seraphim and his devoted worshippers and slaves, the Acolytes. There've been too many plots..." His intense stare met mine, before sliding away. "Also, assassination and escape attempts. None have succeeded and punishments are severe. Prove yourself or submit to the burning love of the Fire God."

Gabriel had been testing us...*was* testing us now.

Yet could I *trust* him?

"If it's so dangerous, why are we leaving our weapons behind and protecting ourselves with pretty jewels?"

"Because weapons show fear that you'll need to use them. If you dress in *pretty jewels*, you look confident that you won't." Gabriel snatched the thong off the bed and lobbed it at me.

I caught it, unable to give Mischief the next order and humiliate him; I wouldn't become that sort of Glory again.

Then Mischief caught my chin, tipping my head, so that our gazes met. He studied me, and I could see his struggle, before he finally nodded.

Why had I wanted him to shake his head, as he said: *don't do this...no...stop...*

And I would've because I loved him, and for the first time in a long time, I had the dominant bitch balanced with my other natures. I shook with the strength of that revelation.

Instead, however, Mischief was watching me with a soft smile curling his lips, waiting for *me* to take charge.

I took a deep breath, clenching my hands so tightly into fists that the amethysts sliced my palms; I welcomed the bright burst of pain.

I pushed myself up, before staring down at Mischief. "Strip."

Mischief scrambled to his feet, before shrugging himself out of his tunic. He didn't look up from the ground, as he slipped out of his trousers. Then, even though he was shivering and naked in the freeze of the moon-soaked room, Mischief insolently cocked an eyebrow as he looked Gabriel up and down. "Enjoying the show?"

Gabriel blushed but he also rubbed his fingers together, materialising a sapphire jewelled bit gag and bridle.

I pinched Mischief's tender upper wing, and he *yipped*, before casting me a sheepish look. "We had a no taunting

64

rule. Let's extend that to when we're bare arsed."

Mischief huffed. "I only see one of us here naked."

I shoved the offensive thong at him. Wincing, Mischief pulled it on, yelping as he wriggled the sapphires between his arse cheeks. I clenched my own in sympathy.

"Good little bastard," Gabriel crooned. *Please let this be an act, or I was going medieval on the Lion King.* "Tonight, you'll learn your place, and your sister will earn her safety within our temple." He swung the bit gag and bridle tauntingly on the end of his finger. "How about we save these for later? There shall be time for plenty of fun games. Istafil's parties are never what you expect and always many times deadlier."

Gabriel held out his arm to me, and I stiffly took it, whilst Mischief followed behind like our slave. Gabriel swept me through the archway towards the party, which would be as dangerous as a battle.

# 7

At the *snap* of a spotted hyena's jaws, I started, stumbling backwards with a *jingle* of beads. The hyena shook its sandy head, *cackling* wildly, although it shook.

Even maniacal bastards with the giggles can sound terrified.

I glanced around the Rose Room: and my official introduction into the life of Court Two.

*Velociraptors, elves, werewolves...*

I hadn't expected any of these to be snarling, scampering, or stalking through the pink spiralling columns, especially as they were on ruby studded collars and leashes.

*Maybe I should've asked to check the guest list?*

But then, this was a realm of gods. Perhaps anything could be *owned* here, even long extinct or mythological creatures?

I still bristled, however, when the Seraphim owners dragged the trembling bastards along the decadently tiled floor or threw themselves down into piles of satin cushions on the sofas that surrounded the raised dance floor, whilst their...*toys*...were shoved onto the floor at their feet.

A pretty naked elf with sky-blue hair that matched his large eyes, looked up from his *kneel* at the feet of a Glory Seraphim, meeting my gaze.

I flushed, shrinking backwards.

Hell, were the collared pets humiliated — tamed — shifters...? Seraphim who were being *taught their place* in public?

*And I'd have to do the same to Mischief.*

My stomach churned; the cloying scent of roses caught in my throat. The garish walls throbbed as if alive; scarlet lines bled snaking into dusky pink petals, like opening mouths.

Even though Mischief had agreed to allow such a violation — a forced shift, when shifting should be something empowering and glorious — I didn't know if I could forgive myself.

**Didn't I tell you to play the politics, Feathery-gem?**

*There are too many bare arses...and pointy-eared elves...for this to be Parliament, J.*

**Here's a dose of hot reality: real politics happens at parties, in bed, and when you least expect it.**

**Dry meetings with even drier assholes are just smokescreens. You need to shake your thing tonight.**

*How?*

*Gabriel's channelling the <u>Cain and Abel</u> vibe with his brother, and the Mongrel Witch is playing the Big Bad.*

**You're the Dragon God: find the power and claim it.**

**Or do you want to end up as the one on a sparkly leash?**

I shuddered, twisting to Mischief.

Mischief crossed his arms over his naked chest, tilting his chin as if to defy the obviousness of being presented to the

Seraphim as Jahael's son in nothing but a thong.

*That took swag.*

Not that Mischief looked out of place: every toy was naked.

For party read *orgy*, Roman style.

"I detest these excuses to flaunt power." Gabriel's dark gaze swept the crowded heat of the room.

Despite his grand robes, Gabriel hadn't made a grand entrance but had slunk into the party next to me, shadow-like. Now he hung back, watching with distaste.

*Slap* — the Glory Seraphim smacked the elf across his pale cheek.

The elf whimpered and bowed his forehead to the floor.

Gabriel's jaw tightened, before he caught himself, straightening his shoulders. "By His glory, Istafil never disappoints. Drink, dance, and indulge."

*How had Gabriel hidden his hatred for Istafil's party so easily?*

I blinked, before rapping Gabriel on the forehead. "Where's the bloke and not the puppet? What happened to your campaign for *elf-help*?"

Mischief sniggered.

Gabriel scowled. "I realised that I was being *elfish*, when I remembered why we're here tonight."

Mischief's gaze shot to mine, before flickering to his brother. "Do tell. Does it involve chocolate fountains and such larks?"

Gabriel seized a naked Seraphim by the arm, who was carrying a tray of sizzling cocktails, before snatching one up and passing it to me. "Drink," he insisted, whilst not raising his gaze to mine. "Believe me, these functions are much more bearable when you're—"

"Pissed?"

Gabriel's lips quirked. "Merry." He grabbed a smoking martini glass and tipped back the lime green drink in one go. *Hell, he was desperate to get merry.* He wiped his mouth,

68

clutching the next glass and gulping the swirling concoction.

When he swayed, the server Seraphim steadied him.

*Why did the servers only have four wings?*

I eyed Gabriel. "You OK?"

He waved his hand dismissively, even as his pupils dilated.

When I stared down at my glass, the sunburst yellow cocktail transformed into violet-and-black, like it'd read my mind, subtly changing to suit my needs, even as I smelled the waft of tequila.

Gabriel had poisoned me before, but a bitch had to drink, and I wasn't in the Angel Games anymore.

*Plus, this was the best bastard drink ever.*

Mischief snorted. "I should've known that it'd only take the bribe of tequila and a party trick. I suppose you're more at home than I am. Don't mind me, go make your *introductions*."

I winced. "You can stick the rest but you're right that the tequila has a one-way ticket to my Throatsville."

Before I could raise the glass, however, Mischief dived for the stem, stilling it. "Two glasses of this toxic...well, you see, we don't even know *what*...and my brother Suleiman the Big-head is flying, whilst in a room with the cast of *Jurassic Park*. How about you don't join him?"

I lowered the glass. Then I noticed the stares, half-concealed glances, and contemptuous looks of the other Seraphim.

We were being watched, just as Gabriel had warned, and by the scornful glances, we'd been found wanting.

Mischief had come here dressed as a toy but he was pushing my drink away from me like the Archduke that he was.

J had been right: this was about politics. I had to tame Mischief for this world of whispers and secrets.

I forced my gaze to become steely, as I wrenched Mischief's wrist away from the glass, ignoring his gasp. "How about *that's none of your business, bitch*?"

I downed the cocktail in one go to avoid seeing Mischief's hurt expression; the alcohol burnt the back of my throat, and my eyes watered. I slammed the glass back onto the tray, whilst the room spun.

My nerves tingled, whilst the sounds of the party were amplified, and the blood bubbled in my arteries. When Mischief supported me at my elbows, his skin seared mine. It was so intimate that I squirmed, desperate for *more, more, more*: every inch of his skin on mine, his mouth, wings, and prick...

*What the unicorn elfing hell was going on?*

Then Gabriel's hands were on my cheeks, as his lips pressed chastely against mine, just once. "Intense, isn't it? In the name of all that's holy, on my first time, I had no one to protect me. *But you have me.*"

Mischief waved his hand in the air like an ignored schoolboy at the back of the class who had a particularly kinky uniform. "Not to be an attention seeker, but she also has me: the angel who she actually loves."

Gabriel flinched, but he didn't let go. He pressed one final soft kiss to my lips, before grabbing my hand. Then he shot a disdainful glance at Mischief, as if he was a disobedient puppy. "Follow."

Gabriel pulled me further into the Rose Room, between a snapping velociraptor and its tiny Seraphim owner. When I brushed against the fur of a grey wolf, each strand lit my nerves on fire, until I vibrated with the ecstasy.

Inside, my violet and black were entwining and enmeshing like they never had before.

*I burned.*

I no longer needed a shank for power: I *was* the power.

*Because I was a god.*

When I laughed, Gabriel spun me. I could hear other Seraphim laughing as well, between the gasps and groans of a swingers' party deep into its swing.

Except, how many of the swingers were consenting? How many were drunk or drugged? Is that what had happened to Gabriel on his first time at one of Istafil's parties when he'd had no one to *protect* him?

I stumbled, instantly sobering. How had I been sucked into this world, even for a moment?

The plaintive guitar grunge of Radiohead's "Creep" burst through the room in all its spinetingling, taunting angst. Gabriel twirled me, before dipping me, like we were salsa dancing. I grinned, lost in his earthy scent, before I caught Mischief's smirk over Gabriel's shoulder.

"Has someone been fibbing to his big brother?" I asked, whilst Gabriel held me tightly: my godly Prince Charming at the Raunchy Ball.

Mischief shrugged. "He asked if you had any *special songs*, with which to court you. I believe he wished for a *romantic moment*. Don't you find the song fitting?"

Whilst a song about an alienated outcast, who aches for someone out of his league, sang through my soul, Gabriel wrapped his wings closer as if he could ward off his own understanding of the insult. I saw the moment that it broke through, however, and he snapped.

Gabriel jerked away from me, his eyes blazing and his cheeks flaming.

Mischief had turned his own humiliation on its head, and I was torn between *whooping* at his epicness and devastation at Gabriel's mortification.

Had Gabriel ever been allowed to choose a lover, whilst trapped in his Gilded Cage? Had he *courted* anyone?

*Whack* — Gabriel backhanded Mischief.

Mischief yelped, sprawling onto his back next to the startled blue haired elf. The elf reached out, stroking Mischief's swelling cheek, as if in Oppressed Seraphim solidarity.

I snarled, slamming Gabriel into a column in a *jingling* blur of amethyst fury, but he reversed my hold, faster than

71

anyone I'd fought before.

*Oomph* — my back hit the column.

I wriggled, but Gabriel held me by the throat, even if his thumb stroked over my fluttering pulse, as he leaned in to whisper into my ear, "They're watching. Always watching."

"I know that I have one squeezable arse, but what's turned me into the prize exhibit?"

Gabriel tensed, as if he was struggling not to say what he truly wanted. *Was he being spied on?* "Didn't you sense it in the Angel Games?" He eased his hand from my throat, tracing over the letters, which wound like rose stems around the pillar: **HOLY, HOLY, HOLY**. "Seraphim love entertainment, novelty, and the unique. You're all three. You must retain that interest, however, by becoming more than the latest show: you become the player, not the played." He sighed. "My father grows bored of watching worlds fall apart and walking as a stranger amongst humans. Yet I wish that I could leave this realm to experience even that."

I traced over his cheek with the back of my hand, and he flinched as if expecting me to backhand him like he had Mischief. "They're watching now?"

He nodded.

I peered over his shoulder: hostile glares, whispers, and hidden glances.

*Yeah, Gabriel, Mischief and I were all on the naughty step.*

Then the Seraphim with four wings, who'd served me the cocktail, was dragged into the embrace of the elf owning Glory Seraphim. Both Seraphims' wings crackled with energy, before the Glory dug her nails deep into the base of the server's neck. He wailed, whilst silver magic jumped from his wings and into hers. I shuddered, unable to look away, as the server slumped to the ground in a puddle of sizzling cocktails, and the Glory laughed.

*She'd stolen his magic.*

I growled, but Gabriel kept me pinned to the column.

"He's an Acolyte," Gabriel murmured. "They worship the Emperor with their service and bodies. How interesting that in his glory my father chooses the most powerful to be slaves." My steel nails shot out, *screeching* down the marble. *I'd kick Jahael's ass, before I'd let him keep gods as slaves.* Gabriel raised an eyebrow. "This doesn't please you? Even though you own a Marked Wing?"

"I don't own anyone. And I'd rather gut myself with my own nails than take a slave."

For the first time that night, Gabriel broke into his genuine smile: warm and glowing. My nails retracted, and I rested my head against his chest. "Well, we can't have that, can we? You'd make such a dreadful mess." I swatted his arm. "Yet we're none of us free." He nuzzled into my hair. "Not yet..." Then he cocked his head, as if listening to something — *or someone* — inside his mind. He blanched. "It's time to tame the bastard Archduke; may the Emperor burn all away in love."

**You know how this works, hooker, you've been listening to me since you were crawling and sucking your sweet thumb.**

*Jahael is talking to the Archduke inside his mind? Just like you talk to me...?*

**Not the same as my fabulous self.**

**I'm seeded: part of you. But Jahael can do the telepathic thing with any dick Seraphim that he wants.**

**He's everywhere in the shadows: worshipped, loved, and feared.**

I stared at Gabriel. "Jahael's messing with your head right now?"

Gabriel's lips were pinched, as he nodded. "I'm honoured that he's chosen to speak to me. If he's seeded you..." I shifted from foot to foot under his scrutiny. "Then he should see and hear everything that you do, unless..." Hell, why wasn't I able to slip on a mask as quickly as Gabriel could?

73

"You're blocking him somehow or the seed is choosing not—"

"Are you done with the Agatha Christy moment because I have a unicorn to break."

Gabriel pushed closer; his eyes were wide and panicked. "Be careful. He'll know and—"

Suddenly, Gabriel's eyes clouded, before blazing. Then he shoved me against the column; his arms and wings boxed me in. He kissed me: hard, demanding, and passionate. It was the sun to the moon of his previous kiss.

The intoxicating musky scent of agarwood bled through his magic.

*Wait...agarwood, rather than amber?*

It didn't make me want to cherish, rather pressed at me to bow before him and *worship.*

I quivered and gagged, whilst I recoiled.

*He wasn't Gabriel...*

"Now you're getting it. I'll spank your perky arse, if you're hiding anything from me, darling." I shot backwards at the sound of Jahael's voice murmuring out of Gabriel's mouth.

Gabriel stared back at me with anguish in his eyes, just as Jahael's laugh bubbled out of his lips. *Jahael was using Gabriel like a Seraphim puppet.* "This is *my* temple, hooker. I'm the daddy: I can take over anyone's mind or body. Their adoration belongs to fabulous me. I created you. That means I *own* you."

Gabriel slumped, and I caught him.

What would it feel like to be possessed? To be truly controlled by another? To never know when you'd lose control again?

When Gabriel raised his gaze to mine, I caught the apology. Before he could voice it, I shrugged. "I wanted an audience with the Emperor. I guess that I got one."

Gabriel rubbed his fingers together, and the jewel bit gag and bridle appeared. "You're not alone: he owns us all," he said, softly.

I steeled myself because it was time to humble Mischief: The Emperor was watching.

Turning, I forced my gaze to become flinty as it raked over Mischief, who was teaching rock-paper-scissors to the elf and losing. "Up," I barked.

Mischief jumped, before casting a final smile at the elf and straightening; his shoulders were tense, as he prowled to my side.

I followed Gabriel through the drunken crowds towards the dance floor, which thinned at our arrival in excited anticipation.

*Golden curls, creamy skin, and satin like the night sky.*

I hesitated, staring at golden-haired triplets who were dressed in sparkling satin dressing gowns and squirmed on the sofa next to the dance floor under a swarthy Seraphim with a sweeping oiled beard, which flared all the way to his leather boots. His black military outfit looked straight out of Fascists Weekly, apart from the ornate sword strapped to his back.

Except, they weren't triplets: they were clones.

*Drake's.*

I dragged the closest Drake clone away from Mr Oiled Beard, desperate with the joy of finding him safe, at the same time as vibrating with the fury of someone else touching the angel that I loved: son of the Mage, Marked Wing of the Matriarch, and Commander of the angelic armies. Yet here used as nothing but a plaything by the Seraphim bastards, along with his clones.

*And his clones were innocents.*

The clone holding my hand smiled with such yearning, even as he glanced anxiously back at Mr Oiled Beard, who still had his other two clones...or the real Drake...crushed under his huge bulk.

Mr Oiled Beard spread his wings, stroking them along his Drakes' necks. "Do you mind, daughter of the Burning One? They'll be no touching of my novice without permission, and I haven't finished here."

"You have now," I growled.

"Guardian," the Drake in the centre of the sofa, beneath Mr Oiled Beard — the Guardian — pushed himself up onto his elbows, and at once I knew that he was the *real* Drake: drawing attention to himself to save his clones and me. "I apologise for her uncouth interruption. Allow me to make it up to you…?"

The Guardian's dark brows furrowed, before he held out his hand to the clone who was clinging to me.

The clone whimpered.

Drake and I had developed a method of communicating via body language, when we'd been banned from speaking to each other in the Legion.

Drake lifted his eyebrows, which roughly translated meant: **What in la-la land, bitch?**

*Roughly*.

I nodded at the Guardian: **You want me to take him out?**

Drake looked down, with a shake of his head: **No way to do the hit now. Let me play the good boy, until I get the chance to be the bad boy.**

*Very roughly*.

Drake was trapped with the Guardian, even as bile burnt my throat at the sight of the Guardian's possessive hand on Drake's wing, and his smug reply, "I shall certainly enjoy your attempts to make it up to me, novice. You're always creative: my compliments to both the Matriarch and your father. They trained you so thoroughly, I have precious little breaking left to do."

*Yeah, and I was going to break the Guardian's dick.*

Gabriel's eyes swept over Drake, as he nodded a curt greeting to the Guardian — he so hated him as much as I did — before Gabriel tugged me onto the dance floor.

*Silence.*

76

The Seraphim fell back, encircling Gabriel. They'd known that this was going to happen: we were the grand finale.

Mischief bowed his head, clasping his hands behind his back, although he couldn't hide the way that his shoulders shook.

In a searing blast of flames, Istafil materialised above us; her snapping ribbons flared as brightly as her hair.

Had she been here all along — invisible and watching?

*Had Gabriel known?*

"Burn with love!" Istafil smiled, but it was cold and deadly. "Fun and games, dear hearts, can also teach us our place in divinity. So, tame your brother and bring him to worship."

I took a deep breath, forcing myself to walk steadily towards Mischief, even though inside I was screaming at the *wrongness*...

When Mischief met my gaze, I'd been expecting anger or accusation but instead there was a steely determination. Because we were in this together: Istafil was trying to break all three of us.

*The gods wouldn't break any of my fam.*

"Unicorn god-out," I demanded.

Mischief smiled, just for a moment, before he smothered it. Then he transformed into a Shetland pony sized version of a unicorn. Not a killer war horse; he barely came up to my waist.

One of Drake's clones chuckled.

Istafil hissed but before she could whip flames towards Mischief, I snatched the bit gag and bridle, slipping them over Mischief's lowered head.

Mischief whinnied sadly, as the sapphires bit into his brow, and the bridle magically tightened to fit. I fiddled with the straps, using it as an excuse to kiss his mane. Then I fixed on the bit gag, which rubbed the soft sides of his mouth; I flinched at the pained shake of his head.

*Hoots and cheers.*

The Seraphim clapped the gagging of their long-lost bastard Archduke. Yet standing proud, in a transformation of his choice, I thought that Mischief had never looked *more* of an Emperor's son.

Suddenly, Istafil shrieked, twirling around. "You did not have invitations to my party. All Non-Divine shall feel the Fire God's wrath!"

*Maybe she'd drunk more than two of those Happy Hour cocktails...?*

Then a flaming spear exploded into the dance floor.

Mischief reared backwards from the raging fire, whilst the Seraphim scattered in uproar.

*What the hell was happening?*

Seraphim wrapped in mismatched cloths in the same sunburst yellow as my cocktail, which even covered their faces, shimmered into the Rose Room. Clutching flaming spears, they were the invaders without the invites.

This wasn't play or entertainment: *it was war.* And we didn't even have our weapons to defend ourselves because we hadn't wanted to show our *fear.*

*Except, I was bastard afraid now.*

"Who are these Mad Max freaks playing at buttercups?" I demanded.

Gabriel paled, seizing my arm. "They're outlaws: The Damned."

"So, not an intimidating name at all."

A yellow figure materialized in front of me. Its violet wings flared, as its silver eyes met mine.

Then a fiery spear dug into my throat.

# 8

J had warned me about the dangers outside the temple. Now one of them in sunburst yellow had their spear sizzling at my throat, as the Damned attacked my party in the Rose Room.

*Bastard gate crashers.*

How clever did the *no weapons and only pretty jewels* look now?

I wet my lips. The bone-tipped spear nicked my neck, as I swallowed; blood traced down my throat. The stink of ash and black smoke from the burning sofas and upturned chairs mingled with the sickly rose scent of the room.

*Shrieks, snarls, and screams.*

Velociraptors, werewolves, and Seraphim wildly charged at the Damned, whilst they blinked in and out, stabbing in surprise attacks.

The blue haired elf crouched against the column, hugging his knees; he'd been abandoned in the carnage by his owner. Our gazes met for a moment, and despite the spear at my neck, I shook my head, flinching as the spear dug deeper: *don't bastard fight; stay where you are.*

The elf nodded.

"By His holy fire, you shall not touch my sister, Damned," Gabriel bellowed over the howling chaos; he squeezed my arm. "She's a prisoner: spoils. Aren't I the prize that you seek to sully?"

The Damned's gaze flickered to Gabriel: these outlaws must've chosen to attack Istafil's screwed-up Welcome to the Gods for a reason. And that left Mischief or me. Especially since Istafil had vanished, either abandoning us or invisible.

The bitch claimed responsibility for raising and *correcting* the Emperor's sons, but she didn't have their back.

*That wasn't fam.*

Behind me, Mischief snorted, lowering his head. I bet he wished that he'd transformed into killer unicorn mode now. Then he'd have been able to fire from his horn and take out the Damned, just like he'd assassinated the vampiric leader of the Pure.

Instead, he'd become a pony that looked like he should be pulling a cart in a Victorian mine. *But why wasn't he changing back into an angel?*

"Your sister has always been the prize," a cultured female voice purred from behind the yellow mask.

When the Damned pressed harder with the spear, my ancient powers stirred along with my magics to burn these invaders from the inside for *desecrating my temple, defying my will, and harming my Divine.*

*What the hell...?*

Those were Jahael's echoed thoughts and outraged screams that blasted through every Seraphim: their lips moved, mouthing the same words, from which J's shields couldn't protect me.

Then the Damned with the spear at my throat was staggering backwards, whilst the pressure at my throat lifted, because Drake's arm was hooked around *her* neck from behind.

Despite Drake's satin dressing gown, he was all deadly Commander. His pale eyes gleamed. When the Damned rammed her elbow backwards, he spread his wings, soaring over her head and blocking her path to me.

The Damned stabbed the spear through Drake's shoulder.

Drake howled, as the Damned twisted, before pulling out the spear with a *squelch* and vanishing.

I caught Drake, as he crumpled to the ground, hovering my fingers over the oozing wound. He grunted; his breathing became shallow.

"It's of no consequence," Drake murmured. I pushed back a golden curl, which had fallen over his eyes. "You're safe, and I'm away from the Guardian, who discovered how to force us out at will and..." He shuddered. "Drake tells us that it's impolite to beg but please, would you kiss me? I do not want the memory of the Guardian alone on my lips."

*This was one of Drake's clones?*

Once, in the Legion of the Phoenix, Drake had told me that he'd tricked the Matriarch that his clones could only be called out in battle to save them from being violated as bed slaves.

Yet the Guardian's magic had been too powerful to deceive, and now the clones were no longer safe.

I loved Drake, how could I not love his innocent shadows?

Above me, Gabriel shifted with a hiss of impatience, scanning the mayhem. I ignored him, pressing my lips to the clone's with as much softness as I was certain he received roughness from the Guardian. His kiss was tentative and sweet. His feathers brushed up and down my cheeks, and he melted against me in a way that the real Drake would never allow himself to...but now I wondered whether it was what he dreamed about.

"Enough. I believed we had an agreement on not dominating my shadows. Allow me to congratulate you, however, on the kiss. Have you been practising as much as you made *me* practise?" The real Drake stood with his hands on his hips, staring down at me with the third clone next to him.

Both had matching injuries on their shoulders. They were also as flushed as the clone who was draped in my lap, with matching hardness tenting the front of their dressing gowns.

*How could I've forgotten that they all experienced the echoes of each other's pain and pleasure?*

"He asked for it *himself.* Or are the clones your slaves?" I demanded.

Drake recoiled. "Never... I only wish to..." He dropped onto his knees before the clone, who whimpered until Drake *shushed* him. "Hush, now. Our Queen is right. If I'd been able to grant you more freedom and keep you safe, I'd have done so." Drake pulled the clone from my lap onto his own, tenderly kissing his forehead. Frankincense wound around me: rich and so intensely *Drake* that I leant into him. "It appears that you've upped my tally as well." He struggled to hide his smile. "I truly have lost count how many times it is now that I've saved your life, my Queen."

"Drink, music, dancing...none of that is *romantic* enough for you, but a battle, blood, and angelic clones, and you're having this *moment*, of which my brother spoke?" Gabriel snarled, yanking me to my feet with a harsh *jingle* of beads.

"What can I say? I'm the Bitch of Utopia not Shakespeare's Juliet."

Drake held out his hand to his third clone, before merging back into one, shuddering back to himself. He slunk to his feet with cold fury. "Be silent and unhand my Queen, Firstborn." To my shock, Gabriel dropped my hand. *Someone had been trained to take orders...or maybe needed them.* Drake blinked at him, as if the Seraphim's obedience had been equally unexpected. "Good. Now, remove that despicable bridle and allow your brother to transform, so that we can retreat somewhere safer."

"I can't." When Drake raised his eyebrow, Gabriel flinched. "Only the one who put it on, can remove it."

"Wait, it stops Mischief shifting?" I clenched my hands. Forcing Mischief to transform and humiliate him had been a violation, but to trap him in that form stole every shred of his control. *Had Mischief known?* "You're messed up. How could you...?"

"Turn around." Gabriel commanded. Reluctantly, I twisted, as Gabriel pointed at the elf, who was sobbing and hiding wedged into the corner beside a column. "Shepherd was my friend when we were Diniel's age, or as much of one as Istafil ever allowed me." Drake shot a questioning glance at Gabriel; his expression softened. Drake had been my brother's only friend in the Legion of the Phoenix. He knew what it was to care for imprisoned and lonely royalty, and how solitary confinement could twist you into the monstrous. "Until one day I was insufficiently grateful for her correction, and as punishment Shepherd was transformed into that...weak creature. Those in ruby collars can only be freed by Istafil's will or death. Thank His wing that Mischief's punishment is only temporary."

"If Shepherd's your friend and whipping boy," Drake said, his voice vibrating with a pain that I understood because I shook too, remembering Drake as Anael's *whipping boy*, "then I propose that you refrain from insulting him and instead, respect his sacrifice. Ensure the safety of your brother first, then your friend. Maybe after that, you'll at least start to look like a true Archduke."

*Hell, Drake had just invited Swirly Eyes to the party...*

Yet Gabriel only studied Drake for a long moment. "I like this one. He reminds me of the spirited Halfling."

I turned to Mischief, before I could snigger at Drake's spluttered outrage. I ran my hand down Mischief's nose, wincing at the flecks of blood wherever the sharp edges of the sapphires on the bridle or gag had sliced into his flesh. Gently, I eased them off his brow and out of his mouth.

If I hadn't removed them, Mischief would've been stuck as a unicorn permanently.

*All those in red collars and leashes were Istafil's slaves.*

I hurled the bridle across the dance floor, as Mischief changed into his angelic self, stumbling into my arms.

"Back with us, Sparkly Pants?" I stroked my fingers through his hair, whilst he steadied himself. "No unicorny thoughts still? Urges for glitter, horns, or shiny hairclips for your mane?"

"Do kisses, blood, and painful death to the Damned count?" Mischief arched his brow.

"You're both hot and freaky right now, you know that?"

"Aren't I always? I must try harder." He turned to Drake, who held his hand over his wounded shoulder. "We're separated for a short time and already the golden child is injured." Mischief sniffed, but I didn't miss the affection underlying his jibe.

"And you've already been a gagged unicorn, so I win." Drake's pout reminded me of his clone: why hadn't I seen this hidden side of him before? Why hadn't I *allowed* myself to see it?

"It's not a bastard game." I glanced across the room at the shaking elf. "Get your arse over to Shepherd, Aslan."

Gabriel nodded, even as he rubbed nervously at his sapphire pendant. Yet before he could turn, a Damned took shape behind him in a haze, raising her arm.

"Brother..." Mischief yanked Gabriel to the side.

"Mischief..." I hollered, reaching for him, whilst my ancient powers howled in terror.

*Crunch* — the spear sliced through Mischief's neck, snapping his spine.

*Bastard, no... Please, please, please... Don't let him be...*

Frozen, I couldn't even move to catch the body.

*No, not the body, never that... Mischief, Mischief, he'll always be...*

The corpse's vacant eyes stared up at the ceiling.

"Be warned, Firstborn, the prize can change." The Damned vanished, even as Gabriel launched himself on her with a roar.

Arms and wings were around me, holding me: soft curls and gentle touches. Salt wet on my cheeks and someone else's. *Words, words, words...* fractured, broken, and meaningless.

*What the hell did anything matter now?*

Dead.

I hadn't saved... There was no way.... *He couldn't be dead.*

My powers burst from me in red-hot rage and grief, until everything burned.

# 9

No one should ever have to cradle their brother's corpse in their arms.

It was only as I stood, shaking with adrenaline and the silver high, which had burnt the remaining Damned to charred ash, beside the clouded glass gates through to Court Three and the Holy Audience Chamber, that I realised how much taller Gabriel was than Mischief, as Gabriel held his brother to his chest.

*Than Mischief <u>had</u> been.*

I furiously swiped at the tears on my cheeks, but I couldn't stop them falling. A rosewater fountain tinkled in the high walled courtyard like a gushing firework, masking with its scent and noise anything beyond. My mind was lost in a fog of pain and loss...*and this couldn't be real.*

It had to be an illusion.

*Please, hell, let this be another test.*

Yet Gabriel's red-rimmed eyes, his slumped shoulders, and the way that he clutched Mischief like he'd only just understood how precious he was told me that it wasn't.

This was real, it wasn't a test, and I wouldn't wake up from this nightmare.

I'd craved to have an audience with Jahael: my creator. But not like this, carrying his dead son. If Mischief's death was the price of admittance to the Inner Court — the sacrifice — then I'd never have paid it.

*But I hadn't been given the choice.*

**Hold your thing together, Feathery-honey. I'm here.**

*J, I couldn't... I tried to... I'm sorry.*

**Don't you dare apologise to me, girl.**

**My son fought at your side and he chose to save his brother. He's been screwed by skank Glories and asshole mages, but he died a hero.**

**You don't go taking that away.**

*I need him.*

**You need to slap yourself back to Sense Land because you're about to meet Jahael, and he's the snake with his fangs in the temple's sweet throat.**

**You don't want your biteable ass to be next.**

*Then don't abandon me.*

**I can't risk the Emperor controlling me.**

**I'm the free and fabulous diva who he never intended to create, rather than a shadow, and you're the bitch who helped me blossom into Divahood.**

**You'll have to face Jahael alone.**

**Remember, the end can be the beginning, and the beginning can be the end.**

I shuddered, wrapping my arms around myself. My vision blurred through the stream of tears; I couldn't blink them away quickly enough, as I shivered with uncontrollable chills.

Suddenly, I couldn't bear anyone touching Mischief.

Why was *Gabriel* holding the body? Not the *body*, I meant Mischief...*his name was Mischief.*

I growled, before I could stop myself, barging Gabriel into the gate.

*Clink* — the sapphires woven into Gabriel's hair smacked against the glass; I winced.

Gabriel, however, only studied me with an understanding gaze. "By all that's holy, I'm grieved that—"

"Don't."

He blinked at me. "What?"

"Say his name. You don't get to say his name, when you only called him *bastard* to his face."

Gabriel flushed. He looked unexpectedly young and lost, whilst he stared down at Mischief like he'd never seen him before, or bothered to. "I don't deserve anything, after he saved my life, and I treated him like..." His eyelashes matted with wet, as he took careful breaths, before continuing, "You have no concept how hard it was to see a new son, who could challenge my hard fought for position at court, waltz into the temple with so much...*freedom*. He'd lived outside. Yet I've always been caged, since my mother's death. She was the Emperor's wife, the only one he's ever taken, despite Istafil's deluded dreaming. After that, I've known nothing but the Gilded Cage." He hugged Mischief closer. "Why would he save me?"

"Because that's the legend he is... I mean, *was*," I burst out, unable to hold back the sobbed grief any longer. Gabriel had hurt Mischief out of jealousy for an imagined life that hadn't even been real; my chest ached at their lost opportunity because they couldn't ever discover the similarities of their childhoods, or a sibling bond: Gabriel had left it too late. "Is it my turn to tell you about your brother? Mischief was as trapped as you in the Legion of the Phoenix; they kept him like a servant. How envious are you now?"

Gabriel paled. But his sorrow didn't lessen mine. Somehow, I needed him to share my hurt: to know just how special Mischief had been and who I'd lost, so that he'd live.

"I d-didn't know—"

"Did you know that Mischief led a rebellion in the Under World? Helped me depose Lucifer? Or that he took on Rahab, the most powerful mage in the Legion to free the slaves... Yeah, and the Children of the Seraphim...that's *your* people, who Mischief always put first. Did daddy not tell you? *Because he saw all of it.* You're the Firstborn, but it seems to me you're being kept in the bastard dark."

Gabriel frantically shook his head.

*Had I pushed him too far?*

"B-by my w-wing, I had n-no idea..."

When the fountain shutoff, I glanced at the gate, expecting it to swing open. Instead, the ground tremored.

*Rumble.*

I crouched in the archway. Gabriel continued to stand, however, as if nothing was happening.

*Slam.*

I clenched my jaw at the jolt, which was followed by a shrieking *roar*, like the entire temple had picked itself up and then had set itself down again with a bump.

I gaped at Gabriel. "What in the Space Dragons MC world of freakery, was that?"

"We've moved."

"Try again, bro, because that sounded like—"

"The Burning Temple: it teleports." He swallowed, unable to rub the fresh tears from his eyes, because his brother's body was in his arms. "I may be trapped, but the temple moves freely from place to place because it's hunted...*we're* hunted. It senses plots, assassination attempts, and threats. What do you imagine triggered it this time?"

I sprang up, thrumming with fury at the sarcastic

89

bastard, but his lips were pinched, and his mask was back in place but fragile: I could shatter it with a word.

I hesitated, uncertain whether I wished to be the one to shatter him or to protect him so that he never broke again. At last, I said, "It must've sucked as a kid never knowing if you were safe."

Gabriel's eyes widened, as if he'd been expecting a clout, rather than sympathy. "It was simply the truth. The Emperor's sons aren't shielded from harsh reality. But that's better than playing pretend." *I knew what someone sounded like who'd spent years convincing themselves of a lie: I'd done it myself.* "No one can move the pawns about the board, if in blissful ignorance, they don't even know that they're in the game."

I stared at Gabriel, as something about the attack nagged at me. The way that the Damned had spoken to Gabriel, and how he'd commanded her... "You knew the bitch who stabbed Mischief."

Gabriel's eyes widened even further. "How could I? She's one of the Damned: brigands who plague the burning love of our majestic—"

"Enough of the *adore the Holy of Assholes* spiel. She at least knew *you*. What do these buttercup bandits want?"

"To return from exile." Gabriel glanced at the gate behind us warily. "To butcher my father and steal his Crown. Isn't that how the game is played? Doesn't every enemy hunger for power?"

"Freedom," I whispered, stroking Mischief's cold cheek with the tips of my fingers. "Sometimes you rebel for freedom."

I staggered, as at last the great glass doors behind us creaked open, through to Jahael's Inner Court and Holy Audience Chamber. I caught Gabriel's eye, before he gave me a nod, and we walked in together, to meet for the first time the most powerful god in the Realm of the Seraphim, bearing the corpse of his son.

I choked on the sweet clouds of incense, which fogged the immense silver domed Holy Audience Chamber in potent clouds: my head spun, and my legs became heavier on each *clattering* step down the diamond and pearl encrusted centre of Court Three. My eyes stung, as I peered through the haze at the chamber, which swam in and out in blurred visions of grand murals and brilliant tiles. The walls glittered like snake-skin; I shuddered.

*Jingle, jingle, jingle.*

My beaded belt rang out like wedding bells, whilst Gabriel cradled Mischief in a bridal carry: together, we made up a freaky wedding party.

The Acolytes were both guests and choir: naked, they ranked on either side of us in worship, as Gabriel and I walked down the aisle between them. They knelt on the hard floor (and hell, it must've been more agonising than kneeling on rice), with their heads bowed; crimson whirls like the realm's savage sun had been daubed on their backs and wings. They held out their arms, which trembled with the effort of holding up a flickering firefly swarm of candles in the fog.

*Holy, holy, holy.*

I shivered at the beauty of their chant, which echoed up to the high roof. The adoration plucked at my new godly powers, until I vibrated, thrilling on their devotion: *thirsting* for it.

*Slam* — the Acolytes cracked their four wings against the floor.

Their shoulders tensed, but they didn't make a sound.

*Slam, slam, slam.*

I cringed, whilst Gabriel grimaced.

The red on their wings wasn't paint: it was blood from their repetitive *slamming* in devotion for their god.

Hell, why had I craved *that*?

Shaking my head, finally it was clear again; my powers settled.

*Had the incense been intoxicating me?*

I was here to meet my creator, but that no longer mattered. Mischief had died because of Jahael's divisions and battles with other Seraphim: Divine or the Damned. Who decided and what did it mean, except death and loss?

"Don't fight," Gabriel muttered. "It's worse if you fight."

"What...?"

A white cloud rushed towards me: a multitude of butterflies. Their wings glistened like polished metal. I gasped, as they alighted onto every amethyst inch of my skin, until I glowed like the moon.

Then they lifted me off my feet, propelling me forwards.

"Let go, freaky Snow Whites." I struggled, flapping my arms, until sharp nips, like pin pricks, forced me to still. *The bastards were biting me: now I knew why Gabriel had told me not to fight.* "What are you, Vampire Butterflies?"

*If insects could snicker, that was a bastard snicker.*

At last, the Vampire Butterflies dropped me in a yelping heap at the foot of a lime green divan, before flying up to the roof. I rolled onto my back and stared up at the Seraphim who was lounging along the divan in a diamond robe — *or was it a dress?* — that was slashed to reveal his hairless thighs: The Emperor, Jahael.

The Fire God was more transcendently beautiful than any angel or vampire I'd ever seen.

*And they were all beautiful bastards.*

Yet now my pulse thundered, and my mouth dried. I clenched my hands to hide their shaking because I was already swept along by it — the *adoration* — even whilst the black inside rebelled, spitting in rage at the subjugation.

*Was this why I craved to cherish Jahael's Firstborn?*

An Acolyte with curly silver hair knelt beside the divan over a bowl of woodchips; he lighted each one individually, throwing up a musky scent. He risked a glance at me with a small smile; his eyes twinkled, despite the pain that he must've been in. Mr Twinkly had a **J** stuck to his chest in pearls: *Jahael liked to mark his property.*

I took ragged breaths, whilst Jahael studied me. His silver hair was as long as Istafil's, but Jahael wore it loosely caught up; iridescent strands fell around his face, which was sharp and calculating, despite the childlike way that he toyed with his hair.

My mind buzzed with the desire to *kneel* just like Mr Twinkly Acolyte...

"Don't you recognise, worship, *love* me, my Violet-darling?" Jahael leant forward. He sounded like J, but also colder and *crueller*.

I shoved myself onto my arse, battling down another sickening wave of divinity worship. *Why did it feel like this was finally home?* "One out of three, bitch."

I expected fire, lightning, another round with the Vampire Butterflies...and I welcomed it because then there'd be *pain* that I could fight, instead of one that pummelled my insides at Mischief's death.

Instead, Jahael smirked, waving his hand airily. "You can't lie to the most fabulous of holy ones, girl. I've seen everything: that's omniscience, darling. I've watched you since you were a baby; I know you've cried out to me to save you. Here I am, answering your call."

I jolted, trembling.

I *had* called out to the angels to save me in Jerusalem Children's Home. I'd always desired parents, a family, and a home.

Could Jahael be what I'd needed all that time?

I bit my lip, refusing to let Jahael see my distress, but his smile was knowing. "You're too late, bro, I saved myself. Then my fam and I saved the bastard world."

Jahael thought that he'd seen everything but he was wrong. J had hidden behind the mental shields that I'd built from Drake, the Matriarch, Lucifer, and then Rahab. Now he was blocking Jahael altogether. Jahael knew me before the supernatural had birthed within me, as the orphan on Utopia Estate, the geek gamer pretending to be the tough girl, so that her sister and she survived, never trusting anyone...or loving them.

Abandoned by everyone.

*The bitch thought that he knew me?* Then the surprise would bite him in the arse.

Finally, Gabriel joined me in front of the divan; Jahael's gaze flickered to Mischief, but then away.

*What the hell...?*

Gabriel and I had arrived with the Emperor's dead son, yet Jahael hadn't even *yelled, wailed,* or *howled...?*

Couldn't Jahael have bothered with at least a fake sad face and trite condolence?

When instead, Jahael stretched like life was too much of a bore, I snapped. "Or were you too busy hiding in here behind your slaves and bodyguards from assassins to protect me?"

One moment Jahael had been lounging on the divan, the next he'd clutched me by the neck, dragging me to my feet: *hell, he was fast.* I held back the whimper, as he wiped his finger through a trickle of blood between my tits from the Butterfly Vampire bites. Then he licked it across his long tongue: his lips were cherry red, like they were painted with rouge. "You can't blame my fae for wanting a taste. Your blood has always been special."

When he dropped me, I staggered.

"So, they're not Vampire Butterflies...?" I glanced upwards at the fluttering cloud above my head.

Jahael made a very Un-Emperor like snort. "BAM! I'm gagging on that deliciousness. They're my bloodthirsty Knights of the Seraphim. Here, Anael, stop lurking in the shadows. Come watch your sister's hysterics, my cutie pie prince."

*Anael — my brother.*

I forced myself not to rush forward but to blank my face, as Gabriel had mastered: to hurt me, you had to hurt my family. The less Jahael knew that I cared for my half-brother, the less hold he had on either of us; I hoped that Anael realised that.

Gabriel had lost his brother: I couldn't lose mine.

Anael had never been allowed outside Castle Drake until now, however, trapped in a single room. He'd moulded friends and lovers out of iron because he'd only had Drake, who was as close to a sibling as I was.

How would Anael cope in this devious Seraphim world?

When Anael prowled from the shadows, imposing and savage, even wrapped in rich satins and diamonds that matched Jahael's like he was the Emperor's consort, he still looked as haughty as when I'd first seen him in the Legion: royal, in a way that I could never pull off.

Why had I been anxious that Anael couldn't play this game? It looked like he'd been playing it better than me...but then, he'd had a lot of practice with psycho dictators under his adoptive dad: Rahab.

Anael cast one glance at Mischief's still body, before tossing his brunet tresses and winding his arms around Jahael's neck. "Bored." He sighed, pouting. "Why do I have to listen to a Glory?" *Anael was only hiding our closeness, wasn't he?* Hell, don't let him have transferred from one despot of a dad to another. I'd only just started to break Anael's conditioning, when Mischief had brought us here. What if Jahael had started his own fresh brainwashing of veneration? "You promised to let me play with Purah if I was good."

Mr Twinkly's head shot up, and his hand trembled. Or *Purah*, I assumed.

"Father, by all that burns," Gabriel growled, even as his gaze ached with anguish, "this angel...Non-Divine...has no right to use an Acolyte—"

"Surely you're not speaking about *me*?" Anael rested his chin on Jahael's shoulder, playing with a diamond on his robe. "Was it an *angel* who failed to protect his own sister's first party, save his brother, or demanded to see the Emperor, almost like he considered this *his* Holy Audience Chamber? Or that we didn't already know...?"

My breath hitched.

I'd forgotten what a cruelly strategic bastard my brother had learnt to be in the Legion.

Gabriel opened his mouth as if to say something, then closed it again, as he looked between Anael and his dad.

Jahael gave his son a considering look. "Naughty boys don't get treats. But good ones..." He swung to Anael, patting his cheek. "Purah's all yours, cutie."

Gabriel's shoulders hunched

"You lost one dad, and now all you crave is a daddy," I spat. Anael finally glanced at me, even if it was with a flat indifference that clawed. "Or is it a *mummy*, since yours would've rather murdered you, than birthed a son?"

Anael's eyes widened, before at last flaring with hurt.

Jahael shoved me, and I tumbled onto my arse. His eyes burned like twin suns; silver crackled along his vast six wings, which spread the span of two columns in his rage, whilst he shielded my own brother from me.

*Because I was the bitch who'd hurt him.*

My ears roared with bellowed chants of *holy, holy, holy*, and the words bled from the walls. My magic thrashed in desperation to submit.

"I taught you to shank with words, girl, but here's where I break it down to you: they'll be no slaying Anael because he's my Advisor. I protect my Advisors, and I'm one fierce bitch." At last, Jahael's wings folded back. "I've loved you longer than you know, but your hoochie mama ass has to know how to love back."

I blushed, peeping around Jahael at Anael. When the chants quietened, my magic calmed. "I know how to love," I whispered...*don't think of Mischief*... "But I don't even know you."

"You've got that right." Jahael *tutted*. "*Mummy*? Freedom, Violet-darling, is choice. As a shifter, I can be male, female, both...or neither. Pure Seraphim can choose."

Jahael batted Anael away as he slunk closer to me with a swing of his hips. His robe tightened into diamond studded trousers, and his jaw-line hardened, but I could still tell that it was Jahael; he was equally as beautiful. He flashed me a grin, before his face softened, and his body blossomed into curves. A Glory fluttered her long eye-lashes at me, before with a flap of her wings, Jahael was back as his androgynous self again in his robe. "Most Seraphim choose their primary form at birth, but *I* choose to be neither...and that, sweet of my life, is *freedom*." For the first time, his scrutiny fully fell on Mischief. "Pretty little thing... One of the flaws in my bastard kids is that they never can hold their shifts for long enough to choose their form." Something darker swept across Jahael's mild curiosity as he studied Mischief's — dead — body. "Pity. Or this one wouldn't have been stuck as a Wing."

"*His name was Mischief.*" I pushed myself up into a crouch. "And he was your son. He suffered because you couldn't keep it in your pants."

"His name was...that's right, it doesn't matter because *he's dead*." Jahael's eyes sparked. "Now put...*that*...down, Gabriel, you're already in daddy's bad books."

*That...?*

Tears burned, as I leapt up, but Gabriel caught my eye and shook his head warningly.

Gabriel laid Mischief down on the cold floor, brushing

back Mischief's hair from his forehead, as if helping his little brother to prepare to meet his dad for the first time, not for his funeral.

A sob caught in my throat. "Don't dare to lecture me about love again, when your son's corpse is lying in front of you and you're dry-eyed, you heartless bastard."

"Will weeping bring him back?" Jahael fainted backwards in full Drama Queen mode, and Anael caught him. Black rose up in me to slap off the fake grief from his smug face. "Or do you crave punishment for those responsible?"

I nodded, not understanding Gabriel's groan.

Jahael straightened, his lips curling into a vicious grin. "Then there shall be atonement. Purah, hold the taper and don't let it go until it burns out."

Purah froze, trembling, but he grasped the taper between his pinched fingers.

*What the hell...? When it burned down, it'd sear Purah.*

"Look, all cured. No more craving for punishment." I spun around, patting myself down. "No need for him to burn himself, yeah?"

Gabriel paced closer to Purah in agitation, leaning forward as if about to tear away the taper; Purah whimpered at the heat. "Please don't punish Purah for my mistake—"

"This isn't punishment: it's atonement, submission, and worship. How many ass whippings does it take to make you understand your role as my Firstborn?" Jahael howled. "Are you feeling guilt, Gabriel? Because you didn't keep your sister safe? Because your brother lies dead like a sparkly sacrifice?"

And now I saw it: Jahael's sorrow unleashed as fury. A shifter, he wore as many faces as Gabriel.

Desperate with agony, Purah doubled up, letting go of the taper before it burnt out. Terrified, he bowed lower in apology.

Jahael simply nudged a second taper towards him.

"By my wing, it's enough," Gabriel snarled.

"Must I insist *every* Acolyte joins Purah in atonement?" Jahael raised his eyebrow.

Gabriel shook his head.

Purah picked up a second taper with trembling fingers, lighting it from a candle. This time he held onto it, sweating, even whilst it burnt itself out on his blistering skin. With a whine, he collapsed.

"I owe my brother a debt," Gabriel said, unable to look away from Purah, yet I couldn't help noticing that Anael had stiffened as well, hugging his arms across his chest. "*He* saved *my* life."

Jahael swept around to Gabriel; his gaze sharpened like he'd realised a sudden advantage over his son. My guts clenched. "All debts are cleared with death, jackass."

"That's not true." Gabriel's gaze was steely, as he raised it to his dad's. "By all that burns with the holiest love, I swear—"

"Don't," Purah gasped, forcing himself back onto his knees. "Don't, don't..."

*What the hell was this oath?*

"I swear that I shall serve you as you see fit, if you resurrect Mischief," Gabriel begged.

*Resurrect?*

A surge of glorious hope swept through me. My pulse pounded so rapidly that I swayed with dizziness. My silver magic crashed in tidal waves, frothing with joy that it might be re-joined with Mischief's.

*And yet...*

I hated that the hope could be false. I'd never come back from it: losing Mischief twice.

I'd promised Rahab *anything* to save Rebel's life. Gabriel's sacrifice was a dangerous one: he'd just bound himself to serve his dad — to do anything Jahael wanted — to save his brother.

I loved Gabriel for that, and yet I couldn't allow it. And

that broke my heart.

"Not bastard happening." I fought hard not to let my voice waver. "I brought Mischief's brother back from the dead as my Phoenix slave — Firebird — and I don't think Mischief ever truly forgave me. He called me a *monster*, and he was right. No way am I doing the same to him. He'd have chosen death, and as you're all about *choice*, you'd better let him have that at least, or I don't care how Big Bad despot you are, I'll kick your arse."

Jahael *clicked* his fingers, and Gabriel lifted Mischief back into his arms, following his dad across the audience chamber. I darted after them.

"Do you imagine I'm some shady floozy?" Jahael gasped in mock horror. "I'm the original resurrection: life and death. Phoenix is the pale imitation. Sorry, cutie pie!" He shot a kiss over his shoulder at Anael, who lounged on the divan, stretching out feline-like.

"If it's so easy," I tugged at Jahael's robe, "why didn't you simply conjure Mischief alive and—"

"Did I say it was easy?" Jahael paused in front of a mural of a snarling sabre-toothed tiger under a boiling sun, in a valley of bones. Just for a moment, I thought that the tiger winked at me. I took a step back, but Jahael clasped my hand. "Rebirth demands a sacrifice." Then he clutched Gabriel by the scruff of the neck, digging in his thumb until Gabriel winced. "You take vampires as spoils, my naughty son. Get my kids killed. And now make demands of resurrection by oath. What you need is another special learning experience. So, let's take a trip to Monster Hall."

The mural shimmered to life.

Jahael shoved Gabriel through, before dragging me after him, whilst Gabriel wailed in terror.

# 10

As a kid, *monster* had been sneered at me as an insult, and I'd hidden my mismatched eyes behind sunglasses. On Angel World, I'd thrown off my sunglasses — and my shame — owning both the angelic and vampiric natures battling within me.

I'd thought that I was the most dangerous monster out there.

*I'd been bastard wrong.*

I stumbled in the dark, catching my foot against something oozing like rotting leaves. My nose wrinkled, and I shied back. The heat beat down in oppressive waves, blasting the decaying stench of Monster Hall against my face. I gagged, holding my hand across my mouth.

Gabriel's wings beat in frantic, crackling arcs through the

gloom; his breath came in panicked gasps.

The *flap — flap — flap* of Jahael's giant wings overhead lit the low ceiling in silver sparks.

"Is this a lame arsed learning through stink lesson?" I growled. "Because if it is, I swear, lesson learnt. Let's get with the resurrecting, or does hurting your living son matter more to you, than saving your dead one?"

Gabriel gasped. I turned towards the sound and sweep of his flaming wings in the black. But I couldn't see Mischief's wings because his spark had been put out.

*Please let us be able to light it again.*

My magic wound around me in desperate coils, soothing me, even whilst it squirmed in its own anxious grief at the loss of Mischief's magic.

"A good father and a strong leader knows that to save, you must hurt, Violet-darling." Jahael's voice was even colder and more dangerous than it'd been in the Holy Audience Chamber: *Jahael truly was nothing like J.* "Does this look like Snuggly Bunny Land? To survive in a realm of monsters, even a god must become monstrous. And hooker, nobody talks to me like that."

I shrugged. "Maybe I'm nobody."

*Sizzle* — light sparked from Jahael's wings and along the roof, illuminating the hall.

Jahael swooped down, landing in front of me. "Girl, you're *everything*. Your cunning as a button brother understood his place here straight away, but you just need the guiding hand of your creator. Luckily for your sweet ass, you have my son to watch as an example."

Gabriel cringed, backing into the centre of the room away from the glimmering murals that were on every wall: *monsters*, real or magical, hybrids or evolutionary possibilities torn from the Gateways. Bristling werewolves, giant apes, and millipedes the size of cars prowled and writhed as if brought to life by the light.

*Howls, grunts, and shrieks.*

Gabriel trudged to an altar in the centre of the hall, which was soft with black mould; when Gabriel placed Mischief onto it, I shuddered at the obscene *suck*, as Mischief sank into its hold.

"The Guardian built Monster Hall, when Gabriel was still the tiniest kid because no amount of wing whippings could kick the rebel from Gabriel's adorable ass. Until *this*."

"Was my oath not enough?" Gabriel pressed the back of his hand to Mischief's cheek. "Must I also atone with humiliation and...?"

"Terror?" Jahael wound a strand of hair around his finger, before *squelching* through the floor towards me. Only then did I realise that his feet were encased in ballet shoes like mine. "That's why you were always locked in for the night, my naughty son. So that you could suffer the spinetingling anticipation...*the waiting*...never knowing which horrific creature would escape from these walls and—"

"Enough with the Hammer Horror dramatics," I snarled.

Tremors ran through Gabriel, as he leant against the altar; his breaths became ragged. His gaze was glazed like he was lost back in Childhood Nightmare Land.

*Had he truly been locked here — in the dark — waiting for the monsters to crawl from the walls?*

We'd both been attacked as kids by monsters at night, but Gabriel's had been *real*.

Jahael rolled his eyes. "What do you think lies outside my Temple, Violet-darling? A god either extinguishes their fear or they're burnt to ash by it." He swept all six of his wings around me, shrouding me in their intoxicating scent of agarwood. "There are just as many monsters in my court." His whisper was too hot against my ear. *Too close, too close, too...* I couldn't escape his hold, yet the preciousness of his touch and attention sank into my bones, illuminating me with *fervour*: my creator saw and loved me...

103

*Holy, holy, holy...*

*Why were my eyes suddenly so heavy?*

Jahael's lips curved against my cheek. "Yet the monsters in this temple wear smiling faces. Even you, girl. What makes an Emperor god any different...? Only this: *I admit what I am.*" His wings tightened to the point of pain. "Choose, Gabriel."

Gabriel started, before inching towards one wall, then changing his mind and backing towards another. He screwed closed his eyes, reaching out his trembling fingers.

"Bastard stop," I struggled in Jahael's hold. "What do you want? A sacrifice tossed into the volcano to appease you?"

Jahael snorted. "That'd be a start."

Gabriel's fingers traced the warping wall.

Lava burst out, knocking Gabriel onto his back and covering him head-to-toe. Except, it wasn't lava, rather thousands of tiny *fire* scorpions.

Gabriel screamed, thrashing wildly, whilst the scorpions' stingers flared in the gloom, searing him. Yet he didn't try and fight back.

Horrified, I hollered, squirming against Jahael's feathered bondage, but he hushed me.

"*Shhh* now, don't be a scaredy-cat. There are more creatures in the supernatural worlds than you've ever dreamed of. No, don't look away..." He gripped my chin, forcing me to watch, whilst his son writhed in agony. "Vampires and angels? They're the sweet cream on the top of the cake. Every bite from now on and for every day of the rest of your life, you'll discover something richer and so much darker now that you're a god."

"Then this is me officially handing back my god card." I hated the way that tears traced my cheeks, and even more, the way that Jahael licked at them.

"Why would you reject your fabulous divinity?"

"I'm a rebel, yeah?"

"*You're a monster.*" I couldn't help the wince. "Both your

104

brother and you are the monsters that shouldn't be: Fallen and angel, shadow and light. Plus, you have a special seeded extra that makes you divine, which means that you need the same lessons. So, choose."

I blinked at Jahael, even as my ancient powers surged in fury at Gabriel's screams.

"Do you wish one son resurrected or the other burnt?" Jahael whispered.

I jolted; my breath caught.

*Hell, he couldn't mean…?*

I peered over his shoulder at Gabriel, who'd stopped moving under the mass of scorpions, except for the twitch of his wings.

I bit hard on my lip to hold back my rage. How could Jahael make me choose between brothers? Was he truly prepared to sacrifice one son to teach me a lesson?

My gaze swung to Mischief on the altar. *All I had to do was say his name, and he'd be alive again…*

I shook my head. "I'm not choosing between who lives and dies. I shouldn't have that power; I don't care if I am a bastard god."

Jahael's eyes flared. "Then they both die."

I stiffened. Every instinct screamed at me to cherish and protect Gabriel, but I *loved* Mischief. I opened my mouth to whisper his name, when Gabriel's pained whimper caught me; fire scorpions were stinging his wingtips, and he couldn't shake them off.

Monster Hall had been Gabriel's hell since he'd been a kid; he'd been trained to fear it, just like Mischief had been conditioned to fear the Lower Vault and snakes. I remembered Mischief telling me about growing up protecting his little brother, Nathanael, who'd become my Phoenix slave, Firebird, with his memories of Mischief stolen.

Mischief had spent his life protecting his brothers: he'd never want me to sacrifice Gabriel to bring him back to life.

And he'd never forgive me if I made that choice.

I bit my lip harder, tasting the sharp blood. "Let me go."

At once, the weight of Jahael's wings were lifted. I darted across the hall, roaring at the scorpions like I could extinguish their fire by fear alone, before tumbling Gabriel round and round on the sticky floor.

*Stamp — stamp — stamp.*

I squished the stinging bastards, even as my own hands blistered. I patted Gabriel's seared wings that still glowed with embers; his face was blackened.

*Hell, don't let me be too late...*

Then Gabriel groaned, and a sudden godly rushing power inside reached out in protective joy that I'd saved him, even whilst it ached at what I'd given up.

*Mischief.*

"My brother...?" Gabriel forced out through swollen lips, and I winced because it was the first time that he'd called Mischief that with full sincerity.

When I soothed my fingers through Gabriel's feathers, I was caught in the velvety embrace of his amber scent. I wished that I could hold him without hurting him because his dad had already hurt him enough for a lifetime.

*Yet, did I crave to burn both my enemies and lovers because of Jahael's seed inside me...?* Wasn't *I* a Fire God too? And why in this moment of both rebirth and death, did I shudder in my need for *J*'s comfort?

"I had to choose," I explained, unable to stop my impotent tears. "Mischief would've gone crazy unicorn on me if he'd died to save you, only for me to steal his free will."

Jahael huffed. "What's with all the diva waterworks? So dramatic..."

He stalked closer, considering us both, before he shoved me backwards. When he pressed his hand onto Gabriel's sapphire choker, the jewel blazed awake: an opening eye.

Gabriel juddered; the tendons on his neck stood out. I shielded my eyes against the brightness of the magic bleeding from the choker and knitting across Gabriel, whilst he arched in agony, paling him from charred to dusky skinned once again. His swollen face was restored in moments back to sweating perfection, although he panted, as Jahael pulled away his hand from the sapphire and patted him on the head.

"There, there, all better now, Gabriel." Jahael rubbed the hem of his robe over Gabriel's cheeks, wiping away his tears. Then he raised his eyebrow at me. "You believed that I'm the sort of angelic asshole to have designed Monster Hall for my son, but not a way to heal him afterwards?" He pouted. "Girl, you disappoint me."

I stared at the pendant around Gabriel's neck, which had faded and was no longer glowing. Everywhere he went, Gabriel wore a reminder of disappointing his dad: Jahael's *power* over him. No matter how hurt Gabriel was during his night here, he could be restored back to perfection the following morning.

Yet Gabriel had stood up to his dad to save Ash and Lucifer, as well as to demand resurrection for Mischief. Only now did I understand what that meant. And I wouldn't forget what terrors he'd faced to have my fam's back.

"By the fire, have I atoned?" Gabriel didn't raise his gaze.

Jahael held one hand out to his son, and one out to me. Reluctantly, I allowed myself to be pulled to my feet alongside Gabriel; Jahael's skin felt drier than I'd expected: reptilian.

"Don't worry your pretty little head; you're all atoned up. What fills me with sweet as cheery pie tingles is that our precious new god here chose *you* to save." Jahael's fingers tightened around mine, as he led us to the altar. I couldn't look at Mischief held motionless in the centre. "I must insist on all your attention; I'm a narcissist, I really am." He slammed Gabriel and me down over the altar; our cheeks touched Mischief's cold chest. I forced panicked breaths through my nostrils, unable to stop my body shaking. When my knees buckled, Gabriel slid his hand into mine; his gaze anchored me. "How about if I told you that your choice was a test of my son's powers?"

"Father, you *promised* that I'd atoned..." Gabriel's fingers stroked across mine in panic.

"The freaky lion shifting?" I hated the feel of Mischief's skin against my cheek. *Why couldn't he at least have the respect of being dressed?* Yet I'd been the one to order him to *strip*...

Jahael massaged his hand down my neck. "His godly power to inspire followers to treasure him, just as they worship me. To *protect*." *Had I sacrificed Mischief only because I'd been under Gabriel's power?* "BAM! She's finally gagging on the truth like a low market hustler."

I crushed Gabriel's fingers between mine, before hurling his hand away from me.

"On all the divinity of love, I didn't mean to... I never chose to use it..." Gabriel looked away miserably. For a moment, I wished that our hands were still touching. "It called to you in a way that it never has to anyone before. I didn't mean to trick you."

"Epic fail."

Gabriel flinched.

"Oh, don't sulk," Jahael said. "Now I know that you're loyal to my Firstborn, even over the one you love for *real*..." Gabriel flinched again. "Let me ask you this: what would you do to get back your sparkly lover from the dead?"

*There was still a chance to resurrect Mischief...?*

My breath ghosted in desperate gasps over Mischief's chest, as my steel claws shot out, sinking into the altar.

Anything: hell, I'd do *anything*.

"Don't," Gabriel hissed. "I've already given my oath and—
"

Jahael dug his fingers into the base of Gabriel's neck, and

108

he shrieked.

"What's all the fuss, naughty boy? Are you begging to touch another mural?"

When the walls glimmered as if in excitement at the treat, Gabriel shook his head, biting his lip to keep in the pain.

"I'll resurrect Mischief, if you give your oath to join the Order of my Knights of the Seraphim, Violet-darling."

Gabriel struggled. "Wait..."

"On all that burns...*blah, blah*...pompous oath...*blah, blah*, I swear to become one of your knights if you resurrect Mischief. Will that do it?"

Jahael's smile was long and luxuriant, as at last he let go of his son's neck. "Fabulous."

Gabriel roared in frustration, booting at the altar. "By His wing, do you imagine my brother would wish your sacrifice anymore than he'd wish mine? Every new knight undergoes a Test by Monster: three days outside the temple in the Bone Plains."

"So, I go sightseeing tomorrow. What's the problem?"

"No one who isn't fae has ever survived."

*Yeah, I got the problem.* Unless I transformed into Tinkerbelle I was screwed and I didn't think having my own fam of Lost Boys counted.

"Then I'll be the first."

"That's the spirit." When Jahael kissed my shoulder, I shuddered. "Why would my creation fail me? And not to dump even more steaming reality on you but if you fail...there's no place in a realm of gods for mere vampires or angels."

I twisted around to Jahael. "What in the Neverland are on you on about?"

Jahael's gaze darkened. "Gabriel's spoils of war: the vampires." My mouth dried: *Ash and Lucifer.* "I'd toss them back into the Abyss." He twirled, spinning his robe with a giggle. I clenched my fists, remembering my *oath*, and how

109

Gabriel had tried to stop me. He'd known that there'd be a *cost*...and the power that his dad would have over me. "Along with that Phoenix, who is nothing more than a travesty of a science experiment raised on my cutie pie prince's blood."

"Firebird's the most innocent bloke in this temple."

Jahael's eyes narrowed. "Maybe that's why Quinn, my Chief Knight, loves the *taste* of him. I've barely seen the Phoenix, but then Quinn is so possessive." I hadn't realised that I was growling, until Jahael gave a cold laugh. "Girl, he's not the only one. You should be kissing his feet because if he hadn't claimed the Phoenix's ass, I'd have erased his false resurrection as a gift for Anael. I do so love to treat your brother."

My eyes were burning, but I refused to let any more tears fall in front of Jahael. I had to win the Test by Monster: how could I let Mischief's brother die, after I'd already raised him as my slave? "Don't bastard touch him."

Jahael chuckled. "A delicate flower like him will be most...popular...in the Abyss. But then so will Commander Drake amongst all those vampires..."

Fire surged in uncontrollable fury under my skin and down my arms at the thought of Drake at the mercy of his enemies: an angel amongst vampires. The injustice of it spiked my righteousness, until I vibrated with violet.

Only Gabriel's arm around my waist, dragging me back, stilled the storm. His rich aroma overlaid the fury, calming me, even whilst I shivered that this could be Gabriel's Angelic Power. Yet it was working symbiotically, winding around my ancient powers: it didn't feel wrong or controlling, but rather like part of me that I hadn't even known had been missing.

A gentleness not to be dominated, but to be cherished.

"She understands, father." Gabriel met my gaze, suddenly grave. "We shan't fail you."

"We?" Jahael queried.

"I made an oath to you as well." Gabriel tilted his chin.

110

"She doesn't know the rules or this land and shall inevitably do something foolish..."

"It'll do your overentitled ass good to serve as a knight rather than my Firstborn." Gabriel blushed at his dad's jeer; everything Gabriel had suffered had been to hold onto his position in court but now he'd been demoted to knight. "It's about time you did more than party and skulk in the shadows. Quinn can guide you. At least then, I'll believe the reports."

Gabriel lowered his gaze; he reddened an even deeper shade.

Jahael swooped above the altar, stretching out his wings; his feathers sparked.

Gabriel and I twisted back to Mischief, as my heart pounded with desperate hope; I studied Mischief's still face.

*Open your eyes...*

Above the altar, Jahael flapped his wings harder.

Suddenly, Jahael transformed into Mischief.

I gasped, looking between the two angels. Slowly, silver tendrils spun from the False Mischief like life from one to the other, before in a spray of light Jahael became himself again.

And Mischief opened his eyes.

I didn't breathe. Speak. Look away.

*Silence.*

Had Jahael raised Mischief wrong? Had he wiped his memories? Did Mischief even know who I was...?

Then Mischief grasped hold of me, burrowing his head onto my chest and drawing in gasp after painful gasp of air. I never knew how much I ached to hear his breaths but each was more precious to me than my own.

"I shan't ever let go again," Mischief rasped.

"And I won't let you go again," I murmured, stroking his hair.

He was warm, safe, and in my arms. Everything was worth this moment.

Gabriel awkwardly shifted from foot to foot. "Then how will I get a hug from my little brother?"

Mischief raised his head; tears glinted on his eyelashes. "*Brother...*"

*Oomph* — Gabriel rushed closer, wrapping his wings around us both so tightly that the air was pushed out of us.

Mischief squirmed. "Get off, you feathered..."

I caught his smile, however, before he could smother it, and Gabriel only rested his chin on my shoulder.

"There's the sugar sweetness that makes me love being Emperor." Jahael soared closer; his shadow swallowed us. "I'm looking forward to some quality time with my bastard son, whilst you're away, in case you fail. You see, the one who raises from the dead, owns that life and can snuff it out with a thought." When Mischief paled, I clasped him closer, just as Gabriel's wings cocooned us. "Don't make me take back my resurrection."

I shook with despair.

I couldn't lose Mischief now that he was back — alive — in my arms. Jahael had dangled this treat before us, only for the punishment to be worse when it was taken away.

There was one night remaining before I'd undertake the Test by Monster on the deadly plains. Mischief's death, and my vampire and angel fam's suffering in the Abyss, would be my fault if I failed.

Yet no one but fae had ever survived.

# 11

Once, I'd had a crush on a posh boy at school. He'd been the perfect pretty boy with two parents, a home, and no idea what a shank felt like slicing through skin.

Me? I'd been Miss Invisible to Perfect Posh, until suddenly — one day — I hadn't been.

Perfect Posh's ice blue eyes had twinkled, as I'd passed him in the corridor; he'd blessed me with a smile that'd been all for me, and I'd guarded it as the only truly special thing that I'd owned.

J had warned me not to go soft and let a bloke become my weakness. Yet I hadn't listened because I'd had *that smile* to light me.

Then Perfect Posh had whispered, "Trust me."

When he'd pulled me after him into the alley behind the playground, I'd burst with glee that at last I'd been *seen*.

Until...

*Sniggers and jeers.*

Perfect Posh had pulled away from me to join his mates,

who'd huddled at the end of the alley.

*I can't believe she fell for it... The bitch actually reckoned I was into her... Who'd want to touch a freak like her...?*

I hadn't bastard cried. But I hadn't trusted again.
Ever.


Gabriel clung to me, before twirling me across the tiny cell in a dance that was all feathers, passion, and desperation. My boots clattered across the cold marble, whilst Gabriel's eyes glimmered in the gloom; the only light in the windowless chamber bled from the grilles on the floor through to the Acolytes' sleeping quarters.

Nope, not feeling the trust from Jahael: he'd dragged Gabriel and me away from Mischief and locked us up for our last night in the temple.

In less than an hour, I'd set out to the Bone Plains for the impossible Test by Monster, so now I'd dance with Gabriel to the heart wrenching operatic rock of Queen's "The Show Must Go On" because if we were going out, we'd do it in style.

Mischief had a serious sense of irony when he'd passed on my *special songs* to his brother, and Gabriel had more control over his imprisonment than I'd thought that he could serenade me even in this cell.

Although, as Gabriel's wings surged their power through me until I shuddered, caught between his jagged spikes of energy and my own answering howl of shadows, I wondered if this was more *his* special song than mine.

**The Firstborn Aslan wears more faces than I do, Feathery-doll. How much makeup do you think he slaps on to survive in the show at court?**

*I saved Mischief but the cost—*

**You know this tune. You chose it. Did you think**

114

**that the Shady Dick Me wouldn't demand a sacrifice?**

**But you're a god too. Demand one right back.**

*Who do I trust...?*

**Haven't you worked it out yet?**

Gabriel gripped my elbows with bruising force. His gaze was anguished but also determined; his chin tilted, even though his lips trembled. He dragged me close, whispering into my ear, "Trust me, and I shall worship you." I gasped, drawing back. His eyes lit with painful hope. "Take my Crown, body, soul—"

"I don't want a bastard slave." I shoved him against the wall.

The godlike powers inside burnt bright at his temptation: to claim an Archduke and future Emperor, just as his rich amber scent begged me to stroke the distressed sparks on his feathers and *cherish* him, rather than force him to his knees, whilst he worshipped me.

I wasn't the shadow of my mother, no matter the Glory that she'd tried to mould me into, *and I wasn't Istafil,* although that was all Gabriel had known.

Gabriel cocked his head. "Then *rule with me.*"

My eyes widened.

*He wanted me to be the future Empress?*

"I'm not some Imperial Favourite who needs the bauble of power held out to me. Help me live through this test and you'll have my trust. I don't need to *take* anything from you."

"And what if I willingly give it?" Gabriel slipped his arm back around my waist, gently kissing my jaw.

His magic sizzled from his lips in a tingling line: I gasped, juddering into his hold, as finally the tremoring shock of Mischief's death and resurrection connected us.

Here was true peace, not slavish worship.

Until Gabriel growled, plucking a flitting butterfly from behind my ear.

*A fae Knight of the Seraphim: the sneaky bloodsucking*

115

*bastard.*

"Game over," I smirked. "Prepare to say hello to Mr Boot."

The knight *squeaked*, before hanging limply between Gabriel's finger and thumb. Cold tendrils squeezed my guts with guilt: *the poor little bastard...*

Gabriel rolled his eyes, whilst shaking the knight. I stared at him in shock. "The fae have been bound to serve His holy glory for centuries. Surely you didn't imagine my father's power all his own?"

The knight snarled, beating his wings. The tendrils of guilt receded: this was one feisty fairy. Especially when he twisted, biting Gabriel's thumb.

Gabriel yelped, dropping the knight who whizzed in a metallic blur around our heads. Then the knight transformed in a shower of gold into a full-sized steam-punk military officer, whose wings burst in burnished gold through the slashes in his coat; a decorative scimitar was slung around his waist.

I startled, staggering backwards, whilst the knight's lips curved upwards; the deep emerald of his eyes danced with a dangerous malevolence that made my hands twitch towards the non-existent weapons at my waist.

Emerald eyes that matched his hair, which was pinned up with flamboyant gold clips, scrutinized me. The knight's grin widened in the translucent alabaster of his skin, revealing sharpened teeth *like fangs*.

It put a whole different spin on the bastard Tooth Fairy.

I shuddered. "Is Fairy of the Fangs here safe?"

Gabriel barked with laughter. "Of course not. By the bones, why ever would you think any of the fae *safe*? You don't survive by avoiding danger, but by understanding that there are dangers you can never tame."

The knight swept to Gabriel, slamming his hands against the wall to box Gabriel in and nipping kisses along his jaw.

I growled — not at the kisses — but at the way that

Gabriel sighed, relaxing under the knight's demanding caresses.

How long had they been *lovers*, whilst I'd only just been admitted to this realm?

Yet Gabriel had offered me *everything*... Had he meant it or had it simply been another move on the board?

I snatched the knight by his hair, digging his clips into his scalp, whilst he hissed and twisted, and dragging him back from Gabriel. I knew, however, that he was *allowing* himself to be manhandled, as I tossed him to the floor: his coiled strength hummed through me.

Gabriel caught my arm. "Aren't we all prisoners, sister? Everyone's a spy in this temple: we're all ensnared whisperers together. And Quinn—"

"This is the Chief Knight?" I gazed down at Quinn, who was sprawled on his back, staring at me unblinkingly. I trembled with eddies of violet rage. If Quinn had touched my teenage Phoenix, I'd cut off his bastard balls. "Where's Firebird, bitch?"

Quinn flicked his fingers at me, and a burst of rainbow sparks shot out, before fizzling away.

"Impressive kiddie show, but as an attack...? Epic fail." I stalked closer, but Quinn only raised an eyebrow. "Cat got your tongue?"

Frustrated, Quinn pushed himself to his knees, shooting another arc of colours at me: rusty reds and oranges this time.

Gabriel *tutted*. "Your coarseness will get you nothing but a spanking, young fay."

The look Quinn cast Gabriel was sultry as he crawled towards him; Gabriel backed away.

I glanced between them. "Am I missing the part where Rainbow Fairy here's...you know, *talking*?"

Gabriel stroked his hand down Quinn's cheek, as Quinn rested his head on Gabriel's thigh. "The fae's voices were stolen by my father. He sought to control and isolate them,

117

so that only he'd be able to talk to them inside their minds. Yet, the fae are rebels..." Quinn sniggered. "They found their own way to communicate and they taught me."

*The rainbow colours were Quinn's voice...?*

A bottle green crept blushing from the tips of Quinn's fingers.

Gabriel sighed. "Thank you for your trust and...she knows that you wouldn't hurt the Phoenix." Gabriel glanced at me, and I read his plea: not to hurt Quinn.

I bit my lip. "You've been protecting Firebird from the Seraphim, yeah?"

Quinn nodded.

"There are many tribes of fae, and the ones that my father bound to him..." Quinn pushed himself to his feet, bursting rainbows so brightly that my eyes ached. Gabriel caught his hands, stilling them. "Why, even now so frightened?" Quinn struggled to back away, but Gabriel held on tightly. "My sister shan't reject you: the ones that she's claimed as family are bastards, Addicts, Halfings, Seducers, and vampires. I promise, she will not believe that you deserve your fate: she is not your father, nor mine."

Why had Quinn and his tribe been bound? Why was Quinn so ashamed?

I nodded. "My fam has my back, and I have theirs. I don't care about your past, only who you are now."

Quinn's eyes widened, before he gestured from himself to me.

Gabriel smiled: it wasn't the radiant one that made me feel alive but soft and thoughtful. "She is indeed a rebel like you. Quinn's entire warrior tribe was hated and feared for their difference. When they were defeated in battle, they were given to the Seraphim as punishment."

"I wish I could kick some fairy arse for you."

"Quinn will *kick arse* for us on the Test by Monster." Gabriel dropped to his knees, pulling Quinn with him and wrapping him in the nest of his wings. Then he glanced up at me. "Fae need skin contact — touch in their world is power. My father forbids it but by my feathers, I'll not deny them."

"Lamest excuse for sexy times ever." I cocked my head. "So, they're Snuggle Fae?" Quinn's brow darkened, until I shivered. "OK, got it, don't piss off the Snuggle Fae."

Then to my surprise, Quinn held open his arms, welcoming me into their snuggle fest.

I dived into Gabriel's wings, allowing myself this comfort. Soon, we'd be taken out of the cell to face monsters.

Ones that weren't me.

*Creak* — I jumped, as the oak door swung open.

"Only me," Purah, Jahael's Acolyte, ambled into the cell, still naked as he'd been in the Holy Audience Chamber, except for the **J** stuck in pearls on the centre of his chest. "I couldn't let you fools go wandering about on a holiday without a final cuddle."

*I guess the holy adoration schtick didn't extend to the Archduke.*

Gabriel scrambled up, grasping Purah around the shoulders, before spinning him. Then he snatched his hands, examining his blistered fingers with a guilt, which I understood from every time that my decisions and mistakes had hurt *my* family.

Hell, Quinn and Purah were Gabriel's *family*: a slave and a bound fae. Yet why had an Archduke chosen the enslaved? Had he truly been that lonely? Had he been scorned by the Seraphim or had he allied himself with those that he wished to save?

*Was he as much a hero in the shadows as Mischief?*

Gabriel kissed the seared tips of Purah's fingers. "By all that burns, you have my apologies a thousand times over. Tell me how to atone..."

Purah tilted his head, and his curls fell into his eyes. "Nothing says sorry like a back massage; my shoulders are killing me. Our Holy Emperor used me as a sodding foot stool for hours."

"Your wish is my command."

Then Gabriel dragged Purah down in a flurry of wings, massaging his shoulders, whilst Quinn licked up his neck. Purah wriggled down with a sigh.

*Purring.*

Purah's contented *purr* thrilled through me, like Rebel's always had.

*Hell, I missed Rebel.*

As if sensing my sorrow, Purah waggled his foot at me. "There's enough loving to go around. How about a foot rub?"

Gabriel paused in his massage, glancing at me uncertainly.

What did he expect me to do? Blast his little Acolyte for his insolence?

This was Gabriel's *family*: Quinn and Gabriel were spoiling the slave to try and make up for the abuses that he suffered.

*I was bastard down with that.*

"I'm God of Foot Rubs." I slipped into their tangle of feathers, dark and pale skin, and snuggles, whilst I picked up one of Purah's small feet and stroked its arch.

"On all that's holy, I'm worshipping your arse." Purah writhed, *purring.*

*Yeah, I have magic hands.*

I glanced through the grille at the Acolyte's sleeping quarters: it was identical to our cell, except for a row of sinks and marble baths. The Acolytes huddled together on the floor without even blankets, sleeping like a pile of puppies with wings.

Gabriel noticed my sad grimace. "At least they don't sleep alone."

Sprays of blues from cerulean to cobalt shot from Quinn's palms.

"Buzzkill," Purah muttered.

120

"Quinn just wanted to make certain that you knew we have three days only to complete the test, and if we don't...we can't return." Gabriel stroked his thumb along Purah's wingtip, and he whined. Hell, that was why Purah was here: *This was a goodbye.* Yet I hadn't even been able to say my goodbyes to my family. Gabriel's assessing stare made me squirm. "Defeated already? Aren't you my father's mighty creation? A *god*? The test is to hunt the monsters, not be hunted. To succeed, you bring back a trophy for my father's cabinet."

Quinn sprang up, military smart. He wove his hands above his head and sparkling creatures sprang to life in the gloom: a sizzling serpent that wound around the cell.

I scrabbled back against the wall, but the snake passed through me, ghostly. Quinn's eyes glittered, as a tiny image of him sprang to life: a doll next to the hissing snake. They circled each other, before the Doll Quinn swung his scimitar in a wide arc, slicing off the serpent's head.

*His trophy.*

Quinn gave the universal gesture for *ta da*!

*That's what I'd be facing...monsters like that...?*

My lips thinned. "Cheers for the motivational video. It's filed under Monsters I Never Want to Meet."

Gabriel brushed his fingers across mine. "The monsters aren't what you think. Some were brought through the Gateways and others..." He looked away. "Remember, my father has demoted me. I fight by your side."

I clasped his hand tighter, just as Purah hugged onto us both, and Quinn rested his hand on our heads. I wasn't alone, but in moments I'd be taking on a test that no one but fae had ever survived, for the sake of my family, who'd die or be tossed into the Abyss if I failed. And I didn't have my true fam at my side, but the Emperor's son and the knight who was loyal to him.

Would I discover that it was even more dangerous outside the toxic court of the temple, amongst the plain's feathers and bones?

The ghostly curve of the valley's bones glowed like a violet river carving a snake path through the mountains of feathers. Hardness between the soft; beauty and decay. A realm that had lived in my mind and haunted me as visions.

Beginning *and* End.

I shook my head, squinting through the blaze of the scarlet streaked sun from my perch at the entrance of the bone cave, which was hollowed like a giant had sucked out the marrow.

In this freaky realm, maybe it had.

*Come on brain, conjure a pissed off Pikachu, rather than a marrow sucking Cyclops...*

I sighed, wiping the hem of my golden robe over my nose to block out the musty stench.

Just before we'd left The Burning Temple, Quinn had tossed a monk-like robe at me, which had moulded to my body in a way that'd been so intimate, I'd squirmed. Then he'd grinned as he'd strapped Flight and Star around my waist ceremonially: a welcome into the order.

I'd only needed a light sabre and I could've blamed the dark side for my new god-like cravings.

Quinn leant against the cave's wall, scanning the plains on sentry duty but looking like a conqueror surveying his new kingdom, whilst the true kingdom's heir sprawled at his feet next to me.

Gabriel nudged a bottle of water and a tin of baked beans towards me from his pack. "Eat, sister."

He smiled hopefully.

I picked up the tin with a grimace. "Cheers, these never grow old."

Quinn glanced at me. Then neon pinks sparked from his fingertips.

Gabriel laughed.

122

*Had I even heard him laugh before...?*

I stared at Gabriel, who was relaxed on his elbows next to me. He looked different — younger — than he had in the temple: *free.*

*Why did I crave to be the one to make him laugh?*

"See how much I tremble at your threat to turn me into an omega cub!" Gabriel pointed at Quinn, who attempted to frown, but his lips unwillingly quirked into a smile. "You fae would coddle me like a snuggle bug. You need lessons on intimidation from my father; he's Emperor of Terror."

I gaped at Gabriel. He'd just disrespected Jahael: where was the *holy, holy, holy,* and the *in His glory* fawning...?

Why had Gabriel just called down punishment on himself?

*Clank* — I slammed down the tin; I winced, as the beans slopped over my hand in a cold tsunami.

"What the hell, Monsieur Viv La Revolution?" I growled. "Are you just begging for another trip to Monster Hall?"

Gabriel blinked at me in surprise. "The rules change outside the temple. Here?" His smile was easy and open. How often would he smile if he was liberated from the Gilded Cage? "Father can't get in my head or use me as a puppet. I can say...what I truly think."

I glanced between him and Quinn. "Then what's with fairy boy?"

Gabriel turned away, gathering up his pack. I knew evasion when I saw it. "Quinn doesn't believe that we should be here; he's masterful in his opinions."

"Isn't this where I slay the monster?"

Quinn snorted.

I stiffened. Not to get conspiracy theory on their arses, but my shadows coiled inside that although this was my Test by Monster, there was more danger than the creatures roaming the plains.

"Don't you trust me yet?" Gabriel asked.

I studied him. "If you save my fam, I'd die for you."

123

Something shuttered in his face. "So quick to die?"

"So quick to save my fam."

Quinn marched to Gabriel, dragging him up by the front of his robe. Quinn's rainbow colours illuminated Gabriel's chest, pulsing over his heart. Gabriel whined, but didn't pull away.

"On my oath, when we return — and we shall survive to return — all your family who I have control over will be given to you, sister." Gabriel eased Quinn's fingers away, and the colours died. "Quinn promises Firebird as well."

"Ash and Lucifer too?" Gabriel hesitated too long. "I'm the Dragon God, do you want to piss me off? Because as *my* omega bitch, you'd be leashed, not coddled."

Gabriel's eyes became flinty. "By my wing, if I believed such of you, I'd not give a single angel into your power."

I deflated, licking at the beans on my hand with a shudder. "You got me, bro. I won't be that sort of god. But you *will* free all my fam — and that's vampires too."

Quinn nuzzled against Gabriel's neck, and Gabriel sighed.

"You may have the vampire whore," Gabriel conceded. "But Lucifer is too dangerous—"

"You're acting the pussy?"

"I'm saving him," Gabriel burst out, "for you. My father wished him *dead* or severely punished at the climax of the Angel Games: you were to be victorious through the death of your own father. It would've been the washing clean of your Fallen past and the entry into your new godly role. Do you imagine the Emperor so furious with me over fripperies? Before your arrival, he believed me the most obedient son in all things. Since it...I have defied him at every turn. *You shall be the death of me.*"

I stared at Gabriel, as Quinn held him to his chest, stroking his back.

What the hell did I say? *Sorry I've screwed-up your life?*

"Good word: *fripperies*. Like flibbertigibbet, kerfuffle, or

124

pernickety..."

Gabriel raised his head from Quinn's chest; his eyes were glazed with tears, but he still smiled weakly. "I hope you're aware how impossible you are?"

"Yeah, Mischief makes sure to tell me that in daily doses of snark."

"I shall claim Lucifer as my personal Acolyte. It's the only way to keep him away from other Seraphim and stop him from being tossed into the Abyss. Does that save me from beating?"

I nodded, licking the final stripe of beans off my hand, before chucking away the tin.

Gabriel's brow furrowed. "I was clear with the Guardian to source human army rations." He untangled himself from Quinn's possessive hold, crouching down opposite me. "Did I fail you?"

My breath caught at the honest rawness of his tone.

How often had he been made to feel a *failure*?

Unexpectedly, the velvet caress of his amber scent wound around me: a silent plea for *mercy*...

I craved to pull Gabriel closer and kiss away the panicked look, pulling the lip that he tore between his own teeth and bite it instead between mine...

"You couldn't fail me." I forced on the most fake smile of my life. "Beans are the food of the gods: delicious as triple chocolate cupcakes smothered in nectar."

Gabriel's shoulders slumped with relief. "I'll have the Guardian fetch you more as a treat once we're back."

*The tangled web of lies...*

I bit back a groan. "Awesome."

"Although..." Gabriel seized my hand; his wings flapping in sudden agitation. "You'd do better with blood."

I jerked my hands away from his. "Listen here, Sultan's boy, I'll never drink human blood."

"Who said anything about human? A Fallen's blood, especially of a bonded, is the most potent...a Marked angel's

125

has almost equal power. Don't you sense it: the *pull*?"

My gums itched at the phantom taste of blood. Rebel's was candy sweet heaven: its strength had juiced me, as well as bonded me so close that I could shoot emotions through to Rebel and even control him on a thought. But I wouldn't do that to him without permission because I wouldn't make him my puppet.

Plus, his blood was addictive.

If Ash's had an even greater kick, how much more addictive would it be?

"Don't get *blood craving* on me." I inched backwards. "My sister's a Blood Lover, and I'm not forcing that type of twisted love on Ash."

Quinn leant over Gabriel, cradling his arms over his neck, before tipping him back and licking down his throat.

Gabriel peeked through his thick eyelashes at me. "How strange that you assume it'd be *unwilling*? What if he secretly longs to bond b-b-but..."

"If you're going to start rapping about your love of big butts..."

Gabriel blanched, staring fixedly at the wall behind me.

**Turn around, Violet-death.**

*How about a hell no...?*

**Would you rather know the dangers in the shadows, hooker, or hide in blindness?**

My pulse racing, I slid my hand to Star and unsheathed it, as I shuffled around. The *scrape* of my arse on the bone floor was painfully loud in the sudden silence.

I forced myself to look up.

A black scorpion, the size of a crocodile, clung to the wall. Its sharp twin pincers snapped; its soft mouth gaped. The huge bulbous stinger on the end of its tail swung, as its back arched.

I held back the scream at the sight of the Giant Scorpion, which was as instinctive as the tremors that ran through me, whilst edging backwards towards Gabriel. I threw a quick glance over my shoulder at him.

Gabriel had frozen in terror at his nightmare from Monster Hall come to life but grown into its Big Daddy.

Quinn, on the other hand, had straightened into a wild warrior: thrilling and menacing in equal measure. With a spray of golden sparks, he drew his scimitar, before firing it in a sweeping arc over my head; a thousand tiny crystalline swords shot from the tip.

*Hissing.*

The Giant Scorpion scuttled further up the wall onto the roof, dodging the attack, even as it curled up and lifted its stinger higher.

With clammy hands, I raised Star above my head, rasping in rapid breaths.

Then the Giant Scorpion dropped onto my back.

Clawing feet, tearing pincers, and smothering coldness.

The alien wrongness of the Giant Scorpion's weight trapped me. I couldn't breathe under its arachnid questing.

My chest hurt; I shook.

Gabriel's hollers, Quinn's sparks, my own flickers of violet.

The Giant Scorpion's bulbous stinger swung around, piercing my shoulder and pumping venom into me, whilst I howled.

# 12

Added to my Least Favourite Ways to Wake Up: paralysed by venom from the shoulders down.

*Blindfolded.*

Wetting my lips, I twisted my head to the side, before yelping as something pointy dug into the back of my head, *cracking* like...*wing bones.*

*I was laid out on the dead.*

When I drew in a deep breath to control the panic — when the hell had Giant Scorpions taken prisoners or developed the ability to put on blindfolds with their claws? — I flew on the sudden overwhelming scent of amber: *Gabriel.*

Where was Gabriel and Quinn? Had they slayed the Giant Scorpion and taken it as their trophy? Or had it slain them?

*Don't even think it...*

When I choked back a sob, the velvety scent cocooned me from the...*blindfold.*

I blinked at the soft cloth blinding me in midnight blue: a fragment of Gabriel's robe.

Hell, what *had* happened to Gabriel...? Was he even still

in the rest of the robe? How could I just lie here on the long deceased, whilst Gabriel could be naked and at the mercy of whoever had snatched us?

I struggled to twitch my fingers: nothing. I snorted in frustration. Even though I'd been paralysed by magic before, being trapped in my body by the Giant Scorpion's sting felt different because the venom was in my blood.

I forced my sluggish tongue around my mouth. I couldn't see or move, but they hadn't taken away my sharpest weapon: my snark.

**Before you unleash your pussy power, remember that gods are shifters with many faces and all of them jackasses. If you had the power to change yourself to survive, wouldn't you?**

*Cheers for the philosophy lesson, but scorpion sting and blindfolded, equals... Emergency, bitch.*

**Keep your luscious tits on, hooker, of course it's an emergency, you're dying.**

*J, did you just say...?*

**Dead like flares and dabbing.**

*Don't ever become a doctor; your bedside manner sucks.*

**How about this then? The venom is slowly causing your heart to fail. You could have hours...minutes...or only seconds left.**

***Now* do you have the drive to survive?**

At the *snap* of footsteps, I stilled, forcing myself to quieten my breathing. At least it didn't sound like a freaky gang of Giant Scorpions who could also truss up prisoners.

*Time to play dead.*

"I still think that we should feed her to the Terror Bird and be done with it." A gruff male voice growled above my head: commanding and assured.

This must be the top boy...*and Terror Bird didn't sound anymore hugs and kisses friendly than a gang of Giant Scorpions.*

"Didn't I warn you that your sister was the prize?" I

129

couldn't help the way that my head jerked backwards *crunching* against the bed of bones at the woman's sophisticated sneer: the same bitch who'd crashed Istafil's party and slaughtered Mischief. Violet and black warred impotent to snap her neck, just as she had my lover's, yet I laid helpless at her feet at the mercy of the Damned. "Yet you, Firstborn, bring her here like she's the—"

"Saviour. By my wing, it's because my sister *is* our saviour. Please, Rachiel, allow her but a chance to prove it."

*Gabriel...?*

My pulse raced; Gabriel was safe. Yet he'd also delivered me to the outlaw Damned.

Feathered outrage spun me thinner than glass: had Gabriel been seized by the Damned like me, or had he been in league with these murdering outlaws all along?

*Where was Quinn?*

Heavy footsteps *snapped* across the bones, coming even closer: *one, two, three...*

"I know that you're awake, girl; cut out the sleeping act." The Damned Top Boy nudged my cheek with his toe. "Don't worry, we voted 60:40 not to feed you to the Terror Bird."

Thrumming with righteous rage, I stretched my jaw. "Cheers for not chopping me up and using me as pet food."

A deep chuckle. "Oh, you wouldn't be dead when we fed you to her; she likes a little fight in her dinner."

I paled. "Down here, amongst the non-psychos," I shook my head from side to side, "take off this blindfold."

"Tell me first why you and the bastard Archduke came to our realm? What do you hope to gain, eh? Another notch to your tumbled worlds...or somewhere bigger and better to conquer?"

"Hold up, you've kidnapped me because you're *scared* of Mischief and me? You think that we're the next tyrants? Last time I looked, you weren't even in power, bitch."

*Crack* — the Damned Top Boy booted me in the face; my cheekbone shattered.

130

I hollered, gasping at the sickening wave of pain, which shuddered through me, even whilst I was unable to curl over, move away, or even protect myself.

*Did Gabriel know that I was dying?*

"Will you watch your words now, girl?" The Damned Top Boy crouched over me; his fingers trailed down the cheek that was swollen and bruising under the force of his brutality; I shivered at his freezing touch. "Will the Emperor elect the bastard or you over Gabriel as heir?"

"Wait...just turning on my psychic mind reading powers..."

The Damned Top Boy's fingers gripped harder into my skin; I flinched.

"Please stop, uncle. I didn't bring her here for this," Gabriel's voice was tear tinged.

*Uncle...?*

*The leader of the Damned was Gabriel's uncle and the Emperor's own brother?*

**Gabriel is his father's son, Violet-cakes. Intrigues are in his blood, as much as the venom is in yours.**

**Except, anti-venom could purge you. Can anything purge a Machiavelli?**

I scowled at the sound of Gabriel's pained whine. "Always too frightened to dirty your pure hands, Firstborn." Despite my rage at Gabriel's betrayal, I couldn't bear to hear the bitch, Rachiel, who'd attacked Mischief, hurting Gabriel, not whilst I was cradled in his scent; it was all that held me together. "At our last raid, Ariel, this pampered puppy acted as if he didn't even know our intentions, even though we'd sent him the sign through the yellow cocktail."

"That's because you, Rachiel, laid waste to innocents without sending me any warning."

My awesome cocktail at Isatfil's party before the attack, which had sizzled from yellow to violet-and-black tequila, had been meant as a sign for Gabriel...?

Only, *I'd* drunk it.

I couldn't help the smirk. "Your little spy game went wrong; *I* got your code drink."

Ariel's — the Damned Top Boy's — fingers slipped to my jaw with the burn of ice. Then he slipped off my blindfold.

I gasped, closing my eyes against even the dim light of the Damned's bone cavern. Carefully, I opened them again.

Ariel's burly bulk blocked out almost the entire cavern like a reverse eclipse in sunburst yellow; he wore the same ragtag cloths as the Damned who'd attacked the party, although a wide necklace of wing bones also hung around his neck and silvered shards pierced both his ears: Mad Max meets caveman. His beard was as military short as his hair.

When I remembered the longhaired flaming Seraphim in their exquisitely decorated outfits in Court Two, I got Rachiel's jeer about *pampered*.

Hell, which was worse: Divine or Damned?

I squinted past Ariel at the roof above, which was a giant ribcage. What size had the creature been if we were inside its bones? Had there been true giants once roaming this realm?

Between the ribs hung colossal black cocoons that rippled, as if whatever was inside them was struggling to be born.

I swallowed. *What the hell sort of creatures transformed in these caves?*

"There you are, now my overly soft nephew can stop fretting, and you can explain why you've been sabotaging our plans." Ariel's gaze was hard.

"For real? You've overestimated a bitch's mind reading powers again."

"Uncle, she had no way of knowing any of this," Gabriel insisted. "I'm at fault. Please, if you do not trust her to help, then allow us to win her trophy and—"

"So quick to wish to return to your father? Maybe you belong by his side? Now I'm seeing how it truly is, lad." When Ariel tossed the fragment of Gabriel's robe between his hands, like he had Gabriel in the palm of his hand — his

132

toy — I couldn't help the growl.

Ariel cocked his head, examining me, before crushing the slip of satin in his fist.

"I shall never belong at a dictator's side." I was shocked at the force of Gabriel's words, although they couldn't hide the pain beneath. "But how could you allow an attack on the temple that threatened the life of my brother and sister? I'd sacrifice much to depose my father, but I will not harm my siblings to do so."

*Yeah, tell that to my heart as it burst in my chest...*

Ariel snorted. "She's only seeded with Jahael."

"Which means that I'm free to love her as more than a sister."

My breath hitched. *Love?* Did Gabriel mean it or was it simply more games?

Ariel swept around, marching further into the cavern towards Gabriel.

At last, I could see the whole cavern: walls that were decorated with glowing feathers and an arena, which was carved out of the bone.

Quinn perched on a high ledge like he was watching outdoor theatre, resting his chin on his elbow. He nodded his head at me in greeting.

*Quinn had known about the Damned; that's why he hadn't wanted to come this way.*

And Gabriel...?

My gaze shot immediately to his torn sleeve; which was uneven on one side, where the cloth had been ripped to make my blindfold. He stood, shoulders slumped, next to a Damned with shorn hair and high cheekbones: Rachiel. She was lean and as tall as Gabriel. She leant on the same bone tipped spear as she'd shoved through Mischief's neck.

Rachiel looked me up and down, unimpressed, before sliding her hand onto Gabriel's neck with more dominating menace, than comfort. Gabriel shrugged her off, before allowing himself to be pulled into a hard embrace by Ariel.

"Chin up, lad, we don't fly an easy path." Ariel patted Gabriel's back, whilst Gabriel clung to him in a way that made my inner violet itch to wrench him away: he was mine to hold, protect, and soothe... Yet was that nothing but a lie of his Angelic Power? Tears itched for real at the corners of my eyes. "*I'm* your only true family. *We're* not the Damned but the True Seraphim, don't forget that. The bastard and the half angel aren't even pure Seraphim."

"I'm not like the others; I shall never care about who's pure or True."

Ariel cradled the back of Gabriel's head, pulling him closer. "Did you care about your mother?" Gabriel whimpered. "In her name, I protected and helped you. I'm your saviour — *me*. You think you can trust these newcomers, but I'm the only one you've ever been able to trust."

When Gabriel nodded against his chest, and Ariel petted him like he cherished him, even though his manipulation and control, which was subtler but just as powerful as Jahael's, was the opposite of what Gabriel truly needed, I snarled. Ariel glanced over his shoulder at me. "Tend to your *sister*. Perhaps she'll open up to someone softer."

I didn't miss the jibe, and as Gabriel grimaced, neither did he.

Ariel snatched Rachiel's arm, dragging her to the back of the cavern. Gabriel nodded at Quinn, who soared down from the ledge, carrying the pack.

Then Gabriel marched to my side. He always had responded well to orders but then he'd had first class training from Jahael, Istafil, and it appeared also his uncle...

Quinn crouched next to my head, lifting a bottle of water to my mouth. I pursed my lips in protest, despite the dryness of my throat and the aching heat of my forehead. When Quinn raised his eyebrow, I sighed, opening my mouth and taking deep swallows. Cool water licked down my throat.

At last, Quinn pulled back the empty bottle, with a shrug

of apology, whilst Gabriel prowled behind him.

"So, are you in on this too, Betrayal Fairy?" I demanded.

Quinn blushed. He touched my bruised cheek, and his sparking fingers stroked my hair. But he still nodded.

"Quinn says," Gabriel's clipped voice translated, "that his people are slaves because they live under an absolute monarch. It's his duty to free them. Wouldn't you rebel?"

And that was the point. Hadn't I already rebelled?

"Then why didn't you tell me? Why the secrets and scheming?"

Gabriel dropped to his knees, wringing his hands in his lap. "I thought that my uncle would welcome you as one of us..."

Quinn blew a raspberry.

I grinned. "Quinn's right: you're a wallad."

Gabriel rocked on his heels. "The courts fly on whispered outrage against my father's dictatorship, but whispers don't overthrow dictators. To take arms against a dictator as the True Seraphim — those who the temple's Seraphim defame the Damned — a hurt must be personal."

I stared at him. *He didn't bastard mean...?* "You intentionally showed me Istafil's cruelty and had me tame Mischief to make my outrage against your father *personal*?"

Gabriel gave a tentative nod. "Quite the moral outrage you have worked up. But would you have wished to overthrow your creator on *my* grudges and those of slaves alone, if your family had not also suffered?"

"You've got one thing right," I snarled, "it's bastard personal: against *your* sneaky arse."

Gabriel shrank back, and Quinn slipped his arm around his shoulders. A rainbow bubble slipped around them both, before popping in a glittering spray.

Gabriel sighed. "She has every reason to hate me, Quinn. Let her vent her poison; I can take it for our cause."

Yet he still gave me a hopeful smile like he was bastard Robin Hood.

Frustrated, I slammed my head back with a *crack* because Gabriel's plan *had* worked. I'd thought that I'd been saving Gabriel, whilst he'd been plotting to turn me to the side of the Damned.

Except, his distress over Mischief's death had been real.

Whatever his uncle's reasons for fighting against Jahael, Gabriel believed himself a freedom fighter, freeing his people in the same way that Mischief had freed the Children of the Seraphim.

*How frightening must it be for Gabriel to live in the Gilded Cage as a secret resistance fighter?*

I forced Gabriel to meet my gaze. "Freaky idea here, but you could've *trusted* me. You're all about betraying your father for his brother, who seems an even bigger bastard..."

"Wouldn't you, with how my people suffer? Or do you revel in the power, games, and slavery?"

I pinked, remembering my own choice in Angel World with my mother: to rule at her side as a princess, or to abandon her and free her slaves.

*There'd been no contest.*

Yet how long had this civil war between brothers been going on?

"I get it."

"You don't," Gabriel hissed. "How can you conceive what it was to grow up under Istafil with no mother amongst the Beloveds to protect me? My mother had been Empress but when she died and my uncle was exiled, I had *no one*. I was a child amongst jackals and snakes. My uncle had raised me with kindness and attention, whilst my own father..." Gabriel leant further into Quinn's embrace; Quinn hummed into his hair. "He moulded me with threats and punishments: a pretty shadow to be seen and not heard, trapped in my Gilded Cage and presented on special occasions to flatter him by my beauty and good behaviour. My uncle...*saw me*." Gabriel's pained gaze met mine, and hell did I understand. Any love, no matter how toxic or controlling was precious in

136

a lonely childhood. "Before her death, I'd be allowed in my mother's chambers; often, I'd discover my uncle there. He'd take me on his knee and play with a set of angel, vampire, and human dolls. He taught me how to play the game. Now, if he were to become the Emperor instead of my father—"

"Everything will be lollipops and fairground rides?"

"I wouldn't — my people wouldn't — live in fear."

Was Gabriel right? Or would he only be toppling one idol to replace it with another...who could be even worse? Because so far, Ariel wasn't like Gabriel.

*He was a bastard.*

"If Ariel's not the next despot in waiting, why the Gestapo methods?" I blinked through the haze that'd crept up on me; my skin felt too tight. *Dying was a bitch.* "You wept over Mischief. Are you just going to watch my heart go BOOM?"

Gabriel drew back, whilst Quinn's eyes widened and fiery reds shot in blistering sprays from his fingertips.

"He wouldn't lie..." Gabriel denied, even whilst he stumbled to his feet.

I let out a breath that I hadn't known I'd been holding: Gabriel hadn't been in on the Murder Violet Plan. Despite my impending death, the ache that'd been worming at my heart eased.

"Uncle," Gabriel hollered, and Mr Swirly Eyes was back because *he was pissed*, "you told me that she was merely paralysed. By my feathers, give her the antivenom."

Ariel barked with laugher. "What little birdie's been whispering into the bitch's ear? The seeded can't be trusted; Jahael's bred inside them."

Gabriel spread his wings in flaming arcs. "The antivenom."

"Are you threatening me, lad?"

Gabriel shuddered, slowly lowering his wings, before he shook his head.

Ariel stalked closer. "Good, because I wouldn't like to

137

have to remind you again that you're Firstborn to Jahael but Rachiel will have that honour to me after the revolution." Rachiel smirked, and Gabriel stared carefully at the ground. *Gabriel was prepared to throw away his Crown?* Hell, he truly was like me. "If the insolent and impure girl truly matters to you, then tell me what you'd do to save her."

Gabriel didn't hesitate. "On my oath: anything."

It was the same oath that Gabriel had promised his dad to save Mischief.

*Why had I doubted his love or sacrifice?*

Ariel grinned, stroking his neat beard. "You'll know when I call on your word."

Ariel strode to my side, slipping a vial out of his pocket, but I couldn't see where he dipped to my shoulder, only suddenly that feeling in a dizzying and agonizing rush spread through my limbs, along with the questing tendrils of his cold magic, restoring life.

I juddered, cringing from his freezing touch as it kickstarted my body and drew out the venom. At last, he pulled me to my knees, then staggering to my feet. I swayed, and he held onto my elbow.

*That was one hell of a headrush.*

"I guess you need this one to pass the Test by Monster." Ariel shook me for good measure; I slammed my hand over my mouth to stop myself puking. "One trophy coming up."

He yanked me over to the arena. Woozy, I stumbled, slipping down the smooth sides like a slide at the playground at his push.

Then I stared up at him.

*That bastard couldn't be serious...?*

I scrabbled at the sides of the arena, but they were too smooth to climb; I wished that I still had my wings. Now I understood how bugs felt who were trapped in the bath.

Gabriel darted after Ariel, hollering at him to *let me out*, but Ariel towered over him, before shooting out ice from the tips of his wings. Gabriel froze like a tortured ice statue.

Quinn fluttered in distress above him.

*Roar.*

I froze as still as Gabriel. Then clenching my jaw, I reached for Flight with tremoring hands, who hummed as I unsheathed her and spun around.

Fierce yellow eyes scrutinized me from the shadows of a tunnel.

*Roar.*

Two sharp, long canines glinted, as the creature paced forward into the arena.

*Roar.*

The sabre-toothed tiger shook its head, as it circled towards me; its powerful body was coiled to spring.

I clutched Flight so hard that the hilt bit into my palm; weak still, my legs buckled. I caught a final glimpse of Gabriel and Quinn above me.

Then the predator leapt.

# 13

The *twang* as the sharp canine, which I'd hacked from the slain sabre-toothed tiger as *my* trophy, sank into the divan only an inch from Jahael's head, thrilled through me: *who was the predator now, bitches?*

It silenced the *holy, holy, holies* mid-adoration from the kneeling Acolytes, shocked Anael into stillness as he curled big-cat like on Jahael's lap, and stole the Emperor's breath.

*Now he knew what it bastard felt like.*

I'd fought and killed a monster out on the Bone Plains. Yet now I'd returned to face the true monster who'd been the shadow across our lives all along. And I couldn't tell my family that truth because inside this temple the omniscient bastard would hear me.

I marched down the incense-fogged aisle of the Holy Audience Chamber in Court Three with Gabriel at my side: returning warriors this time, rather than bride and groom with the dead body of our brother. Quinn soared above us like a gold and white butterfly.

*Clatter, clatter, clatter.*

My boots rang loud in the silence, and my eyes watered with the stinging incense. A furious buzzing swarm of fae bled out of the haze; no one attacked the Emperor.

Even a new Knight of the Seraphim: like me.

Quinn arched rainbows over the fae, but they ignored him. Quinn was their leader, but they were under Jahael's power; I'd understood that they were bound by blood, but only now how much that enslaved them.

Jahael chuckled, however, waving his hand. "You go, girl! A pretty gift for me?" The fae nipped at my shoulders, shepherding Gabriel closer, until he sheltered me in his wings. Jahael sighed. "Enough of working the tough bodyguards schtick; see, not a feather on my fabulous wings harmed. Stand down, soldiers."

The cloud of fae whined, before flitting around Quinn with bursts of emerald kissed apology, then back behind Jahael, who ushered us forward with a lazy twist of his wrist.

Gabriel wiped away a trail of blood on my neck, before absentmindedly sucking clean his finger. Then his eyes widened, before his horrified gaze met mine.

"I told you that your blood was special," Jahael gloated.

Gabriel dropped his gaze, flushing.

I seized Gabriel's hand, squeezing it: caught between his dad and uncle — two men at war with each other who he could never please — Gabriel had developed an Angelic Power that begged to be protected because he could never imagine that he'd be *loved*.

I didn't trust him...but maybe I could *love* him?

Gabriel and I reached the base of the divan, whilst Quinn landed in the shadows to the side, silently stepping back.

I frowned; Jahael was using two naked Acolytes — Purah and a second Acolyte whose head was bowed low and to my surprise had only two wings — as footstools; their crimson swirled backs were slicked with sweat and quivered under the pressure. "We passed your test. So, that's one family safe from the Abyss. Two new knights in your imperial army. And one legendary unicorn shifter resurrected and no returns."

When the two-winged Acolyte snorted, Jahael ground his heel between his shoulder blades. I winced.

"Bam! You've impressed the...robe...off me. Maybe you do have the same skills as your cutie pie brother." Jahael stroked tenderly through Anael's hair, before cupping his cheek. "Not exactly the *same* skills..." When he licked up Anael's neck, Anael clasped onto Jahael's shoulders, whilst his eyes smouldered, half-lidded.

The shadows inside seethed to burst out in waves of phoenix fury and burn Jahael's touch from my brother. Instead, I smothered them, forcing on the mask that I'd known I'd have to wear on our return.

Jahael's smile was wide, as he turned from Anael to the tooth sticking out of the divan. He fixed his gaze to mine as he tongued the tooth, streaking it with the rouge from his cherry lips like blood, as if it was an engorged...

Nope, not thinking *that*.

Gabriel pinked because who needed their dad putting on a show? I'd had enough of that with Lucifer.

At last, Jahael drew back with a satisfied *smack* of his lips. "You'll have what was promised." I tensed, as he leant forward; there was danger in the softness of his tone. "But here's the problem, when you worship, you submit all of yourself. Seraphim fly on my holy grace alone. But you, sweet of my life, *hide*."

My hand inched towards Star, whilst my pulse raced. Had the bastard seen through the mask and discovered the plot?

"Must we always waste time on a Glory?" Anael pouted. "As your Advisor, I advise that she's of little importance. Let your son play with her."

*Why the hell did those words sting so much?*

"My cutie pie prince," Jahael kissed the top of Anael's head, "do I love you because you're innocent, beautiful, or ruthless? Your sister is *everything*: beginning and end and..."

Jahael shoved Anael tumbling to the floor on top of the Acolytes, then darted to me almost before I'd seen him move. He snatched me by the back of the neck, cradling me close to his chest, as he traced down my back.

I shivered, caught in his hold.

"Burning in your worship, father," Gabriel begged, "my sister comported herself with the utmost honour throughout the Test by Monster. She's hidden nothing—"

"Naughty boy, you wouldn't be lying to the Fire God?" Jahael raised a manicured brow.

Gabriel paled. "On my feathers, I know not—"

"You're my seeded Seraphim, Violet-darling, why would you shut me out?"

I jumped. *This was about J?*

I fought to hide the relieved untensing of my shoulders under Jahael's massaging fingers. "Why do you get your jollies from being a Peeping Tom?"

When Jahael wrenched back my head by the hair, I yipped. "Hold the attitude. No seeded has ever evaded my watch. I created you; I *own* you."

*Own me?*

My new god-like power rose up in outraged sparks: no one owned the Dragon God.

Silver sizzled across my skin, bursting out to blast Jahael backwards. "I won't be your Truman Show," my voice licked with fire, raspy and low; it smoked from my lungs. "I've caged the *seed*. And I'm in charge."

Jahael screamed, as fire danced across his skin, before he put it out with a sweep of his hand.

I froze, waiting for the descent of the fae bodyguard, as well as the alarm bells and chaos at the attack on the Emperor, but Jahael merely shook his head, before clapping his hands in delight. With a shimmer, his charred skin was restored to perfection once again. "At last, the deity is in the

143

house!"

I juddered, still riding high on the flush of power: *dangerous* power. I'd made a god scream, and in that moment, I could've taken over worlds and rejoiced in their trembling.

Is that how Jahael had become warped into a dictator? Would I become one too if I was tempted with my Seraphim side?

I shook my head, as if I could deny the truth.

Jahael only smiled slyly. "You feel it, don't you, Violet-darling? The call to adoration? *Power*: it's on your lips, ripe for kissing the world to its knees. You're my true daughter and creation of my soul." His eyes became cold, as he glanced at Gabriel. "You should be taking notes on your sister's divaliciousness, or else you won't long be the Firstborn."

*Don't do that to Gabriel, not in front of everyone, please...*

Gabriel stepped towards Jahael, even though he shook. "Father, tell me how I could better please you?"

Jahael cocked his head, before reaching down to drag Anael to his feet and placing a kiss to his nose in apology. "Even when you succeed, Gabriel, there's always someone who succeeds just that little bit *better* than you."

I winced; how had my triumph, ended up as Gabriel's shame?

Gabriel hunched his shoulders; his eyes gleamed wet, as he refused to meet my gaze.

I didn't bastard blame him. Now I truly was in line for the Crown because I hadn't been able to control the forces inside.

*Rebel would be ashamed of me.*

Jahael kicked the naked two-winged Acolyte, who was smeared in red whorls; the Acolyte groaned. "I've been training up this bastard for the last three days; take him as your personal Acolyte. Your hoochie mama ass needs to learn to be worshipped."

The Acolyte crawled to my feet. At last, he raised his head, and I saw his face.

*Mischief*: bruised, exhausted, and pissed off. But alive and now mine.

What Jahael would never understand, however, was that I didn't desire my blokes' worship, only their love.

*Even if we'd have to play pretend to survive.*

"And now I feel bad because I've nothing to give you."

"Of course you do: you're a Knight of the Seraphim now. You can give me your service."

"I'm sketchy here on the details."

"You relish collecting pretty things, like me, so you can guard my Beloveds along with Gabriel. I'm appointing Quinn as sponsor to you both; if you fail, he'll suffer." Jahael resettled himself on the divan, planting his feet onto Purah's back again; Gabriel flinched on Purah's groan.

I took a careful breath to control my rapid heartbeat: Rebel was trapped in the Forbidden Court with the Beloveds, one of the *pretty things* that I'd be guarding. Finally, I'd have my chance to see him and work out how to rescue him.

What had been done to Rebel in all this time as Jahael's toy, under Istafil's control?

Jahael clucked his tongue, as if my hitched breath had been reluctance. "Accept who you are — and the delectable love of others in their service — and you'll be a true god, rather than a monster hiding in the shadows."

I nodded.

Yet Jahael was the monster, and if I let in the true god side of my nature and sought worship, rather than love, I'd also become monstrous.

*Splash.*

Rainbow snakes of water sprayed out of the pool beside the Acolytes' Training Pavilion at each *whack* of my palm.

145

Firebird giggled, diving beneath my attack, which changed colour at each swipe.

Skinny dipping in the Fire God's Holy Pool at night, underneath the huge domed roof, was the first fun that I'd experienced, since I'd been trapped in this realm.

If I was a god, then this was how I bitching received worship.

Firebird's amber eyes peeked over the skin of the pool, as he crocodile stalked me; his hair had started to grow in, after its mandatory buzz cut at his resurrection as a Phoenix. I longed to rub my hand over it to reassure myself that Quinn had allowed him that at least: the return to his old identity, even if he couldn't remember it.

That once he'd been Nathanael, Mischief's angelic little brother.

Instead, I allowed him to play our game in the final hour before my first shift working in the Forbidden Court. He circled me in the water, whilst the chants of *holy, holy, holy*, floated like incense-fused nursery rhymes from the wooden arches of the Pavilion, which towered in gilded spires.

Suddenly, Firebird dived. Then arms were wrapped around my waist, and I was launched high out of the water, gasping and spluttering with laughter. Firebird's golden wings wrapped around me, as he spun me above the pool.

Focusing, I concentrated on our connection, thrumming with joy as crimson tendrils spread between us and in the blood that we shared.

The bond between Phoenix and the Lazarus Mage who'd raised him.

"*Are you picking up my frequency?*" I sang telepathically.

Firebird wrapped his wings tighter. "*I can hear you, my Feathers.*" His voice — as soft as I remembered it and as achingly similar to Mischief's, yet steeled with a new strength as well — wound into my mind like it'd always been there. Like it was always meant to be. "*I feared that I'd never*

146

*hear you again. I missed you very much."*

My throat was dry. *"You're my epic Firebird. I'd never abandon you. You know that, yeah?"*

Firebird gave a hesitant nod, before lowering us into the water, which changed to a swirling gold and violet.

I drew back, grasping his chin and tilting his head to force him to meet my gaze. *"You're fam, and that means I'll always have your back, like you'll have mine."*

This time, Firebird's nod was more confident.

*"Did those freaky arsed fae hurt you? Do I need to go spank the Chief Knight?"*

Firebird's leonine eyes widened, as he clutched at his own arse like I'd threatened to bend *him* over my knee. *"Please, Quinn protected me from the bad gods. He's...the one who's hurt."* I blinked the water out of my eyes. Why did that roil something in my guts: the idea of such a wild warrior *hurt* by the decadent Seraphim? *"He tries to shield it, but he's as melancholy as the Defender."*

Firebird tipped his head towards Mischief, who sat with his arms around his knees on the edge of the pool *guarding* our clothes. He was dressed only in a pair of bejewelled leather trousers that belonged to Gabriel because no Acolyte of mine was parading around naked; the trousers were too large and hung off Mischief's hips. When I'd suggested stripping for a swim, he'd refused because he wasn't a *teenager, drunk, or suffering from a midlife crisis.*

*Yeah, buzzkill.*

Yet he watched us with such bittersweet longing because Firebird was his brother, who could no longer remember him as anything more than the Defender of his kind.

*Melancholy?* I'd be bastard sad too.

When a wicked grin stole across my face, Firebird shuddered, experiencing my emotions across the bond. The same mischievous grin widened his mouth. Then Firebird and I launched ourselves towards the edge of the pool...and Mischief.

147

Mischief gaped, before he scrambled back. But not quickly enough.

Firebird snatched one of Mischief's ankles, and I snatched the other; together, we heaved.

*Splash.*

Mischief tumbled into the pool with a flutter of wings and hiss of outrage. "You foul rascals..."

Firebird and I howled with laughter.

Hell, how had I gone so long without...*this*?

Mischief stood up, dripping wet. "Oh, how delightful, you insufferable fiends think to join forces against me?"

Gabriel and I edged closer together, before we nodded.

"I believe the words that you're searching for are," Mischief sniggered, "*game on.*"

Underneath the pool's surface, Mischief circled his hands, until the water glowed. Distracted, I didn't notice his scaled merman tail, until it'd wound out and caught me around the waist, dragging me into Mischief's embrace, even as silvered seaweed tendrils entangled Firebird.

Firebird whined as he was netted and pulled to his brother's side, but he giggled at his brother's ruthless tickles. I nibbled at Mischief's neck, and his tail *thwapped* in warning across my hip.

I'd forgotten Mischief was ruler in the water. Why hadn't he wanted this fleeting chance to escape from his new role as my slave in worship?

When Mischief met my gaze — the crimson whorls bleeding from his body like he was already my sacrifice — I read the truth behind his melancholy: I'd brought him to life, but he still doubted me.

I bit at his lip. "Looks like you've won, Sparkles."

"My, you almost sound honest in your defeat." Mischief sniffed. "Except, you're conspiring even now, aren't you?"

I tangled my fingers through his hair, drawing him in for

148

a deeper kiss. His candyfloss fizzed through me in silver bursts. I longed to tell him everything, but instead I had to hide behind the same glittering masks as Gabriel.

Except, Mischief had guessed anyway. He'd taken after Jahael as much as his brother, and if anyone knew about scheming it was him.

When I drew back, I shrugged. "That depends. Are you still in Sulk Mode?"

To my surprise, Mischief shoved away, tumbling Firebird into my arms. His tail thrashed violently. "How many times must you risk your life to save me?"

My gaze hardened. "How many times must your damsel life need saving?"

"Damsel?" Firebird blinked at Mischief, before reaching for him. "My apologies, Glory, I had not realised—"

Mischief swatted away his hand. "What do you believe this is: Touch Up Mischief Day? I am not...a Glory or feminine or...and I only needed saving because my brother..."

Mischief let out a growl of frustration, before stalking to the edge of the pool. He transformed back into his angelic self in a silver spray, before pulling himself out onto the edge, and kicking the water off his soaked trousers with a grimace.

Wet leather? *That was going to stick in all the wrong places.*

Firebird hugged his arms around himself; his lashes were matted with tears.

I stroked my hand across Firebird's shoulder, whilst sending a calm reassurance across our bond that relaxed his muscles. He sank into it like a kid after a scare at the movies.

"I distressed the Defender," Firebird muttered. "Please punish me for my failing."

"That tempest tantrum was all on me, bro. You didn't do anything wrong; you're my good Firebird. Stay out here and play, and I'll go cheer up Mr GrumpyPants."

Firebird smiled, stroking the water until it sparkled neon pink, then dived under the surface. I waded back to the marble shore, dragging myself up next to Mischief, who pretended to ignore me.

Finally, Mischief glanced at me from underneath his eyelashes. "You're good with my little brother."

"What did you reckon I'd do to him? Shut him in the dark? Burn him to ash? Feed him with—"

"Hurt him." Mischief stared out at Firebird, as the Phoenix laughed in the rainbow pool. "As Glories have always hurt me."

"Cheers for the vote of confidence." I swallowed down the pain of Mischief's shanking, until he caught my hand between his.

"But that's my mistake because you're not merely a Glory." Mischief slid his fingers between mine. "You're much more. Although, I shan't allow you to become insufferably big-headed. Already, I'm astounded that you can walk around with the weight of your ego balanced on your neck." I bumped his shoulder, and he bumped mine back. "Thank you for taking care of my other...arrogantly alpha...brother as well, whilst I was on my knees adoring my father. I imagine you had to save his *damsel* hide during your test...?"

I stiffened. "You've no idea."

Two shadows darkened the sky, as Gabriel and Ash swooped over the spires of the pavilion, looped over the pool, and then landed in a *whoosh* behind us.

Just for a moment, I thought that I saw the words **LOVE ME** picked out in midnight blue across the surface of the pool, before they faded.

When I startled, the words lingered in the intensity of both Gabriel's flush and gaze, as he folded his wings, cocking his head as if assessing whether I'd caught his message.

I forced myself to look away. When I glanced up again, there was only lingering pain in Gabriel's eyes, which he hid by crossing his arms and glowering.

150

"Peacocks." Mischief rolled his eyes. "It makes one wonder what they're hiding under the ostentatious fanning of their tails."

"Is that an offer, angel?" Ash smirked, leaning down to steal a kiss on my cheek. Mischief drew back, wrapping his wings around himself. "You're not leaving much to the imagination yourself in those kinky trousers; they suit you."

Mischief reddened.

Ash sprawled across the floor, resting his head in my — naked — lap.

I cleared my throat. "Comfortable?"

Ash wriggled his arse. "Getting there. All I need now...? Cup of tea. Game of *Shadow of the Colossus*. Bed."

"Like we don't know you'd actually be shooting your way through *Call of Duty*," Mischief huffed.

Ash grinned. "And you'd be right there next to me."

"As if you don't die as fast as you spawn."

Ash shoved up from my lap, affronted. "As if you don't—"

"Sorry to break up the geek fest." I grabbed Ash by the hair and clamped my hand down on Mischief's thigh. "Yeah, not sorry. This isn't gametime, and Jahael isn't a second-rate Big Bad."

"Not arguing on the Emperor, but why's Lucifer still shut up?" Ash's charcoal eyes sparked. "Lucifer swore that he'd see through his sentence and he needs me. The Matriarch broke him into little pieces, and I could rebuild him, back to how he was before the pressure of trying to save every Fallen—"

"Turned him into a genocidal tyrant?" Mischief offered.

"Free him," Ash commanded, "and he'll never be the Wing that he was, but he could become—"

Gabriel shook his head. "He's too notorious a Fallen."

Even though I'd known Gabriel's answer, I hated the thought of Lucifer alone in his imprisonment. It was as agonizing as the hope that Ash truly could *save* Lucifer.

Ash twisted his hair out of my grip. "What? And the dark

151

Brigadier isn't, mate?"

Gabriel tried to hide his smile behind his richly embroidered sleeve. "Your infamy is equally renowned, Fallen whore. Shall I lock you up as well...?"

Mischief arched his brow. "Now doesn't it look better to be cloaked in shadows?"

"So, you were dead then?" Ash asked, softly.

Mischief's mouth tightened. "Astute."

"What was it like?"

My breath caught in the back of my throat: that was the question, which I'd been desperate to ask, but hadn't been able to bring myself to because it was too flaying.

*Did I even want to know the answer?*

Yet the wistfulness in Ash's voice calmed the bubbling black inside me because I knew that he was thinking of his murdered little sisters, just as I was.

At first, Mischief didn't answer. Finally, however, he replied, "Dark."

In the silence, Ash's face looked as stricken, as I'm sure mine must've done.

I never thought that I'd be thankful Rebel wasn't with me but I'd lied to him that death would be like rising into the light and if there was one lie that I never wanted him to learn the truth to, it was that.

"Brother," Gabriel crouched down, "I swear, I shall never forget the debt that I owe you. No one has ever valued my life more highly than their own who was not enslaved to me."

"I didn't judge your life more highly," Mischief shrugged. "I beg temporary insanity."

"Of course," Gabriel patted Mischief on the head, "as you say."

Mischief scowled, but I looped my arm around his neck, pulling him closer. My chest was tight; my throat as raw as if I'd been sobbing for hours. "You're in the light now, and we'll none of us let you slip into the dark again."

Gabriel wrapped his wings around Mischief on one side,

152

whilst Ash enfolded him with his on the other.

"Unless you suffocate me," Mischief protested.

Yet as Mischief squirmed out of the feathery embrace — blushing down to his chest — he had to duck his head to hide his smile.

Gabriel slipped a single violet feather into my palm. "Diniel insisted that I play messenger boy. Does he risk so much for prattle or is he wiser than I?"

Rebel's love burst in hot waves of longing from the magic feather, whilst I stroked along its length. I sank into the bond, sending back my devotion and aching need: that I hadn't forgotten Rebel even for a bastard moment.

"Your brother's a brave kid," I murmured. "And he's an epic judge of character."

I trembled, as the feather's message floated into my mind, *"Reasons Why I Should be Off Your List of Asses to Kick: Number Two. You love me. Now, that isn't the same as me loving you. Sweet Christ, you have no idea how long I've loved you. But you — my Feathers — loving me...? I'm bad, banjaxed, and my bleeding wing doesn't even work, but when it's dark, you still hold me, until I can believe that we'll make it to the light. That I can be your light. No one's ever made me feel that. Love has always meant pain. Your love could mean death. But I'm not afraid of death because you freed me. By all the saints, you know that I'm not awful good with this blathering. I just need you to...let me die for you this time. If it saves you...let me die.*

Mischief caught my hand, as the feather tumbled from it. Ash leant closer on the other side. When I glanced between their concerned faces, I realised how much they loved Rebel too.

When I saw Rebel, I'd kick his arse just to show him how much he was still on the list for suggesting that I'd ever sacrifice him.

The ancient powers seethed at the threat to my Marked Wing. "I'll be guarding Rebel as soon as my shift starts. What

153

if he thinks I'm working for the Big Bads now? That I've—"

"He's an overly possessive angel who needs a serious lesson in pop culture, but he's not stupid." Ash nestled closer in comfort, whilst I tangled my fingers in his hair.

In my grief, Ash's aromatic scent drove the black spiralling higher, whilst my gums itched.

I wrenched back Ash's head, sniffing at his throat.

*Thump, thump, thump.*

I could hear the blood pounding through Ash and smell the citrus spice of his blood; I licked up his furiously beating artery.

Ash was hollering something, but I couldn't hear him over the rushing in my ears, the burning across my skin, and the sudden tearing in my gums.

I howled, my steel nails shot out, and my fangs were birthed.

Then I sank them into Ash's throat.

# 14

Citrus blood fragranced my mouth; I rolled the last drops around, tonguing at them and sucking at my fangs. I traced the outlines of my canines, still high on the fresh transformation and the heady surge of Fallen blood, as well as the desperate need to taste Rebel again and mix our bloods: three united at last.

Lucifer, J, and Gabriel...they'd all been right. Hell, who *hadn't* urged me to welcome both sides of my nature and feast on both vampire and angel?

*Ash...he bastard hadn't.*

I retracted my fangs with a growl. Quinn frowned at me, nudging my shoulders straighter, as we stood on duty in the Forbidden Court.

I struggled through the thrill of Ash's blood to clasp my hands behind my back, just like Gabriel beside me, who was in perfect toy soldier mode. We were both dressed up as Knights of the Seraphim; our gleaming uniforms didn't look half as badass as Quinn's, who having adjusted our military parade positions, lounged against the pink wall of the Forbidden Court, twirling his scimitar.

Yeah, he was now top boy: *message received*.

I rolled my eyes, sinking into the cloyingly sweet scent of rosewater, which curled from the bathing pools around the court. My boots sank into the silk-cushioned floor, as if Beloveds couldn't possibly place their bare feet on anything harsher than silk. The walls of the Forbidden Court blossomed outwards into rounded archways around a sunken middle, like a wilted rose, whose petals were falling away in the throes of its dying. And under each archway on a pile of satin cushions lay a naked Beloved — male and female — and I couldn't tell if they writhed in agony or pleasure.

Quickly, I looked away.

There were no windows in the chamber: for all its opulence, it was still a gilded birdcage.

If Rebel wasn't here in the central court, where the hell was he? And how could I rescue him, if all I could do was stand to attention, listening to the moans of the Beloveds?

I elbowed Gabriel, but he stared straight ahead like he was guarding the Queen of England. "Aslan, don't you think you're taking the method acting too far...?"

"Silence," Gabriel hissed. "Did stealing your Fallen whore's blood without permission to bond addle your mind? We're knights in Istafil's kingdom, and wisdom dictates that we do not draw her attention."

I recoiled.

Even though I still juddered on the power of Ash's blood, it smarted that Gabriel had shanked where the guilt lurked in my belly: *without permission to bond*.

"Why didn't you *ask*?" Ash had gasped, as he'd laid pinned under me, and I'd licked over the fang marks in his throat. Tears had fallen down his cheeks, but he hadn't noticed them, as he'd demanded, "A Blood Bond is never equal if it's forced. I would've said *yes*..."

I hadn't been able to answer him because I hadn't known *why*, only that my fangs had grown in with an overwhelming force, amplified by the god-like Seraphim power that'd urged

156

me to *take*.

And we'd *both* lost my chance to ask.

Would I truly be able to forge a new type of god? To become something different to Jahael, even though he was seeded inside me? Or would I take what I wanted, creating worlds, blokes, creatures in the form that *I* wished: playing with them, as I'd once created avatars for computer games?

*Sobbing and howling.*

I glanced over the Beloveds.

In a petal-shaped alcove at the back, a teenage Wing struggled in a heavy wooden structure; the lattices strapped down his wings. He shuddered with pleasure edged with pain, and his eyes were glazed like he'd been drugged. He thrashed as if he was being punished or trained in pleasure.

My hands clenched into fists.

The kid's hair flamed as red as Rebel's: he reminded me of Haman, who'd been caught by the Matriarch in Angel World.

Did my mum put Haman through similar torments?

*Don't think it...don't...*

**Cool your Violet-Hulk ass down. You made a choice to sacrifice the punk angel's brother and the Seducer's sisters too.**

**That's the fluffy lollipop sucking end of leadership: you want the shiny crown, you make the dick decisions.**

*No more sacrifices.*

*I ripped away Ash's choice; I stole his blood and bond, just like I stole Rebel's.*

*I don't even know if I'm behind the wheel of the Violet bus anymore.*

**That's a hoot, girl. All this time you actually thought that you were...?**

Violet flared on my fingertips.

157

Gabriel grabbed my wrist in alarm, until I suppressed it. Breathing hard, I shook him off.

Was the kid trapped in that torture device Sablo, who Rebel had mentioned in his first feather note? I couldn't rescue Haman, but I could help all these Beloveds and not just Rebel.

*Why did it surprise me that the Mongrel Witch was a sadistic bitch?*

I choked, as a sudden waft of Damask rose caught in the back of my throat. A shadow peeled off the archway closest to Sablo with a swing of its hips, burning into Istafil.

A ripple of terror ran through the Beloveds, who scrambled to the back of their alcoves or covered themselves with their cushions like that would be any protection.

My shoulders tightened, but I forced myself to stillness, playing the perfect knight, just as Gabriel was next to me. Even Quinn had slipped his scimitar back into its scabbard and paced behind us.

Istafil hovered over Sablo, who whimpered, shrinking down as far as he could under his restraints. Istafil clicked her tongue reprovingly; her ribbons weaved excitedly around her. "My Flame, why do you still fight against your chastisement?"

"P-please, I d-don't." Sablo begged; his words were slurred and confused through his drugged haze. "My apologies, Favoured One."

A single flame ribbon whipped across Sablo's cheek.

*Swish — crack.*

The jewelled tip sliced a crimson gash; Sablo wailed.

I took a step forward at the same time as Gabriel.

Quinn, however, caught us both by the scruff of the neck, holding us in place. It didn't matter that I couldn't translate his sparking indigoes: I understood now that guarding the Beloveds didn't mean protecting them from Istafil.

158

The Knights of the Seraphim were the Beloveds' defenders from the Damned, but the true monster was already inside the cage with them.

"I don't believe you," Istafil singsonged, stroking her nails through the scarlet streaming down Sablo's cheek.

"In His g-glory, please p-punish me."

*Swish — crack.*

The ribbon struck again, slashing open Sablo's other cheek.

"I don't believe you," Istafil sang again, before sighing. "Don't you want to become a good toy for your Emperor?"

Sablo nodded miserably.

Gabriel stiffened next to me; his hand clasped mine like he imagined he was no longer alone, as he had been throughout his childhood. How many times had Istafil played this game with Gabriel? Hurt him, until he'd begged with sufficient sincerity for his own punishment?

I squeezed Gabriel's fingers reassuringly. My fam had grown up separated and alone: Anael, Mischief, and Gabriel. Each one of us knowing that something was missing but not knowing how to find it...until now.

*I would never let a single one of them go.*

Despite Sablo's agonized whines, I smiled at Gabriel.

Lucifer and Rahab had once had *pets* and *boys*. Yet although they'd trained them, they'd loved them in their own twisted way. For Istafil, however, it was about power alone: The Beloveds were reduced to toys and each one could be crushed underfoot on her path to becoming Empress.

Gabriel pulled me closer as he whispered, "Please, sister, Istafil has dominion here. Do not talk to her, unless spoken to, never touch a Beloved, and remember not to spill an Imperial Favourite's blood. She has my father's love over all...even his own sons." He rubbed his forehead against mine. "By His holy face, Istafil is charged with breaking the

159

toys. They are harshest who were once the lowest and fear losing their status. If my father were ever to choose a new Favoured One, Istafil's fall back to Beloved would be hard indeed. Imagine what she'll do to avoid such a fall...?"

From Fire Shadow feared over her kingdom, to naked sex slave hated by every Beloved, who'd be itching for serious payback? It'd be like a prison governor arrested for abusing the prisoners and slammed up in the same prison.

*No wonder Istafil fought so hard to remain the top bitch.*

Quinn shook us both, before backing away.

I straightened my shoulders, even though my pulse pounded, as Istafil soared towards us on flaming wings. She circled Gabriel and me, before her ribbons smoothed over my uniform. I fought the urge to recoil at their invasive inspection.

"Gabriel, my little lamb, this role suits you much better than the false costume of Firstborn." Istafil tapped him on the shoulder.

When Gabriel didn't reply, she turned his head with her ribbon. "Don't you think?"

"Yes, Favoured One."

"And what a pretty knight *you* make, dear heart," the smug edge to Istafil's taunt made me want to curb stamp *her* pretty head. "It appears that you can be well trained."

*Not a question, so not answering...*

My fangs shot out, and I bit my own tongue. I couldn't contain the *yelp*, whilst sucking on my tangy blood for comfort.

Istafil chuckled, before prowling silently across the Forbidden Court towards its sunken rose centre. Then she met my gaze with a lifted brow, before she clapped her hands. "And where's my newest toy?"

The roof blossomed open, and spools of scarlet silk cascaded down like blood changed into the showy artifice of the harem. And tied in knots of silk, displayed on show —

naked — was Rebel.

I gasped, shaking with the *anguish, shame,* and *pain* that slammed through Rebel's bond. Yet also a *forced lust* that burned.

I ached to shoot love and comfort back through the bond but with Ash's blood still aromatic on my tongue, how could I risk violating Rebel in that way, even to let him know that I was here and hadn't abandoned him? Because Istafil had blindfolded Rebel, casting him into the dark.

Before I could launch myself forward, Quinn's butterfly wings wrapped themselves around me. Then he rested his head on my shoulder, raising his finger, which glowed olive, to silence me.

Reluctantly, I nodded.

Flame red silk, which matched his hair, held up Rebel, spreading his wings like he was pinned on a wall by a collector; it cut across the paleness of his skin that was sheened in sweat. I hated that Istafil must've taken off his collar.

Rebel tremored, and his prick stood as stiffly on attention as me.

*What the hell was the Mongrel Witch doing to him?*

Istafil slid her hand down his chest, rubbing over his nipple. Rebel arched away from her touch and then into it. She smiled, tracing her fingers down his back, before twisting his pink nub viciously; Rebel whined.

"What was that, my Irish lamb?" Istafil purred. "Did I just hear you beg your Favoured One for more?"

"No, plea—" Rebel bit his lip hard enough to bead blood to stop himself begging for real. He was still battling her: I couldn't help the flash of pride that he wouldn't submit to her, as he would to me.

"Beg, then you shall have pleasure, as well as pain."

"Not a chance, Mongrel Witch," Rebel's voice shook with strain, but he still managed a crooked smirk. "Get off on my pain if that's your kink, but you're madder than a box of frogs if you think that I'd get any pleasure from being touched by the likes of *you*."

Only Quinn's hand slammed over my mouth contained the *snigger*.

Then I noticed how Istafil had blanched, and the wildness of her flaming ribbons: *hell*.

"You do not relish my *touching*?" Istafil twisted Rebel spinning in the silk, until I could see the back of his neck and the pearl that'd been sunk over *my Mark*.

Violet rose up in a snarling wave of horrified possessiveness that Istafil had dared touch my Mark, desecrating it. I vibrated with the need to taste Rebel's candy blood and see him on his knees before me...

*Mine...mine...mine...*

I struggled against Quinn, panting with the effort of holding in the static, which was building up and down my arms.

Rebel's lips pursed in confusion. "Violet...?" He whispered like a prayer.

Istafil twisted the pearl, and Rebel's back bowed, as he grunted.

"Are you ready to beg yet, Irish lamb?" Istafil stroked a sweaty strand of hair behind Rebel's ear, before her ribbons *thwapped* out, wrapping around his hard prick; Rebel quivered at their silky strokes. "The Pleasure Pearl is resonating whatever *I* wish throughout your entire body. If you'd only begged...I might've allowed release. But now, your pleasure belongs to the Fire God alone, and if you release, you'll be punished."

When Istafil touched Rebel's wingtips, his prick pulsed, desperate.

The bitch was setting him up to fail, and by the way she didn't look away from me, this whole demonstration was for my benefit: a claiming.

**You said no sacrifices, but there are battles you can win...and ones where your for the gods arse will**

162

**be turned into chunky salsa.**

**Guess which one this is?**

*Rebel knows that I'm here.*

*How can I stand by and watch him tortured? His Mark violated? See him possessed by another Glory?*

**What's more important, Feathery-kiss? Your punk bitch angel or a realm of gods?**

Istafil pressed harder on the pearl, at the same time as her ribbons tightened around Rebel's prick. Rebel sobbed, as a translucent arc striped his stomach.

Istafil *tutted*, in faux disappointment. "What did I say about release? Now ask me nicely for punishment."

Flames burst out across my skin; Gabriel hissed, letting go.

Immediately, I lunged for Istafil, blasting a firebolt at her in my *release* that was equally orgasmic.

Istafil shrieked, stumbling backwards, before blinking invisible.

*Sneaky bitch.*

I dived to Rebel, not understanding the way that Gabriel and Quinn hung back. I pressed my lips to Rebel's in a reclaiming that was equal possession and craving. I licked up the copper candy of his torn lip, until he tentatively kissed back.

"Violet?" He whispered, this time with more certainty than vain hope. "Blessed Mary, tell me that you're real, woman."

"I'm real, pretty boy." I ripped off his blindfold, prying off the Pleasure Pearl with my steel nails. He blinked at me through the light; his eyes were smudged with kohl, whilst his eyelashes had been darkened. I licked over the Mark in desperate joy that it was undamaged underneath the pearl. "Good try to get off my List of Asses to Kick."

"Get on with you, how am I still on it? All the saints above..."

I couldn't help my lips curling into a smile. I cut off his

163

indignant response with a kiss. "You're right, though: I do love you." I sliced the ribbons holding Rebel up, and he tumbled to the floor. Yet when I turned to Gabriel, he only stared back at me, his lips thinned. "Why'd you look like I have wraiths on my arse?"

Suddenly, my back seared with blisters.

I screamed, as Istafil materialised, clinging to my shoulders in shadow form. She twisted me, hurling me into the hanging silk ribbons, which *hissed* and tangled around my arms, even whilst I slashed at them with my nails. Rebel rushed at Istafil, but she flared flames across his naked chest.

I choked; the ribbons wound higher around my throat. Is this what it'd been like for Rebel? *How had he fought back against this helplessness?*

I trembled with rage that the other knights hadn't fought with me. But then, they didn't know or love Rebel. Maybe they had my back, but could I truly ask them to risk their arses for an angel that they didn't know?

*Risk an entire revolution?*

Rebel dropped to his knees before Istafil. I clenched my jaw, whilst inside my ancient powers surged in grief that Rebel would kneel for anyone besides me.

Yet every time my powers attempted to break out, the ribbons heated, searing my throat in warning.

"Please, don't punish her; punish me." Rebel bowed his head.

"*Now* you beg?" Istafil sneered. "Bad toy."

When Rebel looked up at her, his eyes sparked with righteous wrath. "I thought that I was bad for a long time. Here's the thing of it: someone convinced me that I could be something more."

My chest was tight: *hell, I loved Rebel.*

Istafil traced her nail delicately under Rebel's chin. "Oh, my Irish lamb, you'll be bad for me. I'll teach you such wicked things."

164

"This is our first day as knights," Gabriel burst out, marching to Istafil. "You truly would self-combust to grant any one leniency or compassion."

Then Gabriel's eyes widened, as if his mind had just caught up with his mouth.

*I'd been wrong that he wouldn't fight for me.*

"Compassion?" Istafil asked, dangerously low. "I could demand your sister's hand for daring to touch a Beloved. Is it not compassion that I do not?"

Gabriel nodded, carefully.

"Then why are you not also on your knees in gratitude?"

Gabriel's gaze slid to mine; it burned with fury. I paled: *What had I just set him up for?* "My apologies, Favoured One. Thank you for your benevolence."

"But you don't know what you're thanking me for yet, do you?" Istafil strolled towards an empty alcove. The other Beloveds watched with dark and frightened eyes. Istafil clicked her fingers at a wooden structure with an iron lever that hovered after her back into the centre of the court next to Gabriel. I swallowed: *never bastard good.* "Thank me for breaking you."

Gabriel blinked. "I'm not a toy."

"Thank me."

Gabriel took a deep, steadying breath. Then he growled, "Thank you."

Istafil smiled. "For what?"

Gabriel clutched his hands together tightly on his lap. "Thank you for breaking me, Favoured One."

Istafil nodded, before snapping her fingers at Quinn. "Here."

"No, no, no...breaking *me*, not..." Gabriel swung around in panic. "By His holy wing, Quinn tried to stop my sister... He has no fault—"

"He's your sponsor." Istafil studied me. I swallowed with difficulty around the ribbon collar. When I'd thought that I was risking no one but myself, I'd forgotten that I'd been

165

risking my fae superior in the Knights of the Seraphim. By punishing one of us, Istafil could punish us all. "If one of you fails, he takes the punishment. Or shall I refer this to the Emperor?"

Gabriel let out a shaky breath as he shook his head. "My father need not know our failings."

"Then take the position, Chief."

Quinn's shoulders straightened, whilst he trooped towards the wooden device. He pointedly didn't look at me, as he lay next to Gabriel, allowing Istafil to roughly push his butterfly wing inside the box. When he winced, Gabriel snatched his hand and held it to his face. Rebel stared at his knees, unable to look up.

*What the hell was that contraption?*

"Pull the lever, there's a good boy." Istafil's stare at Gabriel was predatory.

Gabriel leant over Quinn, readjusting the golden pin in Quinn's hair; his tenderness broke through me in a devastating wave like he could save Quinn from the brutality by at least making him look his best.

"Not me..." Gabriel muttered. "Don't make me..."

"Are you broken yet?" Istafil crowed.

"I am a god." Gabriel knelt back on his heels; his eyes swirled with silver. I shivered at his strength. "I don't break."

Then he pulled the iron lever.

Wooden rods burst up through the box, tearing through Quinn's wing.

Quinn screamed, arching in agony, whilst tears chased down his cheeks. Gabriel kissed Quinn's cheeks desperately, lapping at the wet, whilst chanting a litany of *sorry, sorry, sorry...*

Istafil waltzed towards Rebel — ignoring Quinn's torture — seizing a handful of Rebel's spiked hair and dragging him to my feet. "My Irish lamb's not a god: he's already broken. He weeps every time I take away the light." Istafil pressed her lips to mine, before whispering, "Yet you've given him too much resistance to please the Emperor. Shall I crush *his* damaged wing and ensure that he never flies again? How prettily do you think he shall beg then?"

I nutted the bitch.

Istafil howled, staggering backwards. She held her broken nose, swiping at it with her fingers, whilst her flame ribbons whipped around in outrage.

Then she held up her crimson fingertips. "Blood," she murmured, stunned. "No one causes the Favourite to spill blood." The freaky smile that crawled across her face chilled me worse than any of the horrors in the Forbidden Court. "Now you get to choose, my Flame, do you suffer alone willingly for this crime, or do all your family suffer through Guilt by Association?"

I shuddered. I should've remembered the reason that Gabriel hadn't moved to back me up: the ruthless system that meant he couldn't fight for me, whilst also protecting Diniel. "That's not even a question: cuff me."

"Now the Head Poisoner shall break *you* in her Citadel in Court Five. You think that *I* lack compassion? I let toys remain who they once were, but the Head Poisoner takes you apart and moulds you as she wishes. Say goodbye to those you love, dear heart, because these are the last moments that you'll ever be *you*."

I could hear Rebel and Gabriel's terrified pleading, but it was drowned out by the pulse thrashing in my ears.

If I had nothing else, I'd always been Violet Feathers; I'd rather die than forget my loved ones, like a Phoenix.

Yet who would I become if the Head Poisoner broke me?

# 15

I'd never expected to be poisoned with such delicate precision that my mind was stripped layer by layer, whilst I was strapped onto a throne of feathers and bones — *nope, not missing the irony* — in a Citadel of polished obsidian, which forced me to witness my shattering in mirrored glory.

Or that the poison would be presented in crystal cocktail glasses with encrusted rims, which smelled of tequila.

I sniffed at the latest poison, which bubbled in swirling salmon with a deeper curl of sienna, whilst underneath the mask of tequila burnt the whiff of sulphur.

I gagged, holding the hissing glass further away from me, whilst wriggling my ankles against the bone fingers that clasped my ankles into place on the throne.

I pouted, thrusting the drink back at the Amitiel, the Head Poisoner.

Amitiel sprawled elegantly on the only other piece of furniture in the obsidian room: a silver throne opposite mine that was set up to watch the show. Her hair wound in a spiral on top of her head like a sleeping cobra, just as she curled in the chair: dangerous but waiting to strike. Her ebony skin melted into the dark, along with her oily black dress, until she was nothing but piercing eyes, scrutinizing me in the dark.

*Taking me apart.*

I licked out my tongue; a drop of poison leapt from the glass — there's always one overeager bastard. It was hot this time and it burnt.

Why couldn't Amitiel *force* me? Why always this ritual of willing sufferer?

*J, should I drink...?*

*I don't even know what it'll do it to me. What I'll lose this time. If I've already lost...me. The ancient powers or...?*

*Who I am...?*

*Please, J, are you still even bastard there?*

*Silence.*

I trembled; the glass shook in my hand.

J hadn't answered since I'd drunk the last cocktail.

*Had I lost him forever?*

I bit down the sob. How long had I even been locked in this never-ending darkness?

*Take the drink... Drink it... Then wait for something new and terrible to happen... Take the drink. Drink it. Then wait for something new and terrible to happen...*

How many times had I repeated the cycle and not even known?

The edges of my mind blurred. *How could I lose more?* I raised the glass. "Cheers, bitch, but where's the umbrella and slice of lime?"

Amitiel's serpentine wings swept around her. "You don't approve of your latest drink?"

I hesitated.

I'd been given intoxicants, stimulants, and hallucinogens. Poisons that took control of you piece by piece. I never knew what was in each one or what it'd do before I drank.

And rejecting it wasn't an option.

I knew that because at the start, I'd smashed the pretty glasses, hurled them against the sparkling walls, and spat bubbling mouthfuls into Amitiel's shocked face.

It'd been worth it...until the moment that the Official Taster had been dragged in to drink in my place: *Purah*.

Purah had knelt, whilst Amitiel had stroked his hair with a familiar tenderness that'd torn at me, tipping him onto his back and feeding him the poison that'd been meant for me, even though I'd hollered that I'd *drink*.

*I'd been too late.*

Purah had writhed in a haze of desire, heated by the aphrodisiacs that'd laced the alcohol. I hadn't cared that it would've been me, blissed out and brought to agonised completion *over and over and*...until Purah had begged for Amitiel to stop, but she'd only massaged his wingtips, wringing more from him and taking control of his body.

When Amitiel had soothed Purah afterwards, kissing his hair and cheeks, Purah hadn't shoved her away, but rather had clung to her like his salvation.

After that demonstration, no matter what the drinks would do me, I'd drunk them with swaggering bravado.

Yet as I lost myself, forgetting just a sliver of why I hated Amitiel and beginning to look to her for comfort like Purah had, it grew harder every time to force the poison down my own throat.

"You have a hardon for experimenting on poor bastards, until you can see how they tick. Why your obsession with control?" I smirked. "Are you about to bore me with a sob story about how daddy was a bastard and mummy never loved you?"

Amitiel's smile slipped. Then she leant forward, her fingers tapping on her chin. "That's what we call projection. And it's time for your drinky-poos because if it's not to your taste... My, my what a shame indeed, when I went to such

170

lengths to design it for you." When I gasped in mock horror, Amitiel's eyes narrowed. "Drink, please. After all, you *chose* this, my perfect project. Or shall I call back the Official Taster?"

I downed the hissing tequila in one go.

Then I spluttered, choking on the foul aftertaste of sulphur and liquorice.

The glass vanished — like always — whilst my throat burned.

Amitiel chuckled. "The Archduke detested my drinks too at first; they are, after all, an acquired taste."

I stared at Amitiel. *Gabriel had been broken by her?*

Amitiel sighed, catching my horrified glare, as if imagining an impossible dream. "Oh, if only. The Emperor has never allowed me to play in his son's mind — yet. The Favoured One, however, orders my drinks for her gatherings; she always selects something extra special to be used on the Firstborn—"

"You're sick," I growled, remembering how Gabriel had told me that he'd had no one to protect him at Istafil's parties. "Can't you get a bloke without drugging him?"

"Where would be the fun in that?" Amitiel straightened in her throne: deadly elegance. "Especially when my reward was the first taste of the Archduke."

I howled, struggling at the skeleton fingers that held me into the chair, but they only dug bruisingly deeper. Silver swelled on dragon-wings, but it was muted; confused under a rising fog.

"Why are you angry?" Amitiel asked. "Do you even know?"

"I-I..." *Why was I angry?* "You said... You hurt..."

Amitiel's intent stare was the only thing anchoring me in a blur of confusion. I stared around, lost.

*Where the hell was I?*

"It's all right," Amitiel soothed. "You don't need to fight to remember...or even to fight. All that pain no longer

171

matters. Why be angry, when you can be happy here with me, *hmmm*?"

When she smiled, it was like comfort, safety, and home.

It was the only thing to cling onto, and I smiled back, desperate to keep hold of the calm joy that was spreading through me.

Wasn't this better than the rage, shame, and despair that I'd been feeling before?

I jolted. Why had I been unhappy? It'd been to do with...*family*. Something important and just out of reach. I didn't want to forget it... I couldn't lose that... *lose me*...

I panicked, whilst my pulse pounded. "I-I can't...my fam."

"Who?"

In the haze, there were fragments of faces...blazes of battles...twists of kisses and love...

*Was this what fam meant?*

My temples throbbed; my forehead burnt as hot as the drink had been. "I won't forget my fam."

"Are you sure?" Amitiel's smile widened. "All I see is pain...betrayal...and lies. Your past? It's not something anyone would want to remember. Let yourself forget and free yourself."

"Forget what?"

I blinked around myself in confusion.

*Who the hell was I to be strapped to a throne?*

"Who am I?" I murmured.

Amitiel laughed. "My perfect project."

Then I tumbled into darkness.

When I opened my eyes, I gasped against the pulsing migraine behind my eyes.

*I'd forgotten my past, fam, and myself.* And that felt like the betrayal of myself.

Even though my memories floated far back in my muddled mind, I watched them — detached — as if they belonged to someone else.

172

Had I ever been the Bitch of Utopia? Vampire Princess? Queen of Chaos? Silver Queen or Dragon God?

Now, I was numb and alone, except for Amitiel who watched me: a scientist tinkering with their latest creation.

When the fresh poison materialised in a crystal glass in my hand — gluttonous layers of cold chocolate with a chilli edge seeping down to crispy vanilla — I chugged it without even looking up.

*Click, click, click.*

Amitiel shattered the deep silence of the Citadel, as she strutted towards me on metallic heels; her dress flowed behind her like tar. When Amitiel straddled my lap, I didn't draw back. But her dress slicked up my thighs like it meant to swallow me.

Maybe I was the mammoth: next to be extinct.

I giggled.

*The mammoth slays the sabre-toothed tiger, then is trapped in the tar...*

Now that was a bitch.

I giggled again.

*Slap* — Amitiel's palm cracked across my cheek.

I yelped, but the blow sobered me: *bastard hysteria.* Except, it'd slowed the crawl of the poison, which crept into the dark places inside.

*And now it howled.*

I shuddered, clutching onto Amitiel's shoulders, like she was my rescuer, rather than my tormentor.

"What's the problem, my perfect project?" She cooed.

"They're coming," I whispered, clinging more tightly. My heart pounded. "Help me, please, please, please... *Hide.*"

I stared horrified at the air in front of me: Rebel and Ash in towering glory stood with flaming wings. Their gaze sang doomsday judgement. Love transformed to hate. And they clutched shanks.

173

*They'd come for me.*

Amitiel stroked my hair. "Why are we hiding?"

I whimpered. Then my waking nightmares struck at me in a flurry of strikes: Rebel and Ash roared, carving me bloody. The worst betrayal of love.

And I screamed, whilst I died.

Amitiel held me down, petting me, as I thrashed.

At last, the nightmares faded, and I wept. Amitiel wrapped her wings around me. Shaking with a terror that spun the world, I tremored, unable to speak. There was nothing but me and Amitiel.

*Had there ever been anything else? Anyone?*

"*Shhh*, now," Amitiel lifted my chin, pressing a kiss to my lips. "I'll protect you from those nasty Wings. You don't need to be alone because you're loved here."

"I am?"

Amitiel slid her wings reassuringly up and down my back. "My, my, you must learn that the god who is love itself holds you in highest regard. Of course, he loves us all. So, we must worship him; it's only fair."

I nodded, tentatively.

When Amitiel slithered off my lap, I tried to grasp onto her dress to stop her, but she shook her head. "Time for a visitor and worship. You don't want to go back into the place with those nasty Wings, do you?"

I shook my head frantically, as I clutched onto her hand.

Amitiel smirked, pulling free of my clasp and turning to a beautiful Seraphim in a pearly robe. "They're all pulled apart as easily as butterfly wings in the end, Emperor, and just as beautiful. Be gentle with this one: she's one of my best."

The Emperor studied me, before reaching out his hand and gently untangling a knot in my hair. "Such a darling."

"Do you love me?" I asked

I couldn't work out the confusion of love and hate that mingled inside at the sight of this Seraphim: it was like he was everything and also the end of all as well.

174

The Emperor startled, before continuing with his work on my hair. "I love all my fabulous creations, Violet-darling. But you're one special hooker." Then he paused, before continuing more softly, "You worship only me now, right? Like your brother does?"

I jolted, pulling back from his touch.

*Brother?*

Hell, I did have a brother...and didn't I have a sister too? And those Wings, were they truly the monsters that the vision had created...?

I schooled my expression to blankness, whilst I nodded.

Strands of the Emperor's silky hair tickled my cheeks, as he bent closer. Why did my chest constrict with panic? "You're the balance that worlds are built on. My Lazarus girl." His breath gusted across my lips. "Simply worship me, and I shall raise you beside me for eternity. *Adore me.*"

"I adore you," I parroted, although the words rang hollow. The Emperor drew back, however, with a delighted grin, snapping his fingers at Amitiel to follow him, as he swept from the room in a rush of incense through the melting wall. "Wait...don't leave me..."

I beat against the skull arms of the throne, whilst fat tears wept down my cheeks.

*Abandoned.*

At last, the skeleton fingers snapped open around my feet, and I tumbled out of the throne, retching in the endlessly repeating obsidian room.

*Who the hell was I?*

I looked up at the soft pad of footsteps, followed by the gleam of a military uniform that burst like sunshine into the night of the Citadel.

Had a guard been sent for me? Where was Amitiel and the one who loved me? Why had they left me behind?

*What had I done wrong?*

Yet when I raised my arm to ward off the guard, I focused on my own golden uniform, which matched the

175

guard's.

Had I always been dressed like this?

The Golden Guard crouched down, brushing the hair out of my face. A sapphire pendant shone around his neck.

*Why were his eyes so sad?*

When he pressed a silver cup into my hands, I sniffed it warily: the clear liquid had no aroma, but sometimes they were the worst.

The Golden Guard sighed. "It's not...it won't do anything. I swear on all that's holy, it's only water. Trust me."

*Trust me.*

Silver tendrils burst through me on shadowed phoenix wings, lighting deadened nerves and numb powers, until I juddered with the sudden awakening.

I didn't know who this Seraphim guard was, whose amber musk made me quiver with desire to *cherish* him, but I knew that he was *mine*.

Yet I also didn't know whether I trusted him.

The Golden Guard cradled me with his wings. "I'm... My name's Gabriel." He pushed the cup to my lips again, and I took a cautious drink: water.

I swallowed greedily, washing away the bitter taste of vomit. Then I peeked up at Gabriel. "Do I worship you too?"

"By blistering love!" Gabriel cursed. When I cringed, he hurriedly soothed a wingtip down my cheek. "Peace, I'm not angry at you. Amitiel does this to the Acolytes as well... She did this to Purah." He nuzzled my jaw, and I realised that he was tremoring as much as me. "I brought Purah back from such treatment and I shall bring you back as well. All your family will. Because the truth is, *I worship you*."

I clutched Gabriel, desperate to believe it, whilst the silver chased in stronger waves through me. "I don't have fam. Only the Emperor loves me."

Why did the silver shock me in furious bursts at the words, which suddenly rang so false?

Gabriel's gaze darkened. "My father requests your

presence. Then you'll see just who loves you. Rebirth is painful, but not a single one of your true family will let you break."

Gabriel dragged me up, hauling me after him towards the melting door. I struggled, terrified to discover what was outside the obsidian walls.

Inside the Citadel, I only had to drink. Here, I was Amitiel's *perfect project* and the Emperor's *darling*.

Yet outside, with a family that I didn't remember and this towering Seraphim with swirling eyes, I had the threat of an agonizing rebirth.

# 16

The Emperor's smile was one of love and ownership. I smiled back with blazing adoration.

Standing looking up at the Emperor, I drifted on a safe wave of *worship, worship, worship....*

Why would I want to be reborn into something that would bring me pain? Remember a past that dragged me from this comforting cocoon?

The Emperor's bedchamber was like being delivered into dreamland after the darkness of the Citadel: giant murals of the Emperor in shifting forms — male, female, and a mixture of the two — were painted in-between the rippling silver scales of the walls, whilst the fire breath of dragon statues blew in braziers, heating the room. It wasn't cold, like Court Five had been, and I basked in the warmth of my god and creator.

The Emperor sprawled, with his six wings regally spread out, on a vast bed, which rose above a cage. I jolted, when a naked angel with flame red hair crawled to the front of the cage.

The Caged Wing clutched the bars, before hissing at the

burn of the heated iron.

*...Doomsday judgement... Carving me bloody... The worst betrayal of love...*

I blanched, as the smile died on my lips. *The Caged Wing was one of the bastards who'd shanked me in my nightmares.* Was that why the Emperor had imprisoned him? To protect me or to punish him?

"Feathers, thank all the saints... I've been woeful worried..." The Caged Wing's black eyelashes curved onto his cheeks, as he peeked out at me.

When the Emperor slammed his wings down on the bed, the base of the bed heated. The Caged Wing shrieked, falling back from the bars.

"Toys should be seen and not heard," the Emperor scolded, before slamming his wings down again, lowering the heat.

Why did the Caged Wing's whimper tug at me? *Pain, humiliation,* but also *love...* How did these foreign emotions spiderweb across my mind?

When the Emperor beckoned, I abandoned the guard, Gabriel, with the sapphire pendant, at the foot of the bed. Gabriel remained ramrod straight: he hadn't smiled at the Emperor. But then, the Emperor hadn't smiled at him.

Maybe the Emperor didn't love guards, like he loved his *darling*?

I clambered up onto the satin sheets, ignoring the Wing who was trapped beneath me, even though he never stopped staring at *me*. I wound my arms around the Emperor's neck, breathing in his rich scent like it was life.

*Holy, holy, holy...*

I shook with desperate fervour; my eyes fought against a sudden heaviness, as I lost myself in the memory of the Emperor's comfort and fought to forget the bitch who was whispering in my brain, trying to break out.

The Emperor stroked my cheek: I shuddered at the reptilian dryness of his skin. *Had I always hated his touch?*

"That's right, Violet-darling. Do you recognise, worship, and *love me* now?" His voice became cold and hard, as he gripped my chin.

I shivered. I knew the answer; I'd answered before, hadn't I...?

It slipped out of reach, until all I could do was nod.

The Emperor loosened his grip. Then he elbowed the richly dressed angel, who lounged next to him on the bed. "Anael, my cutie Advisor, you owe me a sweet slice of your pie for counselling against my Head Poisoner. She builds worlds and nightmares with simple drinks, tearing down the old to create the blessed new."

*...Shattering glass... The whiff of tequila... Screaming, screaming, screaming...*

When I quivered, the Emperor closed his wings around me: a Venus flytrap snapping shut.

I struggled, but the sudden surge of agarwood aroma overwhelmed me; I sank onto the Emperor's chest, smothered in his wings and murmured pleas for devotion.

*Why the hell should I worship him?* The bloke kept Wings locked beneath his bed. Would I truly love a freaky god with a slave kink?

I met the dark gaze of the angel, Anael, through the Emperor's feathers.

Anael shrugged. "Or maybe you owe me a night with Purah because she's *faking*." Anael played with the clip that held back Jahael's hair. "Why do we waste time with a Glory? Throw her to your son who pants like a bitch in heat for her."

Why did Gabriel flush? His wings flared behind him in a furious arc.

"Gabriel, do you need to atone in Monster Hall again?" The Emperor demanded.

Gabriel shook his head, forcing his wings to fold back in defeat.

The Emperor smirked over my head at Anael. "Watch how your most glorylicious god plays the game, my cute prince." He tapped the bed with his foot, and the iron below heated again. When the Caged Wing whined, I winced. "This is where I put naughty toys. Yet this toy must be dear to you. After all, you risked your licksome arse for him."

*Had I?*

Yet a litany of *mine, mine, mine* roared through my blood, boiling it until I gritted my teeth against the pain.

Who the hell was the Caged Wing? But then, who the hell was I?

Hesitantly, I shook my head. "How can a toy be worth anything?"

*Clank* — the Caged Wing smashed his fist against the bars, despite their searing heat.

"Sweet Jesus, woman, would you listen to yourself?" He hollered. "The Violet Feathers I know would kick her own arse for that bollocks."

*Violet Feathers....*

When I jerked, the Emperor's arms only tightened. I sweated; the fires blazed higher from the dragons' mouths. The murals bled brighter and taller: endless clones of the Emperor in multiple versions.

When the cage heated higher, Rebel keened, and the Emperor's lips quirked.

I forced my expression to blankness. Even if the Caged Wing was a toy, did that mean his torment was *play*? Could I love a god who delighted in cruelty?

*Was I truly a monster?*

I gasped, as the prettiest angel in a blue dressing gown stumbled into the Emperor's bedchamber ahead of a swarthy Seraphim with a sweeping oiled beard. The pretty angel had creamy skin, pale violet eyes, golden curls...and a purpling bruise across his cheek.

Anael stiffened at the same time as I did.

When Mr Oiled Beard pushed the Pretty Angel to his knees far more gently than I'd been expecting, I was suddenly consumed with...anxiety? Unease? *Fear*?

Yet why the hell did I care about *this* angel? No bond of emotions shivered across him to me. No ripple of memories.

Then why did my guts roil at the danger that I sensed he was in? Just as my palms itched to snatch my sword and slice him free from it?

*And what in the dwarf throwing heights of craziness did that mean?*

Was I the Big Bad here, not truly the Emperor's most loved? Was that why he'd been forced to shut me away in the Citadel in the first place?

When I struggled, the Emperor allowed me to crawl out of his embrace to the end of the bed. I hugged my arms around my knees, whilst I studied the Pretty Angel. Away from the overwhelming agarwood, I could breathe freely; my mind started to clear.

The Pretty Angel cocked his head and blinked, like this would mean something to me. When I frowned in response, his face became shuttered.

The Emperor's eyes narrowed. "Toy or not, my Beloved must be precious to *you*, novice Drake, to chance the Guardian's not inconsiderable wrath by attempting to aid him?"

Drake was in trouble because he'd tried to help the Caged slave? Why did that boot me in the gut as all types of wrong?

Drake nodded.

The Emperor rolled his eyes. "Verbal answers, jackass."

"Yes," Drake's clipped response was cold; his gaze didn't flinch from the Emperor's. "He is of worth to me."

The Caged Wing crawled closer to the bars. "You're a muppet, Commander. I'd dwell in an eternity of dark for every one of my family, but instead, you throw yourselves on the fire to try and light my way."

Drake's jaw clenched.

Did these two angels...*love each other*?

"Your golden curled beauty could be trained well by Amitiel..." The Emperor soared off the bed, prowling around

182

Drake.

The Guardian rested his hands on Drake's shoulders, almost like he was protecting him. "Burning One, my apologies, but this novice is talented...in many areas. Also, his magical potential is great, but only if he remains *unbroken*."

Drake's gaze softened, glancing back at the Guardian as if to catch the lie in his compliment.

*Who had made him doubt himself like that?*

Yet why were they so terrified of Amitiel? She'd held...comforted...saved me from the pain of my past.

*She hadn't broken me, had she?*

Anael launched himself after the Emperor, catching his arm and kissing down it. "This angel and I were raised as brothers; we both learnt fiendish games. Wouldn't you like a taste?" The Emperor raised a brow, but Anael's gaze slid to me. "My cherub held the Addict prisoner for forty years; no doubt he only wants to play. If he amuses you, why not allow him the bothersome Beloved?"

I didn't miss Drake's slight nod, or the exchange of glances between Anael and him: a secret code.

Why did jealousy blossom hot at their closeness like *I* should have the same code, instead of the numbness, which deadened me?

When Drake rubbed his fingers together, a cat o'nine tails appeared coiled around his hand: a rope whip with nine lengths of knotted cord, spiked with metal balls.

My temples throbbed. I rubbed them, whilst my skin itched like it was fighting to peel away to reveal something new inside.

The Emperor threw himself backwards in faux horror. "Oh my! There's going to be a flogging."

Then he *clicked* his fingers.

The bars of the cage slid back, the murals bent and warped, and coils snaked down from the scales on the ceiling. The coils wound around the Caged Wing's wrists,

183

dragging him out, before stringing him up onto tiptoes and dragging his wings wide.

My breath hitched, as Drake untangled the tails of the whip, shaking them out, before testing his arm.

The Caged Wing panted, shaking.

I *was* a monster. How could I take pleasure in his fear or pain?

Drake hesitated; his lip tremored, before he froze to a studied blankness.

I wrung the sheet between my fists; my steel nails shot out, slicing through the bedding.

Why was Drake making the poor bastard...*and me*...wait?

*Just do it: hit him, hit him, hit...*

Then Drake drew back his arm.

*Swish — thud.*

The Caged Wing bit back the scream, as the metal balls sliced into his skin, lashing a bloody path across his shoulders.

Candy sweetness hit me in a dizzying rush, and I was at another flogging, but this one had been in the Bailey of a castle...

*The Caged Angel's name was* Rebel, *and this had happened to him before because of me.*

Jahael didn't love me, I didn't adore him, and I *did* have a bastard family.

I tumbled onto my side, clutching my arms over my head as if that'd slow the onrush of memories: an upload of epic proportions. Overwhelming, devastating, and blinding. Pain and yet also joy because the pain was *mine*.

Violet, black, silver, and shadows...they crashed over me in majestic waves, binding me in magic and my true nature.

I'd been free, yet I'd been lost. Now I was shackled but I knew who was I was: A Dragon God.

*And I was bitching back.*

Now I just had to hide my true face from Jahael.

Yet rebirth *was* agonising. I writhed in the satin to the *swish — thud* of Rebel's flogging, and I floated in the new dark world, whilst it spun.

# 17

The worst Big Bads don't believe themselves the villains but the heroes.

When Jahael had his poisoned claws in my mind, I'd seen his visions of glorious godhood, and I'd been the golden bitch ruling beside him.

I groaned, pressing at my head. My eyes were too heavy to open. *Heroics hurt.*

**You're a hero now, are you, Violet-bliss?**

*J, you're back? Hell, don't go radio silence on me again.*

**You think being stripped like a low market call girl on a stag night was my deathbed wish...?**

**But then, you even forgot your loyal little punk: Bonded and Marked, the angel in eyeliner still fell away in the throes of fervour.**

**So, now that you've drowned in the Emperor's crazy, are you simply the latest Big Bad with an origin story?**

Golden curls tickled my nose, as I opened my eyes and blinked up into Drake's serious face. My head rested in his lap, and his fingers stroked over my cheek compulsively.

I wriggled on the soft covers in the Imperial Bedchamber, sniffing in case I could catch Jahael's scent. Instead, the sweet tang of Rebel's blood caught in the back of my throat, and I gagged.

"Calm yourself, Zachriel's suffering is over. You're safe." Drake's fingers paused in their stroking; instantly, I missed their touch. "Allow me to reassure you, my Queen, we are alone."

"Apart from me." Rebel popped up over Drake's shoulder with a grin that although too fragile, still managed not to waver. "I'm in tatters, but you recognise my muppet arse...?"

Drake huffed. "Patience. Our Queen hardly remembered her own insufferable self an hour ago."

"You know what I haven't forgotten?" I snorted. "What a brat you are, Genie of the Lamp."

I twisted, rolling off Drake's lap and booting him off the bed.

Drake yelped, tumbling from the high stand in a flurry of feathers and satin. His dressing gown fell open, exposing his creamy chest and perky prick. Flushing, he wrapped the gown around his middle again, before pulling himself tall in indignation. "Extraordinary. You're already back to the impossible Glory that I..." He bit his lip, before continuing more quietly, "I imagined that Zachriel's blood spilled in the same trauma as the Bailey would call to you. Blood and love to battle the Head Poisoner's false reality. Welcome home."

*Home*: not the temple, but the love of my Wings. They'd spilled blood — suffered pain — to save me. Because we were each other's *home*.

I edged Rebel around, until I could see his lashed back. My shaking hand hovered over the welts like I could heal them, but this time there was no Mischief to take away Rebel's pain. Yet I noticed that none of the lashes overlapped, and few had drawn blood.

Drake had been careful, but rage roared through me still at each carved weal. No one hurt my fam, and to repeat such a flogging deliberately was a calculated cruelty.

It didn't matter that Drake's actions had been to save me.

I leapt off the bed, slamming in front of Drake. Startled, he backed towards the cage. He winced, as his shoulders seared against the hot bars.

"I'm home, bitch. And blood and love are about to be visited on your girlie arse."

Rebel scrambled down from the bed. "Cop on! The Commander's a bad bastard sometimes, but I trust his plans. He did what he had to; he always does. So, lay off him."

"Plans?" Frustrated, I seized the front of Drake's gown, wrenching him closer, but Rebel dived between us. "What's with your Rescue an Ice Commander routine?" I stared from one to the other. "Wasn't this just another one of your Beat the Addict sessions?"

"Is that not my place, to always play the villain?" Drake sneered.

I paled at the pain shanking through Drake's gaze and the way that his clenched fists tremored.

Rebel glanced up at me from underneath his eyelashes. "Mind yourself, Feathers. You don't know—"

"Zachriel," Drake whispered, low and desperate, "we promised each other never to tell."

Rebel spun to Drake, clasping him by the neck. Why did such a simple touch suddenly look so intimate that I shuddered? Hadn't they always been enemies?

Yet before, whilst I'd been drugged, I remembered the spark of *love* that I'd witnessed between them.

*What in an alternative universe of screwed-up shipping was going on?*

"Secrets?" I snarled, and Rebel flinched. "From the moment an angel's punk arse fell into my lap, all I wanted was the truth, but instead I've been *poisoned* on lies."

I wiped angrily at the tears with the back of my sleeve.

**You don't always want to know the answers, Feathery-candy, even if you need to.**

*I can't be blind anymore.*

*Drake and Rebel have known each other for centuries; they're part of a war and allegiances that I've only just begun to understand.*

**Truth is a bitch.**

*So am I.*

Drake pressed his soft lips to Rebel's with as much yearning as he ever had to mine.

I held my breath, unable to look away, whilst my skin tingled. My violet thundered at the outrage, and I shook with the effort of holding the flames inside, along with my wails.

Rebel clasped his hand tighter around Drake's neck, whilst he melted into the kiss. Then he shoved away, with the murmured, "By all the saints, I can't."

Drake's gaze froze to ice. "My apologies. Our Queen pretends love but she thinks so little of me in truth, and now you... I'd forgotten that I was to be alone."

"Don't," Rebel said, sharply.

Drake flinched like Rebel was *his* Commander or like he'd never truly been Rebel's gaoler.

I snatched them both by the hair, ignoring their *owws*, as I bent them close. "Listen up, lover boys," my voice shook, but I didn't let go of either of my Wings, "one — or both of you — is spilling on what's up with the snogging, or you won't like the Violet Monster under my skin."

"Get on with you: Violet Monster is hot," Rebel sniggered.

I shook him by his hair, and he yelped. "Unless... Jahael's listening on this frequency?"

"Be calm," Drake ordered. "The Emperor's omniscience is a lie; his propaganda outstrips my father's. He can only watch those that he possesses, or through his spies and seeded. Are you shielded?"

I nodded.

Drake exchanged a glance with Rebel, before he said, more softly, "I'm the disappointment of a son, Marked Wing to the Matriarch, and whipping boy to Prince Anael. I commanded the angelic armies, whilst being moulded into a zealot by my father and the Matriarch. Truly, even now you consider me only deserving of receiving pain or delivering it."

The objection died on my lips. Isn't that exactly what I'd accused him of in the flogging of Rebel?

Drake's expression tightened. "Consider how everyone sees either what they wish to or expect."

"Not following."

Rebel growled, twisting in my grip. "Jesus, will you let us go, woman."

I loosened my grip on his hair and Drake's. They both slipped under my grasp, ducking away. Drake smoothed down his curls.

"We're screwing up the tale." Rebel crossed his arms. "It started ages ago, when we were young ones, and my da...murdered my slave." I startled; I hadn't forgotten the story of Rebel's dad's brutality. "I swore that I wouldn't let another Wing be hurt but I was alone and different to the others..." When Drake rolled his eyes, Rebel nudged him. "So were you, *Commander*. That's when I discovered you bawling and trying to hide it—"

"Irrelevant." Drake slammed his hand over Rebel's mouth. "I apologise for his digression. I'd been gifted as Marked Wing to the Matriarch, as you know and—"

Rebel bit Drake's palm; Drake hissed, drawing away his hand. "The Commander was bawling, so he was, although hiding because he never let anyone see that he was hurt. But I found him and promised to protect him."

I stared at them. They'd known each other since they were teenagers?

Yet Rebel was *Drake's protector*?

What Judas level bastard was Drake that he'd gone on to hunt Rebel and torture him in the dark, simply because Rebel had become a Human Addict? "You became best pinkie mates, yeah?" I growled.

Drake eyed the violet swirling on my palms uncertainly. "Of a sort. When he was away, Zachriel would visit me in my dreams and console me. We both had fathers who were—"

"Bastards," Rebel finished, like they were an old married couple.

"And in the next episode...?" Flames hissed and sparked down my arms; the air scented violet.

Rebel licked his lips nervously. "My da took me to visit Angel World again. This time, what Drake told me changed my promise into a pact."

Drake's gaze met mine. "I begged him to help a shut away prince."

I gasped. "My brother?"

Drake nodded. "And later, Barakiel. In the frenzied days when the angels Fell, neither Zachriel nor I rebelled because of that pact. I regret..." Drake grasped Rebel's hands; only then did I notice how much Rebel shook. "Allow me to be scourged of this guilt: because of me you lost—"

Rebel kissed Drake to stop his words. This time, unlike their first kiss, it was tender and gentle, singing forgiveness. Then Rebel drew back and smiled. "Stop sticking thorns up your own arse. My family view me as a traitor, but I made that choice, not you. And if I hadn't..." He glanced at me. "When the Matriarch was after forcing Lucifer to create a child, as she had Phoenix, I wouldn't have been able to make the same pact for *you*. Except, I became a Human Addict and..."

I stumbled backwards.

Drake and Rebel caught me on either side, lowering me to the floor. The world spun, whilst the fire fizzled out.

*Rebel and Drake had been my protectors jointly all along?*

What. The. Hell?

My gaze swivelled between them. "I don't...? You're bastard kidding me."

191

Drake smirked. "Eloquent as always, my Queen."

"And you're two-faced as always, pretty boy genie. What's been with the Severus act? The whole Hunt the Addict?"

Drake's face became grave. "Patience. It was no act. Zachriel truly became addicted, and I was tasked with his capture..." Rebel looked away, his cheeks pinking. "We had to play our parts, and we suffered for them. I was the villain in your eyes, and Zachriel the bad angel in the world's."

In a sudden flurry of feathers and yelps, I clutched Drake and Rebel, pulling them on top of me and tumbling us around in a tangle of limbs. I kissed their cheeks, noses, necks, and wings... I basked in the mix of their candy sweet and rich frankincense aroma. I laughed, even whilst the tears streamed down my cheeks.

*Rebel and Drake were both the true heroes of the story.*

For centuries, they'd been connected to Anael, sacrificing their families and love to protect him — and then me. Yet like Mischief, they'd worked from the shadows, suffering the humiliation of being Marked Wing and Son of the Fallen.

*Then what did that make me?*

If I was neither the hero nor the Big Bad? No way would I be the damsel, after all.

"You're not narked at us for fibbing?" Rebel ventured.

I licked along the length of Rebel's feathered shoulder blade, and he shuddered. "I'm proud of you." I nibbled at Drake's lip, as I read the insecurity in his gaze. "Both of you. And I love you. You're my heroes, and I'll never let you be alone again."

Drake quivered, tightening his hold around my waist. "Yet we shall all be suffering heroes if we don't discover Anael's long game; after his behaviour with the Emperor, I assure you that he has one. The Guardian has shown me but a slice of the Emperor's power, yet even so, it dims that of other worlds: he can see multiple possibilities at once, alternate universes or resurrect anyone...or *versions* of them."

"Sorry, I'm not fluent in geek."

"Firstly, I believe that you are and secondly: I shall show you." Drake untangled himself from my hold. "The deadliest court in the temple is its final one: Court Six. The Gateways in Infinity Court would make Harahel swoon, but are just as likely to eat us alive. Shall we?"

He held out his hands to Rebel and me.

Rebel met my gaze, then gave a bright grin as he bounced to his feet. "Brilliant! I've always wanted to know what came after infinity."

I took Drake's hand, gently rubbing my thumb over the back of his knuckles.

His breath hitched, then he pulled me up. "Good. Now come with me. We have one hour before the Guardian returns, and if he discovers us, we shall wish that the Gateways *had* devoured us."

One hour to venture into the most dangerous court remaining in The Burning Temple: the centre of Jahael's power.

What did Jahael see in the Gateways, or bring through? Why did my silver quiver in terror? Was it out of fear I'd discover that all along I hadn't been the hero, villain, or damsel of this story, but rather the *monster*?

# 18

I'd never heard a star scream, until Drake flew me into Court Six, Infinity Keep.

I wrapped my arms around Drake's waist, nestling into his frankincense kissed feathers, whilst he soared above the spiralling staircases and crystal walls to the highest point, under a domed ceiling of infinitely pulsing stars.

*And every one of them screamed.*

What the hell was up with the freaky universe?

I shuddered, as my mind fractured under the onslaught, until Drake whispered, with enough quiet pain for me to know that he suffered too, "Icarus flew too close to the sun; the stars sing to warn us."

He circled down to the floor, which was blood pooled by the sun that streamed jewel bright through the walls.

Rebel panted as he dragged himself up the final staircase. Drake had pushed his influence as the Guardian's novice to retrieve Rebel's clothes: red bondage trousers, black ripped t-shirt, and studded leather jacket. Plus, his spiked black collar that Rebel had refastened around his own neck like a votive offering. He'd strapped on his sword, Eclipse, with a grin that even had Drake grinning back. Now Rebel had more swag than me. "What's with all that blessed racket? If the infinite bawls at me, then I'll bawl back."

When Drake scowled, I couldn't help the snigger. "Zachriel, this is the most dangerous court in the Emperor's temple. How do you excel at always reducing the glorious to the mundane?"

Rebel tapped his chin. "Like this...?" He raised his middle finger.

"Wallad," I muttered.

Yet Drake burst into laughter: a fresh light peel of joy, which elated me at the same time as it tugged at a buried sadness. Because I'd never heard Drake laugh like that before, or sound so free.

Drake had hidden every smile before like they'd been a crime, only allowing himself to play a role.

*Had I ever even known him?*

I prowled to Drake, swinging him around.

Drake let out a surprised *oomph*, before laughing again: I guarded that laugh as *mine*, even though Rebel snatched Drake's other arm to spin him too.

"Stop this childishness," Drake giggled.

Hell, the Ice Commander *giggled*...?

*Grrrrrr.*

A growl rumbled through Infinity Keep.

I glanced over my shoulder, just before Drake shoved me to the side.

A giant Gateway — a pulsing slab of stone with a sharp point at its centre like a nose, which the angels used as books, but this one was a hundred times larger than the Gateways in Harahel's library on Angel World — melted out of the crystal world and slammed towards us.

I gasped, as the Gateway clipped my shoulder.

*Slam* — it crashed into Drake, who gritted his teeth and

slapped it.

*Harrumph.*

The Gateway backed away with a shrug, as if frustrated to have missed its prey: *me.*

Why the hell were these freaky *Land of the Giants* sized Gateways in attack mode?

Then with a sudden *grating* and *grinding*, Gateways roared from above us and below in a crimson throbbing stream.

Rebel hollered, drawing Eclipse and standing back-to-back with me. We dodged between the clashing stone blocks, whilst Drake hovered above, diving down and hauling us dangling in the air, or cracking the blocks with his magic.

For some reason, the Gateways feared Drake.

Drake had warned that the Gateways would try to devour us; he hadn't been bastard wrong.

*Grrrrrr.*

A Gateway forced me against the wall, slicing me with its nose.

I winced; this one was a mean bastard. "Let's dance, StoneFace."

*Snarls, rumbles, bellows.*

*Way to piss off the psycho blocks.*

I grimaced at the wetness down my cheek, wiping my hand through the crimson. When I glanced up, I caught Drake's horrified gaze.

"You dare to steal my Queen's blood without permission?" His voice boomed, echoing through the keep; it was colder than the stars.

Immediately, the gateways *hummed,* shuffling

backwards.

"Remain still when I'm talking," Drake commanded. The Gateways froze. "Good. Now show my guests respect or the Guardian shall know of it."

The Gateways whined but didn't move.

Hell, *there* was my angelic Commander, towering over the bully blocks.

I edged around the Gateway that'd pinned me to the wall — could I get away with a quick boot to its stone balls as I passed? — and Rebel pulled me by the hand into the centre of the keep. Only two Gateways had invaded this part, underneath the loudest stars.

*The two tallest.*

I eyed Drake. "So, you're like the Gateway whisperer?"

"I'm the Guardian's novice." Drake pulled on his sleeves. "In here, I have some borrowed power because he considers me gifted."

"You *are* gifted." Rebel rubbed Drake's shoulder. "Only your idiot of a da couldn't see it."

"And being top boy in the court, from which Jahael draws his power...?" I stared around the Infinity Keep. Gabriel might put all his trust in his Damned uncle, but despots were taken down from within as much as from without.

To destroy a monster, you had to understand it.

"I have access to knowledge that most Seraphim never learn. And it is terrifying." Drake's wings curled around himself. "Jahael believes himself Emperor of gods because he can see through these Gateways infinite realms beyond his own...infinite evolutionary possibilities...as well as those supernatural beings that many consider gods. Yet herein lies the danger: a shifter seeing so much will never be happy but strive to shape themselves and others to greater perfection, never-ending. Yet more, the Guardian has the power to resurrect from the past, as easily as does the Emperor raise the dead. Does this make them gods?" Drake shook his head.

197

"What is a god, after all?"

"Screw the philosophy." My heart beat hard in my ribcage, my shoulder blades tingled, and my gums itched like my fangs were about to shoot out. "What's any of this got to do with a gamer from Hackney?"

Rebel linked his pinkie with mine. "I've been known to say it all arseway, but that was your human skin, and that's shed now. I never told you before about..." Drake hugged his arms around himself. "...That muppet Commander over there being a hero, even if he won't see it himself, because I wanted you to be free to choose, not out of duty or a young one's pact." When Drake winced, Rebel shot him an apologetic glance. "Blessed Mary, I've lived what it's like to carry the burden of knowledge, and I just...wanted your wings light, so that you could fly."

My eyes burned, as I rubbed my pinkie against Rebel's.

"Yet again I am the bad guy, am I not?" Drake ran his hand up and down the Gateway. "Because now you must share our burden. These control life and death: *like you*." I startled: *what in merry hell?* "You're the balance of worlds. You shall end or save us all."

"What in the actual...?"

*Eeeeeek, eeeeeek, eeeeeek.*

The Gateways shrieked in discordant unity. I fell to my knees, clasping my hands over my ears.

**Hide your feathery ass, Violet-cheeks. The sorcerer is home, and the apprentice has been a bad boy playing with spells again.**

Violet tendrils shimmered around Rebel and me in a shield, before bleeding away and leaving us invisible, just as Drake had once protected us in Angel World.

"Keep silent," Drake hissed.

Drake stumbled, gripping onto the Gateway to hold himself up; casting his Angelic Power over others always left him vulnerable, and he couldn't cast it on himself.

Rebel held me close; his face was as pale as my own.

On Angel World, I'd left Drake to face his attackers alone because then I'd only known him as my guard and Rebel's gaoler. But now I loved him — not with the aching devotion that *he* loved because he'd been alone for so many centuries — but with a need that insisted that he was *my* Wing.

And I could show him what it was to no longer be *alone*.

When the Guardian soared into the keep and slammed onto the floor in front of Drake, crimson-soaked in the bloody light, Drake cringed.

"My talented novice," the Guardian stroked his beard, whilst his wings twisted with energy, "why do you invade the sanctity of the infinities without me and disturb the Gateways' slumber?"

Drake forced his expression to blankness, unravelling the tie of his dressing gown, so that it swung open; flashes of skin were revealed like slices of sweet heaven on each step, as he sauntered to the Guardian.

Drake knelt before the Guardian, rubbing his head on his thigh. "My apologies. I wished only to hear how bright the stars could sing. To make you proud, Guardian."

I stiffened, as the Guardian traced the tip of a wing down Drake's cheek. "And you shall hear them sing until you learn your lesson."

Drake's eyes widened. "Allow me to..."

With a flick of his wrist, the Guardian hurled Drake flying in a hissing spray towards the stars.

Drake howled as he was sucked into the ceiling.

Even I could feel the stars' maddening draw like my mind was being pulled up into Drake's agony.

When I glanced at Rebel, he simply nodded. Then together we stepped out of Drake's shield: at least I got to play the ghost card.

"*Boo,*" I yelled.

The Guardian comical staggered, losing concentration.

The stars' screams died, and Drake fell from the sky onto Rebel and me.

*Oomph* — I stared into Drake's dazed gaze, as he lay across our laps.

The second angel to fall into my lap, but this time I'd chosen him.

I tucked a curl behind Drake's ear and glared at the Guardian. "Enough with the Saruman routine. We sneaked in here; you caught us. And yeah, I know, curiosity killed the freaky violet-and-black eyed cat."

The Guardian's wings sparked, and the two tallest Gateways scraped closer, surrounding us. "To make *me* proud?" He mocked Drake, who refused to look up. "Why, naïve novice, you did this for *them*. Your misguided attachments are holding you back from becoming something great. I've risked myself with our Burning One, arguing your place as my apprentice. Maybe when I show the seeded who she truly is, you'll desist in your folly and devote yourself to the study of the never-ending."

"And perhaps your pompous arse will explode into sprites singing "Purple Haze", but we don't always get what we want," I smirked.

The Guardian snarled, smashing his palm on first one block — I flinched as the sharp point speared him and blood trickled — and then the second.

I didn't understand why Drake encircled his wings around me.

The first Gateway bellowed and pulsed, then an angel staggered out.

And that angel was *me*.

# 19

When you cover yourself in nothing but *choice*, you parade in the Emperor's new clothes: naked and vulnerable.

Nobody's battles are unique; we're all caught in the same turf war between our darker primal natures.

But me? I got to bastard face-off with mine.

"*Who are you?*" I gasped, at the same time as...Imposter Me.

Imposter Me crouched in the mouth of the Gateway with Star drawn in her palm. How the hell did she have the same weapon as me? Had Rebel gifted his dad's dagger to her as well, and why did the thought of that shank me?

Light shone through the crystal walls of Infinity Keep, anointing Imposter Me. Rebel and Drake's wings were soft around me, whilst the tiled floor was hard underneath. The stars' screams had been muted to whisperings.

Imposter Me inspected me back with the same intensity that I examined her.

*Well, I was one hot bitch.*

Imposter Me was also an *Angel Me*: A golden Glory with neatly coiled hair, who was dressed up like she was in my computer game, *Angels vs Vampires*, with top score and highest level of perfection. A gleaming ideal of satin violets and armour. When her violet-and-black wings stretched out behind her, I cringed at the tingling in my shoulder blades and the loss of my own wings. Her domineering sneer was straight out of Angel World: a true baby bird Matriarch.

My mum would be proud; Angel Me could rule worlds.

The Guardian slid behind the Gateway, leaning against the keep's wall, readying himself to watch the show.

I prodded Drake. "You *cloned* me?"

Drake hunched his slight shoulders. "I wish that was all, which had been done to you, my Queen."

I closed my eyes, whilst I steadied my breathing. On the count of three Angel Me would've vanished: *one, two, three...*

When I opened my eyes, Angel Me was still there.

**What did you reckon, Feathery-puff, you'd been sucking on the crazy juice and *she* was just a delusion?**

*Here's hoping.*

**You wanted answers; you were never going to like them.**

**Sometimes people wear masks not to protect themselves, but to protect *everybody else*.**

Angel Me stared back superciliously. "What villainy is this? To which strange realm have I been dragged out of the long dark? Who dares...?"

Then she sniffed.

Her expression softened, just for a moment, before it hardened, as her gaze fixed on Rebel, with such possessive desire that I shuddered.

Is that what I looked like when the violet howled *mine, mine, mine*...until driven by its hunger, I'd touched, Marked, and bonded Rebel against his will?

How could Rebel submit to such terrifying, unbridled dominance?

Angel Me *clicked* her fingers.

I clasped Rebel's arm, but he wriggled away. He glanced between the two Violet versions, before wandering to Angel Me like his dreams and nightmares had collided. My pulse pounded in panic at the loss of him and the *slam* of his sweet scent.

*Angel Me was stealing my candy.*

I couldn't miss the love, as Rebel's gaze met Angel Me's, even though I wished that I could.

Angel Me sheathed Star, reaching out her hand to Rebel, who blinked in confusion. He still tipped up his long neck, however, in supplication.

*Crack* — Angel Me backhanded Rebel, slapping his cheek crimson with such brutality that his eyes overflowed with shocked tears.

I snarled, shoving Drake off my lap, as I scrambled up and stalked towards her.

"Kneel, Wing. Must I instruct you in such simple submission again?" Angel Me's harshness made me shiver: how close had I come to transforming into this Glory?

*Was there a side of her even now inside me?*

Rebel knelt, bowing his head. "Forgive me, princess."

How could Rebel kneel to *her*?

Whatever part of me was close to this angelic bitch raised its head and roared to beat Rebel bloody, until he knelt before me, rather than this imposter wearing my face.

*How could Rebel abandon me?*

Angel Me stroked her hand through Rebel's hair, like petting a dog. "What has become of you? These clothes? Collar? Your wing?" He flinched at her unexpectedly tender investigation of his damaged wing. Then flinched again, as she tipped forward his head, brushing aside his hair. She traced the Mark with shaking fingers; Rebel whined, arching away. His distress tore through the bond. "The pox on you all! Who has dared do such a vile thing?"

I curled my hand over Flight's hilt: nobody should touch

203

Rebel's Mark, not even this freaky angelic doppelganger. I let out a ragged breath, before raising my hand. "That'd be me. So enough with the touching."

Angel Me punched me in the nose.

"OK, I'm leading with the *ow*, and following with the *back off, bitch: he's mine*."

I should've known to duck Angel Me's second punch.

*Slam* — I hit the floor with a *crunch* of ribs.

Drake prowled closer, but I waved him back.

Rebel hovered over me, staring up at Angel Me with his patented puppy dog eyes. "Whip my arse, princess, but don't hurt..."

"You'd give me orders, Zachriel?" Even my guts churned in fear at Angel Me's icy threat.

Rebel paled. "Never, princess. But she—"

"Marked you." Love — yearning, protective, and *real* — broke through Angel Me's frustrated expression. *Yeah, I'd have kicked my own arse for that decision too.* "She desecrated your trust."

I blanched. *Angel Me knew how to shank with words as well.*

I forced myself up shakily again. "I also saved his life, the world, and love the little Irish bundle of bondage."

"You talk like an Apothecary," she sneered.

"And you talk like a bossy bitch." I shoved her back against the Gateway. "You're the new kid here, not me. This is my turf."

"We look alike, although you lack wings." Angel Me's eyes narrowed. Her own wings widened in an alpha display. Rebel watched us anxiously. "But you're shamefully dressed as a servant. You wound and Mark my Wing like that makes you strong, but indeed it only dishonours you as weak. I imagine you to be nothing more than a beastly, sluttish Glory, unable to control a Wing without breaking him. You truly aren't me at all, are you?"

My jaw clenched; I cupped her cheek, stroking across the

soft skin. It was freaky to be staring into my own black-and-violet eyes: they weren't ugly, like I'd always thought, but beautiful. "You have no idea," I said, "how much I'm not you."

My steel nails descended, *screeching* into the stone just beside her cheek, at the same time as my fangs shot out.

Angel Me didn't scream, although her chest rose and fell more rapidly, and her eyes widened. "Fallen," she hissed.

"Half right," I smirked.

When I scraped my fangs along her throat, she stiffened. Her artery throbbed, and the vampiric powers surged higher than ever before at the thrumming of blood beneath her skin.

*My skin.*

Powerful, special, and important blood. I craved it... I licked across her throat.

Then I felt the sharp point of her shank pressed to my gut.

"Villain," she murmured into my ear, "we appear to be in a quandry."

I couldn't help smiling against her neck. The brush of her hand against the back of my head, almost as she'd petted Rebel, was a surprise. I couldn't supress the shiver, or the second smile.

"I'll lose the fangs and claws, if you lose the shank," I bargained.

"How shall I trust the word of a Fallen?"

"Do you trust yourself?"

When Angel Me nodded, I pulled in both my long canines and nails, and stepped back, as she sheathed Star.

Rebel and Drake dragged me into their arms in a fuss of feathers, kisses, and whispered reassurances. Until Angel Me *clicked* her fingers, and Rebel reluctantly drew back to kneel before her again.

I forced myself not to haul him away from her.

"I do so hate to dwell in ignorance, Zachriel." Angel Me's

205

expression was hard and inscrutable. "Explain what is occurring, and be on your guard because I have little patience."

I nodded. "Yeah, Cliffnotes now, punk boy."

**I warn you, Violet-mirror, the Guardian has resurrected this past self to force you to look at your reflection.**

*Resurrected? What the hell...?*

**I told you that there'd be answers you wouldn't like. Don't let them fracture you.**

**Whatever happens, you're still *my* Violet Feathers: The Bitch of Utopia.**

**Remember that.**

Rebel shifted on his knees, before peeking up at Angel Me and then glancing at *me* as well. "Here's the thing of it: I'm yours...*both* of yours." He dug his thumbs into his thighs. "By all the saints, I *loved* you..." When he stared up longingly at Angel Me, my knees buckled and only Drake's arms held me up. "But I love *you*."

Rebel stared up at me now: his despairing confusion swirled through the bond. I ached to wipe the tears from his eyes, but was he even *mine* anymore?

"How can you love this Glory?" I growled. "She looks like me, but I'm the one who loves you."

*Why had it sounded like such a plea?*

Angel Me cocked her head. "You love like a Wing, rather than a Glory. You claim that he belongs to you, yet you act as if *you* belong to *him*."

The Guardian slow clapped from the shadows behind the first Gateway. Then he pushed away from the wall, sauntering between us. "Your father considers you worthy of his attention....as does my novice...but you haven't even guessed it yet, daughter of Lazarus." He raised his hands above him to the wail of the stars. "I wield the power of the infinite: life, death, and the world in-between. Special ones, like you, I can even resurrect."

206

Had I truly wanted to know the *truth* behind the secrets and whispers?

I forced the words out past dry lips, "You can't resurrect what hasn't died, necromancer. I never went down the whole dominatrix Glory route. I rebelled."

The Guardian grinned with vicious delight. "*You* didn't die. *You* didn't choose the angelic path. *You* rebelled, which is an interesting twist that we're all just thrilled to watch play out, since you've never reached the Realm of the Seraphim before. But you're the spark who kindles the rebellion between the angels and vampires, so that the war doesn't go out; Rahab didn't even need Phoenix blood with you. Reincarnation of your sort is a much rarer gem." The Guardian's voice rose in excitement. "How could the *original* you have been allowed to die and not be raised again?"

My startled gaze met Angel Me's, then Drake caught me, as I fell.

"You're lying..." I muttered over the roaring in my ears.

*Except, I knew that he wasn't.*

How many lives had I lived, acting out a part? Being jerked around as a puppet of the Seraphim?

Birth and death... I was as much a Phoenix, as Firebird was. Rebel didn't belong to me.

*Did any of my fam?*

Gabriel had been terrorized and injured in Monster Hall only to be put back together like nothing had happened by the sapphire pendant. I'd died and been restored as a baby like these bastards could point the glowing eye of their sapphire at me and I'd be Violet Feathers anew.

Yet Gabriel *had* been damaged by those psycho trips to Monster Hall, even if he looked perfect on the outside. And the Seraphim *had* stolen my past lives and memories, leashing the different dominant natures inside me, so that I'd grown up at war with myself, never knowing who the hell I was: alone and abandoned.

*No one could simply wipe clean the past.*

Frankincense and copper candy: how many times had I forgotten the taste and smell?

"You've lived two lives before this one." The Guardian's dark gaze met mine. "Once you chose the angelic path, once the Fallen. It makes me wonder...who will you choose now? Because both times you died during or just after your twenty-first year, so the clock is ticking..."

In this rebirth, what had changed? Rebel's training me as a hunter, Drake's battle to teach me not to fly in the shadow of my mother, Ash's warnings of Lucifer's spark, and Mischief's help to lead rebellions in the Under World and the Legion of the Phoenix...

All of that together? Or had only one tiny moment led me to become a perfect balance of vampire and angel. A monster, but not monstrous.

*A rebel.*

"Enough." Drake rubbed his forehead against mine, whilst I shook. "It's not honourable to mock someone with their past or deaths. She shouldn't..." He wetted his lips. "She should never have discovered this in such a fashion."

"Discovered what, my disrespectful novice?" The Guardian's wings hissed in furious arcs. "That she's the ultimate weapon both sides have fought to seduce for centuries? The balance that the Emperor has used to keep both Fallen and angel in their place? Or that the lovers she's risked so much for, never loved her, but rather her past selves?"

I stiffened, caught in a frantic maelstrom of black and violet. I'd been found as a baby, clutching nothing but a feather, on a grave in a Hackney Cemetery. I'd been named after the woman buried there: Violet Lazarus.

*Hell, that'd been me.*

The epitaph on the grave read:

*Violet Lazarus*
*1896 — 1918*

*I don't die; I sleep.*

Why would a Glory be buried in London....? Unless, she hadn't.

Another version of me had, one who'd chosen the Fallen side and the Brigadier, who'd still haunted her graveside in mourning a hundred years later, only to discover me instead and...

The world greyed; my lungs ached. My chest tightened, and I couldn't pull in air fast enough. Sweat dripped from my forehead, whilst my heart thundered.

Rebel belonged to Angel Me, just as Ash was truly some vampire bitch's.

I needed — loved — both Ash and Rebel.

But what did they see when they looked at me? *A ghost*? A second chance with their loved one, who they'd already lost once?

No wonder they'd been prepared to sacrifice so much for me. Except, not me: they'd never seen *me*.

I'd only been wearing their lovers' skin.

I whined, hiding my face in Drake's wing.

*A rumbling grumble.*

I glanced up at the second Gateway, which was throbbing now.

Then a Vampire Me stalked out of the Gateway: a vision in lace, which was patterned with bat-wings, along with a plum sash. Her hair tumbled around her shoulders like she'd just rolled out of bed, and her eyes were smoky, although narrowed against the light.

Vampire Me had sexy swag and no wings.

I paled at the viciousness of her smile; her fangs descended in a signal of intent.

Vampire Me licked her lips as she looked around at the angels in the keep like they were a platter of treats; her scrutiny lingered on Drake in a way that made me shudder. Her grin widened, whispering of a chaotic wildness, as her gaze flicked between Angel Me...and me. "What high jinks! I've dreamed about tipping the velvet with myself but never with an angel tart and a tomboy." Angel Me bristled in identical outrage to my own. "I shall simply have to rip out your throats."

Then she dived at me, shooting out her claws.

# 20

Just because the resurrected angelic and vampiric versions had worn my body in previous lives didn't make them *me*.

*But it did make them bastard dangerous.*

I gripped the edge of the Acolyte's arched Training Pavilion; the gilded spires cast me in a golden shadow beneath the domed roof.

*Holy, holy — whack.*

A scream echoed out of the pavilion; I shuddered. The *Acolytes'* atonement, worship, submission, or whatever word Jahael had chosen today to justify his ritualised sadism had been going on since I'd strode towards the pavilion.

Even shrieks became nothing but familiar background noise, if you heard them enough.

*Holy, holy — whack.*

I glanced over my shoulder at Vampire Me, who hovered just that little bit too close: the Edwardian lady does anarchy instead of high society balls did not respect the personal bubble.

I smirked at her split lip and swollen eye, even though it was matched by my own slashed cheek. She'd dived on me in the Infinity Keep with more ferocity than *I'd* ever fought with, but had stopped as soon as Drake had leapt on her back and hollered Ash's name.

*Holy, holy — whack.*

A whiff of smoke like a bonfire caught in my nostrils. My eyes widened, before I sniffed at Vampire Me's throat; her eyes danced with amusement, but she stretched her neck to the side in offering.

*Lucifer*: she smelled of her dad — *our* dad.

*Why did that boot me in the gut?*

"By God, you're such a chit of a girl." Vampire Me stroked her lace gloved hand through my hair; I arched closer to her. Then she patted my back. "Neither angel, nor Fallen...not fully one, nor the other. I can sense it. Did you ever grow wings?"

I flinched, drawing away from her. She'd died...at almost the same age as I was now. Yet she seemed so much older.

What had she...*I*...done as a Fallen? As Lucifer's daughter and weapon?

*How many had I killed?*

"I had epic blood wings," I couldn't help the boast: I was owed it. "A bastard mage stole them."

Her gaze darkened: hell, did I ever look that scary? "Rahab, damn his eyes...?"

I nodded.

"Did you feast on his blood?"

I grinned. "Something like that."

Vampire Me gave a satisfied nod. "Maybe you're neither tomboy nor a chit, but a worthy reincarnation who foolishly believes that she's a pippin."

212

I frowned. "An apple?"

Vampire Me laughed. "Someone who wraps themselves in morals like a coat against the cold night. But you can't protect yourself against the creatures in the dark." She leant closer, boxing me against the side of the pavilion. "Because *you're* that creature."

I stared back into a face that was my own and yet now that I studied it, was so different: hungry, twisted, and flooded with the black that coiled in my own belly to meet hers. "I was Champion in Lucifer's Cage, but Lucifer never controlled me with his spark. It seems that you're the one who can't protect themselves."

Vampire Me growled. "Look where your *morals* get you: you should've killed me. Instead, you lead me to our father and Fallen bonded..."

She gripped my chin, turning me to look at the Fire God's Holy Pool beyond the pavilion.

Gabriel marched up and down in an agitated arc, peering above him as if expecting a divebomb attack by his dad, or perhaps another impromptu appearance of the Damned.

My stomach flipped at the care with which Gabriel was guarding both Ash and Lucifer. I couldn't help the soft smile at Ash's military-style laps of the pool — naked — whilst the rainbow water glistened on his olive skin. He'd have rolled his eyes at Firebird and my playing as much as Mischief had, and I'd have dragged him into the splash fest just the same. Lucifer lounged on the pool side in the same tatty leather shorts as he'd worn in the Angel Games, skimming his toes across the surface like he was scared of the water.

Vampire Me gasped, before sliding her hand to grip me by the throat and smash me — *crack* — against the pavilion. "My father is a *king*." Her fangs scraped my neck. Out of ten, what did I rate the likelihood of telling her that in fact her dad had been deposed by me and now was King of Nowhereville...? Yeah, that'd be... *Never out of Ten*. "What bloody swines have dressed him as a peasant?"

213

"Dial down the Fang freak out," I rasped. "This isn't your time: it's mine. And that's *my* dad and bonded."

Why hadn't that felt *real*, until I'd defended the claim?

Vampire Me let out a shuddering breath against my neck; she'd deny that she'd sniffled if I'd called her on it. Then she drew in her fangs as she pulled back. "*I* should kill *you* for stealing them..."

*Nope, Vampire Me not down with the reasonable.*

I stiffened, as she dove for my neck again, but this time she licked it. Then she was kissing me: hard and angry.

If Vampire Me was into kissing girls, then it appeared that I wasn't hating it either. Although, if I was into kissing myself, did that just make me a narcissistic bitch?

"Whether this is my time or not, I'll carve my place here. You pretend that butter wouldn't melt in your mouth." Vampire Me licked over her lips. "But I've tasted you now, and my pippin, you're not fresh, but sour as a lemon. You're *me*, underneath." I flinched back from her lace fingers, which traced down the gash on my cheek. "Still, what a cad my Brigadier is; I'll be certain to punish him for touching another."

"It's not cheating if you're dead."

"*Pffft*, balderdash, and he knew it. Perhaps, it's a little unfair of me." Vampire Me's smile was wide and hungry. "But he knows that I'm a demanding lover. I have a large appetite and could easily add a pippin to my orange. They'd taste delicious together..."

Had Vampire Me just propositioned me...*herself*...to be her third with Ash...?

Dazed, I watched, whilst she spun and sauntered towards the pool and my fam: *to take them away.*

Yet how could I keep her from her own dad and Wing? She'd died and been resurrected with her memories intact. If that'd happened to me, nothing would've kept me from the blokes that I loved.

And she did love them, didn't she?

214

**I never reckoned that you'd be a scaredy-cat, handing over your family like toys just because your new step-sisters demand a turn.**

*They're not the wicked step-sisters: I am.*

*Rebel and Ash loved these other versions, before I was born. I'm just the substitute who they love out of duty and—*

**Hold it, I'm gagging on the pity flood.**

**Every time you rise, you're different. Do you think that simply because I'm seeded from Jahael, I'm the same as him?**

*You're not that despotic bastard: J, I know that.*

**Then why can't you understand this realness: you're not the Violet who chose the Matriarch. Or the one who was seduced by Lucifer's spark.**

**You're only you: right now, the god who's loved by...me.**

I hugged my arms around myself, scowling.

When Vampire Me reached the pool, Lucifer leapt up and spun her around with a *whoop* of joy.

This was the scene of dad and daughter reunited, and she was the daughter who Lucifer had loved and lost. The vampire that he'd tried to find again in me: had ever truly loved *me*?

Gabriel moved in confusion towards them, but Lucifer held him back with a gentle hand, and to my surprise, Gabriel simply nodded.

Ash faltered in his precise laps.

I hadn't thought that I had a Masochistic Bitch lurking inside, but I couldn't stop myself studying the way that Ash's face froze with shock, before it flooded with wonder...and *love*.

When his wings beat, and he dove out of the pool towards Vampire Me, spraying droplets into rainbow arcs of hope, I let out a sob, before twisting away.

It turns out, I'm not enough of a Masochistic Bitch to watch their heavenly snogging.

Rebel and Drake prowled closer from the other side of the pavilion. Through the veil of my tears, they blurred to a kaleidoscope of red, blues, and violet.

"Why aren't you with Miss Angelic Stick Up Her Arse? You don't need to pretend anymore: your epic love's back from the dead." Abandonment clawed at my throat: familiar and bleak. J had spent my childhood teaching me this lesson, yet I'd still allowed myself to be weakness shanked. "None of you need to make do with me: the freak." I spun to Rebel, whose expression shattered like I'd slapped him.

I didn't bastard care: *I didn't.*

Drake's hand curled into Rebel's.

"You're a muppet." Rebel's voice shook, but his anguished gaze met mine. "I tried to give you the chance to make things different this time. You're different, and I love—"

"Which of me did *you* have?" I shoved Drake in the chest. His back thudded against the wooden pavilion, whilst his fingers fell from Rebel's grasp. "Because it turns out that my fam all loved *past* me, but I can't remember it. So, which version of me was yours? Did she like your kissing?"

Drake turned his head, refusing to meet my eye, as he flushed. "All those centuries, and you never wanted me."

"But *you* wanted *me*...?"

Suddenly furious, Drake thrust away from the wall; his eyes blazed, whilst they gleamed with tears. "It wasn't *I* invading *your* dreams... Zachriel and you stole away my nights... I betrayed my family — world — for your brother and you. I still do. *And you've still never wanted me.* Not as I do you."

"I do," I said, gently. Drake's eyes lit with such hope that my chest ached: *why hadn't he believed it before?* How many centuries had he played his part to protect others, suffering alone and unloved? "I love you, Drake."

The tears caught on Drake's eyelashes, and I caught them with my lips, before they traced down his cheeks. Then I

216

kissed him tenderly, willing him to read the love in each touch of my tongue.

Rebel drew his wings around both Drake and me, although there was a tentativeness to his kisses along my shoulders like he didn't know if he was still welcome in this feathery sandwich.

"By all the saints, *I don't love her*," Rebel blurted.

I arched my brow as I glanced over my shoulder at him. "You knelt for her."

He pouted. "Dry up, so would you if you knew how hard she spanked." I winced. Rebel nestled his head on my shoulder, like he could become part of me, whilst he snatched Drake's hands in his. The spikes of his collar dug into me, but it was reassuring because it meant that he was with me and not with her: *he'd chosen Drake and me.* "I'll always love her, but now I'm *in* love with you. Here's the thing of it: I'm not the angel she loved either; I'm bandjaxed. She's not like you; she's a Glory from a woefully stricter time. An Addict with a damaged wing and fear of the dark...? I'm reduced to Imperfect in her eyes."

I slipped my feet around Rebel's ankles, dragging him even closer, whilst pressing my mouth to Drake's again like our kiss could cleanse Angel Me's cruelty. "You're *mine*," I panted, between kisses, whilst Rebel rubbed the tips of his wings across Drake's and *hell, were they both purring...?* "And you're both bitching legends."

"Room for a fourth?" I froze at Ash's quiet question from behind me.

"Where's Fang Me?"

"Spending some quality time with her dad." Ash shook water off his sable mane as he sidled closer; I shivered at the cold splash of the droplets. "Didn't you think that I'd notice you lurking, Violet?"

I shrugged: not easy with a punk angel glued to my shoulder.

Ash snorted. "Let's cut short the angst. Yes, I loved her.

217

No, I'm not still in love with her because I'm no longer the dark Brigadier. Vampire You would take me as her pet as soon as she discovered that I'd been broken by witches, kept by mages' as their creature, or had been turned into a Seducer." His smile was shaky. "She couldn't love me like you do; she never did. And I never loved her, like I love you."

My breath caught. The ancient powers inside carolled in ecstasy. Both my angel and vampire bonded had been offered their first loves, yet they'd *chosen* me. The Blood Bonds had been forced, but the love was freely given.

*Their choice.*

For centuries they'd loved me, but we'd been forced apart. At last, we were together. It felt right within each side of my natures and magic. What couldn't we do differently this time united?

*Even save this realm of gods.*

I rested my forehead against Drake's. "Join the party."

Ash's wings *swooshed* wide in a spray of multi-coloured water, before settling damply around us all. Rebel cursed, and I laughed.

Ash slinked against me with a snap of his hips. "Hey sexy."

I raised my eyebrow. "For real, bro?"

Ash smirked. "I wasn't talking to you." When Ash brushed his naked hip against Drake's, Drake's eyes widened. "Has the Ice Commander melted enough to touch a vampire whore now?"

Drake coughed, before turning his head and lightly pressing his lips to Ash's, just for a moment. Then it was Ash's turn to cough.

Rebel let out a bark of laughter.

"Hush, now," Drake said, coolly. "If we are to belong together, I shan't have you describe yourself as anything less than *my* whore."

Now it was my turn to cough.

*Kinky bastard angels.*

Unexpectedly, a holler broke our contented bubble. It wasn't the screams of punishment from inside the pavilion, but Gabriel's howls from beside the pool.

"She's hurting the Archduke," Ash bit out with as much concern as reeled through me, "and he's not fighting back because she looks like you."

He didn't say it, but I heard it: *and the Archduke loves you.*

When had Ash gained such respect for Gabriel?

I nodded, and as one, my fam and I untangled ourselves from each other and turned, dashing towards the pool.

*Agonised howling.*

Vampire Me crouched over Gabriel, who was half submerged in the scarlet water. She'd ripped back his robe and gouged her nails down his chest, Wolverine style. Blood dripped in crimson rivers down his sides.

Lucifer hauled on her arm to hold her back, but with his fires taken from him, he was less powerful than her.

*And it bastard hurt to see that.*

"By God! My father is King of the Under World! Yet you blaggards would keep him against his will, steal his spark, and turn him balmy?"

Gabriel whined, as her nails furrowed deeper.

Lucifer yanked on her elbow. "Yikes, who's an angry little minx? I'm not king anymore. Huh, that only hurt like a hundred daggers in the back, rather than a thousand."

*Crunch* — Vampire Me clouted Lucifer, crushing his nose.

Lucifer gasped, falling backwards into the pool, at the same time as Ash roared in fury.

*And so did I.*

The bitch didn't get to beat on my fam, or reject them because they weren't powerful and perfect anymore.

When I snatched one arm and Ash the other, Vampire

Me gaped at us. Then she grinned. "Crikey, my pippin's a fast one: she does want a taste of our apple and fang pie."

I wrinkled my nose. "Now, if you'd offered a chocolate cake..."

Ash caught my eye. Then we swung Vampire Me backwards, shrieking into the pool.

I held out my hand to Gabriel, and he pulled himself up, whilst hastily rearranging his sliced robe to cover the gashes. I dragged him closer, adjusting the ruined garment. "Don't ever lie there and let a bitch Glory hurt you again; I don't care who she is. And that includes me."

He nodded, brushing his fingers across mine.

When Vampire Me arose, choking and soaked in the now pulsing purple water, she radiated anarchic power in the flash of fangs and steel claws. My own magic squirmed within me, shrouded in shadows at the threat.

"Come on then." I grinned. "I've always wanted to kick my own arse."

Vampire Me growled but before she could launch herself at me, the waters heaved with serpents' coils. I yelped at their scaly graze across my ankles, then they'd wound around me, and I was being dragged up into the air.

I dangled in the hold of the giant serpent, only to lock gazes with Vampire Me who dangled upside down, equally as caught. She was tremoring and pale like she was about to pass out.

*Lucky me, I'd seen more monsters than a vampire.*

"Calm your showboating asses down." Jahael's voice thundered through Gabriel's mouth. Gabriel stood stock-still, once more a puppet for his dad. *How much had Jahael witnessed?* "This gang fighting between angels and vampires is why I created you in the first place, Violet-darling." I couldn't look away from Vampire Me; he'd played both the Matriarch and Lucifer to create Anael and me, even though they'd never known that someone was pushing them around the board. "Here's the newsflash: angels were predatory dicks, hunting humans to extinction. When they became too cruel, their glorified asses were confined to Angel World. But they still needed something to keep them...occupied. Miss Fabulous here *might've* incited a certain charismatic Wing to rebellion..."

Lucifer blanched; pulling at his hair. "*Huh*, even Emperor's lie..." The coils tightened; I struggled to draw in panicked gasps around my cracking ribs. Lucifer's eyes widened. "I take it back, scout's honour."

The coils loosened, and I choked in a breath.

"Civil wars need balance," Jahael's voice continued through Gabriel as calmly as before, like his serpent hadn't just squeezed me until he'd broken bones, "and that's you, Violet-darling." I shivered, at the same time as Vampire Me. "Your delectable cherry pie sweetness has never reached my realm before. I've tried to teach my Firstborn since his birth with Monster Hall, the Guardian's lessons, and Istafil's firm hand, but he's still a weak disappointment." Stricken, I glanced at Gabriel, who chuckled with Jahael's voice, even though his cheeks were tear-tracked. "Oh, he can hear us. And *you'll* be at my side, whilst I create a fresh new world worthy of you."

"New world?" I questioned, cautiously.

*Chocolate Heaven, Planet Rock Out, or Land of Cuddly Cat Halflings...*

"*Our* world: The Seraphim's. I can start again with any evolutionary possibility, and you can bet your hoochie mama ass that I'll shape it into a world — an Eden — which will worship us as the true gods."

"So, not chocolate heaven...? Wait...*start again*?"

Jahael's smile on Gabriel's weeping face was creepy arsed. "You know the story of Noah and the flood?" The serpent dunked my head under the water. I choked, gagging. *Hell, hell, hell...* My lungs were heavy. I thrashed, splashing my hands against the water, whilst Drake and Rebel dragged against the coils. At last, I was hauled upwards, gasping for

221

air. "The worlds — human, angel, and Fallen — need to be cleansed, before my pure one can begin again. You're not just the balance now, girl, you're the catalyst for the beginning and the end."

I closed my eyes, horrified at what I'd done. Every decision that I'd made, which had led me to the Realm of the Seraphim, could mean the genocide of every single world...and my family who lived there.

*Who I loved.*

Jahael was offering me the power to become his Empress in a new world. As I swung upside down, caught in the snare of the serpent, all I could think about, however, was how to save the old one, no matter the cost.

*But what if I was the destroyer?*

# 21

The pulsing scarlet block — Mini Gateway to the Giants skulking in Court Six — hung between Mischief and me in the Gilded Cage.

Rebel clung to Mischief like Mischief would crumble to ash if he let go. I'd expected Mischief to shrug Rebel off with a sharp word, but instead he'd only given an exaggerated sigh, before relaxing into the embrace.

Spark curled at my feet in the shadows; his tail wound around my ankles, as he rubbed his ears against my calf. I tapped on the opal windowsill; sweat slicked my uniform. Monsters crept beneath the blood-red sun outside in the nightmare land of feathers and bones.

Was I meant to rule this realm? Had my visions always been leading me here? A destroyer of worlds, who birthed a new age?

*Screw that.*

Rebel, Drake, Ash, Mischief, Gabriel...*all* my fam...had rebelled against the roles, into which their worlds, leaders, and *destiny* had tried to force them. If they hadn't been able to use weapons, they'd shanked with schemes, words, and even betrayal.

No matter the sacrifice, however, they hadn't allowed themselves to be used as pawns.

*Yeah, the Emperor's Crown was bitching hollow.*

*Grrrrrr.*

The Gateway bucked impatiently like a stallion eager to start the race. Mischief pinched its stone nose, until it stilled.

Mischief hitched up his trousers, which had slipped down his slender hips. He might've been crimson whorled in the marks of an Acolyte but his snarl but was all noble Archduke, "I did not overthrow one tyrant who flooded his own kingdom, only for another to dream of such delusions on a grander scale."

"With you, bro, but why do we need the book from your secret library? I've had enough of being close and personal with their freaky big brothers and I didn't like what they puked up last time."

"She'll hurt me, hurt me, hurt me..." Spark whispered, peeking up at me from underneath his dark eyelashes; his ears pressed to his head in fear.

"Vampire Me...?" I reached down, stroking the silky fur of Spark's ears, until they fluffed up again; he whined. "That bitch won't touch you."

"Aye, right."

He might as well have rolled his eyes and held up a banner printed with **WHATEVER**.

I gripped his chin. "Why'd she be after you?"

Spark closed his eyes as he muttered, "The lass hated me, even as Ash's Fallen friend. She called me *Mistress Spark* and... Nay, don't make me say..."

I hushed Spark, whilst he trembled. How could I hate myself, even though I couldn't remember my past life?

"Now I'm a Halfling too...?" Spark ducked his head. "She'll be after my foxie hide to punish me worse than she's always punished Ash."

I froze.

Dark rage whipped inside that Vampire Me had hurt Ash, as well as Spark.

*Yet, I'd known, hadn't I?* If Vampire Me had joined with Lucifer, whilst Ash had still been Lucifer's righthand man, why had I imagined that their romance had been all roses and moonlight?

Ash loved me because I was *different* to the Vampire version who he'd first loved.

Was Vampire Me still a danger to Ash...and to all of us?

Mischief's eyes narrowed. "At last, the jewel of the realm perceives the peril. Shall we have another kiddies pool party or pause for an orgy perhaps? After all, it's only billions of lives at stake." Mischief waved at the vibrating block. "*That's* why I risked spanking from Harahel by stealing from his Angel World library: if you know what to ask, your knowledge becomes the mightiest weapon. It can even stop the true Apocalypse." Mischief glanced over at the bed, where Gabriel slept under the fur and feather blanket of Blaze, who drowsed draped possessively over him. Mischief had healed the gashes down Gabriel's front, drawing out the pain; tremors still shook through Mischief's hands from the strain. "I warned you that the Emperor wouldn't blast trumpets of welcome for me, but instead he tipped burning oil on my head." I winced, but Mischief's wry smile was all teeth. "Being a bastard, I'm not valued. Being a bastard, I'm not seen. But being a bastard, I can avenge."

Hell, I was glad that Mischief was on *my* side.

"Pull back on the Tarantino. I'll ride the Gateways to discover how to bring down Jahael, but he's a god not a mage, and we're battling the top boy of them all: being pissed off with daddy issues won't save us."

"Oh, it's a start." Mischief seized my hand and slammed it down on the thorn in the centre of the slab.

The Gateway roared, whilst my blood melded with the stone. I thrashed, howling, as I was drawn *into* the block.

225

Electric currents juddered through me.

Torn into a million itty pieces, the Gateway gaped, and I was devoured.


I howled into the void, whilst the silver rainbow of Mischief's gateway spat red-hot metallic drops that sizzled on my skin. I hurtled through the spray of crushed stars, blinking grit from my eyes. My tongue fried in my mouth.

Yet below lay the supernatural world's interactive database, and I'd hacked this bitch before.

It was always about asking the right question...

*Where do I start, J? What do I search for?*

**That depends, Violet-power, what do you want? Now you know the truth, have you chosen a side?**

*Did you really think it'd change anything? That I'd learn that I was Lazarus resurrected and forget fam, humanity, <u>and that I'm the Bitch of Utopia</u>?*

**Hooker, under the Poisoner's toxic cocktails, you even forgot that Emperor Me was a dick.**

*You forgot <u>me</u>.*

*Fair point.*

*I'm back now, however, and so...I've lived before. Those bitches weren't <u>me</u>. This non-psycho version won't choose: angel, vampire, or Seraphim.*

*I'm the Protector.*

*Every bastard and their world are under my protection, the same as my fam. And no jumped up narcissistic megalomaniac is going to wipe them out.*

**Be still my proudly beating heart: was that the spirit of Churchill just with us...?**

*Stick it, hooker, and help me search for a way to stop Jahael.*

**Are you certain that's what you want to ask?**

**You either defeat someone, or else you become their conqueror.**

*I won't be a weapon.*

**You've always been a weapon. The question is whether you're brave enough to use it.**

*I won't...lose myself to the blood lust or the beast inside. Mischief and Ash pulled me back from becoming the beast, just as Rebel and Drake taught me that I could be more than a monster. I owe it to them to find another way.*

**Then don't <u>be</u> the weapon: find a <u>new</u> weapon. Yet are you brave enough to seize it?**

I tumbled lower in the void, before throwing out my arms to gentle my descent. To my surprise, I controlled the fall, whilst the wind that cut against my cheeks whined. The god-like powers, which had burnt through me when I'd tamed the dragons in the Angel Games, surged.

I vibrated, tingling with crackling silver; I grinned, high on the rush. "How do I become more powerful than Emperor Jahael without becoming like him?" I demanded. "What weapon can conquer him?"

*Silence.*

The wind died, and my fall slowed.

My heart *beat — beat — beat* at my heady magics, which whistled through me in anticipation: Seraphim unleashed.

Yet was this what Jahael had hoped for all along? For my divine bitch to rise up, until I became a true sultan's consort?

My Seraphim side was dangerous.

Like Ariel leading the Damned in the false belief that only *they* could be True Seraphim, once I let out my inner god to beat Jahael, would I simply be freeing my combined natures to rule as the next monster over the gods?

Who would be able to stop *me* forcing all to kneel in worship before the Dragon God?

"I take it back," I whispered, before howling out into the void, "I bastard take it back."

*Too late...*

227

A flaming twister burst from beneath me.

I hollered and flailed, struggling to back away, but the flames licked around with a heat that choked me, even though it didn't blister my skin. I screamed, as the twister spun me *down...down...down...*hurling me onto an altar of bone, which was sunk in a valley of glowing violet feathers beside a winding river of fire.

*Crack* — I groaned at the harsh blow to my spine.

The wind died.

At last, I glanced up. My mouth was dry and tasted of ash; my hair smoked like I'd been barbecued. I pushed my hand onto the altar to balance as I stood up, then doubled over with a shriek; I cradled my hand to my chest in shock.

The palm had been branded with a map: The Burning Temple in the centre, whilst an altar stood out in the Bone Plains, which had been marked like X on a treasure map. When the brand started to fade on my palm, I memorised it before it could disappear.

*A metallic flash...*

I gasped, rolling to the side, as a double headed battle-axe sliced down. Flames wound up the weapon's silver haft and ornate crescent head.

Nobody held the Silver Axe, unless the attacker was invisible. Instead, Silver Axe quivered in the air: one warrior squaring off against another.

He swung in the universal gesture for: *Come on then.*

This is what I needed to conquer Jahael? An axe with attitude?

Yet my magic reached out in desperate awe-stricken tendrils towards Silver Axe. I shook with the hunger to hold him in my palm, where he'd fit...had always fitted...where he'd been waiting for me to seize, claim, and wield him...

I took a steadying breath, before stepping forward, but Silver Axe dodged backwards *tittering*: flames burst from his haft, blasting me backwards.

I fell over the bone altar, catching myself on the edge.

*The bastard would pay for that.*

Silver Axe soared up into the air, however, and whirled around, writing out a message in his flames; the letters hung in sparking curls:

*Blood touched*
*With Sacrifice*
*We kill again.*

Always with the riddles...

The words flared so brightly that I covered my eyes, then they died, still haloed against my eyelids. Silver Axe bent forwards, as if bowing.

I couldn't help the smile.

Then Silver Axe stilled; my own magic shifted with thrilled anticipation.

A single word blazed behind Silver Axe in the dark: **GODMAKER.**

I wet my dry lips. "Welcome to the fam, Godmaker. Together we'll kick Seraphim arse."

Godmaker sizzled with flames, whilst he roared: a fierce and ancient warrior awoken.

Yet now I knew the godly weapon that I needed to save all worlds from destruction — including from myself —I still had to follow the map out of the temple and into the deadly plains to quest for it.

And every quest had dangers and a *sacrifice*.

# 22

I prowled towards the bone altar in the valley, booting aside piles of violet feathers. Hot rain drizzled from the crimson sky, dribbling down the back of my neck and plastering my hair to my forehead. I wiped wet strands out of my eyes, slipping on the slick bones that were piled beneath the feathers. Beyond the altar, a river of flames roared; it wound to a thunderous waterfall, which half-masked a cave into the side of a wall of bone.

*The sacrificial altar from the Gateway: the home of the Godmaker.*

Whose blood would the Godmaker demand?

Firebird tugged at my sleeve. "Is this the infernal valley?"

I nodded, battling the urge to glance down at my stinging palm, which had been branded when I'd been in the Gateway; the pain had flared up every time that I'd made a misstep in the wrong direction.

Firebird tilted his chin. "No need to have the same melancholy cast as the Defender. In this bone valley, between the mountains of feathers, we'll claim the weapon that shall make the god who can take the Crown."

My Seraphim magics rose up in answering battle cry. It was lucky that there weren't any towns laying around to be sacked and pillaged.

I curled my smarting hand into a fist. "That's the problem."

When I'd sprawled back through the Gateway into the Gilded Cage, falling to the floor with a *crack* of my kneecaps, Gabriel had rushed to my side, awoken from his rest with Blaze.

If looks could shank, Gabriel would've have slain his brother for a second time: either pissed off that Mischief had secret Gateways or that he'd allowed me to be devoured by one. After all, Gabriel hadn't known that the badass librarian Harahel had trained me in Angel World to survive the trip.

I'd shrugged away from Gabriel, aching with the knowledge that in the secrets and lies of Court Two, I hadn't been able to risk sharing the Gateway's revelations.

Instead, I'd demanded to leave the temple.

*Curses, pleading, scoffing.*

Until I'd howled above my family's hullabaloo:

*Blood touched*
*With Sacrifice*
*We kill again.*

"You're certain?" Gabriel's expression had been troubled. "This is the way?"

Then Mischief, Rebel, and the fox brothers had fallen silent, whilst exchanging glances, before they'd each nodded.

"Oh, in case you're unclear," Mischief had sniffed, "that means we're volunteering to go with you."

I'd shaken my head. "This is a one bitch mission."

"Plus, do you not imagine that my father would notice a mass exodus? His Beloved, my spoils, or his own Acolyte

231

son?" Gabriel hadn't been able to meet my gaze. "The Phoenix, Firebird, however, my father imagines simply belongs to Quinn... He wouldn't be missed..."

Rebel had taken a step forward; his lips curled. "Not a chance, Archduke. I should be the one..."

Mischief had caught Rebel's hand, hauling him backwards firmly against his chest. When Mischief's wings had curled around Rebel in protection, Rebel had cast him a startled glance.

I hadn't understood the sudden grief that had passed behind Mischief's eyes.

Now, as I stood before the altar, I shivered with an inconsolable wave of sorrow, that pulled at my chest, until it ached with the doleful desolation that swept through the valley like a disease. And I couldn't shake the vision of Mischief curling his wings around Rebel, whilst the life died in his own eyes.

The rain beat down harder in scalding tears.

*A sob behind me.*

When I twisted around, Firebird trembled. I gripped his wrist, and he hurled himself into my arms.

"Forgive me, my Feathers," he bawled. "Punish me for my wretched display. I do not know what forlorn spirit has possessed me."

"That'd be me." I jumped at the sweet voice behind me.

When I spun around, unsheathing Flight in a flaming arc, the...*ghost*...perched on the edge of the altar giggled.

"What a fierce barbarian you are, child." The Spirit Seraphim, whose every word sang lamentations through my soul, scrutinized me with the hunger of the truly lonely. Her silk jade robe hung open, revealing her milky thighs, and her silver hair was held up with bronze combs like teeth. Light from the fire river caught the huge pearl that hung around her neck, which shimmered as iridescent as a rainbow. Yet I could see the cave wall on the other side of her, whilst she flickered in and out like there was bad reception. "I reflect

232

my pain onto others...at least, onto the weak."

I bristled. "My epic bloke *takes* pain from others, so your Angelic Power sucks. Enough of the Moaning Myrtle and hand over the Godmaker."

The Spirit Seraphim's large silver eyes, which swirled like she was auditioning for the role of Overseer, narrowed. All at once her pretty mouth twisted into an ugly snarl. "You think to steal such a treasure from Kuhel without *sacrifice*?"

Firebird whimpered.

I swallowed. "What is this? The dragon and the princess moment? Plus, referring to yourself in the third person is insane loner territory."

Kuhel hissed; a blast of wind, scented with mint and honey, blew Firebird and me tumbling backwards over piles of feathers and cracking over wing bones.

"Perhaps we can avoid angering the vengeful appariton," Firebird whispered, caressing his bumped temple; he'd never sounded more like Mischief. "I am ashamed to say that I do not know if I would win against one such as she."

Kuhel rapped her jade nails against the altar with a sickly smile, although I noticed with a jolt that her fingers passed straight through. Then there was the slither of bone chains like guts at each corner of the altar wrapping around it...waiting for its victim.

I bent my neck, whilst chills convulsed me.

Kuhel shook her head. "There's no fight or winner. Still champions come seeking who believe all is bound in strength and power. The only winning is in the *losing*." A surge of sadness shook me, until my teeth chattered at it. "You seek from one who has lost all: *you will take my pain*. So, now I seek the blood of one dear to you."

I pushed myself to my knees; the pounding in my ears was like a death knell.

The bitch would take from me those I loved because she mourned? What kind of screwed-up spirit was she?

I pulled myself onto my knees. "Not happening, ghost

bitch."

She shrugged. "Then no weapon."

**This is it, Violet-death. The moment: are you brave enough to seize it?**

*It's not courage to send others to their deaths.*

**You've no idea, hooker, how much courage it takes to send someone to their death.**

**Dying is easy. It's killing that hurts.**

Firebird pushed himself up, straightening his shoulders, before he marched towards the altar.

*What the hell...?*

I remembered Gabriel's troubled expression and the grief in Mischief's eyes: Firebird had been sent with me as the sacrificial lamb.

*...He won't be missed...*

Cold washed over me. *Had Firebird guessed it too?*

I launched myself up, yanking Firebird back by the elbow. I clutched him, kissing over the fluff of his hair and then across his wet cheeks; he'd been silently crying as he'd walked to his death.

There was no bastard way that I'd ever sacrifice a Phoenix slave who was younger than Jade.

I gripped his cheeks and forced him to look at me. "You are dear to me, but I'd never let you die for me."

"My Feathers," he murmured, and in that moment, I knew that to him, I *was* his creator and god, "let me serve you."

"*Want to take the bitch down?*" I asked, telepathically.

Finally, he smiled. "*Very much so.*"

I wound through the crimson tendrils of our bond, vibrating with the sudden joy that warmed me against the desolate cold of Kuhel's valley. When I sent my strength through the connection, Firebird's wings unfurled, then he grinned, before he soared up into the sky.

I prowled towards Kuhel, who stared back at me, nonplussed, whilst Firebird circled her above. "Hand over the axe now, or we're going Phoenix style on your arse."

Kuhel slipped off the edge of the altar; her hand slid to the pearl around her neck. "Always the barbarians come banging on their chests."

I threw more power into the bond, until Firebird's golden wings flamed. Then he dived.

Kuhel's form thinned until it was nothing more than an outline. Too late to pull out of the attack, Firebird plunged straight through Kuhel, crash landing along the sharp path of bones.

I wrenched back, desperately pulling on the bond to haul Firebird away from the edge of the fire river, before he plunged into the blaze.

*Hell, please...*

In a flurry of feathers, Firebird skidded to a stop, whilst flames licked at him. I scrambled to drag him back from the river's edge. Then I patted over his bruised body, shaking him.

"He's not dead," Kuhel drawled, drawing away her hand from her pearl necklace, whilst she became opaquer again. "Dim children take naps. Fool: this form is only an illusion." Her voice quivered with rage. "I've been...transformed...for centuries. Don't be so eager to see my true form; you'll wish that you hadn't been."

I stroked Firebird's purpling cheek. My eyes were flinty, as I swept up, stalking towards Kuhel. "Now it's just us two bitches. You'll have to take me."

"That's not how the game's played." Kuhel wagged her finger. "Think hard: who's dear to you?"

I stilled: *don't you dare have a Stay Puft Marshmallow Man moment, brain...*

*...Training with Rebel as my Custodian in the glade behind the House of Rose, Wolf, and Fox, whilst the snow kissed us like confetti...a thrilling dance: blade and fire, Sex Pistols and love...*

At Kuhel's laugh, I flinched.

235

"You've made your selection...?" Kuhel crowed.

"No way...no selection...no choosing...and no Irish punk here anyway—"

"Don't get narked, but that's not altogether true." Rebel slunk out of the feather mountain's shadows with his hands in the pockets of his jeans.

I stared at him. "Are you real?"

*Hell, let him be an illusion. Let my Rebel be back in the temple...*

Rebel's laugh was low. "Sweet Jesus, how many times have I wondered that about you? Even now, it's like I'm still in the cell on Angel World, sinking into the dark and nothing's real...only for you to pull me up out of it for bright sharp moments of true life."

"Why are you here?" I demanded.

"*You know,*" Rebel said, shanking me with two such simple words. My heart pounded so rapidly that I couldn't catch my breath, yet I was frozen, statuesque. "There's always a price, so there is, and what kind of bad bastard would I be if I let Mischief's brother pay it? Mischief thought that he could survive such a brutal loss, but I know how much he's suffered for his brothers. It'd break him, and I—"

"Shut the hell up, pretty boy." I stormed to Rebel, dragging him into my arms, whilst the Glory in me roared to punish him for suggesting that he *abandon me.* "The sacrifice doesn't have to be you."

Rebel flinched at the tightness of my fingers bruising his arms, but didn't pull away. Instead, he rested his cheek against mine. "It's always been me, Feathers." I shook, whilst his wings soothed up and down my back. Why was he comforting me? I wasn't the one about to be tied to a sacrificial altar. "I'm sorry, so I am, for not catching up with you sooner after the Archduke let me go, but I'm a selfish ball-bag. I just wanted a few more hours without you knowing, whilst I could still pretend..."

I stopped his apology with a kiss, tearing at his bottom

lip, until he hissed. "There's no need to pretend. I didn't let you die for me before and I won't let you die for me now."

Rebel's eyes sparked. "Wise up! This time I'm not dying for you alone: I'm dying for all my family, Angel World, Under World, and the humans who I swore to save as a hunter...*everyone*." His expression suddenly became haunted. "I die to prove that I can be more than a bad angel, bad Custodian, and bad son...that what Drake and I promised to protect was worth it. Let me have this; on all that's blessed, don't take this away."

I shook my head, but Rebel wrenched out of my grip. I could barely see him through the veil of tears.

Rebel pressed a gentle kiss to my clenched fist. "Hurt me." A second kiss to my fluttering throat. "Kiss me." Then his gaze flickered to Kuhel, before he kissed me for a third time: on my lips. "Burn me."

Then he turned in a *swish* of red-and-black leather and strode to the altar. Before I could stop him, he laid back, allowing the chains to snake out and wrap around his wrists and ankles, jerking him spread-eagled, whilst his wings lay outstretched. He gasped at the pain of being wrenched until his back arched.

Kuhel's eyes glinted with a fierce light. "Sacrifice selected. I shall feast on his flesh, whilst you gorge on my agony."

In a flash of silver lightning, Kuhel vanished.

I launched myself to the altar, tugging on the chains, but they slipped out of my hands. I growled, slamming my fist repeatedly against the links.

"Feathers," Rebel murmured, "take it easy. Just..." He reached with his hand as far as he could in the restraints. I clasped his fingers between mine, whilst I wiped the rain off his face with my sleeve. Then I kissed him more gently than I ever had before, as if that could make up for every bruise and *burn*. Rebel's laugh caught in his throat. "Get on with you, we might've left it on the late side to make love."

I stroked the back of my hand down his cheek; he was shivering. "But if I was asking...?"

His fingers tightened around mine. "I told you back in the House of Rose, Wolf, and Fox to offer again when you loved me." His gaze was steady: it flayed me. "I've always seen you, but now you see me. And knowing that you love me is enough. Sweet saints, woman, I've been ready to die for centuries."

"I've *never* been ready for you to die." I clutched Rebel's collar, like that way I could hold onto him forever; my tears dripped onto his cheeks.

"Take it easy: love is pain." Rebel shuddered, before forcing himself to meet my gaze again with new resolve. "I'm not afraid anymore; soon, I'll be rising into the light."

Why the hell had I lied to Rebel that death was a heaven of light? Yet if I hadn't, he wouldn't be throwing himself willingly into the flames but quaking in fear of the end.

His belief was his saviour, even if it was all a lie.

"Yeah, it'll never be dark again," I forced out.

But it would be: forever dark for both of us.

"Don't leave me." Rebel's plea shanked me in the soft parts that I didn't know I still had. "Not until..."

"Never."

I sniffed, distracted by the sudden sweet zing in the air, just before a lightning bolt flashed jagged at the head of the altar.

Dazzling, the light blinded me momentarily, whilst I stumbled backwards from the blast, losing my grip on Rebel. The spectral clones of the lightning endlessly repeated in front of my eyes, whilst I fought to blink them away.

*Crack.*

I jolted at the thunderclap, which burst above in the stormy sky. I wrinkled my nose at the stench of burnt feathers, before my sight settled, and I was blasted further

238

from the altar by a wall of wind.

Frantic, I fought against it to reach Rebel's side.

*I'd promised not to leave him...*

But the squall held me back. Then from the cave behind the waterfall, in a spray of crimson fire, burst an enormous Jade Dragon.

# 23

The Jade Dragon surged through the bubbling flames like they were water; it's long neck snaked side to side, its horns resembled the ones that Lucifer had once worn on his helmet, and an over-sized pearl was embedded in its scaly neck.

When the Jade Dragon slithered onto the shore past the heaped mountains of feathers, winding around Rebel who was tied to the altar, I hollered. Rebel only stared up at the stormy sky, blankly. He didn't struggle or pull on the chains: he was the princess laid out for the dragon and *ready to die*.

The wind blew harder, as I slammed myself against it. Howling, I fell to my knees amongst the long dead of the plains, unable to look away, whilst the Jade Dragon sniffed at Rebel, savouring the treat: from his hands down to his tight trousers...

"Don't bastard touch him, Smaug." I trembled, hugging my arms around myself.

The Jade Dragon's head turned to me, even whilst its tail whipped over Rebel, stroking down his chest possessively, and its eyes were a swirling silver: *This was Kuhel's true form.*

She was right, I now wished that she was ghost girl again.

Kuhel opened her mouth, displaying her sharp teeth as if in a grin, before she turned back to Rebel and rose up over his left — damaged — wing.

"Close your eyes," Rebel begged. "You can leave me now."

I desperately wanted not to watch, but I couldn't look away because how could I abandon Rebel?

If Rebel was ready to die, then I should be ready to witness his death. I wouldn't take Kuhel's pain, I'd take Rebel's courage, so that it wouldn't be forgotten.

Fire snorted from Kuhel's nose across Rebel's wing, and Rebel shrieked, thrashing in agony.

Then Kuhel opened her jaws...

Suddenly, Jahael in giant form burst through the mountain of feathers, scattering them like violet rain amongst the crimson.

Jahael's hair hung loose, crackling with silver, along with his six flared wings. His robe had been transformed to armour.

Here was a god of old: and he was pissed.

*I'd never thought that I'd be pleased to see the bastard.*

Kuhel reared back; her monstrous face appeared almost angelic again in its longing and grief, before her eyes sparked, and she *roared*. Then she plunged towards Jahael, who caught her in his hands in equal rage like she was no more dangerous than a lizard, holding her snapping teeth away from him, as he brought her down over his knee.

*Snap* — I winced at the shatter of bones.

The tempest died. At last, I struggled up, staggering to Rebel.

Dazed, Rebel stared at me, as I yanked ineffectually at the chains that still held him down, whilst the Godzilla worthy battle of the monsters continued behind us.

Kuhel wrapped her sinuous body around Jahael,

241

squeezing. When she butted him with her head, she gored his chest with her horns. Jahael's bellow echoed around the valley. Then he wrenched back Kuhel's head to pull free the horns; scarlet stained his chest.

I held my breath. *Any moment, fire would snort out of Kuhel's nose and...*

Jahael took hold of the pearl in Kuhel's neck and tugged.

Instantly, Jahael transformed to his normal size, catching Kuhel as she too changed but not into the ghost that'd greeted me. Instead, she became a real Seraphim.

Jahael cradled Kuhel to the ground, kissing her, until she blinked awake: a Seraphim Sleeping Beauty.

Kuhel's eyes widened; the pall of melancholy lifted from the valley. The rain stopped; a rainbow spanned the fire river.

Kuhel whispered, "My dear...?"

*Crack* — Jahael snapped Kuhel's neck.

Then he dropped her to the side amongst the bones and stood, wiping his hands down his armour.

Rebel and I shouted out in the same startled, sick shock.

*Had I cheered on the wrong monster?*

Jahael stalked towards me with his wings beating. I drew Flight, but he knocked the sword flying from my hand with a spark of silver. "I don't think so; daddy needs a little discussion with you, darling." Jahael snatched me by the hair, hurling me onto Rebel's seared wing on the altar.

Rebel's howl was silenced by Jahael's mouth, which slammed over Rebel's in a furious clash of teeth and bite: an attack masked by passion. Only when he drew back, did I notice the tears that had streamed down Jahael's cheeks.

"How does a tempter taste of candy innocence?" Jahael muttered.

I tried to struggle up, but Jahael wrapped his manicured fingers around both Rebel's throat and mine, holding us both down.

I couldn't forget the ease with which he'd cracked Kuhel's

neck, tossing her away like a broken doll.

Jahael breathed hard through his nostrils. "It's enough to make a scaredy-cat even of me, when your Firstborn's weak in a world as dangerous as this. So weak, that I even fibbed and told him that his mummy — the floozy who he doted on — had died." His lips pinched. "BAM! She's dead now."

He turned my head to look at Kuhel.

*The Jade Dragon was Gabriel's mother...?*

"Why the hell was she playing at dragon?" I rasped.

"Not playing, girl." Jahael leant closer; musky agarwood washed over me in an intoxicating wave. "When we came to this realm, we ruled as equals. But then her sweet ass betrayed me because she wanted *more*: no power was enough. *I wasn't enough.*"

I choked, as his fingers constricted.

"Lay off," Rebel demanded.

Jahael scowled at Rebel. "Watch your delicious mouth, my untameable Beloved, or I'll find other uses for it." He eased off my throat, and I gasped. "I ignored my Empress'...indiscretions...as she ignored mine. But tell me this, how could I ignore her choosing my own brother in a coup against me? *Loving him...?*" I startled. Gabriel's own mum had tried to depose Jahael alongside Ariel, who now led the Damned against Jahael? Did Gabriel even know? After all, he thought that she'd died, not been trapped in a cave as a dragon. "Don't look so shocked, girl," Jahael pouted. "I only transformed Kuhel into a monster as ugly as she was on the inside. My court is full of snakes; they hiss plots and venom. But do you want to hear the line that'll bring down the house?" He bent over me; his lips were cold against my ear. "I still loved my Empress: she was my *dearest love*. Now because of you, she's dead. I should take away your *love*, Violet-darling."

I tremored, pulse pounding, as Jahael's fingers stroked over Rebel's throat. "Don't—"

"You were made to adore me," Jahael wailed. "You

should worship *me* as your dearest god. I desire all my children's love because I'm a jealous bitch."

Finally, Jahael leant back from us, letting go, before smashing his hand onto the side of the altar.

*Crash* — the hollow bone caved in, and Jahael hauled out the Godmaker.

The axe gleamed in glory, as Jahael swung it pendulum-like above our heads.

"What a fabulous plaything. Is this what you were after?" Jahael arched his brow, although his hands shook.

Dizzy from watching the Godmaker swing above the tip of my nose — the *swish* of the air as it passed blowing across my cheeks — I was too exhausted to do anything but hum my agreement.

Yet I couldn't help the sting at the betrayal: who'd played us? I hated that I instantly doubted Gabriel.

*Please, let me be wrong...*

"If you're to rule next to me, you need to remember the dangers of pussy power. My son needs a wing whipping just for thinking that he could sneak you out stealthily; Istafil's my Favoured One because she's the most asshole of ruthless spies; she reports every whisper. Nothing happens in the Gilded Cage that she doesn't know about or control." When Jahael paused Godmaker over Rebel, I tensed. Yet I hadn't been able to help the breath of relief that Gabriel hadn't tricked us. Under the sway of Isafil in the Gilded Cage on one side, and his exiled uncle on the other, however, he was at even more risk than I'd realised. "How about my seeded one tells me why she'd want a bauble like this? And I'll play act like I believe her...or not."

Jahael wanted play acting? *He'd bastard get it.*

Now to appeal to the paranoid in him...

My eyes blazed, as I met Jahael's gaze. "You want me to let out my divine side? How can I do that when I have to prove my strength against all those snakes in your psycho court? The only way to stop them plotting and manipulating is to make certain that they know I can kick their arse."

Jahael drew back, uncertain. The Godmaker hung loose in his hand. "They're plotting against you? My own creation?"

"Aren't they?"

The chains melted. I wriggled up on the altar, easing Rebel's bleeding wrists to my lips and kissing the candy copper blood. "From now on you live for me," I whispered sternly, as I drew Rebel into my embrace, stroking along his blackened feathers.

Rebel nodded. "Always."

Jahael's laugh made Rebel pull me closer.

"Aren't you the fascinating Fallen God?" Jahael's dry hand on the base of my neck made me cringe. "Your streak of ambition *is* divine. Yet love for the unworthy leads to nothing but betrayal, pain, and death. Worship is the only true love. You're weakened by your attachments, and now I have your less sentimental past selves to choose from...I can't decide which of your biteable assed versions to raise by my side."

"They're museum relics; I'm the bitch who isn't dead," I snarled.

Jahael waved his hand. "Details. I love a spectacle, and you cheated me of one at the end of the Angel Games. So, you Violets shall fight in the Games against yourselves. The winner gets the Godmaker and to become my heir."

By seeking out the weapon, I could've armed a psychotic vampire or a dominating Glory to become the next ruler.

Maybe I could wield Godmaker and not laugh above the bones and feathers of the dead, but my past selves...? They'd feast on their enemies and delight on new worlds kneeling.

"Not happening, you nauseatingly beautiful yet sadistic despot."

Jahael sighed dramatically. "It seems that your brother's a star Advisor: you're just a naughty faker. Those drinking sessions simply never took, did they? Well, if you don't want the weapon, you only have to say..."

I clenched my jaw. "I'll battle myself. And I'll win. I've had a lot of practice."

Jahael smiled. "You go, girl! Because the losers? They also get dead."

Rebel shook his head, enfolding me in his wings.

Yet this time it *was* my choice: to risk my life to gain the Godmaker. My vision in the Gateway had brought the weapon into this fight, and I couldn't let Vampire or Angel Me become as powerful as Jahael.

I might die in the Angel Games, but worse, my other versions might live. Then a monster even more deadly than Jahael would be unleashed.

# 24

*Know yourself*: especially if you're a bitch.

Fangs sank into my right shoulder, and a shank skewered my left. Both fangs and shank pinned me to the ruby floor in the final room of the Pleasure Pavilion. I choked, coughing pretty patterns of crimson onto my bluing lips. The sulphur smog stung my eyes, whilst I became the hunted prey in the Angel Games.

Vampire Me snarled around her mouthful of flesh, sucking on my blood, whilst Angel Me *whooped* in victory.

I shuddered, clawing at the floor, until my nails broke, but I'd played this level like a newbie: my past selves had formed a pack and brought me down.

*Here, I was the Big Bad.*

Why hadn't I realised that *I'd* be the common enemy? I'd violated, broken, and stolen both their blokes.

*Now payback was a bitch.*

"Will you give us such a poor show, sister?" The Overseer's — *Gabriel's* — superior voice cut through the twin points of agony in my shoulder blades, where my wings once had been.

247

Yet underneath the sneer, I caught the strain, whilst Gabriel held himself back from transforming into killer lion mode and mauling my attackers.

I raised my head, even as one of my bastard selves pressed their sharp knees into my back. I grunted, but caught a glimpse of Gabriel's swirling eyes above me in the blackness, along with his giant pink lips.

There was none of the calmness, joy, or connection that I'd sunk into when Rebel had drunk from me in Hackney Cemetery; Vampire Me's feasting was all about pain and not the pleasure.

*Was this how she'd treated her poor Blood Lovers?*

At the start of the games, my past selves had prowled around the pavilion, staring up at the high walls with the dragon statues, before peering down into the gaping Abyss. Then they'd drawn together, glaring at me.

They'd guessed that we hadn't been gathered for a long overdue slumber party...and that it'd been my fault.

Jahael had shimmered above our heads, riding a dragon statue with a mock salute at me, which had made my stomach turn when I'd remembered Kuhel's raw power, before she'd laid dead at his hand.

Even if the bitch's scaly hide *had* been begging to be ganked.

Yet when Jahael had pontificated with offers of weapons, thrones, and worship, Angel Me had snorted and turned her back.

Vampire Me had sniggered. "Crikey, what a clot you are. We don't care about any of your flash plans or offers. We're not your entertainment."

Angel Me had simply glanced back over her shoulder and nodded.

Jahael had roared. The pavilion had vibrated, whilst thick clouds had plumed from the statues' mouths.

*Any moment, we'd be wading in lava...*

Then Jahael had *clicked* his fingers with a tight smile.

248

Black had hissed in an oily slick out of the Abyss, carrying in its tide two tarred creatures...flame red hair peeked out of the top of one and a sable mane out of the other.

*Hell, no...*

My ancient powers, which had seethed inside my gums, shoulder blades, and claws that had shot out at the sight along with my fangs, had told me that it was Ash and Rebel.

My past selves had howled in outrage at the same time as me: our voices had mingled as one. For the first time, they'd felt like part of me, experiencing the same pain.

Before any of us had been able to dive to the edge of the Abyss, however, the black had receded, yanking Ash and Rebel back down into the dark...

With a shadow fuelled fierceness, I'd swept to Jahael, but he'd simply lifted his hand like a headmaster requesting quiet from unruly kids. "Will you shake your thing now?" Jahael had leant forward, resting his chin on his hands in mock innocence. "I'm super excited to see who wins this angel vs Fallen vs monster knockdown. And because I'm so spectacularly benevolent, whoever wins will not only save their toy, but can also ask one favour of me. The others shall die. Now isn't *that* entertainment!"

Angel Me twisted the shank, burrowing it further into my back; when it scraped bone, I hollered.

Panting, I grasped hard onto the edges of consciousness, whilst my magic lashed out. Flames sparked but then died along my skin.

*J, spark the violet match: I need to go BOOM!*

**What's righteous about barbecuing yourself?**

**Angel You has more righteousness in her left tit, than you have in your entire divalicious self.**

*Then how do I fight both of them? How do I fight myself, when they know my moves?*

**They don't know you, Violet-blade: Hackney, Jerusalem's, or the bitch that you've become.**

**But you've studied their worlds: pretty boy punk and the Seducer have given you a crash course in how you used to be, even if you didn't know it then.**

**Words are the true weapons: shank them where it hurts.**

When Vampire Me tore her fangs out of my shoulder, I screamed.

To my surprise, Angel Me stroked my hair almost in apology, as she too wrenched out Star.

*And hell did that smart: stabbed in the back by Rebel's gift.*

"Perhaps, competitors could take a moment to..." Gabriel sounded panicked.

Then Jahael clapped his hands in fury, and Gabriel's eyes and mouth sparked out.

I shuddered, as my past selves snatched an ankle each and *bang — bang — bang*, dragged me across to the lip of the Abyss.

"I regret the necessity of killing you, half Fallen." Angel Me peered down; her golden armour had tarnished in the sooty air. "You might be a beastly, sluttish Glory but you're still part Glory, and if Rebel was not at risk, I would make that sadly puffed up Wing of an Emperor cry mercy that he ever dared cross us."

*Hell, I'd made a chilling Glory...*

Angel Me nudged me towards the edge; I gasped.

Time to shank with words. If I couldn't fight fair, I could fight dirty.

*Divide and conquer Violet style.*

"I bet you could make him cry all sorts of things." I flicked a glance at Vampire Me, who was pretending not to watch our exchange, pulling at her lace gloves in faux indifference. "Rebel told me that you were known to the vampires as the *Destroyer*."

Vampire Me's head shot up. "You're the Destroyer?"

Angel Me preened. "An honour won upon many a blood

trammelled battlefield."

"Damn your eyes, trammelled with Fallen blood," Vampire Me hissed.

Angel Me laughed. "I fail to see the loss."

Vampire Me let go of my ankle with a growl. I held myself still with an effort.

*Time to stoke the flames.*

"Weren't there also dark amusements to be had with the Fang POWs...?" I asked. "Ash tells me that they were used like the captured angel pets, from which *you* fed, Bitesalot."

A wild stab in the dark that one, but I shoved myself onto my side, raising my eyebrow at Vampire Me. From the way that she'd suckled on my blood, there was no way that she wasn't addicted.

She'd learnt to hunger for angel blood somewhere and it hadn't been on the willing.

Angel Me drew herself up in outrage; her fingers shook around Star. "Villainy of villainies! Not only a traitor to choose the foulest side in the war, but a cruel abuser of prisoners."

"My word, you appear to be describing *yourself.*" Vampire Me licked her tongue over her canines, which still glistened with my blood.

Angel Me roared, towering with righteous glory; she spun away from me, launching herself at Vampire Me.

*Clank* – Star struck steel nails.

My past selves swung in a wild circle: a parody of a dance.

I groaned, shoving myself to my knees. Blood stuck my uniform tacky to my back; my limbs were weak with the loss of it. Stumbling, I reached my feet, unsheathing Flight who *hummed*; her hilt was cool and welcoming in my palm.

Angel Me was a bloody Coriolanus: Mars brought to life. I realised now that even in attempting to bring about my death, she'd been gentle: regretful. Against a vampire, however, she held nothing back; she was a slashing

251

whirlwind of vengeance. At last, she pinned Vampire Me against the wall.

I glanced up at Jahael who watched hungrily; he caught my eye and smirked, inclining his head in admiration.

He bastard knew that I'd caused this.

I pinked, even as I didn't loosen my grip on Flight.

It's a surreal experience to watch yourself die.

One moment, Angel Me was pinning Vampire Me against the wall, and the next, she'd slashed Star so deeply across Vampire Me's throat that her head hung off like it'd been held on by nothing but thread.

Then Angel Me turned: a vision in blood. And she was coming for me.

Flight whined.

All of a sudden, Angel Me hesitated. "By my wing, Flight allies herself with you?" Her haughty voice was subdued, as if the scarlet splattered across her face like a mask had changed her.

"Yeah, she's my main bitch."

Slowly, Angel Me lowered Star. Only then did I notice that she was shaking. Destroyer or not, maybe it'd taken more strength than I'd guessed for her to kill the vampire incarnation of herself. "Riff raff such as you should not be able to hold her; only the most righteous may touch her without being burnt."

"What's up with the *riff raff* disrespect?"

Angel Me eyed Flight, who hummed, jumping in my hands. Then she sheathed Star, before murmuring, "May we speak under a flag of truce?"

I nodded. "Let's parlay."

"First, knock me onto my back and wrap your hand around my throat."

I raised my eyebrow. "It turns out that I *am* kinky."

I smirked at Angel Me's glower. Then I drove her backwards, whilst she grappled with me.

*Whack* — Angel Me hit the floor.

252

I scrambled over her, straddling her chest, whilst leaning over her. I squeezed my fingers around her throat.

"Promise that you shall save Zachriel," Angel Me whispered.

I nodded, confused.

Angel Me's shoulders slumped, as if relaxing into the choking. "I understand little of this time and wish to understand even less. Yet tell me, is Zachriel in much peril from this lunatic Seraphim...?"

"Yeah, and every Glory and Wing in Angel World too."

Angel Me's eyes widened, before they steeled with resolve. "You imagine that I know not that this isn't my time? That Zachriel is not mightily changed? He's...no longer my Wing." I flinched from her pain. "It is a second death indeed to know that he's *yours*. In truth, I'd damn you both, but...perhaps, I too love as a Wing and not a Glory in the end." Tears pricked her eyes, but she clenched her jaw, and they didn't fall. She was all warrior, even now. "I care nothing for the world, but all for Zachriel. There can only be one winner in this battle, and it must be you."

Angel Me lay beneath me, in shining perfection, and she offered her life, so that Rebel would live.

*She truly was me.*

I stroked her cheek. "How'd you want me to...?"

*Kill you...?* How could I even say it?

"Star." Her voice wavered, but she tilted her chin. "I shall remember my Zachriel. It is most fitting."

I fumbled at her waist, pulling out the dagger. I'd held many shanks in my palm and sliced through soft skin more times than I wish that I had. I'd grasped my own Star in battle, but never to take a willing life.

*Never to take my own.*

I held it to Angel Me's throat. "Thank you."

Angel Me grasped my arm; her nails gouged scratches. "You live for all three of us now." I blinked away my own tears, whilst my powers reached out to hers, soothingly. "Be

253

victorious."

I slashed Star across her throat.

*Red...red...red...*

I clutched Angel Me, whilst she died, and I was as Coriolanus coated in death as she'd been. I bathed in the blood of my past selves and I soaked in their strength.

*I lived for them.*

"Well hail the conquering warrior! Weren't you just the cleverest and the fiercest thing? The toys will be so relieved, and Violet-darling, so am I." When Jahael plummeted to land in front of me, ethereally perfect, I raised my savage gaze, and imagined bloody hand prints across every immaculate inch of him.

His step faltered.

Godmaker hung in the air in front of him, buzzing with silver.

I gripped Star, until my knuckles whitened.

*...Blood touched...*

What if the riddle in the Gateway had actually been about this moment? Star had fed on the blood of all three versions of me. *What if he could kill an Emperor?*

I craved to launch myself at Jahael and slash him until he bled out too. Fuzzy brained on the adrenalin high of the fight, grief, and blood, plots and plans were hidden in the haze.

Only the need for more pulsing *blood, blood, blood* throbbed through me.

Jahael seemed to read the thought in my eyes, because he soared up into the dark, just as I lunged. His eyes sparked, as he wagged his finger at me. "*Ah-ah.* Calm down, girl, it's all that new power coursing through you. Time out, Fallen God."

I screamed, as waves of fire blazed through me. Then everything faded to red.

254

# 25

Silver magic tingled in static bursts across the back of my shoulder blades, knitting my shanked skin together and shocking me out of sleep.

Mischief healed me in light touches, whilst he crouched over me. I was lying on my stomach on something hard and cold, but nothing hurt anymore: Mischief had taken the pain into himself. It felt like I'd been asleep all my life, and finally I'd truly awoken.

I knew who I was and had been. I didn't need a Prince Charming to kiss me out of sleep.

I might be Violet Lazarus, but I was also a god. And I had my own blood on my hands: I'd never wash them clean, unless I took down my creator.

"If you wish to feign sleep," Mischief said, leaning down and licking the base of my neck, "perhaps you should retract your claws. Please tell me they were triggered by happy thoughts, rather than beastly ones because I'm too exhausted for a unicorn one-on-one."

I wriggled away from Mischief's wet tongue, turning onto

my back with a grimace at the mild twinge.

I opened my eyes, staring up at the same windowless cell that I'd been held in with Gabriel and Quinn before the Test by Monster; red still bled in streaks through my vision. I blinked to clear my sight but the edges of the cell were blurred with blood. I shakily sat up.

Mischief knelt next to me, his hands resting on his knees. Shadows bruised under his eyes, and his skin was clammy. I caught him before he toppled forwards.

*Taking pain was a bitch.*

"It appears that my brother swoons like a damsel." I startled at Gabriel's teasing voice. He sauntered closer out of the edges of crimson with his hands clasped behind his back.

Mischief pouted. "And it appears that my brother has yet to learn the meaning of *sexism*."

At least they were calling each other *brother*...and bickering. Just like real siblings.

I grinned. "You're both wallads. Now why are we locked up?"

Gabriel and Mischief glanced at each other uneasily.

Then Mischief eased himself out of my arms. "Our oppressive father believes that you need time to calm down and reflect."

*The bastard truly had put me in time out.*

"On how hard I'll curb stamp his face?"

"Oh, that might be on the list, along with your place by his side, the new weapon that awaits you, and how not to transform into the Big Bad monster inside who's high on the slain blood of your own past selves." Mischief's lips quirked. "Be glad that he didn't make you stand in the corner with your hands on your head."

Gabriel nodded. "By my feathers, he does that with the Acolytes."

I sighed. "You're not about to go all *Exorcist* on us again? Jahael can't hear us?"

Gabriel glanced through the grille down into the

256

Acolytes' sleeping quarters, then stilled as if seeking the slither of his dad inside his mind, before shaking his head. "We're safe — briefly — from his possession. The Acolytes are at worship, and the Emperor is distracted."

I raised my eyebrow. "The distraction of dictators never means adorable puppies in bows."

Mischief snorted. "Unless they're adorable puppies awaiting the guillotine."

I winced. "Why did you have to leave us with that visual?"

Gabriel's expression tightened, as he brushed the pad of his thumb over Mischief's shoulder. "My illustration would've been...worse."

I launched myself up. The red had almost receded now from my eyes and beneath the powerful wafts of amber, which begged me to *treasure, treasure, treasure* Gabriel like he thought I'd forgotten him, was another familiar scent, as if a third angel was hiding at the back of the cell.

*The tang of lime.*

"Anael!" I staggered past Gabriel, reaching for the shadow, which bled into my savage prince brother. Then I dragged him into an embrace, even though he stood still like he didn't know what to do with the emotion. I rubbed my hands across his wings, shuddering that at last I could hold my brother like I'd wanted — needed. When Anael continued to stand statuesque, his regal gaze averted, I drew back, gripping his chin to force him to look at me. "What's with the cold shoulder?"

"I slandered you." Anael's mask shattered, as he blinked at me, uncertain. "I hid in the Emperor's court because trapped in my father's Mirror Lodge, I learnt the trick of invisibility in plain sight. I witnessed cruelties, depravity, and cunning that would've made my father blush." At last, he rubbed his cheek against mine. "Sister, this is a monstrous realm, and I had no choice but to play the monster."

"It's OK," I murmured. "I know."

257

He drew back; his feathers bristled. "You jest."

I barked with laughter. "Enough with the shocked cat impression. You're my bro: I knew you had my back."

Mischief cleared his throat. "It's a *little* more complicated than that."

*Nope, not acknowledging the betrayal tingles...*

When I let go of Anael, resting my hands on my hips instead, he leant back against the cell's wall. "Do you not think that we should seize this chance? We've already held a war council—"

"You bastard what?"

"To be fair, you were unconscious." When I glared over my shoulder at Mischief, he raised his hands in mock defeat.

"The Firstborn Archduke is as sly as his brother." Anael's sudden ferocity reminded me just how dangerous he was. I didn't miss Mischief's flinch. *Or Gabriel's.* "He holds intrigues in his hands like cards, merely waiting for the time to play them. Do you believe that the conspiracies he wove with you were the only ones, when the fate of worlds rested on their success? Or that he loves only you?"

Hell yeah, that *was* what I'd thought. I'd hungered for Gabriel to be *my* precious: for his smile, love, and plots...*everything*.

But he'd also been planning to take down his dad with my brother...?

*He'd offered him love...?*

Yet when Anael spread his vast wings — my dark reflection — I couldn't blame him.

*I'd want my brother on my side too.*

Gabriel spun me, shaking me until I looked up. I hadn't realised that my breathing had become ragged. "On all that's holy, I need you *both*. I was caged, and you freed me. My father divides to keep the court weak: he raises up, only to keep his people below him in squabbling petty jealousy with his Favoured One, Beloveds, and Firstborn. There's nothing but conditioned worship. By my wing, we must create a new unifying story, shining a light on a future where the past doesn't simply endlessly repeat itself in cycles of war. A future of freedom and hope."

"Practised that in the mirror a few times, did you?"

Gabriel flushed. "Possibly."

"It was a bitch of a speech, but Jahael can snap a dragon's neck like it's made of glass. We're the ones huddled in the dark."

"Because we choose to be." Gabriel smirked. "My father believes himself flawless: he's not. *Trust*: it's his weakness. He trusts both too little and too much. He trusts in those he breaks to worship him and those he's bound." Gabriel glanced at Mischief and then Anael, before adding, "My father doesn't understand that true love and loyalty can't be broken *or* bound. What that means for us...? Even though we appear Acolytes, Knights of the Seraphim, or nothing but his children, *we* hold the power in The Burning Temple."

Hell, they bastard meant it: *they had a plan.*

Suddenly, the haunting, gentle strains of Eel's "P.S. I love You" wound through the cell with its heartrending epiphany at a funeral.

*Not exactly marching into battle playlist material...*

Gabriel's gaze was so hopeful, however, as he clasped his arms around my neck and waist, swaying like we were back at Istafil's party and this was the last dance at the prom.

I bastard danced and I ignored the fact that this was the darkest love melody...ever. Because it was also about how it takes death to make you seize life.

*And hell, had I learnt that.*

"This could be our courting song." Gabriel pulled me closer; his wings settled on my lower back. "For *our moment.*"

At Mischief's wicked snigger, I glanced over Gabriel's shoulder at him; Mischief had the decency to look abashed at his trick.

"Yeah, bro," I said. "The perfect moment."

259

When Gabriel looked at me with his radiant smile — the one like the sun — I craved to capture it so that it could warm me forever. Yet there was something off about the tremor that ran through him and the way that he clung to me just that bit too hard.

A cold ball grew in my stomach. "You never answered me. Why are we the lucky ones held captive? Are we being punished or kept away from something?"

"The Choosing." Gabriel drew back, unable to meet my eye. "It happens within the hour, and until it occurs, we're simply being kept separate, as you'd divide—"

"Cattle at a market," Mischief said, quietly.

I gritted my teeth. "Choosing for extra pancakes, pony rides, spankings...?"

"A place as the Emperor's Beloved in the Forbidden Court." At last Gabriel's gaze lifted to mine: fury bubbled underneath the fear. "As it burns with love, so the hateful selection occurs each year. The Seraphim must send their most beautiful daughters and sons; it's a great honour to be chosen."

*...Beloveds writhing on satin cushions in wild agony or pleasure... Sablo strapped down in the heavy wooden device and Rebel tortured...*

Yeah, a great bastard honour.

"I'm already his, which is why my taking isn't necessary." Anael waved his hand up and down at his diamond encrusted clothes.

"And we're his own children," Mischief huffed. "Despite my bastard status."

"This Choosing is different." Gabriel gripped my arm like he expected me to run, although I didn't know where he thought I'd escape in a cell. "To test your love and faith as new Empress, he's selecting his Beloved from your family."

I exploded in a whirlwind of enraged violet and black; silver snaked out, whilst phoenix shadows exploded, charring the wall. Gabriel hollered, letting go of my arm, whilst I roared. Flooded with the fresh wash of divinity, my skin hissed with the affront: I wallowed in fury, unable to pull myself back.

Then I was skidding backwards, slamming into the wall.

Silver discs pinned my arms, holding them to my chest. I wailed, struggling.

"Why, the beast still resides within the godly jewel." Mischief strolled closer, twirling his finger to tighten the bonds. I growled, battling his hold, just as I battled to soothe the ancient natures inside. "My father has requested your hot-headed presence at the line-up for the The Choosing. You shall attend as his future Empress, and *our* family shall attend as future Beloveds. Every one of us shall play our part. Unless you prefer that my father keep his crown on his cold-blooded head?"

I panted, whilst the tempest inside me calmed, and Mischief's magic caressed my own. "I won't ask my fam to sacrifice themselves."

Mischief slammed his hand onto the wall next to my head. "Insufferable *glorious* fool, don't you understand? You haven't asked it of any of us. We are joined and together in this. We willingly risk our lives, as you do, to save each other, free the enslaved, and bring down a dictator who's behind centuries of war...who would destroy worlds."

"Can't I just be *glorious*...?"

Mischief sighed, as his discs faded, and he caught me in his arms.

Yet as he stroked his fingers through my hair, all I could think was that in less than an hour, I'd be forced to play Empress to his father at The Choosing.


For such a majestic temple, Jahael's palace had a freaky number of cells. And for a god, I spent too much time trapped in them.

I paced the windowless cell, rolling my shoulders in

261

frustration. I'd been ushered by a swarm of knights to the courtyard behind the Gilded Cage and the line of dark cells that were used to punish the Archdukes.

Then I'd been nipped on the arse until I'd stepped inside.

As soon as the steel door had swung shut, I'd been swallowed by the blackness.

I fought down the panic.

Whilst I lost myself in the void again, outside in Istafil's Forbidden Court, my blokes were preparing to be slave auctioned to Jahael.

Anael had cautioned patience. Yet he, Gabriel, and Mischief had waited centuries for their revolutions: they'd chosen to suffer, until the moment had arisen to strike.

*Screw that.*

I didn't have centuries or even years. Maybe leaders did need courage to sacrifice their own people, but maybe they also sacrificed themselves. And my family were done suffering for this cause.

*Clank* — I booted the steel door and then hopped back, as my toes throbbed.

"*Tsk*, that's a naughty tantrum, missy." Lucifer's whisper from the cell beside mine, stilled me.

I dropped down, exploring the cell's damp wall with my fingers, until suddenly they slipped through a ragged hole. The pads of my fingers touched Lucifer's.

*How long had he been kept in the dark?*

Gabriel had promised to free my family. Had this been where he'd hidden Lucifer?

Sparks shot from my skin to Lucifer's: my god-like power warmed him. He gasped, shuddering. His shock and joy licked me in turn through my power, joining us more closely as dad and daughter than we ever had been.

Like offered forgiveness...and almost like Lucifer allowed himself to believe it.

When I drew back my power, but not the pressure of my fingers against Lucifer's, his voice wavered with tears, "I know that she's dead."

I paled.

How had I forgotten that because of me the daughter that Lucifer truly loved had been slaughtered?

*And that I could never be that daughter?*

I pulled back my hand, and Lucifer whined at the loss. "She battled like a true warrior; the Emperor forced her to fight to save Ash."

"That was my champ." Why did I flinch at Lucifer's indulgent nickname, which he also used for *me*? "She'd have done anything to save her Brigadier."

"I'm sorry you'll only have me now: the bitch who betrayed you." I shuffled away, resting my head against the wall.

*Silence.*

I didn't blame Lucifer if he'd retreated to the back of his cell as well. I'd been conning myself that I'd ever have him as a dad.

I'd deposed him from his throne, and he was a murdering tyrant. I'd told Mischief that he had *daddy issues*, but that didn't even start to cover *my* problems.

"On my bones, have you forgotten that I was the one *forced*? My freedom and fire taken by your bitch mummy because she wanted an heir?" Lucifer's voice bled through, muffled. "Yet here's the good part, see? I loved you from the moment of your birth and... Huh, I'm truly amongst the ranks of the cry-babies now." At his sniffle, I leant against the dank wall, wishing that our fingers were touching again. "I'm proud to call *you* daughter."

His words filled up an emptiness that'd hollowed me out my entire life.

*My dad was proud of me.*

I bit hard on my lip to keep in the sob. "I'm proud to have you as my dad."

And for the first time, I meant it.

Unlike me, Lucifer didn't hold back the sob. "I once told you that as a leader, you can't spank and forget. You have to make an example. That's why my sweet Brigadier is—"

"To hell with your masochistic sessions to thrash out your guilt. I'm proud of you not as the former King of the Underworld, but as my dad who's fam. Nobody's perfect, yeah?"

Lucifer giggled, shuffling closer. "Huh, then as your imperfect family, do I get to stand by your side against the Emperor in the coming Apocalypse?"

I grinned. "Nobody knows the Apocalypse like you..."

*Thud* — Lucifer whacked his fist against the floor.

"Oh goodie, grudge time. Mine was *an* apocalypse, technically. You're not really seeing the difference, are you? By the shadows, I wished to control to keep the Fallen *safe*. It was the angels who wouldn't let us go. What do you think the Emperor will do with *his* power and *yours*? Control or annihilate? What will his brave new world look like afterwards...?"

I shivered, curling my arms around my knees. "Hell..."

"See, you're getting it now," Lucifer purred through the crack. "I'm no longer king, but the Fallen will always be mine. The Matriarch can steal my fire, but my spark will always burn. Just give the order, and anarchy will commence."

I smirked. "Lucifer's back."

Silver spun in a soft strand, winding through the hole from my cell and into Lucifer's. He gasped, as it stroked over his wings in comfort and promise: a sealing of our deal. In the Under World, everything was a bargain or a bet.

*Clank* — my cell door slammed open.

I blinked against the painful light, recoiling. Then my arm was being snatched and I was dragged into the courtyard.

"Time to witness your pretties being chosen, dear heart,"

Istafil sneered.

I choked on the sudden sweetness of her rose scent, after the fustiness of the cell.

I wrenched my arm free and nodded. When Istafil hesitated at the cell next to mine, however, I froze.

*Don't let her know...*

By the predatory look in Istafil's eyes, however, I guessed that *she bastard did*.

Now I understood why Gabriel had hidden Lucifer in the dark; he'd only been trying to protect him for me. In a screwed-up way, that was the most romantic gesture ever.

Yet Istafil was a master spy: she must've simply been waiting for when Lucifer's discovery would hurt the most.

*And that moment was now.*

Toying with me, Istafil's ribbons rubbed over the steel door, as if debating whether to open it.

I clenched my fists. "What are you waiting for? An engraved invitation from Queen Nefertiti?"

Istafil whipped her hair behind her shoulder with a snarl, before yanking open the door.

Lucifer might've been tiny, but he stood against the back wall like he was dressed in his sleek black armour and flaring horned helmet, instead of only a pair of ragged shorts. His wings flamed behind him. He sauntered out into the courtyard, despite the agony of the light that throbbed through his temples.

Istafil took a step back, then her eyes narrowed, and she steadied herself.

Lucifer's gaze flickered to mine, before he looped his arm around my waist.

Was it the first time that he'd hugged me? I flushed, unsure how to deal with the rush of sudden emotion at the naturalness of his affection.

Then Istafil's ribbons caught Lucifer by the chin and tugged him forward viciously. "Did you imagine that I'd forgotten about you, lost lamb? The Emperor will be fascinated with such a rebellious creature and shall enjoy humbling you. Now, naughty brat, come join the line-up: it's time for The Choosing."

The breath caught in my throat. Even Jahael wasn't cruel enough to force me to prove my commitment to him by giving up my biological dad as Beloved, was he...?

Istafil's triumphant grin, as she gripped Lucifer's neck and dragged him with her into the Gilded Cage like a kid on their way to punishment, told me that Jahael was precisely that cruel.

*And that Istafil had planned this moment.*

I darted after Istafil towards The Choosing, whilst my pulse raced: inside, my family waited for the Emperor to pick one to be his new toy and to suffer under Istafil's torments.

# 26

Feathers, teeth, and fur: Jahael checked each thoroughly on my lined-up family like they were no more than animals for sale. He touched my blokes with a cool detachment, weighing his decision in The Choosing: a master chess player making their move.

Yet all I could do was sit on my hands to stop the fire from sizzling out at Jahael, whilst I sank into the pile of rosewater scented cushions under an archway and played my role of indifference.

*Whilst inside I burned.*

Scarlet ribbons, which hung from the petal roof, held each of my blokes' wrists, dragging them up onto their toes in the silk-cushioned sunken middle of the Forbidden Court. Lucifer had been bound next to Ash; their shoulders brushed. Rebel hadn't looked up once.

*Fear, shame, courage...*

The emotions burst through my bond with Rebel more strongly than ever before. Rebel alone knew what it was like to suffer as a Beloved. If Istafil gained control over him again, she'd make sure to break him.

Jahael paused in front of Rebel, tipping up his chin. "BAM! Those baby violets of yours are for the gods. No wonder they all risk their asses for you. Why do you have to be such a brat?" He traced down Rebel's long white neck. "I wonder whether the taming of you would be worth the bother...?"

Rebel's throat bobbed under Jahael's hand, before Jahael shook his head.

Then Jahael swept to Drake, who strained against the ribbons.

I bit my lip to keep silent.

"Then there's you, my golden curled beauty." Jahael ran his hand roughly through Drake's curls. Drake's frosty glare would've terrified his enemies on the battlefield, but Jahael only laughed, flicking Drake's Mark. "My toy's would-be rescuer. I find you intriguing, and it'd be delightful to take apart both a Commander and the Matriarch's Marked Wing to become *my* Beloved."

"As you wish," Drake replied, not looking at Jahael, but rather at me.

Even now, Drake would play Beloved if it was *my wish*. I craved to scream that I *wished* he'd never have to pretend, sacrifice, or be touched against his will again.

But instead, I kept silent. And that killed me.

Jahael glanced between us thoughtfully, before he sidled towards Firebird.

"*My Feathers,*" Firebird frantically whispered into my mind, "*I apologise: I'm frightened.*"

"*Believe me, we're all frightened. And whatever happens, I won't let him...*" I broke off, not knowing how much Firebird even knew about the intimate. He had no memories, and it shook me that these might become his first ones.

"*I'll be strong.*" Firebird scowled at Jahael, who'd lifted his eyebrow in surprise. "*I shall make you proud, my Feathers.*"

I turned away my head, unable to watch.

"Well, it's not like I'd touch a tainted Phoenix anyway. You don't need to glare at me like that, little boy," Jahael grumbled.

I turned back at Blaze's growl.

One of Jahael's hands encircled the tip of Blaze's tail, whilst the other turned Spark's ear inside out. Then Jahael peered inside Spark's ear, which tried to twitch away, whilst Spark whined. Finally, he fluffed out Blaze's tail.

"Two brothers," Jahael pondered, "I've never tried *that* before. Kudos to the pussy with the power, Violet-darling, you created your first race here; I always love a taste of a new breed. Daddy's impressed."

"Second race, actually," I forced out.

Jahael laughed. "Watch yourself, girl, your divinity's showing." He let go of Spark's ear, running both hands down Blaze's tail. "Wild foxes that need caging and leashing...the idea's giving me shivers."

"Inflated sense of self-importance, insincere charm, and a lack of empathy. Anyone ever tell you that you're a psychopath, mate?" Ash swung nonchalantly from the ceiling like he was on a kinky ride at the fair, even though I could see the tremoring strain in his shoulders.

That's when I realised that my fam wouldn't only walk into the flames for me: they'd walk into them for each other.

When I'd been knocking back tequilas in a dive of a bar in London for my twenty-first birthday, with no family to even celebrate that special date, I'd never have guessed that I'd discover such an epic fam...or that we'd build one together.

*That's what Jahael would never understand.*

Jahael turned from the fox brothers with a *swish* of his robe, stalking to Ash. "Has anyone ever told you that you're already a toy?" When Jahael slipped his hand down to the front of Ash's jeans, Ash stiffened. Then Jahael cupped his hands around Ash's balls like he was weighing them.

"Seducer, pet, and creature... Why, you wouldn't even need to be trained on leashes and cages." He leaned closer, tightening his hand around Ash's balls, until Ash yelped. "Drop the showboating, pet, you'd crawl behind me as my Beloved with submissive joy in your broken heart."

Lucifer wiggled his arse in his tight leather shorts.

Jahael glanced over at Lucifer with an amused quirk of his lips. "Hello there, sweet Star. Is someone jealous?"

"You don't need to save me," Ash hissed.

"Naughty pet." Jahael gave Ash's balls a final twist, before letting go. Then he spun to Lucifer, caressing Lucifer's chest with a surprising tenderness. He traced over the branded **FIRE** with a regretful shake of his head, before pressing his finger to Lucifer's lips. Reluctantly, Lucifer opened his mouth, and Jahael pushed in his finger; flushing, Lucifer sucked. Jahael grinned. "And we have a winner."

"You what?" I launched myself up, scattering the cushions.

Jahael couldn't truly expect me to rule at his side, whilst my own dad sat at his feet as his toy? His *bed slave*? Or did he intend to control *me* through him?

"King — sorry, my *oopsie*, — *ex*-king of the Underworld, already instructed in the Matriarch's dark amusements...? How could I not choose Star?" When Jahael pulled out his finger from Lucifer's mouth with an obscene *pop*, Lucifer's shame radiated from his quivering form. Lucifer didn't know our plan: *he hadn't consented to this*. "I'm all agog to discover his fun tricks."

At his words, the ribbons holding up Lucifer fluttered to the floor; Lucifer fell forward into Jahael's arms: The official choosing made.

"No bastard way." I shook with the effort of holding in my powers. "Choose again."

Jahael hurled Lucifer to the side, before darting to me with a speed that had me gasping. He snatched me by the throat, throwing me against the archway's column. "I am

270

Emperor of the Seraphim!" He roared in full majestic god-out. "I listen to all — advice, worship, and whispers — but every choice is *mine. You're* mine, girl. I am the creator, but I know how to tame." He shook me, and I held back the hiss, as my head banged against the column. "Here's a portion of harsh reality; don't choke now. No one had ever bound fae...before me. Once, they were the wildest kickass angels." My eyes widened. *Quinn was an enslaved angel?* Jahael misunderstood my shock, laughing in delight. "Violet-darling, you're my monstrous daughter for certain. Did you reckon them *lower* than you...lesser? Let's just say that the fae's glittery arses were demoted, which left them stranded between both Fallen and angel. You never wondered why they loved sampling your delicious blood?"

*I hadn't been far wrong with my guess of Vampire Butterflies...*

I shrugged. "What's with the history lesson?"

Jahael's lips pinched. "*You* are the history lesson, hooker, can't you see? You're not the only bitch that I bound and created. It's what I do. Soon, it's what we'll both do: a whole new playground for us." I stiffened, as he gripped my chin, turning me to look at Lucifer, who was sprawled on the floor. "We both donated our seed to make you, but that jackass was unwilling. Me? I've *chosen* to make and remake you. To raise you from the dead. Look at your so-called family weak before me."

I trembled, staring down the line of my fam hanging in bonds; they stared back at me silently. Each one of them had *chosen* too. Just as I had. Yet that didn't make this moment any easier.

I simply nodded. "I see them."

Jahael smiled like that was a victory. "Let the worthless assholes worship us both, whilst we become tamers of worlds." I couldn't help the curl of my lip, although I quickly fought down the flare of silver. Jahael frowned. "Why, do you still imagine yourself the hero? Back off, girl, that role

271

has already been taken by fabulous me. You're the Big Bad: the spark and kindling for the civil war. I created you for death." I recoiled, but Jahael pressed a gentle kiss to my forehead that made me shiver. "I know you feel it. How exhausted you must be, darling, fighting your true nature. Give in because you're also wondrous *life*. Be both destroyer and saviour. Let me take the weight of being the hero, and *choose* me as your new...and only...father."

Lucifer whimpered, but I couldn't look away. I forced myself to nod. "I've been battling myself for so long...never knowing what bastard side to choose. I can't do it anymore." At last, Jahael gentled his hold on my chin, and I pulled back to look up at him. His expression had softened into something yearning. "You're signed up for daddy duties, and I'll rule as Empress. But I like my pretty toys as well, and I want the rest of my fam to be mine."

*Hell, please let Lucifer and my fam know that I was only playing a part...*

Jahael relaxed against me with a laugh. I realised how tense he'd been. Had it mattered that much to him that I'd chosen him? Had his selection of my dad been more about *replacing* Lucifer than anything else?

"Like father, like daughter. How about we design a new court in the temple for your own Beloveds?"

"It's like you read my mind." *Don't let him catch the Sarcasm Level...* "Whilst you're in the giving mood, how about that *one favour* you offered to the winner of the Angel Games?"

Jahael drew back, his expression instantly darkening with suspicion. "Good try, clever girl, but The Choosing is a sacred ritual and—"

"I'm over that," I shrugged. Lucifer curled up on the floor, wrapping his wings over his head; *he had no idea about my plan*. "I wanted to ask for a party."

"Party?" Jahael echoed, flatly.

This was the moment to start the revolt against Jahael:

272

the one that I'd plotted with Anael, Gabriel, and Mischief in the first cell. They'd never calculated that I'd move the timeframe forward this far, but now that Jahael had picked my dad as his new Beloved, I wasn't waiting.

This was the final game for the Crown.

"The last celebration to welcome me into Court Two didn't end well after the Damned crashed it." My heart thundered; I crushed my nails into my palms to control my breathing. "The Seraphim are all about status and appearance, yeah? Then I need to be seen by your side schmoozing. It'll strengthen your position here against assassinations."

Jahael tilted his head. "You play court life like you were raised here." Then he grinned, flaring his wings in peacock display. "Tonight, I shall hold the most fabulous celebration of our divinity. By its end, none shall doubt either of our glory. Of course, there'll also be time to play..."

I forced myself to smile.

Tonight, I'd pretend to become the Empress that Jahael wished, whilst my fam suffered their part. Tonight, I'd put on a show to impress the Seraphim of my worth.

Tonight, I'd start a revolution.

# 27

To bring down a giant, you must turn his own strength against him because he'll be guarding his weaknesses. That way, he'll never notice the shank, until it's buried in his back.

Bubbles popped on the surface of the cocktails, which balanced on the glass table next to the sofa. Swirls of sunburst yellow coiled, before being swallowed by tequila scented black-and-violet. I grinned, sprawling amongst the cushions in the Rose Room, which throbbed to the wild party that was being thrown in honour of my new status as Empress.

*Even if it was actually the stage for my coup.*

This time, Istafil hadn't been in charge of my outfit. Instead, Jahael had issued a new Knight of the Seraphim uniform, which had been polished and brushed until I gleamed in golden perfection.

*Yeah, not missing the irony.*

Godmaker rested heavy in my lap: a queen's coronation sceptre. Godmaker growled, nudging crossly at Jahael's elegant feet, which also rested on my knees. Jahael lounged next to me on the sofa, wriggling his toes expectantly as if for a foot rub.

When I raised my eyebrow, Jahael grumbled.

*Whap* — Jahael swiped Purah across the back of the head.

Purah startled out of his position in prostrate. When Jahael waggled his foot, Purah dutifully began to massage Jahael's feet, whilst Jahael sighed his contentment.

Acolytes ranked the edges of the Rose Room, kneeling on the tiled floor. A white cloud of knights hovered in guard mode between the columns. Quinn stood on military alert behind the sofa; his damaged wing was folded back, so I couldn't see the holes but I still knew that they were there. I shifted, squirming with guilt, until Quinn gently rested his hand on my shoulder. Rainbow sparkles tingled down me in a fountain spray; I didn't need to be able to understand the words to understand his forgiveness.

The Acolytes and Knights of the Seraphim were a show of power: The Emperor smugly safe, strong, and supreme.

*Let Jahael bastard think that.*

I glanced out onto the dancefloor, where my blokes mingled with the Seraphim: Ash never let go of Rebel, just as Mischief held tight to Firebird. The fox brothers prowled around the edges in red flashes. The Guardian clutched Drake and his two clones, slow dancing with them, as he twirled them like lovers. Anael snatched them in his large wings protectively at each spin, even though he had to release them back into the Guardian's hold.

Suddenly, Queen's "Somebody to Love" burst out in its dramatic operatic joy. I gripped Godmaker's hilt to stop myself jumping up and bouncing onto the dancefloor to boogie along.

I caught Mischief's eye and tipped my imaginary hat to him; he smirked. He was the Archduke of Satirical Song Choices.

Seraphim shimmered in and out of the party in their most opulent finery: a statement of status. They hauled

275

werewolves, spotted hyenas, and velociraptors on ruby studded leashes. The sharp faced Glory owner of Shepherd slapped the sky-blue haired elf to the floor, before tying him to a column like a dog outside a bar.

In a blur of sparking silver, Gabriel tore to the Glory, towering over her. She scowled at him, spreading her wings in automatic shocked defence.

"One would almost think," Gabriel's voice echoed across the Rose Room in full Overseer fury, "that you intended to insult the Firstborn with your vulgar display. But that wouldn't be wise, would it?"

The Glory blanched, shaking her head.

Jahael chuckled. "Well, isn't that a kick in the ass surprise? You're a good influence on my Firstborn, Violet-darling; you've filled his belly with fire." He swung his feet around, narrowly missing booting Purah in the nose, before he leant forward in his seat in sudden regal style. When the music cut off, Gabriel's shoulders tensed. Shepherd whimpered, cowering lower. "What's with the scaredy-cat impressions?" He smirked at the frozen Seraphim, who stared back with wide eyes or sipped nervously at their drinks: their god about to pass judgement. Then he glared at the shivering Glory. "Kneel before your Emperor."

The Glory's lips thinned, but she dropped to her knees...next to Shepherd, who raised his head, meeting her eye for the first time now that they were level. I didn't miss the dangerous spark in his scrutiny.

"Allow me this, father," Gabriel pleaded.

Jahael nodded graciously: favour wrapped in future control. "Daring deserves reward."

Jahael waved his hand, and Shepherd's leash flared. Shepherd howled, clutching at the flaming collar. Gabriel growled, dropping to the floor next to Shepherd and holding him, whilst he wailed.

Godmaker leapt in my hands, wailing in turn.

"What the hell have you done...?" I snapped.

"Returned Gabriel's *dearest*." Jahael's expression was unexpectedly troubled. "And undid Istafil's monstrous cruelty. I've allowed myself to be blind to my Favoured One for too long."

The collar and leash melted in a crimson puddle. Then the elf transformed into a sylphlike Seraphim with untamed hair and dancing eyes, who stared down at his hands in shock, then touched his face, before flapping his graceful wings with a cry of broken delight.

Gabriel pulled Shepherd into his arms, shuddering with suppressed sobs. "By His holy face, I'm sorry, sorry, so sorry—"

Shepherd *thwacked* Gabriel across the back with his wing. "Don't apologise. Ever again."

Gabriel beamed. "Yes, sir."

I couldn't help also grinning to see Gabriel's best mate returned to him: someone who understood his need for orders, but loved Gabriel enough to only order him as much as he needed.

Who wouldn't force him to apologise before punishment, like Istafil.

"I believe *you* sanctioned such *monstrous cruelty* for your brattish sons." At first, there was nothing but a blazing shadow, but then Istafil flamed fully into the room in front of the Emperor, so close that her lips almost grazed his. Istafil had decked herself out in party attire: ruby jewels and ribbons mummified her, although in her outrage, the winding ends stood up Medusa-like and ready to strike. "Do you imagine that it was easy to train them for you, when they're such defiant—"

*Crack* — Jahael backhanded Istafil hard enough to knock her to the floor.

*At last, she knew how that felt.*

The Seraphim watched with calculating expressions. After all, this was Istafil's Court of Whispers: The Emperor's disrespect could destroy her.

I smirked. It'd only have been better if he'd made her *beg*.

Istafil's eyes gleamed, as she reached up to her reddened cheek, before touching her split lip; she stared at her bloody finger in shock.

The Imperial Favourite had been made to bleed.

The Seraphim burst out in excited, gossipy chatter.

Istafil's brow furrowed; her ribbons snapped around her in agitation, before she snarled, "You think that you don't need me, but you rule only because *I* allow it."

*Silence.*

Hell, even I drew in my breath.

Jahael pulled his robe around himself with a dramatic *swish*, before shaking his head as if disappointed at a child. "How can a toy *allow* anything?" Istafil flinched. "You were once my Favoured One." Istafil scrambled to her knees in shock, but before she could speak, Jahael grabbed her chin. "Now...you're just a toy who couldn't even produce an heir."

A tear trickled down her cheek. "My dear one, please..."

*At last, the bitch was begging.*

Jahael *tutted*. "What are you doing out of the Forbidden Court, Mongrel Beloved?" Istafil blushed at the Seraphim's titters. "You'd better hightail it to where you belong, toy, before I spank your sweet cakes right here: we need some fabulous entertainment."

Istafil shot me a venomous look. "I shan't forget, dear heart, what you've stolen. And you'll suffer for it."

Istafil's wings and hair flamed in a furious blaze, before she vanished.

Jahael sighed, before waving around at the room. "Hey, come on, this is a party! My daughter is working her extravaganza as my Empress and my son... Well, you've all seen he's now shaking his thing as my Firstborn." I caught Jahael's proud tone, and so did Gabriel; Gabriel flushed, finally letting go of Shepherd, although they still held hands. "This is the end of the old worlds and the beginning of the New Age of the Seraphim."

*This was it...bastard now or never.*

I raised my hand from Godmaker, who jiggled restlessly on my lap, whilst wisps of flame licked from the crescent head, and picked up the violet-and-black cocktail from the table. I wet my lips at the scent of tequila. "Hell of a toast."

When I passed Jahael the cocktail, however, he sniffed it, suspiciously. I stiffened, as he examined me over the lime encrusted rim. Out of the corner of my eye, I noticed Amitiel sweeping across the dancefloor towards us.

Jahael smiled, although it was crooked, as he grabbed Purah's curls, yanking him to his feet. Then he shoved the glass to Purah's mouth, tipping it up. "My Official Taster gets the first sip of heaven; a hunted Emperor like me can never be too careful."

I bounced my leg up and down, whilst I forced a smile, even though my fangs itched to descend. When Purah spluttered, wiping a dribble of cocktail off his chin, I leant forward. Purah simply folded back to his knees, however, when Jahael dropped him.

Jahael laughed, sprawling onto the sofa. "To the New Age of the Seraphim!"

His throat bobbed, as he downed the cocktail in one go.

*I bastard had him.*

A dark grin — vengeance and justice entwined — spread across my face. Godmaker rose in the air between us.

Jahael recoiled. "W-what did you...? I don't feel..." He glared at the glass. "Traitor..."

*Smash* — the glass rolled out of his motionless hand, smashing on the floor.

Jahael collapsed, paralysed from the neck down; his eyes were wide and terrified.

*And that's how you poison, bitch.*

I remembered the sensation of being paralysed by the

279

scorpion in the bone cave because Jahael had sent me on the Test by Monster: the panic and fear of being trapped inside my own body. I hoped that Jahael was now experienced it too.

Gabriel always had a long game, and building up Purah's resistance to this poison had been the work of decades.

I thrilled on a high of adrenaline and betrayal: *let the revolution begin...*

*Click, click, click.*

Amitiel surged towards me on her metallic heels; her onyx dress slithered behind her. "Do you even know what you've done, perfect project? The Emperor is the balance, control, and love—"

"Stick it, potion master." The Godmaker arced in front of me, curling doodling patterns like he was imagining cleaving through flesh. "It's not my fault that your drinky poos are an *acquired taste*."

Amitiel's dress whipped out in furious tendrils; Godmaker slashed at them, holding them back, until Gabriel dived at Amitiel from behind, wrestling her to the floor. Now it was her turn to be straddled and helpless.

"My, my," Amitiel panted, "if you'd wished for another taste, Gabriel — one that'd you'd fully remember — then you'd need only have asked."

Gabriel's expression became grim, as he reached out his hand to me. When I passed him a cocktail, Amitiel finally began to thrash but she couldn't squirm free.

Gabriel pressed the glass to her lips. "Drink, please."

I shivered: how many times had I heard that in the Citadel?

I caught Purah's eye and realised that he was reliving the Head Poisoner's attempts to break him, just as I was.

Purah crouched next to Amitiel and kissed her hair, like she'd held him close in the Citadel, whilst she'd forced him to suffer; she shuddered. "Why fight anymore, when you can be happy?" He mocked, nudging the glass against her lips.

Her hands fisted, but she reluctantly swallowed the drink. Then her head lolled back, and she was lost in a drugged haze.

Purah scrutinized her in fascination. "What's it do?"

I shrugged. "Nothing worse than she did to us."

Purah allowed himself to be swept into Gabriel's arms, as Gabriel twisted to the silently watching Seraphim. "Shame."

"If anyone's considering aiding my father, they should consider one thing." Gabriel flared out his wings in crackling majesty. The Seraphim backed away from him: even snuggling a slave Acolyte, Gabriel exuded an Alpha persona that would normally make Mischief roll his eyes. Now Mischief was poised with his own magic spinning. "*I am your Emperor now*. Questions?" When the Guardian raised his hand, Gabriel broke into a wide, feral grin. "Oh, it is a true delight that you're the one to challenge me, Guardian. Don't worry, Commander Drake I believe shall answer you."

The Seraphim shifted away from the Guardian, whilst Drake and his clones draped themselves closer.

The Guardian blinked. "But I haven't even..."

The three Drakes gripped their hands around the Guardian's neck and twisted, cracking his spine with a *snap*.

*Screams, wails, whimpers.*

The spoilt Seraphim shimmered out of the Rose Room in a fluttering panic.

Drake sighed, dropping the Guardian's limp body. Then he pulled his clones closer in comfort, sweeping a kiss over both their cheeks, before pulling them back into himself.

I glanced down at Jahael, whose steady stare unnerved me: even paralyzed, stripped of his imperial title, and abandoned by his own cowardly people, he was divine.

Godmaker whizzed above Jahael, flaming a curl of letters

above his head: **KILL?**

The storming silver and shadows inside hissed *death*, just as sharply in answer.

It'd be an execution in answer to Jahael's crimes: untold centuries of them. Yet the unsettled ache in my heart screamed that Jahael was my creator: *love, love, love...*

I shoved it down because how much of that was even *real*?

I edged closer to Jahael, whilst Godmaker trembled at his throat. Jahael's eyes were glassy with tears.

*Yet were even they real?*

"My Violet-darling," Jahael murmured, "I chose you above everyone."

"I know. And I chose everyone above myself."

The axe hung but didn't slice down.

I wasn't an executioner, and this couldn't be a bloody coup. If we killed Jahael, then it set a dangerous precedent; next time, it could be Gabriel's head under the axe.

Jahael let out his breath, when Godmaker pulled back. "You shady dicks think that my strength lies in the Seraphim? BOOM! You're going to be gagging, bitches! Quinn, kick their asses."

Quinn stalked around the sofa; his emerald eyes glowed with a savagery that shook me. He ran his fingers over his scimitar, before black flashed from his fingers like a thundercloud: Jahael was getting a bastard of a scolding.

Jahael stared at Quinn like he was seeing him for the first time, and had suddenly been reduced to a naughty kid before his daddy.

Quinn raised his arm with a fiendish grin, and the fae fluttered down in an attacking bloodsucking wave: Jahael screamed, as they alighted on him like he was wearing a glittering new robe.

Then the fae bit.

At last, Quinn shot out a burgundy arc, and the knights rose back up into the air. They remained hovering about

Jahael's head, however, warningly.

I grinned. "That was some arse kicking."

Jahael's robe was ripped and bloodied, whilst his breathing was ragged. He refused to look at me as he stubbornly persisted, "Acolytes, defend your Emperor. Worship me by killing these traitors."

The rank of Acolytes behind the sofa finally rose to their feet from their position in prostrate, glancing at Purah for courage. But they didn't attack. Instead, they circled, predatory: our army. Their wings sparked.

There were no chants of *holy, holy, holy* now.

What was Jahael without anyone to worship, serve, or love him? Did he need that simply to survive?

At last, Jahael let out a wail. Next to me, Gabriel shifted uncomfortably. I knew the devastation of betraying a dad. Mischief marched forward, resting his hand on Gabriel's right shoulder, whilst Anael prowled forward to rest his hand on his left one.

Jahael looked between them in shock. "Gabriel...sweet bastard Archduke...Anael, my cute prince...*help me.*" In the silence, when not a single one of us moved, Jahael closed his eyes, whilst he shivered. When he opened his eyes again, however, his gaze had become cold and hard. "You nest of scheming vipers."

"Turn down the Shakespearean drama." I met his frosty glare. "This is a game, and you lost."

"I take it back; I might've created you, girl, but you're nothing but your *father's* daughter: a corruptor with a dark spark."

I winced, but looked the Seraphim up and down who would've toppled worlds, as he slumped on the sofa with drool slipping out of one side of his mouth, which he couldn't even wipe away. "Your problem, bro? You underestimate people. Gabriel, my fam, and your legendary knights and Acolytes didn't need me to lead them to rise up against you because they were *by my side* all along."

283

"All hail the conspirators, traitors, and rebels," Jahael snarled. "You have my fabulous self at your mercy. I've feared such a moment all my life and now it's here...I don't feel anything but wretched that it's you, my children."

Gabriel tore at his lip with his teeth, whilst Mischief tightened his grip on him. "No one's assassinating you."

"Don't make promises that you can't keep." I jolted at the gruff voice: *The Damned had arrived*. "It appears that the puppy has big teeth. Why didn't you tell me the plan? You should slit the bastard's throat and be done with it." Ariel's burly bulk materialised next to me in sunburst yellow.

Jahael reddened with both loathing and terror.

I glanced at Gabriel: I'd noticed the coded cocktail, which matched Ariel's yellow rags, at the start of the evening, but I'd hoped that we had more time. After all, Gabriel had just declared himself Emperor, rather than allowing his uncle that honour.

*No way would I allow Rachiel to be Firstborn.*

The Damned considered Gabriel nothing more than the pampered Archduke, who'd be replaced on the return of the True Seraphim. After that, what would actually happen to Gabriel and Diniel? Would they find themselves with their throats slit too or locked in the dark cells forever?

Jahael let out a bitter laugh. "*Brother*...how splendid that the family is all together at last...well, *almost*."

When Ariel's swarthy face clouded and he reached for Jahael, Gabriel lurched forward to block him. "Please uncle, there's no need to harm him. Let me explain..."

"How about why you're giving me orders, eh?" Ariel reared back. "Or why you acted without my permission, lad? Or who are these impure angels and slaves?"

Gabriel's expression hardened. "I give you *orders* because I am now your Emperor. I act without *permission* because despite what you've always thought *I have never needed it*. And these courageous and most true and *freed* angels," the Acolytes *whooped* and stamped their feet in
284

celebration, "are my family who I trust more than I've ever trusted you. I will not give up my Crown."

Ariel gaped at him: a puppy transformed to lion. "Lad, I shall make you regret every word that's yapped out of your impudent mouth. I warned you that your sister and bastard brother had come here to tumble this world, and so they have. I protected you and your mother both. You're an insolent fool if you believe your sister the saviour. Plus, have you forgotten that you promised me *anything* to save her from the scorpion's sting? Will you also be an oath breaker?"

I glanced at Gabriel, who'd paled. He met my gaze: desperate and pleading.

What did I care if some bitch outlaw cried *unfair*? But Seraphim lived by their oaths. Could Gabriel even maintain his rule, if he broke his?

At last, Gabriel straightened his shoulders. "What is your wish?"

Ariel stroked his beard. "What I intend to have, lad, is the Crown."

Mischief shot silver at Ariel's chest, knocking him back a step. "Sorry, we're all out of those."

Gabriel looked dazed, however, as his hands shook. "Uncle, ask anything else of me."

"I shall be Emperor, Rachiel my Firstborn, and you...? You'll discover what becomes of those who cross me, lad."

Godmaker shot into my hands, but I hesitated, even whilst sweat dripped down my neck. *What the hell should I do?*

Jahael's chuckle made me shiver. "Well, I wasn't expecting such diverting entertainment, but this party has been a blast. Still, I've been a little naughty; you see, I've built up quite the resistance to poor Amitiel's delicious drinkies. Just like Purah, it would appear." I glanced at Amitiel, who writhed on the floor, pawing at herself. My skin prickled with unease. "Funny thing though, I can tell when a drug is the fun sort or the *paralyse you in a plot* sort. And I

285

always find, hookers, that when it's the latter, waiting it out, no matter how staggeringly horrendous, you learn a lot. Like: *who's a traitor*."

"Bastard..." I staggered backwards, hollering a warning.

*But it was too late.*

Jahael — who'd never even been paralysed, only pretending — burst up off the sofa. He smiled sweetly. "Who's winning now?"

Jahael had merely been watching to see who'd shank him in the back and how.

Pretending weakness, when in fact there was strength, was Mischief's trick. I should've known that he'd inherited it from somewhere.

Ariel charged at Jahael, but in a shock of powerful agarwood that choked me, Jahael transformed, growing into a giant silver snake with lustrous scales, which looped around Ariel, scooping him into the air.

When Jahael smashed down, knocking Mischief out of the way, I snatched at Jahael's coils at the same time as Gabriel. Then Jahael's tail whipped out, cracking across my back, until I howled.

# 28

In the game of war there were no winners or losers: there was only the bastard who was left alive.

Except, sometimes it was the dead who freed the living.

Godmaker swung, slashing through the hissing ribbons that guarded entry into the Forbidden Court.

Lightning jags connected my mind to Godmaker's warrior spirit; he dived back and forth, hacking across the petal archway, without my even having to hold him.

Instead, I groaned, wrapped in Gabriel's wings. Gabriel's velvet scent soothed me; I didn't simply want to treasure Gabriel, although he deserved to be loved in a way that he never had been before. I craved to *raise him up* to his rightful place and force him to believe that it was his.

My back throbbed, whilst agony speared up my spine every time that I shifted.

Jahael's serpent tail had whipped across me, before he'd slithered out of Court Two with Ariel squeezed in his coils. For long moments, I'd lain on my back, staring up at the garish roof of the Rose Room, whilst it pulsed as if in sympathy to my agony, and I'd wondered whether I'd be able to walk.

Mischief had dropped next to me, brushing the hair out of my eyes and shivering as he'd taken the pain. When he'd whimpered, keeling over into Rebel's arms, however, I'd stopped him.

Mischief had taken enough pain: I wouldn't use him anymore.

I'd gingerly pushed myself up, battling against the twinges that had shot up my neck. Then I'd battled against my own family, who'd wanted to stay with me. Yet I'd insisted that they follow Jahael discretely, whilst Gabriel and I had freed Lucifer.

*Who the hell knew how Istafil was hurting Lucifer?*

Blaze and Spark had scowled with enough Glaswegian edge, however, to muscle themselves onto the rescue mission.

"You can't mean to leave behind the wee rascal, Diniel?" Blaze's ears had twitched.

"He'll be wanting his foxies!" Spark had nodded, hopefully.

How had I forgotten the brave little Archduke, who'd flinched from my touch after his abuse at the hands of Istafil but had nonetheless smuggled in Rebel's message?

"You'll be after saving Sablo too," Rebel had added with his best puppy dog impression.

My eyes had gleamed. "Just call this the Great Escape, bitches."

"Spoiler alert: that film didn't end well for the escapees," Ash had warned.

"Then we're the legends who'll rewrite the ending."

When Godmaker arced away from the flaming entrance to the Forbidden Court with a satisfied growl, Gabriel smiled at me, although his gaze was steeled with resolve. "It's time that my wicked stepmother learnt the truth of chastisement."

Blaze and Spark smirked, saluting.

I grinned. "Let's burn a Mongrel Witch."

Godmaker led us like a candle in processional into the Forbidden Court. The rosewater scent had soured: the rose withering on the bloom. The first archways and bathing pools were empty. Ribbons coiled from the ceiling into the sunken centre. My feet sank into the floor, silently.

I scanned the darkened court, but Istafil wasn't here, unless she was invisible, which was dangerously likely...

*Whimpering.*

I gasped at the shooting pain in my back as I twisted to the side alcove.

Beloveds huddled on top of each other, shielding themselves with cushions — because when it all went down, Cushion Attack was deadly — and a kid Wing with flowing onyx hair stood in front of them: their tiny defender.

*Diniel.*

When Diniel realised that it was me, he almost fell, only to be steadied by Sablo, who crouched behind him. Then Diniel's expression crumpled like he'd been holding onto his courage for so long that he simply couldn't any longer. Yet he still managed a chorused, "Foxies!"

Blaze and Spark dived to Diniel, swinging him around until he giggled. "Archduke!" They singsonged back.

I no longer minded that they sounded like family because Diniel was *my* fam too.

Gabriel dropped to his knees in front of his brother, who stumbled from Spark's hold. Gabriel wrapped all six wings around him, whilst he nestled closer. "How forgiving of you to hold tight one who allowed your suffering. Don't you detest me as much as the Mongrel Witch?"

Diniel pulled away from Gabriel. He touched his finger to his own wing and then to Gabriel's. "You're my brother; I love you."

289

Gabriel let out a choked laugh. "I am honoured to be such, Diniel. Oh, and I'm waging war to be Emperor: you're all free."

The Beloveds blinked in wide-eyed astonishment, until Sablo flapped his wings and *whooped*.

"Rebel said you were *brilliant*." Sablo flung his arms around my neck, until I winced. He let go with a shy, although self-satisfied, shrug as he flexed his small arms. "Sorry, I've forgotten my own strength."

I fought to hide my grin. "Yeah, you're a gladiator. How about you lead your mates into the Gilded Cage and barricade it? When we're done with the revolution, your friendly new Emperor here," Gabriel ducked his head, "will help you."

Sablo nodded, whipping the cushions off the Beloveds and coaxing them out of their nest.

Diniel's lip quivered with betrayal. "But I want to fight." He gripped onto the bunched front of Gabriel's robe. "What if father hurts you? What if you need me? What if—"

"So many *what ifs*," Gabriel sighed, detaching Diniel's hand, finger by finger, from his robe. Then he played with Diniel's fingers gently between his own. "If only all could be feathered in certainty, would we not fly such a surer path? I cannot make promises, Diniel, because I would not lie to you. But I am the Firstborn and this...what I do now for the Realm of the Seraphim and the worlds beyond...has always been *my* responsibility." He patted Diniel's hand, before pushing him towards Sablo. "Do not wish duty on your shoulders too early; you shall have your own soon enough. You shall be the Champion of Beloveds: it's a shining title."

Diniel nodded. "Am I the Champion of the vampire Beloved too? The Mongrel Witch hurt him."

*Lucifer*...

"Where...?"

Diniel waved to the back of the court.

I gestured to Godmaker to guard over the Beloveds,

before staggering through the forest of ribbons in the sunken middle of the room, which *thwacked* me in the face.

On the other side, in the furthest petal arched alcove, Lucifer was trapped in the same wooden structure with an iron lever that had punctured holes through Quinn's wing.

My breaths came short and fast, as I stumbled to Lucifer's side, crouching next to him.

Lucifer's eyes were closed, although his chest rose and fell shallowly. My eyes prickled with relieved tears that his glorious wing hadn't yet been mutilated for Istafil's amusement.

*And because I'd replaced her as Empress.*

I remembered when I'd had wings, before Rahab had stolen them from me: how sensitive they'd been to the lightest touch. Yet my dad had almost suffered the worst punishment an angel could: just like *Quinn*.

I drew my shoulders up as I ran my hands over Lucifer, checking for injuries, but his pale skin was unmarred. I huffed out a relieved breath, until I slipped my hand to the base of his neck and discovered the Pleasure Pearl. I growled, edging my fingers around it; the pearl was stuck deep into the Matriarch's Mark, covering the **ML**.

I tugged again.

At last, Lucifer's eyes shot open; he wailed, arching. He turned his bleary gaze on me; his pupils were blown. Then his hips humped the air, whilst tears of frustration leaked down his cheeks. His nipples peaked and his feathers ruffled.

*Istafil was edging him through the pearl...which meant that she was still here.*

Nobody did that to the dad of the Dragon God...

Shadows burst out of me, winding in a whirlwind rage, whilst silver glowed celestial across my skin.

My fangs descended in a snarl, and I dove on the back of Lucifer's neck, sinking in my teeth and ripping out the pearl in one savage twist.

Lucifer screamed.

I spat out the mouthful of blood and tattooed skin.

*I'd removed the Matriarch's Mark...*

Lucifer collapsed in a sweaty heap; his pained gaze finally managed to make out mine. His lips half-quirked into a smile. "You know, you gave daddy a scare, champ. Huh, that is...you *are* choosing me as your father...?"

"You've always been my dad." I eased his wing out of the device. "I just didn't know if you were fam."

He winced. "Always straight for the balls."

I rubbed my hand across his shoulder, before frowning. His skin was hot — *heating* — just as the brand **FIRE** across his chest was fading.

*Did that mean...?*

"You think that you can steal my title of Imperial Favourite?" Istafil crooned her poisoned words into my ear as she materialised behind me. I tried to spin, but my back spasmed, and she caught me, digging her nails into my throat. "After centuries as that fool's toy, I've earnt it."

I choked, scrabbling at Istafil's hands, whilst Gabriel and the fox brothers crashed across the court towards us.

Grey blurred my vision. My breath stuttered...

I reached for my powers, but they couldn't rouse against the lack of oxygen and the pressure on my throat. Istafil's Damask Rose scent sickened me. I called across my bond to Godmaker: his bellow echoed.

*J? Where are you? This isn't the time to go missing in Seraphim Land. I can't... I'm dying... Please...*

*Silence.*

I quivered, alone at the last. My eyes fluttered, whilst I swam in the sea of grey.

Then Lucifer rose in towering fury. He waved his hand once and sleek black armour covered him. His wings burst on demon fire behind him, whilst his horned helmet grew in flaming — terrifying — fire.

*Had I unleashed my saviour or a second destroyer?*

My lungs ached, and my eyelids finally drooped shut, as my shoulders slumped.

Suddenly, there was a burst of heat behind me, which was so hot that it scorched my throat and a light so blindingly pure that it haloed even my closed eyelids.

Then Istafil crumbled to ash.

Lucifer caught me in his arms. I gasped for breath, massaging my bruised throat, before opening my eyes and staring up at his flaring horns.

Lucifer smirked. "I may no longer be king, but I'm still badass."

Gabriel skidded to a halt with Blaze and Spark panting at his heels. Godmaker hovered at his shoulder; fire flickered like a mane around his head. Gabriel eyed Lucifer's transformation into a formidable supernatural — with a horned helmet to prove it. "I don't doubt it. But are you now also bad?"

Lucifer's smile faltered, before he steadied me onto my own feet and slinked closer to Gabriel. When he touched his horn, a fire fairy leapt onto his palm and pirouetted: *hell, I'd missed Lucifer's spark*. "In only the best ways."

Inside, I blazed as brightly as Lucifer's Light; my dad was an army just by himself. "What about the Seraphim who are in Istafil's ruby collars?"

"Istafil's incineration," Gabriel glanced down coolly at the pile of ash, which had once been the Glory who'd tormented him throughout his childhood, "will have freed them. What happens to any wild beast, which has been beaten by its master, when it's freed from its cage?"

Lucifer laughed: it was as dark as Gabriel's answering grin. "*Din-dins...*"

"I'm a wild beast," I snarled, "I've been beaten. And now I'm free from my cage." Godmaker sped into my hand with a howl. "Now I hunger to feast."

Lucifer stared at me with wide — proud — eyes. "*That* is

badass."

Except, all I had to do was fight the most powerful of the Seraphim: *All I had to do was die.*

# 29

I didn't crave power, control, or kingdoms.

In the end, saying goodbye to my family on the day that I'd die was enough. Even though I couldn't destroy my last moments by letting them know the truth: *Dying for them was life*.

I clutched Godmaker, whilst I schooled my expression to a careful blankness. The pain in my back settled to a dull ache. A cool breeze cut across the high walled courtyard outside the Holy Audience Chamber. The rosewater fountain tinkled in mocking calm to the angels and vampires ranked in high treason against the Emperor; its sound and scent blocked out whatever was going on inside.

My blokes had tracked Jahael here, but then the gates to the Inner Court had slammed shut. Firebird had telepathically called me to join them: he'd never had the confidence to do that before. Now the whole gang kicked their heels in the courtyard, apart from Ash, who'd slid out Devil's Trident and winked as he'd marched away.

"Secret mission," he'd called over his shoulder. "Just call me 007."

Who knew if Ariel had already been consumed by the snake?

*Not that he'd be a bastard loss...*

Mischief cupped his ear against the gate's clouded glass, listening intently as if for the slither of Jahael or the *crunch* of a Damned Takeout.

Gabriel raised his eyebrow, but Mischief only shook his head.

"We're engaged on a monster hunt." Mischief rapped *clink — clink — clink* on the gate. "Except, the serpent's trapped in an unbreakable glass aquarium."

"And feeds on live outlaws," Drake added.

Rebel whacked Drake across the back of the head at Gabriel's stricken look.

Drake rubbed at his head, before stiffly nodding to Gabriel. "My apologies. And *may* feed on live outlaws."

Lucifer sniggered.

I glanced between my blokes — enemies in wars for centuries, secret or deposed rulers, and love rivals — yet they all had my back.

*Because fam was fam.*

I sniffled, hiding the tears behind a fake cough and wiping my sleeve over my eyes.

"You all right there, Feathers?" I jerked at Rebel's soft touch on my arm.

*I wasn't ready for this... Just a couple more minutes...*

Finally, I understood Rebel's willingness to die: being this close to death, I'd never felt so alive.

*What use was Godmaker if he wasn't powered by the blood of a god?*

I'd wondered whose blood he'd demand. It turns out, he desired Violet flavoured.

Yeah, I'd always known that it'd come down to a sacrifice.

*Me.*

Ancient weapons couldn't be tricked by trickles of blood:

296

I'd tested it on a slice down my arm.

*Nothing.*

Angel Me had already shown the way, dying for her *Zachriel*. My life would save my family, giving them the weapon that Gabriel could swing — and the grief maddened fury — to hack apart Jahael. At last, I'd break the cycle by becoming both death and life.

Yet...I just needed a moment to say goodbye. And this — in the end — was the greatest secret of them all.

Godmaker floated away above the fountain.

"Never better, pretty boy." *Hell, I meant it.* "I love you. And I know that we're going to win."

Rebel's smile wavered. "Away with you, kiss me, woman."

I laughed, as Rebel pulled me into a gentle kiss; he caressed me with his wings.

"Don't monopolise my jewel." Mischief yanked me into his arms, spinning me, until I breathlessly pulled back.

When Mischief studied me with sudden concern at the tightness of my lips, I twisted away to Spark and Blaze.

"Foxies," I grinned, peppering kisses across their cheeks and stroking their ears, until they nudged me away to Firebird.

Firebird lifted my hand to kiss its back.

I swallowed around the thickness in my throat. "Mischief is your Defender, yeah?" Mischief glanced up startled. "He loves you, as much as I do. Just...don't forget that."

Firebird nodded.

I caught Mischief's gaze; his eyes gleamed with tears, but he mouthed, "Thank you."

When Lucifer burst tiny dancing sparks onto his palms, I held out my hand; they trooped up my palm but they didn't burn.

I laughed at the sparks' jig, before they fizzled out. "I need a helmet like yours."

"As my daughter, after these high jinks, you shall have

one...although, no one has horns as large as mine, missy."

When I stroked Drake's wing, he looked up startled.

"Be silent." He clenched his jaw. "I need no mawkish words before a battle."

"Is that so, Ice Commander?" I bit my tongue. "Then let's not make this a weepie moment. I only wish that I'd truly known — seen — you from the start. Because I bet the real you is a legend."

Drake stared at me, but I hurried past him to Gabriel because it was too painful...

Except, Quinn lounged against the glass gate next to Gabriel, with his hand rested on his scimitar. His emerald eyes sparkled with a dark understanding that made my heart clench.

*He knew.*

I froze, drawing in a panicked breath.

What if he told the others? *What if they tried to stop me?* Instead of quiet, peace, and love in my final moments, there'd be panic, grief, and rage...

*I couldn't even talk to Quinn to beg him not to tell my secret.*

Noticing my fear, Quinn straightened, before casting a spray of ivory, like lilies at a funeral.

*He wouldn't tell.*

I nodded as I touched the pouch at my neck, which held Jade's necklace. My sister was Blood Lover to Wings, Rebel's brother: she didn't need me. Maybe she never had, and it'd been *me* who'd simply been desperate to be needed.

*I'd bastard got my wish.*

I clasped Gabriel, allowing his wings to cocoon me, whilst I rested my head on his chest.

"It's almost as if you imagine that you shan't see us again." Gabriel snuggled closer.

When Anael snorted, I stilled.

*Did Anael guess the truth like Quinn?*

I tugged at Godmaker, edging him towards me.

"How droll." Anael sauntered closer, swiping at Godmaker like a misbehaving puppy. "You are *stupid* like my father."

I bristled: I hadn't expected a statue erected in my honour for offering my life sacrificial but I could've done without the insults.

"Mind yourself," Rebel growled, "or I'll boot your muppet arse."

"You'll try," Anael's eyes darkened. "Perhaps first my sister should answer this: how long has it been since J last spoke to you?"

I stared at Anael: *how long had it been?*

J hadn't answered me when I'd called.

So...since the Angel Games? Since I'd received Godmaker and hadn't been able to use my past versions' blood...

What the hell did that mean?

*J, you're taking this Silent Chicken game way too far. Where the hell are you? You're freaking me out: This is Official Freak Out Day.*

*How can you abandon me?*

*You promised that you'd never leave... That you loved me.*

*I trusted you.*

*I have been bastard stupid. You're the same as Jahael: you raised me and now you've betrayed me.*

I squirmed in Gabriel's hold, but his wings pinned me. He glowered at Anael. "You're not *my* sweet prince: distressing our current Empress will lead to worse than a scolding."

Quinn drew his sword with a deliberate flourish.

"Your brother is a drama queen like you, sister." Anael raised his eyebrow. "J crossed over to me through our blood link because he understood the meaning of Godmaker and its sacrifice." I held my breath: *please, don't let him say it*, not whilst I was nestled in Gabriel's arms. "Or was I merely confused, and you weren't about to fall on your own *axe*?"

299

*Gasps, howls, bellows.*

Caught in Gabriel's hold, I shook, reducing the horror to white noise. I hadn't realised that I'd been shaking, until my teeth chattered. Gabriel stroked my back, whispering nonsense onto the crown of my head.

*And that was why I'd wanted to say my goodbyes in secret.*

I yanked through my bond with Godmaker, swinging him closer. My eyes burned.

Hell, this wasn't what I wanted, but if I slipped out of Gabriel's hold, I could leap onto Godmaker and choose death.

*And life for my fam.*

I trembled, waiting for the right moment.

"Enough!" Drake roared.

*Silence, apart from the tinkle of the fountain.*

Drake marched to Anael, gripping his head until their gazes met. Then he massaged his other hand through Anael's feathers. "If you will not curb your savage spirit for anyone else, then do so for me and speak plainly about why our Queen would...spill her blood."

Anael blushed. "I've missed you, cherub."

Drake blinked, before smiling. "As well you should."

Anael looked down at his hands. "Once J told me what my sister was concealing about Godmaker, I considered how with her martyrdom complex she would likely be foolhardy."

"Standing right here," I complained, muffled in Gabriel's wings.

"Permission to speak denied." Mischief was ghostly pale; Spark wound around him, with his tail drooped between his legs and his ears pressed to his head. Blaze stood close over him in guard mode. "You fight for us, you do *not* die for us."

"Noted," I muttered.

"Ready to *live*." Rebel watched me with wounded eyes.

Anael shrugged one elegant shoulder. "Interesting how ironies work: the Godmaker makes a ruler of gods, by killing a god. Yet unlike my sister, I grew up in such isolation that I learnt to reshape the world into my own playground. Why must the blood be hers? Wouldn't we rather kill Jahael?"

Drake arched his brow. "I apologise for stating the obvious sentiment but...*duh*."

"I repeat," Anael said, meeting my gaze, "how long has it been since J last spoke to you?"

Suddenly, the silence in my mind was devastating. Despairing, I reached for J.

*Please, J?*

*Please, please, please...?*

I shivered, grasping onto Gabriel in the sudden fear of being alone — fully and terrifyingly — for the first time in my life.

J wasn't simply the voice in my head. He'd raised and loved me in a way that no one else ever had.

He'd always been there... *I couldn't lose him.*

A surge of grief overwhelmed me, far greater than the sharp pricking of my own sacrificial death.

*Had Anael already murdered J...?*

I struggled in Gabriel's hold, bursting free and storming towards Anael. "Why can't I hear him? He's not the same bloke as Jahael, just like I'm not my past selves. If you've done something to his sassy arse..."

I snatched Anael away from Drake, but Anael twisted in my hold, dragging me towards the fountain. My back protested the rough treatment, whilst I scrabbled against him; Godmarker growled, swinging in an arc around Anael.

"I've only done what *J* asked. Don't you remember that my blood is as special as yours? It *resurrects*, and I've been working on whether it also brings seeds to life." Anael snatched my hand, crushing his nails hard enough into my

301

palm to draw blood. I howled, but Anael smeared our blood together. "Grant J this choice: to protect you."

"You *ganked* him?"

Anael shook his head sadly as he stepped back. "He has requested that you undertake that duty."

*A moan.*

I glanced behind the fountain, before stumbling to my knees in shock.

Jahael – nope, never Jahael, *my J* – but made beautiful flesh, knelt naked, huddled on the floor. His wings were wrapped around himself, and his hair tumbled around his shoulders. His jaw-line was harder than Jahael's normal appearance with higher cheekbones: this was his more masculine form that J, rather than Jahael, must favour.

*Because J wasn't Jahael.*

I understood that now...when it was too late and all that was left was to swing the axe.

I knee walked closer, whilst J tentatively touched at his face, before running his hand over his wings in child-like delight. "I really am fabulous." I didn't miss the way that his lip quivered. "You have a shady dick Emperor to go kick in the snaky ass, let's not turn this into a soap special."

"Stop it," I whispered, taking his hand in mine for the first time. He jumped at the touch, over sensitive: his first taste of life, and I'd be taking it away from him. "I can't..."

"All my existence, Feathery-love, I've been Jahael's shadow and slave." J wrapped his fingers tighter around mine. They were soft and warm and so unlike Jahael's that I craved to protect such innocent new life: not destroy it. "You'll be freeing me, girl." He rested his forehead against mine. "Blood is love: mine for yours. I've been hiding scaredy-cat in you, thinking of nothing but saving my own hide. But now it's time that I die for you."

I stopped J's words with a kiss: he tasted of our salty

302

tears mingled down our faces, as well as of an unconditional love that I hadn't even understood existed within me, until I had to kill it.

I hesitated for a long moment within the kiss because when it was over, my childhood would be too, and I'd be alone.

At last, my lips drew away, I closed my eyes, and Godmaker cleaved through J's neck.

Silent tears streamed down my cheeks, whilst crimson rivers of J's blood sprayed me warrior painted for the final battle.

J's blood burst through Godmaker in scarlet tendrils lighting it spectral, whilst Godmaker thundered a war cry.

*And J died.*

I shuddered, whilst my hands tightened into fists on my sticky lap.

Then my eyes snapped open.

I leapt to my feet, answering Godmaker's call with a roar of grief and rage; the ancient powers slipped free of their leashes, overtaking my mind and combining in a tempest of sensations that made my tongue heavy and words fuzzy in my mind.

My fam's awe-struck pale faces stared back at me. But nothing registered, except the silver and violet flames, which raced through me; they exploded out, blazing up Godmaker and drawing the weapon in a fizzing arc into my palm.

I thirsted for my quarry: Godmaker quivered, pointing towards the glass doors.

I prowled to the gate, lifted the axe, and struck.

*Smash* — like the walls of Jericho, the gate came tumbling down.

I howled in the wild beserker flame of battle, as I stormed into the Holy Audience Chamber with my fam at my back, J's blood on my cheeks, and Godmaker blazing in my palm.

It was time to unmake my own creator.

# 30

No Acolytes chanted *holy, holy, holy* or beat their wings bloody in worship on the floors of the silver domed Holy Audience Chamber. No incense burned in choking clouds. No fae swarmed in clouds.

Silent, empty, abandoned.

The chamber was as hollow as the Crown...and the Emperor who was settled back in Seraphim form on the divan as casually as if he'd summoned me for a picnic.

I blazed high on the blood haze, flaming with a primal thirst that reached beyond words, twining with the magics inside me and both sides of my nature, which welcomed Godmaker's rage and grief at Jahael's sacrifice. Violet lightning exploded in erratic bursts from Godmaker across the room, blasting the grand murals, as I stalked towards Jahael.

My family marched at my shoulder. I could sense them all now: a nerve rubbed raw, until even their breath rose the hairs on the back of my neck. But still they were separated from me by Godmaker's howling; he'd been awoken and he

304

couldn't rest until he'd unmade a god.

I scanned the chamber. Where was Ariel? Had Jahael thrown him into Monster Hall to torment him? Had he *eaten* him?

I blanched.

Jahael curled one leg onto the divan, allowing his other to swing in a child-like parody. Then he laughed. "Well, aren't I just shaking in my fabulous little boots, darling." Then he tilted his head, thoughtfully. "You're a traitor, but you've also worked your thing with enough underhanded crookedness to make *me* blush." A firebolt whizzed from Godmaker over Jahael's head, and he ducked, before smoothing his hair. "Take a compliment, girl. Your father is offering forgiveness."

When I faltered, Godmaker whined.

Jahael could forgive me, even after my betrayal? He still wanted me to rule by his side? The godhead inside hungered for that power; Jahael's smug smile told me that he *knew*.

Godmaker swung in agitation.

"Do you extend the same amnesty to your cunning Advisor?" Anael brushed my elbow, and I glanced at him, shaken out of the blood trance.

Anael's steely smile steadied me.

Jahael tossed his hair, although I didn't miss the way that his lips pinched and he couldn't meet Anael's eye. "You know naughty boys don't get treats, my cutie pie prince. And you've been very, very naughty."

Anael pouted. "I'm wounded."

Then Gabriel's fingers curled around my right shoulder, whilst Mischief's curled around my left. Their touch anchored me — melding Godmaker's divinity with my other natures — whilst we clattered the final steps to Jahael's divan.

"How strange that you imagine you can make terms," Gabriel's voice was harder than I'd ever heard it; his gaze boldly met his dad's, "grant amnesty, or offer forgiveness.

305

*You* should be down on your knees begging forgiveness from *us*."

If Gabriel had broken into *Rebellion: The Musical*, dancing and rocking out to a *Jesus Christ Superstar* angst, Jahael wouldn't have looked so shocked.

When the lion cub grows into the lion, he doesn't only roar...he *bites*.

Jahael opened his mouth to say something, then swallowed, and finally tapped his long fingers on his chin. His gaze became frosty, as he turned away from Gabriel. "I'm the Burning One: love isn't gentle, it *burns*. Yet remember this, sweet things, I offered you the choice."

Jahael flicked a tiny *scuttling* thing, which he'd trapped in the folds of the divan. I tensed, tightening my hold on Godmaker. Next to me, Gabriel drew in his breath.

A *scorpion* darted out.

Yet even as Rebel launched himself forwards to one side of me, and Lucifer to the other, the scorpion had transformed into Ariel.

Ariel glared at Jahael, who simply raised a mocking eyebrow. Then Ariel sat straight backed on the divan and stared out balefully at us: a sovereign surveying his disobedient subjects.

*Bastard, no...*

In a single scorpion move, Jahael had changed the entire game.

Now Ariel wasn't snake *din-dins* or Jahael's enemy: he was once again his ally.

Against us.

*What the hell had Jahael offered him?*

Gabriel surged forward, only to be dragged back by Blaze who stroked across his shuddering back. "I suffered, risked, betrayed...and always in your cause's name. *I trusted you*."

Ariel shrugged, like Gabriel's devastation was no more than a kid's tantrum. "You're a pampered puppy, of course you did. Throw you a scrap of affection, and you always came whining back for more. Only now you yowl because you're kicked. Sorry, lad, but there are no more belly rubs."

"Why?" Gabriel whispered.

"My brother offered me something better: to rule by his side." Ariel leant forward, resting his large hands on his knees.

I shivered: now there were two brothers playing Emperor to bring down. I slashed Godmaker through the air. "All he offered was the chance to *die* at his side," the words tore from my throat in a growl.

"Not today Satan, not today." Jahael slithered closer to his brother, who tensed, as Jahael wound his arms around him. "Look at you all — such a pretty righteous army of bastards, toys, Addicts, vampires, whores, and monsters — puffed up in your own self-importance. *You're nothing but a speck in time to me.* Disposable. You think that I can't replace my Firstborn or Empress? I can birth or seed a thousand more."

The one thing worse than being hated was to be replaced.

I could never replace one of my family: I loved each of them in their separate ways — needed them differently.

*They'd never be disposable.*

Suddenly, I knew that no matter the god-like powers surging through me, I couldn't become Jahael. I swelled on my fam's love; sugar and blood coated the back of my throat in honeyed sweetness. I quested through my bond with Rebel, drawing on his strength, whilst plucking the gentle threads of my connection to Phoenix. Taut, I was ready to spring against either brother...but only when Gabriel gave the signal.

I saw it now as clearly as the arcing rainbow after the Noah's flood that Jahael wished to bring sweeping across worlds: Gabriel had the true power. Mine was borrowed in his service. And this was his family that we'd be slaying.

I had to give him the choice.

Blaze wound his tail around Gabriel, steadying him.

307

Gabriel's eyes narrowed at Ariel. "What fun assassination attempts they'll be, when Rachiel discovers your double-cross. The temple shan't be able to stay in a single place for longer than a day."

"You're still worrying for my safety, eh? You'll be dead by then. And the Damned were never more than a tool." Ariel pointed at Gabriel. "Like you."

Gabriel's wings crackled. "You were never protecting me or my mother, were you?"

"And you were never the smartest lad."

Jahael nudged Ariel, slyly. "Well, you can't blame me for that, he is *your* bastard."

My breath hitched. *Hell, no...not like this. Please don't let it be true...*

But even as I glanced between the brothers, I could tell that it was.

Ariel had slept with Jahael's Empress, and Jahael had covered it up to raise the kid as his own.

Gabriel was a bastard, just the same as Mischief.

Gabriel panted raggedly. His gaze was desperate and broken. "You...you and my mother?"

Ariel laughed. "Why did you think I was in her chambers? Your little brat self was always interrupting—"

"Lies..." Gabriel wept.

"When the jackasses became too...cruel with their indiscretions," Jahael untangled himself from his brother and waved his hand, but I didn't miss the way that it shook, "I exiled them."

"Exiled?" Gabriel's sudden hope broke through his tears. "Please, by my feathers, tell me: does my mother live?"

"Well, that's the bitter pill inside the sugary sweetness." Jahael twirled a strand of hair between his fingers as he lounged to his feet. "She *did*: as the fiercest dragon." I stumbled to the side, only caught by Rebel's cool arms, which banded around me. His eyes were sad and understanding. "I killed her because your Violet-darling wanted the most badass weapon of them all."

Gabriel twisted out of Blaze's hold to stare at me...and Godmaker who'd cost his mum's life.

I shook, whilst Godmaker roared.

Yet even as Jahael chuckled, waiting for Gabriel's rampage at me, Gabriel's tears stilled, and his eyes swirled silver. He stepped closer to Jahael. "You always were a terrible father; I'm glad to discover you're not mine."

"He's *your* son," Jahael snarled to Ariel, "what shall we do with the wayward boy?"

Rebel edged back, unsheathing Eclipse.

*Rip* — Ariel lunged up, grabbing Gabriel by the robe, hard enough to tear it, as he hauled him to the side.

The fox brothers and Mischief slinked after them.

"What do I need with a soft son?" Ariel's tone was as glacial as his eyes. "He's a threat to the throne. And you may have enough *love* to allow him to live, brother, but I don't."

Ariel's beard frosted glittering ice, whilst his hands glowed blue. His hair stiffened and froze, and even his eyelashes sparkled with ice.

Gabriel clenched his jaw against the cold that shocked through him.

Jahael chuckled. "I always knew that you were the Big Bad brother."

"Father..." Gabriel murmured.

Ariel shook him. "A bastard is not my son."

Silver discs spun out in rage between Mischief's hands.

Gabriel hung in agony between the torturing freeze of Ariel's hands, before turning to meet my gaze. "*Trust me.*"

I grinned at Gabriel's code words that freed me at last. Time to unleash the *bastards, toys, Addicts, vampires, whores, and monsters* on the Seraphim gods.

I swung Godmaker.

A howling arc of violet lightning blasted towards Jahael, catching his wings. Shrieking, he tumbled backwards.

Mischief released his silver, lassoing Ariel and hauling

him away from Gabriel. Blaze caught Gabriel, whilst Spark pinned Ariel, savaging his calf with his fangs, until Ariel booted him in the head. Ariel crawled away, snapping Mischief's silver like it was a guitar string.

Jahael bellowed, *swishing* to his feet in towering outrage. When he blasted magic towards me, I pulled Firebird spinning like a shield; Firebird's golden wings deflected the bolts back towards Jahael, who dodged them at breath-taking speed, before swapping to silver fire in his attack, before I could pull Firebird away.

In a blur of midnight blue and violet feathers, Drake soared up, clutching Firebird around the middle and turning him away from the flames: *saving him.*

The fire raked across Drake's back instead, and he screamed. Firebird held onto him tightly, gentling their fall. When they crashed to the floor in a crunching tumble of feathers and seared skin, Rebel met my gaze with a concern and fury that matched my own.

"If you'd only worshipped me, I wouldn't have had to break your toys." Jahael paced closer.

"If you'd only... Actually, I'd always have broken you." I raised Godmaker, and fire sizzled across my skin.

Jahael's wings unfurled. "Perhaps, darling, we've already broken each other."

Then he sprang.

Rebel dived in front of me, swinging Eclipse. Jahael batted him away; his wings were as hard as steel. I thrilled as, like a dance, Rebel and I fought back-to-back, whilst Jahael slashed at us with his wings.

When Jahael sliced down my side, I staggered, clutching at the gash. The blood gushed sticky between my fingers. I grasped at Rebel's shoulder to keep standing.

Through my blurred vision, I could see Gabriel and Mischief's battle with Ariel, who couldn't stand after his savaging. The floor was iced like a rink, as my fam slid between the sharp shards that shot from the tips of Ariel's wings. The fox Halflings snapped at Ariel, whenever they could get close enough, and Gabriel tore whirlwinds around him, which Ariel put out like snuffing a candle.

*Ariel was as powerful as Jahael.*

Then an ice shard caught Mischief's shoulder, and Mischief dropped to his knees.

My heart pounded; tremors ran through me. *Why wasn't he getting up?*

Ariel raised his hand to hurl another ice shard.

*Get up, get up, get bastard up...*

Still Mischief hunched over with his head hanging low.

Even though I was struggling myself to stand, I lurched towards Mischief, only for Jahael to shake his head at me as he prowled closer, blocking my path.

Rebel held up Eclipse, glaring at Jahael. "Not a chance. Move or my sword will make you."

Jahael smirked. "Such dirty talk out of such a sweet mouth; it's giving me tingles."

"*Hmmm*, then tell me if this tingles *too* much..." Lucifer rose up on flaring wings, whilst a blinding light shot out of his palms in a winding tendril.

*Thud* — the light caught Jahael in the chest, smashing him against the far wall.

I flinched, expecting Jahael to disintegrate into ash, but he only thrashed, whilst his wailing rose steadily in pitches of agony.

"Too many tingles yet?" Lucifer growled.

When Jahael smashed his fist against the wall, the building shook.

The light wavered, crashing against the floor; I tumbled to my knees at the shock wave, gasping at the pain to my gashed side.

When I looked up, my gaze locked with Mischief's, as he too knelt, wounded.

In the midst of the battle, tiles fell and smashed from the domed roof, The Burning Temple itself tumbled down, and I was steeped in my own blood.

Jahael and Ariel were both gods and monsters and they'd either kill us, or bury us alive.

# 31

Vampires? Angels?

I once thought that they were bastards. And I hunted, ruled, and torched bastards.

Yet now I called them fam, they bled for me, and they sacrificed their lives to spark my Seraphim divinity.

At the dawn of both the Apocalypse and New Age, I was Violet Lazarus: birth and death, the Beginning and End, saviour and destroyer.

*The Fallen God.*

Did that make me merely a player in the game of Crowns? The princess who slayed the dragon? Or the true monster at the centre of the maze?

Silver scaled tiles crashed around me — *slam, slam, slam* — like Rebel's candy sweetness, as he bled for me, they combined in a maddening tribal beat to drag me off my knees in the midst of the destruction of the Holy Audience Chamber and stumble towards Mischief.

War was written on my brow in blood. Terrible, I tasted

death.

Jahael howled, pinned to the cracked mural walls by Lucifer's light. Godmaker twisted furiously in my grip towards his prey, hungry to cleave the Burning One's head from his shoulders. But Ariel knelt behind Mischief; his hand wound around Mischief's hair, wrenching back his head; an icicle shank grew from his palm, tracing along Mischief's throat.

I wasn't Jahael: my family wasn't disposable. And Mischief wasn't bastard dying again.

I battled down the blinkered buzz of Godmaker's call for an Emperor's blood, instead forcing out his fire in a hissing beam, which melted Ariel's icicle shank and scorched his hand.

Ariel bellowed, pressing his other hand cruelly into the base of Mischief's neck. Mischief screwed shut his eyes against the agony as he elbowed Ariel in the guts.

Ariel let go of Mischief and bent over, gasping.

My eyes widened, as Blaze and Spark skidded on the frozen floor towards Ariel, yet he didn't even see them, before they were booting him sprawling away from Mischief and tumbling into Gabriel's path...who'd taken the battle shifter style and transformed into a lion.

The same giant lion with ivory mane and blue eyes who'd fought Mischief in the Shifter Duel.

Gabriel stared down at his true dad, who'd abandoned him to be raised by Jahael and Istafil, using him as a double agent and a means to bring about his own power: nothing but a tool.

Just like I'd been used by Jahael and my own parents as a weapon.

Gabriel shook his mane and lowered his head; his unblinking, predatory gaze met his dad's; Ariel raised his shaky hand, as if to touch his son.

Then Gabriel opened his jaws...

314

*Crunch.*

Never put your hand near a lion: *Basic Safety Lesson 101.*

Ariel screamed.

*Crunch, followed by silence.*

Also, never put your *head* near a lion: *Advanced Safety Lesson.*

Gabriel shifted back into his Seraphim form, dropping to his knees next to Mischief, who caught his wings around his trembling shoulders: Gabriel was as soaked in blood now as me.

The chamber shook, and Rebel caught me around the waist to stop me falling. I clung to his candy copper scent, snuffling along his collar.

Jahael's low laugh echoed around the chamber. "Well, I guess that proves my brother right on the *not trusting you*, Gabriel. Without adoration, kids betray their parents, and parents betray their kids."

"On my fangs, do you never stop whining?" Lucifer rolled his eyes. "I'd never betray my daughter. Even if..." He glanced at me, with sudden understanding, "...She betrays *me* because she's the glorious spark who has to make those choices."

"I'm the *Emperor of the gods*," Jahael roared. "I'm the one who chooses."

I smirked. "Not anymore, bitch."

Jahael snatched hold of the light that tethered him, even though his palms charred. I gagged at the stink of singed flesh. Then he yanked Lucifer towards him, before Lucifer could break the connection, and slammed him against the wall.

At once, the temple's juddering stopped like it'd been freed alongside Jahael.

As one, Rebel and I turned, storming towards Jahael, but he only choked Lucifer, forcing us to still.

"You'd choose this *vampire*," Jahael pressed his fingers more cruelly around Lucifer's throat, "over the most holy of Seraphim to walk amongst humans? A creator and destroyer of realms? Who *seeded* you?"

"He chose me," I said, softly.

When Lucifer met my gaze, he smiled. Then he nodded.

Hell, I knew what he meant, as did Godmaker, who surged with flames in anticipation.

Lucifer closed his eyes.

"And he'd die for me," I added, "that's why."

I raised Godmaker to take the shot that'd take down both Jahael and my dad in the final fiery sacrifice. Except, in a sudden clatter of footsteps behind, *flap — flap — flap* of wings above, and scratching of claws across the walls to the side, the vampires from the Abyss burst into the chamber.

Tortured, bloodied, and starved, they crawled over the diamonds and pearls in their rags: beaten dogs turning on their master. A grey tide of furious revenge more potent than even my own, they hung on every side of Jahael.

And the Brigadier was their leader.

This had been Ash's *secret mission*: to free the vampires who he'd fought alongside in the Angel Games. Not once had Ash forgotten those that he'd left behind.

Ash never did.

Ash marched in, holding aloft Devil's Trident at full length, which glistened in living bone and chanted, "*Death, death, death.*"

Ash scanned the room. Then he pointed the killer fork at Jahael, whose eyes had widened in the first genuine terror that I'd seen from him.

Jahael had inflicted fear on Gabriel since he'd been a kid locked in Monster Hall and called him *weak*. Yet had the debauched Seraphim retreated to this realm because they were frightened of true war? How long had it been since

Jahael had been in a real battle, rather than inciting others to fight for his entertainment or playing at it?

Slaying his dragon wife didn't bastard count.

Now that Jahael was alone, unloved, and outnumbered, Jahael was no god.

*He was a coward.*

"Let's make this easy: I'm the Brigadier, Lucifer's not a choke toy, and you're the wanker who's about to let him go." Ash waved Devil at Lucifer. When Jahael didn't remove his fingers from Lucifer's throat, Ash's flinty eyes narrowed. "I hoped that you'd prefer to make it hard."

"Hold up, asshole..." Jahael hurled Lucifer to the floor.

When Purah and Quinn prowled behind Ash into the chamber, Gabriel grinned, dragging them to his side.

My entire fam was here: the joy electrified me, overshadowing my grief.

*Almost.*

Until Jahael soared into the air, outstretching his six wings that snapped with magic; his hair hung loose from its pins in wild glory and his robe had been reduced to shreds.

But he was still the most transcendent angel that I'd ever seen.

"*Worship me.*" It was no longer a demand but a forlorn plea.

We'd broken an Emperor: a god.

Although Gabriel tried to hold onto his arm, Purah stumbled before Jahael, staring up at him.

How had I expected centuries of Amitiel's training and serving as an Acolyte to be undone? I hated Jahael's superior satisfaction, as Purah raised his wings, like he intended to smash them in ritualised reverence against the floor.

"Worship *this*," Purah snarled.

Purah shot sparking magic from his own wings at Jahael, blasting him *thudding* against the wall. Jahael slid, stunned, to the floor.

Godmaker thundered a victory cry, as I charged towards

317

Jahael, straddling and holding him down.

Jahael stared up at me in shocked horror: at his own Holy Audience Chamber transformed into his execution room, and at the people who he could've ruled.

Only, he'd thrown away their true love for hollow worship.

A mixture of anguish and confusion warred in his eyes, before he gasped breathlessly, "Why do you think you can kill me? I'm the one who decides on life and death. *You're all mine.*"

"We were never yours." I kissed his forehead.

Then I hacked Godmaker across his throat.

Godmaker bayed in the rapture of the hound that rips apart the fox.

I held down Jahael, whilst his legs kicked, and his eyes rolled back. Godmaker burned bright violet; his flames burnt through Jahael's neck, and he feasted on his blood, which tear splattered across my cheeks, just as J's had done.

Blood for blood: it was done.

Exhausted, I fell back on my heels. Godmaker fell silent and sated.

*Whooping, cheering, stamping of feet.*

Then hands were clasping and spinning me around, raising me on vampires' shoulders and bearing me around the room like a hero.

Numb, I was desperate to see my fam. I'd saved worlds, yet there was nothing heroic about death. My skin was tacky, my hair plastered with crimson to my head, and my hands were scarlet gloves.

I craved to wash myself clean.

My past selves hadn't lived long enough to do that. Maybe now *I* would?

I scrabbled away from the crowd, spinning around to discover my blokes, hanging back beside the divan, as if

318

they'd had no part in the victory.

Like we weren't equals.

*No bastard way.*

Crowned in blood, I stalked towards them amidst wild applause with no thought but to run my fingers over each one of them, until I was certain that they might be bloody and battered but they were *alive*.

Godmaker slipped out of my hand, hovering by my shoulder.

"What a shocker: Violet of the bitches makes an atrocious Knight of the Seraphim but an astoundingly good blood monster." Quinn raised a sardonic eyebrow.

Ash lounged against Devil. "A *hot* blood monster."

I nearly tripped over my own feet, whilst Purah sniggered.

Quinn's deep, musical voice was as beautiful as his rainbow arcs: *Jahael's death had broken the spell that bound his speech*. His eyes glittered with tears that he refused to shed, as he met my gaze.

Then I was clutching and spinning him in a mad tangle, dragging him to the floor.

"Thank you," he whispered into my hair, with a kiss.

I'd suffered nightmares over my mistake of teaching Ash's sisters to speak, and now it was like a dream to hear Quinn's words.

"By all the saints, if we're onto the kissing already..." Rebel dived on top of me, smothering my crimson face in kisses. "If I'm not off your List of Asses to Kick now, I'm resigning myself to having my arse kicked."

"Your arse is safe: you'll never be on my list again."

Rebel grinned, wrapping his wings around me.

Halflings, phoenixes, vampires, angels, and Seraphim jumped into the feathery, furry pile: I didn't need glory or power.

*I needed my fam.*

I blinked up at the two angels who were awkwardly

standing on the edge of the celebration like the geek kids at the party, with whom nobody danced: Mischief and Drake.

"Get your angelic arses into snuggle mode," I commanded.

Mischief cleared his throat, before nudging Drake. "We're injured."

I eyed his shoulder, which was no longer ice shanked. "And I'm *not* a scarlet pin cushion...?" I winced as I raised my arms; Mischief winced too. "What happened to the shank in your shoulder?"

Mischief shrugged. "Funny thing about ice: it melts."

"How's your barbequed back?" I was desperate to touch Drake's charred skin and trace the evidence of his bravery.

*Why wouldn't he let me hold him?*

Drake shifted, avoiding my eye. "Funny thing about Mischief," he pushed the curls out of his eyes, "he healed me."

"Then enough of this shy boy routine. *I need you.*"

Mischief and Drake exchanged a look, before diving on top of me.

*Oomph* — I startled, whilst Rebel rolled away.

Mischief and Drake's delighted laughter — something that I'd heard so rarely unrestrained — filled me with both sorrow and a determination to make it ring out just as loud and as often as I could. I twisted between them, pushing back a stray curl, stroking over their wings, and stealing kisses like promises.

*A polite cough.*

I looked up at Gabriel — the new Emperor — who was imperiously peering down at us, as we writhed shamelessly on his Holy Audience Chamber floor.

At least, *I* was shameless.

"Sister, we have an audience." He glanced around at the vampires.

320

I grinned, waving at them. A couple of the vampires grinned and waved back.

Gabriel pinked.

"Fangs are big on orgies; they'll break into one themselves any moment."

Lucifer giggled as he sprawled with his back to the divan. "Now *there's* an idea."

Anael booted Lucifer. "No teasing the Emperor: he bites."

Gabriel's scent wafted across me: it's amber musk that stirred my desire to *treasure* and *protect*. I understood now that that it was his defence.

Blaze rubbed his ears against Gabriel's leg. "Get your haughty backside down here."

Gabriel fought his way over the giggling, wrestling blokes to push his way next to me, snuggling down between Mischief and Rebel. I wiped my fingers across a smudge of blood beneath his eye, and he turned to kiss my hand. Then he pulled me close, holding hard to the back of my head, whilst he shook. The tremors ran through me, as if they were mine.

At last, he pulled back, and I murmured into his ear, "I saw your message that day by the lake. And I do love you."

Gabriel's gaze met mine like we were alone; I knew that he was reading the truth of my declaration. Then he nodded, steeling himself before he drew back.

"The Gateways are open to you," he said, rehearsed and strained, "as they are to the fae, Fallen, Acolytes, and those who Istafil transformed. You may choose any time, universe or world to travel to or...you may stay here and rebuild this realm with me."

*Hell, his hopefulness could've cracked hearts.*

Gabriel turned away his head, screwing shut his eyes, when I crawled out of the comfortable nest of bodies and struggled to my feet. "I'm not a tyrant to make that kind of decision for you all. We still haven't saved the Wings in

321

Angel World or... I'm Protector to everyone; we made promises. But freedom means having choice."

"Here's the thing," Rebel smiled as he too shuffled forward, "choice can be given away, if it's willing."

When he dropped to his knee in front of me, my heart clenched.

Ash knelt next to him, meeting my gaze. "Where you go, Violet, so do I."

I wrapped my arms around myself, as one by one each member of my fam knelt before me, until only Anael and Mischief still stood beside Gabriel.

Mischief's gaze was agonized as it met mine. I didn't even let him speak. "He's your bro, you stay here with him."

Mischief nodded, slipping his arm around Gabriel.

Anael lounged back with a snort. "And I'm *your* brother. I go with you but I don't kneel to Glories."

I stared out at my family, kneeling before me and waiting on my answer. To take them — *anywhere* — in the worlds or time, freeing them from the dangers of this realm. Or to remain and help Gabriel rebuild his empire?

"I don't abandon fam," I smiled at Gabriel and Mischief. "It looks like we have a new Emperor to crown. After that...you're free from the Gilded Cage. Why not go walking amongst humans with us? Our adventures in other worlds are always epic."

Gabriel's face lit up with his sun-like smile; it warmed me with the certainty that no matter the dangers ahead, I wouldn't regret the choice.

Then my blokes were leaping up in excitement, chattering out plans for the coronation, parties, and military strategy.

I grinned, flaming Godmaker through the air towards Gabriel. "You'll be needing this, Emperor Aslan." Gabriel startled as he caught Godmaker. "He belonged to your mum and he's consumed your dad's power. You're the top boss here; you're the one who should wield her."

Gabriel turned the weapon thoughtfully in his hands, whilst it growled.

I looked around at the cracked walls and smashed tiles from the domed roof.

My fam was safe, alive, and free.

Who knew what would happen or how long it'd take to resettle the unbound fae and vampires, as well as to establish Gabriel's authority in such an unstable and dangerous court...?

Afterwards, I'd keep my promises to Angel World and beyond.

For now, the touch of Rebel's pinkie, as he reached to link it between mine, was enough.

There were more supernatural creatures and realms than I'd ever imagined: I'd not even begun to explore them. And they hadn't even begun to discover the Fallen God.

I hauled Rebel to his feet and spun him, as a new dawn broke over a freed realm of gods and monsters.

Whatever our next adventures in these magical worlds, they'd be legendary.


The End
Ready for another instalment in the Rebel Verse? Check out **REBEL VAMPIRES**!

Watch out for the next instalment in the spinoff series from Rebel Angels: **REBEL WEREWOLVES!**

https://rosemaryajohns.com

If you enjoyed **Vampire God: Rebel Angels Book 5,** let me know by leaving a review.

Thanks, you're awesome!

# AUTHOR NOTE:

Thank you for reading to the grand finale of REBEL ANGELS! I love this series. I hope you do too!

It means the world to me when you recommend, review, and pass on by word of mouth about my books because this is how they reach new readers. I started this series knowing the ending and the exciting redemptive journey that I wanted to take Violet on with J... I hoped that readers would come to love her and her fam with the same fierceness that I do!

After all, nobody's perfect...

The next series is set in the same rebel world as Rebel Angels: The Rebel Werewolves trilogy. There'll be a mix of old and new characters who I'm excited for you to meet. This is the series that I've wanted to write for the last five years. I hope that you'll enjoy diving into another supernatural world with me!

Rosemary A Johns

X

# Hooked on the *Rebel Verse?*

### Series in the Rebel Verse

Rebel Vampires
Rebel Angels
Rebel Werewolves

# Love Reading Addictive Fantasy?

Sign up to Rosemary A Johns' *VIP* Newsletter List to be notified of new promotions, secret bonus content, and never miss out on hot new releases.

Plus you'll also receive Rosemary's FREE and exclusive novella "All the Tin Soldiers".

It's our gift to you.

Visit Rosemary's website to subscribe and become a Rebel: rosemaryajohns.com

## Read More from Rosemary A Johns

Website: https://rosemaryajohns.com
Bookbub: https://www.bookbub.com/authors/rosemary-a-johns
Facebook: https://www.facebook.com/RosemaryAnnJohns
Twitter: @RosemaryAJohns
Secret Rosemary's Rebels Fan Group:
https://www.facebook.com/groups/698811356958470/permalink/867211580118446

# ABOUT THE AUTHOR

ROSEMARY A JOHNS is a USA Today bestselling and award-winning fantasy author, music fanatic, and paranormal anti-hero addict. She writes sexy angels, savage vampires, and epic battles.

Winner of the Silver Award in the National Wishing Shelf Book Awards. Finalist in the IAN Book of the Year Awards. Runner-up in Best Fantasy Book of the Year, Reality Bites Book Awards. Honorable Mention in the Readers' Favorite Book Awards.
Shortlisted in the International Rubery Book Awards.

Rosemary is also a traditionally published short story writer. She studied at Oxford University and ran her own theatre company. She's always been a rebel...

Want to read more and stay up to date on Rosemary's newest releases? Sign up for her *VIP* Rebel Newsletter and get a FREE novella!

# Member of a Book Club?

Why not share *Vampire God* with your group?

www.ingramcontent.com/pod-product-compliance
Lightning Source LLC
Chambersburg PA
CBHW051335250626
47155CB00007B/2606